Lakeshore Christmas

SUSAN WIGGS
Lakeshore Christmas

MIRA®

MIRA

Recycling programs
for this product may
not exist in your area.

ISBN-13: 978-0-7783-2689-2

LAKESHORE CHRISTMAS

www.MIRABooks.com

Printed in U.S.A.

First Printing: October 2009
10 9 8 7 6 5 4 3 2 1

To the many librarians I know—
including John, Kristin, Nancy, Charlotte,
Wendy, Cindy, Rebecca, Elizabeth, Suzanne,
Melanie, Shelley, Stephani, Deborah, Cathie—
and to the many more I've never met...
You have no idea how much you enrich people's lives.
Or maybe you do. I hope you do.
Thank you.

Part One

Blessed is the season which engages the whole world in a conspiracy of love.

—Hamilton Wright Mabie (1846—1916),
American essayist

1

The boy came to the edge of town at twilight, at the close of a winter day. Although the snows had not yet begun, the air was brutally cold, having leached the life from the fields and forests, turning everything to shades of brown and buff.

The road narrowed to one lane and passed through a covered bridge on ancient river stone pilings. Through the years, the structure had weathered and been replaced, plank by plank, yet it never really changed. The tumbled rocks and sere vegetation along the riverbanks were rimed by a delicate breath of frost, and the trees in the surrounding orchards and woods had long since dropped their leaves. There was an air of frozen waiting, as though all was in readiness, as though the stage was set.

He felt a quiet sense of purpose, knowing his task here wouldn't be easy. Hearts would have to break and be mended, truths would be revealed, risks would be taken. Which, when he thought about it, was simply the way life worked—messy, unpredictable, joyous, mysterious, hurtful and redemptive.

A green-and-white sign in the shape of a shield identified the town—Avalon. Ulster County. Elevation 4347 feet.

Farther on, a billboard carried greetings from the Rotary, the Kiwanis and at least a dozen church and civic groups. The message of welcome read Avalon, in the Heart of the Catskills Forest Preserve. There was another sign exhorting travelers to visit Willow Lake, The Jewel Of The Mountains. The bit of hyperbole might apply to any number of small lakeside towns of upper New York state, but this one had the earnestness and charm of a place with a long and complicated history.

He was one of those complications. His understanding of what brought him here only extended so far, a narrow glimpse into the mystical realm of the human heart. Perhaps he wasn't meant to know why the past and present were about to collide at this moment in time. Perhaps it was enough to know his purpose—to right an old wrong. Exactly how to accomplish this—well, there was another unknown. It would reveal itself, bit by bit, in its own time.

The main feature of the town was a pretty brickwork square around a Gothic block structure which housed municipal offices and the courthouse. Surrounding that were a variety of shops and restaurants with lights glowing in the windows. The first Christmas garlands and light displays of the season adorned the wrought-iron gas lamps around the square. In the distance lay Willow Lake, a vast indigo sheet under the brooding sky, its surface glazed by a layer of ice that would thicken as the season progressed.

A few blocks from the main square was the railway station. A train had just pulled in and was disgorging passengers coming home from work in the bigger towns—Kingston and New Paltz, Albany and Poughkeepsie, a few from as far away as New York City. People hurried to their cars, eager to escape the cold and get home to their families. There were so many ways to make a family...and just as many to lose them. But human nature was forged of forgiveness, and renewal might be only a word or a kind gesture away.

It felt strange, being back after all this time. Strange and... important. Something was greatly at risk here, whether people knew it or not. And somehow he needed to help. He just hoped he could.

Not far from the station was the town library, a squared-off Greek revival structure. The cornerstone had been laid exactly ninety-nine years ago; the date was seared upon his heart. The building was surrounded by several acres of beautiful city park, lined by bare trees and crisscrossed by sidewalks. The library occupied the site of its original predecessor, which had burned to the ground a century before, claiming one fatality. Few people knew the details of what had happened or understood the impact the event had on the life of the town itself.

Funded by a wealthy family that understood its value, the library had been rebuilt after the fire. Constructed of cut stone and virtually fireproof, the new Avalon Free Library had seen nearly a hundred years come and go—times of soaring prosperity and crushing poverty, war and peace, social unrest and harmony. The town had changed, the world had changed.

People didn't know each other anymore, yet there were a few constants, anchoring everything in place, and the library was one of them. For now.

He sighed, his breath frosting the air as old memories crowded in, as haunting as an unfinished dream. All those years ago, the first library had been destroyed. Now the present one was in danger, not from fire but from something just as dangerous. There still might be time to save it.

The building had tall windows all around its periphery, and a skylight over an atrium to flood the space with light. Through the windows, he could see oaken bookcases, tables and study carrels with people bent over them. Through another set of windows, he could see the staff area.

Inside, laboring at a cluttered desk in the glow of a task lamp, sat a woman. Her pale face was drawn with a worry that seemed to edge toward despair.

She stood abruptly, as though having just remembered something, smoothing her hands down the front of her brown skirt. Then she grabbed her coat from a rack and armored herself for the rapidly falling cold—lined boots, muffler, hat, mittens. Despite the presence of numerous patrons, she seemed distracted and very alone.

The sharp, dry cold drove him toward the building's entrance, a grand archway of figured stone with wise sayings carved in bas-relief. He paused to study the words of the scholars—Plutarch, Socrates, Judah ibn-Tibbon, Benjamin Franklin. Though the words of wisdom were appealing, the boy had no guide but his own heart. Time to get started.

Hurrying, her head lowered, the woman nearly slammed into him as she left the building through the heavy, lever-handled main door.

"Oh," she said, quickly stepping back. "Oh, I'm sorry. I didn't see you there."

"It's all right," the boy said.

Something in his voice made her pause, study him for a moment through the thick lenses of her eyeglasses. He tried to envision himself as she saw him—a boy not yet sixteen, with serious dark eyes, olive-toned skin and hair that hadn't seen a barber's shears in too long. He wore a greenish cargo jacket from the army surplus, and loose-cut dungarees that were shabby but clean. The winter clothes concealed his scars, for the most part.

"Can I help you?" she asked, slightly breathless. "I'm on my way out, but…"

"I believe I can find what I need here, thanks," he said.

"The library closes at six tonight," she reminded him.

"I won't be long."

"I don't think we've met," she said. "I try to meet all my library patrons."

"My name is Jabez, ma'am. Jabez Cantor. I'm…new." It wasn't a lie, not really.

She smiled, though the worry lingered in her eyes. "Maureen Davenport."

I know, he thought. I know who you are. He understood her importance, even if she didn't. She'd done so much, here in this small town, though perhaps even she didn't realize it.

"I'm the librarian and branch manager here," she explained. "I'd show you around, but I need to be somewhere."

I know that, too, he thought.

"See you around, Jabez," she said.

Yes, he thought as she hurried away. You will.

2

Maureen Davenport's cheeks stung after the brisk walk from the library to the bakery. Although she loved the nip of cold in the air, she was grateful for the warm refuge of the Sky River Bakery. Peeling off her muffler, hat and gloves, she scanned the small knot of people crowded around the curved-glass cases of pastries and goodies. More couples gathered at the bistro booths and tables around her.

He wasn't here yet, clearly. It was a singularly awkward sensation to be waiting for someone who didn't know what you looked like. She considered ordering a big mug of tea or hot chocolate, but there was a line. She sat down and opened the book she was reading—*Christmas 365 Days a Year: How to Bring the Holiday into Your Everyday Life.*

Maureen was always reading something. Ever since she was small, she'd found delight and comfort in books. For her, a story was so much more than words on a page. Opening a book was like opening a door to another world, and once she stepped across the threshold, she was transported. When she was reading a story, she lived inside a different skin.

She loved books of every sort—novels, nonfiction, children's books, how-to manuals. As the town librarian, books were her job. And as someone who loved reading the way other people loved eating, books were her *life*. She tried not to sink too deeply into the page she was currently reading because of the upcoming meeting. She kept reminding herself to keep an eye out for him.

Him. Eddie Haven. And he was late.

As the minutes ticked by, Maureen grew paranoid. What if he didn't come? What if he stood her up? Could she fire him? No, she could not. He was a volunteer, and you couldn't really fire a volunteer. Besides, he'd been court ordered to work with her.

Why else would a man like Eddie Haven be with her except by judicial decree? She tried not to be insulted by the notion that the only way he'd ever be found with the likes of Maureen Davenport would be through court order. The fundamental mismatch was a simple fact, perhaps even a law of nature. He was heartthrob handsome, a celebrity (okay, a D-list celebrity, but still) and a massively talented musician. He was almost famous.

Long ago, his had been one of the most recognizable faces in the country. He was one of those former child stars who had rocketed briefly to fame at a young age, and then flamed out. Yet his role in that one hit movie—along with twenty-four-hour cable—kept him alive for decades. *The Christmas Caper,* a heartwarming movie that had captivated the world, had become a holiday staple. She'd heard his name linked with a number of women, and every once in awhile, one of the gossip magazines pictured him with some starlet or celebutante. For quite a while, he had fallen off the radar, but a fresh wave of notoriety surrounded him now. The silver anniversary DVD of his hit movie had just been released, and interest in him had skyrocketed.

Maureen had nothing in common with him. Their lives had intersected one night he didn't remember, though it was seared in her mind forever. He lived in New York City, but came to Avalon each holiday season—against his will. She'd heard he had friends in town, but she wasn't one of them. To her knowledge, he'd never set foot in the library.

Even so, arranging to meet him here had almost felt like a date. The rendezvous had been organized via e-mail, of course. Using the phone would be far too bold and intimidating. She was much better in e-mail. In e-mail, she didn't get flustered. In e-mail, she almost had a personality. So she hadn't actually spoken to him—who needed to talk when there was e-mail?— yet the give and take as they settled on a day and time had borne all the hallmarks of a date. It wasn't a date, of course, because that sort of thing didn't happen to women like Maureen.

Except maybe in books. And of course, in dreams.

It only happened in dreams that a plain, bookish woman caught the eye of someone like Eddie Haven.

Even if the plain woman had once saved his life. She sighed, and shrugged away an aching wisp of memory, quickly stifled.

She hadn't dated anyone in a very long time. She had exacting taste, or so she told herself and her too-inquisitive siblings and friends. She still cringed, remembering her last two dates—an outing with a stamp collector named Alvin, and a very bad concert with Walter Grunion last year. She'd ended up returning home with a headache, and a resolve to quit going out with guys because it was expected of her. She was determined to stop saying yes to men she wasn't interested in just because she was still in her twenties—barely—and "supposed" to be dating.

People coming and going in the bakery barely looked at Maureen, which was fine with her. She never liked being the center of attention. A long time ago, she used to dream of being in the limelight. Life had quickly cured her of that notion. At a mercifully young age, she'd learned that being well-known and recognized was no substitute for being loved and cherished. Maureen was an unobtrusive sort; that was her comfort zone. Flying under the radar took very little effort on her part. She wore a T-shirt that said Eschew Obfuscation and a button in support of intellectual freedom, yet the slogans didn't seem to draw anyone's eye. Maybe the trendy shirt was counteracted by her hand-knit cardigan sweater—a gift from a favorite aunt—and Maureen's tweedy wool skirt, leggings and boots. Though she knew her style of dressing was plain and boring, this didn't bother her in the least. Fashion was for people who craved attention.

Occasionally, her gaze touched someone else's and they would give each other a slight, social nod. She was the sort people recognized only obliquely. She looked vaguely familiar, like someone they occasionally encountered but couldn't quite place.

This always mystified Maureen, because she had a facile

memory for faces and names. For example, there was Kim Crutcher nursing a mug of coffee with her friend Daphne McDaniel, who was nibbling a donut with sprinkles in every color of the rainbow. They were both regular library patrons. So was Mr. Teasdale, who sat on the opposite side of the café, gazing dreamily out the window. He used the library's low vision services on a regular basis. With hardly a stretch, Maureen could name the kids jostling toward the exit with their post-hockey-practice purchases—Chelsea Nash, Max Bellamy, AJ Martinez, Dinky Romano.

She wondered if Eddie Haven liked his notoriety. Maybe now that they were about to be forced to work together, she would have the chance to ask him.

Or not.

The sad fact was, she'd probably be too bashful to ask him what time it was, let alone the way he felt about the vagaries of fame. She knew plenty *about* Eddie Haven. Yet she didn't know *him*. Perhaps over the weeks leading up to Christmas, that would change.

Or not.

She wondered if it was possible to get to know someone without letting him know her. And did she care enough to try?

She read a page of her book, then tried to avoid looking at the lighted neon clock on the wall. A burst of laughter sounded from a nearby table, and the trill of a child's gleeful voice drifted across the busy café. Along with the library, and Heart of the Mountains Church, the Sky River Bakery was one of her favorite spots in town. It was impossible to be sad or depressed in a bakery.

There must be something in the sugary, yeasty scent that imparted serenity, for everyone Maureen could see appeared to be happy.

A girl in a white apron perched on a step stool, creating a list of Thanksgiving pie options and announcing Christmas preorders. Seeing that, Maureen felt a thrill of anticipation. Christmas was right around the corner, and in spite of everything else going on in her life, it was still her favorite time of year.

She made the mistake of glancing at the clock. Eddie Haven was officially late. Seven minutes late, to be precise, not that she was counting—though she was. How long did one wait until the other party was considered "late?" Five minutes? Ten? Twenty? And whose responsibility was it to check in with the other? The wait*ee,* or the wait*er?*

She cupped her hands around her eyes and peered out the window. There were a lot of people out this time of day, heading home from work or after-school activities. A boy passed by, and she thought he might be the one she'd seen earlier at the library—Jabez. He had enormous dark eyes, thickly fringed by long lashes. His poise and formality when he'd greeted her had struck Maureen as unusual in a way she couldn't quite put her finger on. He regarded the rows of bread loaves and pastries, and his hand went inside the pocket of his olive-drab jacket. Then he sighed, freezing the air with his breath, and moved on. She had an urge to call him back, to offer…what? Maureen wasn't given to social impulses, and she doubted a teenager would welcome an invitation from the town librarian, anyway.

After nine minutes, she began to wonder if she had made

a mistake with the time and place of her meeting with Eddie. Just to be sure, she opened her clipboard and consulted the printout of their e-mail exchange. No, she hadn't gotten the time wrong. He was late. Totally, inexcusably late.

By the time he was twelve minutes late, she was seriously nervous. She might need to phone him after all. Good grief, but she hated phoning. Or…wait. She could send him a text message. Perfect. A text message. She could ask him if he was still planning to meet with her.

Yes, that would give him a chance to save face in case he'd forgotten the appointment. Why it was her job to save his face was another matter entirely.

Taking out her mobile phone, she remembered the no-phone rule in the bakery. There was a sign just inside the door, depicting a symbol of a phone with a slash through it. Did that include sending a text message? Maureen was new to sending text messages, so she wasn't sure.

Just to be safe, she stepped outside, feeling almost furtive. Frowning down at the keypad, she composed a text message with too much care. "Come on," she muttered under her breath. "It's not as if this is going to be chiseled in stone." Yet she agonized over the greeting. Did she even need a greeting? Or should she just plunge into the body of the message itself? And what about a sign-off? BEST WISHES? SEE YOU SOON? Was she MAUREEN? M.D.? No, that was weird. Okay. M. DAVENPORT. There.

She hit Send.

At that precise second, she noticed a little flashing icon on her screen, indicating she had a message. Strange. She almost never got text messages.

This one was from—whoops—Eddie Haven, sent about an hour ago.

RUNNING 15 MIN LATE. SORRY. SEE U 6:15.

So now she would look like a neurotic psycho stalker, nagging him over a fifteen-minute delay and too much of a ninny to check her messages.

Staring down at the tiny screen, she stood on the edge of the curb, wishing the pavement would crack open and swallow her up, sparing her this awkward meeting. Lost in thought, she didn't notice the white, windowless van careening toward her until it was almost too late. She jumped away from the curb just as it angled into a parking spot a few feet away, nearly flattening her against the brick building. Rock music thumped from the scratched and dented vehicle for a couple of seconds before the engine rattled to a halt.

Clutching the mobile phone with frozen fingers, Maureen choked on a puff of exhaust. She heard the thud of a door, footsteps on pavement.

A man in black appeared, glaring at her. She looked him up and down. He had the shaggy blond hair of an old-school California surfer. He wore ripped jeans and black high-top sneakers, and a jacket with a ski pass hanging from the zipper tag, open to reveal a formfitting black T-shirt. Eddie Haven had arrived. Wonderful. He was going to think the world of her.

"Jesus Christ, lady. I didn't see you there. I nearly ran you down," he said.

"Yes," she agreed. "Yes, you did."

"I didn't see you," he repeated.

Of course he hadn't. And it wouldn't be the first time. "You should've been watching."

"I was, I—" He raked a hand through his long, wheat-colored hair. "Christ, you scared the shit out of me."

"There's no need to take the Lord's name in vain," she said, then cringed at her own words. When had she turned into such a marm?

"It wasn't in vain," he replied. "I totally meant it."

She sniffed, filling her senses with winter cold, tinged with exhaust. "It's just so…unimaginative. Not to mention disrespectful."

"And self-righteous to boot," he said with a grin, handsome as a prom king. "It's been real, but I gotta bounce." He nodded in the direction of the bakery. "I'm meeting someone."

A soft burble of sound came from…it seemed to be coming from his jeans. He dug in his pocket and extracted a cell phone.

Maureen glanced down at her own phone's screen to see that it said Message Sent.

Then she looked back at Eddie Haven. Despite his easy dismissal of polite speech, there was no denying the man had presence. Although he was almost inhumanly good-looking, the strange appeal went deeper than looks alone. He had some kind of aura, a powerful magnetism that seemed to suck all the light and energy toward him. And he wasn't even doing anything, just standing there checking his messages.

I am in such trouble, she thought.

With a bemused expression, he touched a button. A second later her phone rang. Startled, she dropped it on the ground.

He bent and scooped it up, holding it out to her. "Maureen, right? Maureen Davenport."

"That's me." She turned her ringer off and slipped the phone into her pocket.

"What, you're hanging up on me already?" he said.

"I suppose that would be a first for you. A woman, hanging up on you."

"Shit, no, are you kidding?"

She winced. "Don't tell me you're going to talk like that the whole time."

"Great," he said, "so you're one of those holier-than-thou types."

"I'll bet a convicted felon would be holier than you are," she retorted.

"I've met quite a few felons who were holier than me. Wait a minute, I *am* a convicted felon." He touched the heel of his hand to his forehead. "Does that mean I'm holier than me? Jesus, lady, way to mess with a guy's head."

"I'm sure I don't mean to mess with your head or any other part of you," she said.

He started walking toward the bakery. "So...Maureen Davenport." He pronounced her name as though tasting it. "From the library."

"That's me." She couldn't tell if he was surprised, disappointed or just resigned.

He paused, frowned at her. "Have we met before?" Without waiting for a reply, he said, "It's weird that our paths haven't crossed, in a town like this. I guess we just move in different circles, eh?"

She considered telling him their paths *had* crossed, but he simply hadn't deigned to notice her. Instead, she simply nodded. "I guess."

"This is going to be fun," he said, clapping his hands together, then blowing on his fingers. "And fun is good, right?"

She didn't think he expected an answer to his question.

"I'm Eddie Haven," he said.

"I know who you are," she said. Good grief, who didn't know who Eddie Haven was? Especially now, with his anniversary DVD topping the charts. She knew it topped the charts because the library currently owned a dozen copies, and each of those had more than a hundred patron holds. She wondered what it was like for him to see his own flickering image on the small screen, year in and year out, all hours of the night and day.

She'd have plenty of opportunities to ask him, because this holiday season, she was stuck with him. The two of them had been charged with codirecting the annual Christmas pageant for the town of Avalon. She had taken on the job because it was something she'd always wanted to do, and she was well-qualified for the task. Eddie was her partner in the endeavor thanks to a mandate from a judge ordering him to perform community service. For better or worse, they were stuck with each other.

"Sorry I'm late," he said easily. "I texted you."

"I...sent you a text message, as well." She couldn't quite bring herself to use *texted* as a verb. "And after I hit Send," she added, "I saw your message."

In the bakery, several people greeted him by name, welcom-

ing him back to town. Several more—mostly women, she
noted—checked him out. A group of tourists looked up from
studying their area maps and brochures to lean over and
whisper about him, likely speculating about whether or not
he was who they thought he was. With the publicity surrounding his movie, he was definitely back in vogue.

"Our table's over here," she said, leading the way, on fire
with self-consciousness. There was no reason to feel self-
conscious, but she did. She couldn't help herself.

"Why do I get the impression you've already decided not
to like me?" he asked, shrugging out of his jacket.

Was it that obvious? "I have no idea whether I'm going to
like you or not," she felt compelled to say. "Not a fan of the
language, though. Seriously."

"What, English? It's standard English, swear to God."

"Right." She hung up her coat over the back of her chair
and took a seat. She didn't want to play games with this guy.

"You mean the swearing," he said.

"Brilliant deduction."

"Fine. I won't do it anymore. No more taking the Lord's
name in vain or even in earnest."

"I'm pleased to hear it," she conceded.

"They're just words."

"Words are powerful."

"Right. You want to know what's obscene?" he asked.

"Do I have a choice?"

"Violence is obscene. Injustice—that's obscene, too. Poverty
and intolerance. Those are obscenities. Words are just that—
words."

"A lot of hot air," she suggested.

"That's right."

"Now that we've established you're full of hot air, we should get to work."

He chuckled. "Touché. Hang on a sec. I need to get a coffee." He dug in his back pocket and took out a well-worn billfold. It flopped onto the floor, and he stooped to pick it up. "Sh—" he paused. "How about shit? Can I say shit?"

"I'd rather you didn't."

"Jesus—er, gee whiz. What the hell do you say when you drop something?"

"There are many ways to express dismay," she pointed out. "I imagine you know plenty."

"I'm asking you. What do you say when you get pissed off?"

"I don't get pissed off." She forced herself to use words she'd rather not.

He stood stock-still, as if he'd been planted in the middle of the bakery. She thought for a moment that he might be having a fit or something.

Instead, he threw back his head and guffawed, causing heads to swivel toward him. "You're killing me," he gasped. "You really are."

She tried to ignore the inquisitive stares. "Why is that?"

"Because lady, I can already tell—you were born pissed off."

"You can tell this," she said, scowling a challenge at him. "Because you're…what? Such an amazing judge of character?"

"Because you're not hiding a thing," he said.

"You have no idea whether I'm hiding anything at all," she said. "You don't know the first thing about me."

His gaze flicked over her, assessing practical boots, the plain cloth coat, the handknit accessories, the glasses, her stack of books and clipboard.

"I know everything I need to know," he said.

"And what's that?"

"Ray Tolley says you're the town librarian."

Ray, who played keyboard, was in charge of music for the pageant. Maureen tried to decide whether or not she was pleased Ray had discussed her with Eddie Haven. "That's not exactly classified."

"You're a big reader, and freakishly organized," Eddie said, eyeing her books and papers.

She sniffed. "You're stereotyping me. Not to mention being completely wrong." He *was* wrong. She cleared her throat and glared up at him. It was then that she noticed he wore an earring. A single, sexy golden loop in one earlobe. He also had a tattoo that rippled when he bent his arm. She could imagine how it looked as he stroked the strings of his guitar. Obvious signs of a person craving attention.

"Okay, then you live a secret life, moonlighting as a dominatrix."

"That's no secret," she said.

He chuckled again, his eyes shining. "Right." He headed for the counter. Halfway there, he turned. "Do you want anything?"

She tried not to stare at the earring. "No. No, thank you."

With his weight shifted to one hip and a charming grin on his face, he chatted up the counter girl, whose eyes sparkled as she made small talk with him.

Clearing her throat, Maureen organized the papers on her clipboard and adjusted her glasses. She wished she didn't wear glasses. It was just so…librarian-like. She owned a pair of contacts, but they irritated her eyes.

Her sisters and stepmom had insisted that she opt for trendy Danish-import frames and a good haircut in order to avoid being regarded as a total cliché. But she usually ended up pulling her hair back and not bothering with makeup. The end result was the impression of a librarian trying not to look like a librarian, which was ridiculous.

She eventually surrendered to who she was, and for the most part she was comfortable in her own skin, with a cozy apartment, two cats and plenty of books. She hadn't always been that way; her contentment was hard-won. And when someone—like Eddie Haven—came along and threatened that, she went into defensive mode.

He returned with a mug of hot coffee for himself, and a cup of hot chocolate. "For you," he said. "I know you said you didn't want anything, but I figured I'd give it a shot."

"Thank you. How did you know I'm a hot chocolate drinker?"

"Who doesn't like hot chocolate?" He gave her a smile that made her feel as if she were the only woman in the place. "Whipped cream?"

"No," she said quickly. "That would be a bit much." She went back to feeling self-conscious. People were probably wondering what the hot guy was doing with the geeky girl. Some things never changed. Everyone who saw them together would assume he was with her out of some kind of obligation, not because he was attracted to her. Getting attention from Eddie Haven was like being the dork in school, having her pigtail tugged by the cutest boy in class. She was ridiculously grateful for the attention, even if he was taunting her.

Five minutes with this guy and she'd regressed to junior high. Just for a moment, she wished she could be someone else. That was probably unhealthy in the extreme—to be with a person who made you dissatisfied with yourself.

She patted the papers on her clipboard. It was always a safe bet to get down to business with someone who made you nervous. "I've made you copies of the audition schedule and the rehearsal times and—"

"Thanks. I'll look at it later. Give me a break, I just rolled into town."

"Where are you staying?" she asked.

"At a place by the lake. It belongs to some friends who go to St. Croix for the winter. Hell, I'd like to be in St. Croix right about now."

"I hope you settle in quickly," she said. "This Christmas pageant has to come together in a shockingly short amount of time."

"And yet it does," he said, "like a miracle, every year."

"So it's been your experience that a miracle occurs."

"Hasn't failed us yet. I'm not exactly new to this," he said.

She was aware of his entire history with the pageant, including the infraction that had earned him his sentence of community service. It was a known fact in the town of Avalon that Eddie Haven had begun his involvement in the town's annual pageant by judicial order. Following a terrible Christmas Eve accident, he'd been sentenced to help with the program, year in and year out. "It's been my experience that miracles work out better when they're preceded by a lot of hard work and preparation."

"Me, I got faith," he said easily.

She regarded him skeptically. "Are you a churchgoing man?"

He laughed heartily at that. "Yeah, that's me. I'm a real regular." He toned down the laughter a bit. "Trust me, I can deal with the pageant without divine intervention, okay? And how did you end up with this job, anyway? Did you volunteer or were you drafted? Or maybe you're a felon like me."

"Nobody's a felon like you."

"Ouch," he said. "Okay, I can tell, you're going to be a barrel of laughs."

"It's not my job to amuse you."

"Come on, be a sport. Tell me more about yourself, Maureen."

"Why should I? You've already declared me a boring person obsessed with books and cats—"

"I never said boring. I never said obsessed. The books were a no-brainer and the cats—every chick likes cats. Lucky guess. Come on. I really want to know. Are you from around here?"

He did this thing, she realized. This magnetic thing that made her want to…she wasn't sure what. Give him little offerings from herself. It was the strangest sensation. Strange, and maybe dangerous. "I was born and raised here," she said. "I went to college in Brockport, came back and became the town librarian." She swallowed. "No wonder you said I was boring."

"Hey. I did not say boring. And it sounds to me like you didn't have to go looking for your heart's desire."

She actually *had* gone looking, but she wasn't about to own up to that, not to him.

"And what about you?" she asked, feeling bold. "Are you looking for your heart's desire?"

"No need. I know what my heart desires. It's just a question of finding it."

"Really? And what is that?"

"I just met you. I can't be telling you that."

During their conversation, something unexpected occurred. Against her will, she started to like him. As a person, not just as an amazing-looking guy, a guy who was so far out of her league, he might as well be on another planet.

Planet of the Fangirls, thought Maureen, as three women approached their table. They were all nudging each other and exchanging bashful smiles.

"Excuse me," one of them said. And it was completely clear they weren't addressing Maureen. "You're…Eddie Haven, right?"

"*The* Eddie Haven?" her friend clarified.

He gave them an easy smile. "I guess that would be me."

"We thought so. You look the same as you did in that movie."

"Oh. Not good," he said.

"No, you were adorable." The three women looked jubilant. "And we saw you on *Extra* just last week."

Here was something that always seemed to be true. Attractive women tended to hang out together. Each of these had the looks of a former cheerleader—bright-eyed and smiling, in jeans and high-heeled boots, fitted sweaters.

"So…would you mind if we got a picture together?"

"Actually, I'm kind of in the middle of something—"

"Just a cell phone pic," she said, whipping out an iPhone and thrusting it at Maureen. "Here, would you take it?"

Before Maureen could reply, one of the women showed her how to point and shoot. The three draped themselves around Eddie and—it had to be said—he lit up like a Christmas tree.

"Thanks. You were really cool about that." The woman addressed Eddie as she saved the image on the phone. "And I know you must hear this all the time, but I loved you in that movie. I still love you in that movie, every time it airs."

"Thanks," said Eddie. "Nice of you to say so."

She handed him a card. "Here's my number. For, you know, if you ever feel like hanging out."

"You bet."

The three took off, putting their heads together and scurrying away, giggling like schoolgirls. Maureen felt a little stunned. The woman had hit on him right in front of Maureen. For all they knew, Maureen could be on a date with him. She wasn't, but still. The thing that hurt—and she hated the fact that it hurt—was knowing the women looked at her and clearly did not consider, even for a moment, that she might be…with him. His date. His girlfriend. Instead, they had treated her as if she was his assistant or secretary.

"Sorry about that," Eddie said. "Now, where were we?"

Maureen shook her head. "I have no idea." She'd never witnessed anything quite like that before. It was slightly shocking, like an ambush. "That happens to you a lot, doesn't it? People—women—just appear out of the blue and ask for an autograph or picture."

"Not sure what you mean by a lot," he said.

"Has it happened before?"

His face confirmed it.

"More than once constitutes a lot," she said.

"I wish they hadn't been so rude to you," he said.

She was surprised he'd noticed.

"I should have spoken up," he told her. "I should have pointed out they were being rude."

"Thank heaven you didn't," Maureen said. "That would have been flat-out embarrassing."

"And you don't like being embarrassed," he observed.

"Do you? Does anybody?"

"I've been a performer all my life, and like it or not, being embarrassed on a regular basis comes with the territory."

"I wouldn't know," she said. *Thank goodness.* "But don't be embarrassed. They called you adorable."

"Hell, I was adorable," he said with a curious lack of vanity.

"I know. I've seen *The Christmas Caper.*" Maureen paused. It was strange, knowing more about him than he knew about her. Generally speaking, that was the librarian's role, to be the woman behind the desk. The woman no one wondered about or speculated about.

As for Eddie's movie, she'd not only seen it. She watched it every year with rapt attention. She had already bought the just-released commemorative edition DVD and had played and replayed all the special features, paying particular attention to the interviews with the grown-up Eddie. She'd memorized every frame, every word of every song in the film. She loved that movie so much it was ridiculous. "Would it make you feel old if I said I saw it when I was in the second grade?"

"Nah, because I was six at the time of the theatrical release."

"Oh, I see."

"Yeah, I peaked at age six and it's been downhill ever since."

There was something about his smile. Something that made Maureen understand why grown women would approach him for a picture, giggling like schoolgirls. The other thing about his smile was that when she looked at him, she could see the precious little boy who had captured the hearts of America more than two decades ago.

He had played little Jimmy Kringle in *The Christmas Caper,* which was universally acknowledged to be one of the most sentimental Christmas movies ever made. Yet he'd transcended the stigma, taking a character who was trite and absurd and transforming him into a little boy everyone could believe in. And did, for years to come, thanks to the wonders of digital remastering, DVD extra features and the unending routine of round-the-clock cable.

"It can't have been easy, being made a star at such a young age," she observed.

"Wasn't so bad, back in the day. But nobody saw the Internet coming. Or cable TV on this scale."

Maureen was getting much too interested in him on a personal level. "We should finish up," she suggested.

"Can't wait to get rid of me, eh?"

"Yes, I mean, no, but—" Flustered. She was getting flustered, talking to this guy. Which was ridiculous. She was an established professional in her field. Still, she couldn't help getting unnerved over Eddie Haven, with his sexy attitude, his earring and his too-pretty face. He must think she was a total loser. She didn't like being around people who thought she was a loser. She liked people who propped her up. Her family. Library patrons. Children.

"I have a lot to tell you about this production," she said. "For starters, it's going to be filmed for a PBS special." It still excited her, just saying it. "A production company from the city is coming up to cover it as part of a story about small-town Christmas celebrations."

"Cool," he said, but he didn't look thrilled.

"It doesn't really change our plans, but I wanted you to be aware of it." She handed him a printed document. "Here's the program I'm planning. You can take a look at it tonight." She'd spent weeks finding the perfect combination of story and song for the traditional Christmas Eve celebration at Heart of the Mountains Church. It was a wonderful program, designed to bring the magic of Christmas to life. She had envisioned the ideal pageant for a long time, ever since she was small. She conjured up images of an evening aglow with candlelight, the air infused with incense and alive with song. It would be the quintessential celebration, one that would soften even the most jaded of hearts and remind people that the joys of the season could be felt all year.

He took a cursory look at the script and song list. "Sure, whatever. But it doesn't lead with the angels," he said. "When Mrs. Bickham was in charge, we always led with the angels."

Ah, the ghosts of Christmas pageants past, thought Maureen, clasping her clipboard to her chest. She was going to be haunted by them for a long time. "Not this year."

"It's your show," he said. "Hell, I don't even like Christmas."

He was so obnoxious, she thought. But so ridiculously good-looking, in a shaggy-haired, skinny-jeans, tight-T-shirt way. A lethal combination. "Nonsense. Everyone likes Christmas."

He laughed. "Right. Okay, I guess I didn't explain this very well."

"Explain what?" In spite of herself, she was intrigued, and found herself leaning toward him, hanging on his every word like the most hopeless sort of Fan-girl.

"This whole Christmas thing."

"What about it?"

"This is probably going to throw you for a loop, but in case you haven't noticed, I'm not a big fan of the holiday."

Maybe, she thought, he appealed to her because he challenged her. It had been a long time since anyone over the age of five had challenged her. "Don't be silly. Everybody loves Christmas."

"You slay me, Maureen. You really do. News flash—everybody does *not* love Christmas." Then his gaze slipped down the list of songs. "I'm not seeing a lot of variety here. Nothing new."

"We could always add 'The Runaway Reindeer' from your hit movie. Your fan club would love it. Would that make you happy?"

"That would make me gag."

The meeting was going so badly. She wished she knew how to bring it back on track. "Here's the sign-up sheet for auditions."

"Ought to be interesting. Everybody wants to be a star."

"So it seems. We'll try to be as inclusive as possible. We should remind everyone that there are no small actors—"

"Only small parts," he finished for her. "And everybody knows that's bullshit."

She winced, wondering why he felt compelled to antagonize her. Her friend Olivia would say it was because he liked her. The notion intrigued Maureen far too much. She busied herself with her printouts, hoping to disguise her nerves. "And then we'll go right into rehearsals. Here's a schedule."

"Got it, boss."

"Are you patronizing me?"

"I'm trying to, yeah."

"It's not working. I won't be patronized. Let's not lose sight of our goal. This program isn't for us or about us. It's for the children, and for everyone who wants to celebrate the holidays." The more nervous she got, the more cranky she sounded.

"Honey, you're taking this way too seriously."

"Honoring Christmas should not be taken lightly." Oh, Maureen, she thought. When did you turn into such a dork? Olivia was always telling her to relax and have fun. But Olivia was pregnant, and hormones made her completely unreliable these days.

"Got it," Eddie said again. "Are we done here?"

"Yes," she said. "We're done." She hesitated, then screwed up her courage, struggling to conquer her nerves. They'd had a rough start. Maybe, she thought, they could fix things over dinner. "Listen, Eddie, let's try not to start off on the wrong foot together. The bakery is about to close, but I was thinking, maybe we could go somewhere else, get some dinner and talk about this some more. I'd like to hear your ideas."

There. She'd said it. She had blurted out an invitation to the best-looking guy ever to sit across a table from her. Putting herself out there like this was so contrary to her nature that she nearly hyperventilated, waiting for his reply.

To his credit, he didn't smirk or anything. He simply rejected her in the most straightforward manner possible: "Maureen, thanks for the invitation, but I can't. I have to be somewhere." He glanced at his watch. "In fact, I better go, or I'll be late. Maybe some other time."

She wanted to die. Right there, right then, she wanted to curl up and die, turn to ashes and blow away on a cold winter wind. What had she been thinking, inviting him to dinner? Of course he didn't want to have dinner with her. He was Eddie Haven, for goodness' sake. He didn't have dinner with people like Maureen Davenport. Nor would she want to, even if he'd asked. He was crude and deliberately provocative, so far from being her type that it was laughable. The next several weeks were going to be excruciating.

Somehow, she kept a lame smile on her face as he practically bolted for the door. She pictured him heading home to get cleaned up, probably for a date with a woman who didn't know a library from a lobotomy, but who knew how to fill the gaps in a conversation as well as she could fill a sweater. Maureen pictured the two of them on their dinner date, gazing across the table at each other at a candlelit restaurant, whispering "Cheers" and clinking their goblets of fine wine together.

3

"Hi, my name is Eddie, and I'm an alcoholic."

"Hi, Eddie." The people in the group spoke in unison, their voices warm and quiet in the small meeting room in the basement of the church. It wasn't like they didn't know who he was. The greeting was part of the ritual of recovery, and the unvarying repetition held a certain comfort for the participants. Whenever he was in Avalon, he came to this group, and they all knew him. Everybody in the group knew who everybody else was because they'd all been coming here regularly, some of them for many years. There were sometimes a couple of new faces, yet the core membership was fairly stable. He recognized a red-haired college kid named Logan, a high school teacher named Tony, and an older guy, Terry D., who had helped Eddie a lot through the rough years.

When Maureen Davenport had asked Eddie if he was a churchgoing man, he'd answered in the affirmative. It wasn't a lie—the building was a church. But he knew that wasn't what she meant. He hadn't started going to church thanks to some divine inspiration. Following a spectacular screwup on Eddie's part, he'd been ordered by a judge to attend 12-step meetings. He hadn't expected to like it. He hadn't expected to discover the deepest truths about himself in a group of strangers. But something had happened. He hadn't found salvation the way most people did. He'd found it in the shared fellowship of people like him, renewing their commitment every day to stay sober.

On many levels, he told himself, the night of his DUI had been a blessing in disguise. For Eddie, it had been the start of a new way of living. A new way to spend Christmas, too. He still couldn't stand the holiday, but at least he could get through it with clear-eyed sobriety instead of through an alcoholic haze.

He'd started the journey—very much against his will—one snowy Christmas Eve. He was no longer that lost, desperate man who had shown up with a chip on his shoulder and his arm in a sling. But whether he was at his place in the city or here in Avalon, he still came to meetings for the support, the friendship, the chance to serve others. And sometimes, like tonight, he came to think about things that were bugging him.

Like Maureen Davenport. He could tell she was not going to be a picnic. She had that whole prim-and-proper librarian thing going on, which only made him want to tease her, undo her hair, remove her glasses and say, "Why Ms. Davenport, you're beautiful!"

That was the way it might happen in the movies, anyway. He doubted Maureen would play her role, though. She'd probably just tap a pencil on her clipboard and insist on getting back to work. She promised to be weeks of Christmas pageant hell.

He missed Mrs. Bickham already. Mrs. Bickham had made his community service obligation bearable, because she'd been so easygoing. Eddie had barely had to lift a finger for the pageant. However, this Maureen chick was no pushover. She might actually make him do some work. Eddie didn't really mind doing work, but he'd never been fond of taking orders from bossy females.

The people around the room came in all sizes and shapes, all ages and all walks of life. They sipped coffee and waited for Eddie to speak.

"The topic of tonight's meeting is perspective," he told them. "Yeah, that's a good one for me at the moment. I need to remind myself to keep things in perspective. I first started coming to these meetings as a result of a judge's mandate. I thought I didn't belong here. The fact was, I didn't *want* to belong here. I didn't want to be a member of any club where you couldn't drink your face off every single night."

Sympathetic murmurings circulated through the group.

"The judge knew me better than I knew myself. She knew the value of strong medicine—in my case, a lifetime membership in this fine fellowship right here."

Sometimes when he closed his eyes and thought about that night, those moments of terror, Eddie believed he was remembering it all exactly as it happened. He could still feel the glass neck of the bottle in his hand—Dom Perignon, of course.

Nothing but the best on the night he would propose to the woman he loved. It was Natalie's favorite and nothing else would do. Natalie Sweet. She was the perfect woman—a few years older, a lot more sophisticated, a journalist. What's more, she'd been sending out "ask me" signals for weeks, he was sure of it.

He'd planned the evening out. Avalon was the perfect location, between New York City and Albany, where Natalie's family lived. She thought he was taking her to her folks' for Christmas, never guessing the surprise he had in store. He wanted to get engaged on Christmas Eve. He had issues with the holiday, thanks to the way he'd spent all his Christmases growing up, his parents dragging him from town to town with their Yule-themed road show. So to overcome those issues, he would supplant the bad memories with something good. He would transform the holiday from a time filled with painful associations to something joyful—getting engaged to be married.

He knew about the town of Avalon thanks to his family. The town was the home of Camp Kioga, where his folks used to park him each summer when he was a kid, while they traveled from place to place, performing at Renaissance fairs. Through the years, the town had come to feel like home to him, as much as any place had. He'd even pictured himself and Natalie getting a weekend place here one day. That night, he'd booked the best table at the Apple Tree Inn, the one overlooking the Schuyler River. In winter, the rocks were encased in ice and the banks crusted with snow, sparkling in the light streaming down from the restaurant windows. He'd requested all their favorites for the menu and even gave the restaurant manager a list of songs to play throughout the evening.

He remembered the expression on her face when she tasted her dessert—a silky eggnog crème brûlée—because it was the same face she made in bed sometimes. In fact, her dreamy look had been his signal that the time had come.

Although they'd already polished off a bottle of wine, he ordered champagne, noting the lift of her eyebrows and taking it as a good sign.

In retrospect, maybe it was apprehension.

Pleasantly buzzed from the wine, Eddie forged ahead with his plan. Natalie was almost secondary, a bit player to his starring role. That perception in itself should have been a clue. When the moment stopped being about Natalie or even the two of them as a couple, it could only mean trouble.

The sommelier poured two glasses. Eddie offered a toast— something about their future, about a lifetime of happiness. The time had come.

He was a traditionalist at heart. Unabashed by other Christmas-Eve guests, he went down on one knee and took her hand. At that moment, the theme song of *The Christmas Caper* came on the stereo. Maybe he should have recognized it as a bad sign.

The song had definitely not been on Eddie's playlist. The manager might have thought Eddie would like hearing the sweet, sentimental tune. Eddie would never know. Many people assumed that such a beloved movie must be loved by him, as well. All he knew was that the hated song intruded on the moment like a choking spell in the middle of a gourmet meal.

And to top off the moment, this was the most heinous version in existence—the one recorded by an a cappella group known as the Christmas Belles, which had become a sensa-tion on the Internet. The rendition was so sticky-sweet, he thought he might gag, just listening to it.

But he was down on one knee. He was committed. He had to go through with this. There was no turning back now.

He had carefully scripted the words, then memorized them so they wouldn't sound scripted: "I love you. I want to be with you forever. Will you do me the honor of being my wife?"

That was her cue to weep for joy, perhaps to be so overcome she couldn't speak, could only nod vigorously: *Yes, yes, yes, of course I'll marry you.* All around the restaurant, people would sigh over his performance.

Then he would lift the lid of the small velvet jewel box, and a fresh wave of emotion would wash over her.

It was perfect. It was unforgettable. It was going to turn Christmas into the happiest time of his life.

There was one problem. Natalie didn't follow the script. There were no joyful tears. No reciprocal declaration of love. Only a stricken expression of horror on her face.

"Magic can happen, if only you belieeeeeeeeve," sang the Christ-mas Belles in the background.

Natalie didn't nod. She looked nauseous, shook her head no. "I can't. I'm sorry," she said, getting up from the table and making a dash for the cloakroom.

Eddie had dropped a too-big wad of cash on the table, grabbed the champagne bottle by the neck and left, despite knowing it was illegal to leave an establishment with an open container.

Not caring.

She was walking as fast as she could toward the train station.

"Can we at least talk about this?" he asked.

She kept walking. "I'm sorry if I ever gave you the impression that I'd be open to a proposal."

"Hell, you were sending out signals like Western Union," he said. "What was I supposed to think?"

"I have no idea what you're talking about."

"Yeah, excuse me all to hell for thinking you meant it when you said you loved me."

"I did," she protested. "I *do*. But I'm not ready to marry anybody, and neither are you."

"Don't tell me I'm not ready."

"Fine, I won't. But here's what I think. I think you don't want to be married so much as you don't want to be alone."

"Hey, it's one thing to turn me down. Don't psychoanalyze me on top of everything else."

From there, the argument devolved into a rehashing of each other's faults, and after she boarded the Albany-bound train alone, he was ready to concede that yes, he had probably been hasty in proposing marriage.

By the time he returned to the restaurant parking lot for his van, he'd already made the transition from feeling hurt to feeling pissed. At her but even more at himself. Why had he made some big public production out of it? Why had he set himself up for failure like that?

As he drove through the streets of Avalon, the small town looked deserted, a ghost town. Most people had headed home early to be with their families on Christmas Eve. Others were at church, filling the night with song and worship.

Eddie planned to spend the rest of the evening with a man of the cloth. Specifically, a monk named Dom Perignon. Since the bottle had already been opened at the restaurant, he started drinking as he drove. Hell, it was Christmas Eve and there wasn't a soul in sight. He'd just been dumped and he was desperate to numb the hurt and blunt the anger. And he was driving slowly, anyway. He didn't have anywhere he needed to be. His parents had invited him home to their place on Long Island as they did every year, but Natalie had given him the perfect excuse to decline the invitation. Now he was out of excuses.

The snowstorm began in a lively flurry, feathering across the windshield. Within minutes, driven by a lake effect, the flurries blossomed into thick, relentless flakes that were strangely mesmerizing as they hurled themselves toward him. He decided to swing by the Hilltop Tavern, see if anybody was still around. He had a few old friends in Avalon who went way back to his days at summer camp. The small town never changed. He passed cozy-looking houses with their windows aglow, businesses that were closed up tight, the country club that crowned the top of a hill. The most impressive light display belonged to the Heart of the Mountains Church at a bend in the lakeshore road.

The oblong building twinkled with lights along the roof line. An elaborate, life-size nativity scene occupied the broad, snow-covered grounds. He rolled down the driver's side window to feel the icy air. Big snowflakes whipped into the van through the gap.

The faint, distant tolling of bells drifted in through the window, and it was the loneliest sound he'd ever heard. He chased away the mournful noise by turning up the radio, which was playing Black Sabbath's "Never Say Die."

For Eddie, music was more than just sound. It was a place he went, familiar and safe. Amidst the chaos and uncertainty of his childhood, music had been his retreat and solace. Over the years, his affinity had only deepened. When he was a teenager, it became a way to sort out the confusion, almost as calming as drinking a stolen six-pack from his parents' fridge. Later, when he was a student at Juilliard, it was a form of expression that finally made sense to him, the perfect accompaniment to the wine he loved to drink before, during and after performances.

He heard music in his head, all the time. It surprised him to realize this was not the case for other people. Maybe it was a form of insanity.

Years later, when he reviewed the events of that night, he could never separate the sounds and images in his mind from those that had actually existed. He recalled a curious rhythmic beating noise, like the rotors of a helicopter, and a deepening of the already-dark sky. And then something—an animal? A tree limb?—crossing his path.

Operating on pure reflex, he swerved to avoid it.

Mission accomplished.

But in the next moment, everything was ripped from his control. The van hit a patch of black ice and careened off the road, exploding through a snowbank and jolting down a steep slope. The brakes and steering were useless as he cut a swath through the churchyard. Everything in the van—sound equipment, CDs, gear, the empty champagne bottle—was swept up in a tempest.

As the speeding vehicle smashed through the nativity scene and barreled toward the church, only one coherent thought slipped out. *Please, God, don't let me hurt anybody.*

★ ★ ★

"That night changed everything for me," he told the people in the room. "And for that, I'm grateful. I'll remind myself of this in the weeks to come. Because something tells me I'm going to face some challenges. I always do, this time of year."

"Thanks, Eddie," the chorus murmured, and they went on to the next speaker.

His life had really begun the night it had almost ended. That was when he finally had to admit that drinking wasn't working for him. He'd had to transform himself entirely. Music was still his life, but now he worked behind the scenes, a composer and producer, and he also volunteered for an after-school music program for at-risk kids in Lower Manhattan. Life was good enough for him, under the radar like that.

His ancient but still-in-effect contract with the production company had limited his earnings from the movie to a pittance. To this day, he had no idea why his parents had allowed it. That same contract called for him to participate materially in promotion of the movie—which meant he had to appear in DVD extras. Creating those segments earlier in the year had reminded him of the things he disliked about fame—knowing he wasn't the person everyone saw and loved on screen. Having to hide who he really was.

Being a composer kept him involved in music, though by choice, he was mostly anonymous, creating soundtracks and jingles to order. It freaked him out that people recognized him, and that interest was renewed thanks to the DVD. He only hoped it would blow over soon.

The part of him that still loved to perform found satisfaction, as well. He visited Avalon frequently to play with a group of his friends in a band called Inner Child, and they had the occasional gig at local festivals or a neighborhood club. This year, he agreed to be the guest host for a local radio show, "Catskills Morning," consisting of news, talk and music of his choice, five days a week. The regular host was on maternity leave.

His life was a far cry from the orgy of fame and fortune he'd once pictured for himself. But it was a much better fit.

The meeting ended as it always did, with the serenity prayer and a quick cleanup of the coffee service; then Eddie prepared to head home for the evening. He stopped at Wegmans and treated himself to his favorite take-out dinner—a pimento cheese sandwich, a big fat dill pickle, a bag of chips and a root beer soda. On the way out of the store, he encountered one of the earliest signs of the season—a Salvation Army bell ringer.

The insistent clanging of the bell was both annoying and impossible to ignore. Scrounging a crumpled bill out from his pocket, he stuffed it into the painted red bucket.

"Thanks," said the bell ringer. He was young, just a boy, really. Something about him was familiar in a vague, distant way. The teenager reminded Eddie of some of his students, back in the city—hungry but proud. Maybe the kid had been in previous Christmas pageants. But no. Eddie was pretty sure he would remember that long, dark hair and soulful eyes, the slightly bemused smile.

"I'm Eddie Haven," Eddie said.

He gave a nod. "Jabez Cantor."

"New around here?" Eddie asked.

"Kind of. I've been away for a while. Just got back to town."

"Hey, same here."

Another kid came out of the store, staring down at a handheld game as he walked, oblivious to everything. By the time Eddie realized where he was headed, it was too late. Both he and Jabez said, "Watch out," at the same time, but the kid had already crashed into the tripod holding up the collection bucket, knocking it to the ground with a clatter.

"Sorry," he said, stuffing the handheld into his pocket and dropping down on his knees to retrieve the spilled coins. "I wasn't watching where I was going."

"It happens," said Jabez, stooping down to help.

Eddie pitched in, too, scooping coins from the pavement. He couldn't help noticing the scars on Jabez's hands. They had the taut shine of very old burns, imperfectly healed.

An older guy with iron-gray hair and a long overcoat came toward them. "Cecil," he said in a voice grating with disapproval, "what's going on here?"

"I knocked this thing over," the boy named Cecil said. "Sorry, Grandpa."

The older guy looked exasperated. Cecil worked faster, trying to round up the spilled coins while Jabez reassembled the tripod. A couple of minutes later, everything was back in place. The grandfather strode away toward a sleek Maybach. The kid started after him, hesitated and dug a dollar bill from his pocket, stuffing it into the collection bucket. Jabez thanked him, but he probably didn't hear as he rushed to catch up with his grandfather.

Eddie studied the boy named Jabez, who was staring thoughtfully after them. Actually, a lot of people were staring at the Maybach, since you didn't see a car like that every day, but Jabez seemed more focused on the older guy.

"He looks familiar," Jabez said.

"Everything all right?" asked Eddie.

"Sure," said the boy.

"You hungry?" Eddie held out the sack.

"No, I'm good. Really. But thanks."

Eddie had learned not to push for too much information. That often resulted in a kid running off and disappearing for good. "You like doing volunteer work?"

The kid indicated the Salvation Army bucket. "Guess so."

"Good. A group of us are going to be putting up a nativity scene Friday night—you know what that is?"

The kid chuckled. "Yeah, I know what a nativity scene is."

"Just asking. Anyway, they could use more volunteers." He scribbled the time and a place on his white deli bag, tore it off and handed it to Jabez. "Maybe I'll see you there."

Jabez took the slip of paper and put it into his breast pocket. "Maybe you will."

4

After her meeting with Eddie Haven, Maureen was convinced of at least two things. First, Eddie was going to be a big problem in the weeks to come. And second, he was not the worst thing she could expect to happen this week.

She felt an ominous sense of apprehension as she stayed late at the library the next day. An important board meeting would convene at closing time. Although not a member of the library board, she was a key participant in their meetings. While waiting for the small group to arrive, she went through the usual ritual of securing the building. When she reached the main entrance, she stepped outside, breathing deeply of the crisp, empty air.

A light snowfall would be nice, she thought, surveying the parklike surroundings. In a side garden with an ancient yew rumored to have been brought from the yard of Cadbury Castle in England, there was a smallish, lonely-looking block of granite with a commemorative plaque. It was an unassuming monument to the unknown boy who had died in the library fire a hundred years before.

The trees had long since dropped their colorful mantles of leaves. The grass had gone dormant and lay dry and beaten down, as if it would never grow again. An air of bleakness hovered everywhere, giving the place a sense of waiting. A good, clean snowfall would change everything. Situated on the east side of Willow Lake, the town of Avalon usually received early and copious snow. But the weather came in its own time, and a simple wish would not hurry it along.

Enough moping around, she told herself. It would take a lot more than Eddie Haven or even a fiasco at work to ruin her Christmas.

Time to go inside and get ready for the meeting. As she passed beneath the library building's arched portico of figured concrete, she could still feel an echo of reverence. The entry to the library was designed to inspire it. Chiseled into the concrete were the words *Make thy books thy companions. Let thy cases and shelves be thy pleasure grounds and gardens.—Judah ibn-Tibbon (12th century)*. Which was a diplomatic way of saying, Maureen supposed, that it was all right to have no life.

She wasn't being fair to herself. She did have a life, a life in books and in the embrace of a large, supportive family. This was more than many people had, and she was grateful.

She grabbed a yogurt from the tiny fridge in the break room and called it dinner, which she consumed while reading a publisher's advance copy of an upcoming self-help book called *Passionate Living for Shy People.* It was filled with advice no one in their right mind would ever take, like signing up for salsa dancing lessons or participating in touch therapy. Reading about such things was so much safer than actually doing them. Losing herself in a book usually brought the world back into balance, but it didn't always work. By the time she finished her yogurt, she was feeling decidedly unsettled. The topic of today's meeting was the budget, and she knew the news would not be good.

The library's executive board members arrived, heading into the meeting room with their laptops and briefcases. The four of them stood up when Maureen joined them, waiting in a line on the far side of the table, as solemn and intent as a firing squad.

She draped her coat over the back of a chair. "It's not good, is it?"

An uncomfortable silence hung in the air. Mr. Shannon, the president of the board, folded his hands on top of an official-looking document. "Worse than not good. Unless we can pull a rabbit out of a hat, we're done. The facility is closing at the end of the year."

"Please, Miss Davenport, have a seat," said another board member.

She sank down onto one of the molded plastic stacking chairs, folded her hands in her lap. She knew the facility had been operating in the red for a long time. It was no one's fault, simply the fallout from a disastrous system-wide finance crisis, exacerbated by rising costs and hard times for the entire area. When revenues shrank, hard choices had to be made. Priority funding went to life-or-death agencies—police, fire, EMS.

Maureen might consider the library vital to the life of the community, but to many people, already feeling overburdened, it was expendable.

Mr. Shannon summarized the dilemma so the secretary could include the discussion in the minutes. After the original building burned down, the library had been rebuilt by Mr. Jeremiah Byrne. Although the building and grounds remained in the family, Byrne had extended a 99-year lease to the institution. Now it fell to a Mr. Warren Byrne to extend the lease.

And he had, but there were conditions attached. The lease would not be renewed until the library could fund itself, and that meant coming up with an entire annual operating budget before the end of the year. The library board secured a grant from the city, coupling this with donations and public monies, and for a time, the crisis seemed to be averted. The grant money for the next fiscal year had not come through, and the shrunken tax base had caused a budget cut. The library had been cut off like a bleeding artery.

Maureen tried to focus on what the head of the library board was saying. She was trying, actually, to hear anything but what he was saying.

"We're out of money" could only be interpreted in one way.

Her heart sank. The library? *Closed?* It was impossible to imagine Avalon without its library. The public library was one of the most revered and recognizable institutions in any town. Avalon's had always seemed special. Following the fire that had taken the boy's life, the devastated community had pulled together, raising the new building as a monument to the spirit of resilience. For the next ninety-nine years, the place had endured, seemingly as permanent as the granite rock formations around Willow Lake. It was an illusion, though. Soon all of Avalon would know they were celebrating the library's centennial by announcing its closure.

"I knew there was a budget crisis," she said, trying to keep panic at bay. "I didn't realize it was so dire." Yes, *dire*. It wasn't a word she used every day. Unfortunately, it was the right word for the current situation. Fixing a determinedly pleasant smile on her face, she said, "We can send out an emergency appeal. Do another fund-raiser. A whole series of them. What about an urgent letter, a capital campaign? An auction or event—" Her smile sagged as she surveyed their bleak faces. "I know. We've done all that."

"And frankly, we don't even have the money for postage," said the treasurer.

"What about emergency funds from the county? Or the state—"

"Despite what we all think, Ms. Davenport, this is not considered an emergency like a wildfire or flood. The sad fact is, our expenses greatly outstrip our resources, and they have for quite some time." He indicated the large, intimidating figure printed boldly in bright holly-red. "We're not going to make it."

"There has to be something more we can do," she insisted. "What about asking Mr. Byrne to renegotiate the terms of the lease? Or ask for an extension until we can come up with more funds."

"Warren Byrne? He's the stingiest man in town."

"And the richest," she pointed out.

"He got that way by being stingy. He's never given the

library a penny." Mr. Shannon shook his head. "We've asked, and he's refused. The sum we need is out of our reach, pure and simple. Our major donors have been more than generous, but there's a limit to what can be done with private funding. Without the grant, we're out of options," he said with a weary sigh. "Times being what they are, even our biggest donors are overcommitted—or tapped out. Perhaps if the recent bond issue had passed, we wouldn't be in this position, but the voters declined to approve it."

Maureen gritted her teeth. A small but vocal group of tax protesters had convinced people that the library was not worth saving if it meant a small added sales tax. She had campaigned hard for the bond, but it had failed.

"Our state assemblywoman requested a budget variance on our behalf, and so has the city council," Mr. Shannon was saying. "But the money is not there, not for this. There are other matters ahead of us in the queue."

The treasurer passed out her latest report. "Under the circumstances, we can't come close to meeting our operating budget for the next year. We have until year's end to close our doors and transfer all assets to the main library branch in the county."

Maureen saw her own despair reflected in their faces. "What's going to happen to this place?"

"Most of the collection and assets will be distributed among other library branches. The property is likely to be sold to a developer. Thanks to a building preservation ordinance, the space will be used rather than torn down."

"Used for what?" Maureen asked. She pictured the venerable old place, converted to a craft shop or B & B. Not that she had anything against craft shops or B & Bs, but this was a *library*.

"You're giving up, then," she said. "Just like that."

"Not just like that," Mr. Shannon said, his voice thin with weariness. "We've left no stone unturned. You know we've been working nonstop."

"I do know, I'm sorry. But…it's the library," she said in her broken whisper. She gestured around the room, its walls hung with old photographs depicting the library's history. The arched doorway framed a view of the main room. In the half light slanting through the windows, the neat stacks and polished oak tables gleamed.

"And that's the problem," Mr. Shannon said, donning his overcoat and flat driving cap. "It doesn't matter to enough people. Most people I've talked to don't see letting one library go as a total disaster. It just means a few more people will have to drive an extra twenty miles to get books, or wait for the Bookmobile to show up. Hardly the greatest of catastrophes in times like these."

Maureen felt a chill, knowing he was right. "Yes, this is just one library, but our situation is being replicated everywhere. They just barely managed to save the library in Salinas—John Steinbeck's hometown. Philadelphia lost eleven branches last year. An entire county in Oregon shut down their system. It's all part of a slow erosion. When will it stop?"

"The city council had to fund public safety," Mr. Shannon pointed out. "Do they monitor misdemeanor sex offenders or pay the library's light bill? There's really no choice."

"I understand," she said. "I'm…trying to, anyway."

"Thanks for meeting with us," he said. "I wanted to tell you in person as soon as we heard the bad news."

She stood up, walked with him to the door. "I appreciate it." Everyone else followed, silent and somber. Maureen felt shell-shocked, like an accident victim. She'd always pictured herself spending her entire career here, serving the institution she loved. Now, she realized, in a few weeks she'd be out of a job.

Mrs. Goodnow, the board secretary, said, "We're planning a potluck for the closing ceremony at the end of the year."

Maureen tried not to sway on her feet. "Yes, all right," she managed to say. She shut the double doors to the meeting room behind her.

Mr. Shannon paused at the exit, draping a muffler around his shoulders. "Are you coming?"

"I'll be a few minutes more. I need to check my e-mail and rearrange a few things on my schedule."

"Take care, Ms. Davenport."

"You, too, Mr. Shannon."

He hesitated a moment longer. "You don't look well."

She felt a nauseating wave of grief. "This library is part of the fabric of the town. We can't just close." She thought about the children who came for story hour. The seniors who came for book clubs and computer classes. The adult literacy program. Then she pictured its doors being closed and locked forever. And something inside her curled up and died.

"Can I get you something before I go?" Mr. Shannon offered. "A glass of water or—"

"A miracle," she said, forcing a smile. "A miracle would be good right about now."

★ ★ ★

In the empty quiet of the library, Maureen didn't check her mail. She didn't even go near her desk. Instead, she went to the stacks, walking slowly between the tall oaken shelves, running her hands across the spines of the books. She'd always considered the library a sacred place, a place of ideas and art, a safe place to let dreams take flight.

A library—this library in particular—had always filled her with reverence. It was a cathedral for the most diverse elements of mankind, where all of humanity could find its place. She'd practically grown up here in this historic Greek revival building, with its marble halls and leaded windows, the polished mahogany railings and casements. In the center of the building was a sky-lit atrium, featuring a winding staircase leading to the children's room. When she was very small, climbing the staircase had felt like a special rite of passage, like ascending to heaven.

It was fitting that Maureen would one day become a steward of the institution. Oh, there had been a couple of years in college when she'd been bitten by the theater arts bug, dreaming instead of a future on stage, as if such a thing could actually happen to a girl like her.

A disastrous adventure abroad had cured her of that notion. Even now, years later, the memory of her semester in Paris made her shudder. The life lesson had been slammed home with the force of a tidal wave. She'd learned quickly that she was made for a quieter, more mindful life. Working at the library offered her exactly that. She could be here doing work that mattered, that made her feel vital and alive…and safe.

Yet soon, this place would cease to exist. The county system might assign her to the bookmobile, she thought with a shudder. The one time she'd served in the bookmobile, as an intern, she'd gotten carsick. She could probably find a position in another town, or at the college in New Paltz, but working in this particular place was so much more than a job to her. And it was about to be taken away.

She couldn't imagine her life without this library. What would she do every day? Where would she go? Who would she be? She refused to imagine it. But that was just denial, wasn't it? It was time to face the cold, hard facts. By year's end, the library would be closed. She had to quit hoping for a miracle.

As she put on her things and prepared to leave, her gaze slipped once again over the dimly lit stacks. The wisdom of the ages lived there, philosophers and scientists, poets and playwrights and novelists, the best minds of humanity. Shouldn't the answers lie in one of these books?

Wandering between the rows of shelves, she went through a ritual she'd been enacting since she was a girl. Whenever she had a problem or question turning over and over in her mind, she would close her eyes and select a random book from the shelf. With eyes still closed, she would let it fall open, and without peeking put her finger on a passage. Then she'd open her eyes and read the book's advice. It was just a game, yet it was uncanny how much she'd learned simply by opening her mind and opening a book.

She couldn't imagine what advice might possibly save her from her current troubles, but force of habit ran strong. She shut her eyes and skimmed her fingertip along the spines of the books, stopping between heartbeats. She quickly extracted a volume from the shelf. She heard another fall to the floor, a corner of the book hitting her foot.

"Ow!" she said, her eyes flying open.

Now she had a dilemma. Which was more random, the book in her hands or the one at her feet?

She let the book in her hands fall open and, without looking, ran her index finger partway down the page. Then she looked down to see what would be revealed to her.

There is a theory which states that if ever anyone discovers exactly what the Universe is for and why it is here, it will instantly disappear and be replaced by something even more bizarre and inexplicable. There is another theory which states that this has already happened.

"Thank you, Douglas Adams," she murmured to the late author, flipping the book over to check out his photo. "You're no help at all." She reshelved the book, carefully lining up its spine on the old oak shelf. Then she picked up the book that had fallen to the floor: *Words to Live By: A Compendium.*

Well, that didn't even belong here in adult fiction. It had been misshelved.

This was a common occurrence in any library, but there had always been rumors afoot that the place was haunted. In a building like this one, filled with whispering marble halls and papery echoes, such fanciful talk couldn't be avoided.

As she hastened to the aisle where the book properly

belonged, she glanced down at the page that had fallen open, read the line indicated by her thumb in the margin.

If you never did, you should. These things are fun, and fun is good. The statement was attributed to Theodore Seuss Geisel—better known as Dr. Seuss.

Fun is good. A tiny chill touched the back of her neck. Maybe her thumb was really pointing to the next entry: *Life shrinks or expands in proportion to one's courage.—Anais Nin.*

Snapping the volume shut, she put the book away and left the library through the staff-only back door, locking it behind her.

As she headed into the dark night, her mobile phone sounded with her sister Janet's ring tone—"Shattered" by the Rolling Stones. She pulled her glove off with her teeth, fished out the phone and flipped it open. "Hey."

"Hey, yourself. I was just wondering if you'd had dinner yet."

Maureen's stomach was in knots. She couldn't imagine eating anything. Ever again. "I've already eaten."

"Oh. I just wondered if you wanted to drive over and grab something. Karl is going to be late tonight, and I'm all by my lonesome."

That was Janet for you. Her younger sister was the baby of the family. Though she was as loyal and loving as a person could be, she was never happy in her own company. She'd gone from her college sorority house to marriage, and was already expecting her first child.

"It'd take me an hour to get there, Jan," Maureen said. Janet and Karl had moved closer to the city to make his commute shorter.

"There's no snow in the forecast."

It always bothered Maureen that she was the default sister. When anyone in her family needed someone to be instantly available, Maureen was the one they called.

They didn't call Meredith, the oldest. Meredith was a doctor in Albany. She was always on duty or on call and at any given time, she was considered too busy to bother. Renée, the next oldest, had three kids, which meant three thousand reasons Renée could never be the go-to girl. Their brother, Guy, was, well, a *guy,* reason enough to leave him be. That left Maureen, the middle sibling. She was the one they called when they suddenly needed something—companionship, an errand runner, someone to chat with on the phone, a babysitter.

Here was what drove her crazy—not that she was the one they called, but that they assumed she never had anything better to do.

"We could get takeout and watch goofy old holiday movies," Janet wheedled. "Come on, it'll be fun. You remember fun, right? Fun is good."

"What?"

"I said—"

"Never mind. I've got something I'm doing tonight," she told Janet.

"Really? What's going on? Do you have a date? Oh, my God, you have a date," Janet exclaimed without giving Maureen a chance to respond. "Who is it? Walter Grunion? Oh, I know. Ned Farkis. He ran into Karl on the train and asked about you. Oh, my God, you're going out with Ned Farkis."

Maureen laughed aloud. "I'm glad you have my evening all

figured out for me. Ned Farkis. Give me a break." Ned was a pharmacist's assistant at the local Rexall. He'd asked her out several times, and she'd never said a clear no, but she never said yes, either. Then she felt guilty about her scorn, because she knew there were guys out there—many, many guys—who had exactly that kind of opinion of her—*Maureen Davenport? Give me a break.*

"Seriously," she said to Janet, "I'm meeting Olivia. We're going to the church to help construct the nativity scene."

"Oh. I didn't know you were on that committee, too."

"I'm not. Not officially, anyway. But since I'm working on the pageant—"

"I get it. Today the pageant, tomorrow the world."

"Very funny. You could join us," she suggested.

"Us?"

"The volunteers at church."

"It's kind of a long drive for me," Janet said.

Yet she'd been perfectly willing for Maureen to drive it. Maureen tried not to feel exasperated. "Have a nice night, Janet," she said.

"Sure will. Love you!"

Maureen was blessed to belong to a family where everybody loved each other. Her parents had been college sweethearts who made their home in Avalon because it was a place of natural beauty, a place where they wanted to have lots of kids and raise them surrounded by small-town safety and the richness of nature. All five of their children still lived in or near Avalon.

This was not to say life for the Davenports had been easy. Far from it. Her mother had died of a virus that went straight to her heart. Stan Davenport, a high school principal, had been left with a houseful of kids. Maureen was just five years old when it had happened. She remembered the livid pain of loss, a memory as stark as an old photograph. Meredith had cried so hard, she'd made herself throw up, and Guy had turned their mother's name into an endless string of tragic sobs: "Mama. Mama. Mama." Their father had sat at the dining room table with his head propped in his hands, his shoulders shaking, Janet and Renée clinging to him, too young to grasp anything but the fact that in a single instant, their world had exploded. Maureen understood everything, young as she was. Dad had looked like a stranger to her. A complete stranger who had wandered into the wrong house, the wrong family.

In time, they had all learned to smile again, to find the joys in life. And eventually, her father had married Hannah, who adored the children and mothered them as fiercely and devotedly as if she'd given birth to them. One of the reasons Maureen loved Christmas so much was that Hannah always set aside time at the holiday for each child to spend remembering their mother. This meant there were tears, sometimes even anger, but ultimately, it meant their mother lived in their hearts no matter how long she'd been gone.

Only now, as an adult, could Maureen truly appreciate Hannah's great generosity of spirit. They were a close family, and this time of year was the perfect time to remember the many ways she was blessed. Even in the face of the biggest professional disaster of her career, she could still feel blessed.

Maureen loved everything about Christmas—the cold nip in the air and the crunch of snow underfoot. The aroma of baking cookies and the twinkle of lights in shop windows and along roof lines. The old songs drifting from the radio, sentimental movies on TV, stacks of Christmas books on library tables, the children's artwork on display. The cheery clink of coins in the Salvation Army collection bucket and the fellowship of people working together on holiday projects.

All of this made her feel a part of something. All of this made her feel safe. Yes, she loved Christmas.

5

Eddie Haven couldn't stand Christmas. It was his own private hell. His aversion had started at a young age, and had only grown stronger with the passage of years. Which did not explain why he was on his way to help build a nativity scene in front of the Heart of the Mountains Church.

At least he didn't have to go alone. His passengers were three brothers who had been categorized at the local high school as at-risk teens. Eddie had never been fond of the label, "at-risk." As far as he could tell, just being a teenager was risky. Tonight, three of them were his unlikely allies, and at the moment they were arguing over nothing, as brothers seemed to do. Tonight was all about keeping the boys occupied. One of the main reasons they were at risk was that they had too much time on their hands. He figured by putting their hands on hammers and hay bales, they'd spend a productive evening and stay out of trouble.

"Hey, Mr. Haven," said Omar Veltry, his youngest charge. "I bet you five dollars I can tell you where you got them boots you're wearing."

"What makes you think I even have five dollars?" Eddie asked.

"Then bet me," Omar piped up. "Maybe I'll lose and you'll get five dollars off me. Five dollars says I can tell you where you got those boots."

"Hell, *I* don't even know where I got them. So go for it."

"Ha. You got those boots on your feet, man." Omar nearly bounced himself off the seat. He high-fived each brother in turn and they all giggled like maniacs.

Christ. At a stoplight, Eddie dug in his pocket, found a five. "Man. You are way too smart for me. All three of you are real wiseguys."

"Ain't we, though?"

"I bet you're smart enough to put that fiver in the church collection box," Eddie added.

"Oh, man." Omar collapsed against the seat.

Heart of the Mountains Church was situated on a hillside overlooking Willow Lake, its slender steeple rising above the trees. The downhill-sloping road bowed out to the left near the main yard of the church, and a failure to negotiate the curve could mean a swift ride to disaster. Eddie slowed the van. No matter how many times he rounded this curve in the road, he always felt the same shudder of memory. This was where the two halves of his life had collided—the past and the future—one snowy night, ten years ago.

Tonight, the road was bare and dry. The iconic church was the picture of placid serenity, its windows aglow in the twilight, the landscape stark but beautiful, waiting for the snow. This, Eddie figured, was the sort of setting people imagined for weddings and holiday worship, community events—and of course, AA meetings.

He pulled into the church parking lot. "I'm officially broke now. Thanks a lot."

"I heard you used to be a movie star," Randy, the older brother, pointed out. "Everybody knows movie stars are rich."

"Yeah, that's me," Eddie said. "Rich."

"Betcha you're rich from that movie," the middle brother, Moby, pointed out. "I saw it on TV just the other night. 'There's magic in Christmas, if only you believe,'" he quoted. It was a famous line in *The Christmas Caper,* uttered by a wide-eyed and irresistible little Eddie. The damn thing aired endlessly like a digital virus every holiday season.

"Now you're officially on my nerves," said Eddie. "And FYI, I'm not rich from the movie. Not even close."

"Huh," Moby said with a snort of disbelief. Moby was his nickname, based not on his size, but on the fact that his given name was Richard. "Your movie's huge. It's on TV every Christmas."

"Maybe so, but that doesn't do me a bit of good."

"You don't, like, get a cut or anything?"

"Geez, don't look at me like that. I was a kid, okay? And my parents didn't do so hot, being in charge of finances." The Havens had been incredibly naive, in fact. Against all odds and conventional wisdom, they'd managed to fail to make money off one of the most successful films of the year.

Maybe that was why he avoided his folks like poison ivy

around the holidays. Oh, please let it not be so, Eddie thought. He didn't want to be so shallow. But neither did he want to try figuring out the real reason he steered clear of family matters at Christmas.

"Did they, like, take your money and spend it on cars and stuff?" Randy asked. "Or make stupid investments?"

"It's complicated," Eddie said. "To make a long story short, they signed some contracts without quite knowing what they were agreeing to, and none of us saw any earnings. It was a long time ago," he added. "Water under the bridge."

"Didn't you, like, grow up in some kind of compound?" Moby asked. "That's what I heard, anyway."

Eddie laughed. "Commune, not compound. There's a difference." His parents had caught the tail end of the radical sixties, and for a time, they'd dropped out of society. They'd spent the seventies on a commune in a remote, rural area of the Catskills, convinced that simple living and self-sufficiency would lead the way to Nirvana. Eddie had been born in a hand-built cabin without electricity or running water, his mother attended by a midwife and surrounded by chanting doulas. He wondered what the Veltry brothers would say if they knew the actual name on his birth certificate. It was a far cry from Eddie. "A commune is based on the idea that the community raises the kids, not just the parents," he explained to them. "I was homeschooled, too. The group kind of fell apart after a while, but by then, my folks had created a traveling show. We were on the road a lot."

"Musta sucked for you," Randy said.

Eddie had thought so, but working with kids like the Veltrys had shown him everything was relative. Compared to the three brothers, Eddie's problems had been nothing. At least both of his parents had been present. According to Eddie's friend Ray Tolley, who was with the local PD, the Veltry boys were in foster care more than they were out. Eddie didn't know the precise reason and he didn't want to bug them by asking. They'd never known their father, and they had a mother who couldn't manage to stay out of jail.

When Eddie was their age, his biggest worry had been how to survive his parents and the legacy of the Haven family. He came from a long line of entertainers dating back generations, to Edvard Haszczak, a circus acrobat who stowed away on a freighter from the Baltic Sea. Upon arrival in America, Edvard had changed his unspellable last name and founded a family of performers. Eddie's great-grandparents had been vaudeville singers; his grandparents were borscht-belt crooners and Eddie's parents were a semifamous couple who had starred in a cheesy variety show in the 1960s called *Meet the Havens* when they were just teenagers themselves.

During their counterculture years, they'd dropped out of everything, but trying to bring up a child woke them up to the reality that they couldn't always depend on the commune for everything. They couldn't raise money for doctor visits and clothes for a growing child in the communal garden. So at a young age, too young to be consulted about it, the youngest Haven carried on the family tradition of show business. After appearing in a couple of commercials, including one featuring him as a bare-bottomed baby, he scored a box office hit which had become the Christmas movie that would not die. His delivery of an unforgettable line, and his performance of an iconic song—"The Runaway Reindeer"—ensured his fame for decades to follow.

Although he landed a couple more movie roles—a horror flick, a stupid musical, voicing a cartoon—Eddie never cared that much for acting and the projects flopped or never made it to release. Yet no matter how many hats he subsequently tried on—serious music student, edgy grunge rocker, soulful singer/songwriter—the child-star persona stuck to him like melted candy. He grew up in the shadow of a little kid who had no idea what he was saying when he mouthed the lines that defined him for a generation of viewers.

His parents continued to perform, featuring Eddie in an act designed to cash in on his popularity. "Meet the Havens," as the trio became known, spent every Christmas season on the road. This left Eddie with little more than a blur of unpleasant memories of the holiday season. His parents insisted Christmas was the ideal time of year for a traveling ensemble. People tended to get nostalgic, and in the grip of the holiday spirit, they opened their pockets. From the time he was very small, he'd been obliged to head out with his parents the day after Thanksgiving, playing a different small venue every night, right up to New Year's Day. They stayed in nondescript motels and ate their meals on the fly, often skipping dinner because it was too close to showtime.

Eddie had hated it, yet every single night when he stepped out in front of an audience, he did so with a smile on his face and a song on his lips. But it left a bad taste in his mouth about Christmas.

He didn't let on to the three Veltry boys, though. He honestly wanted them to regard Christmas with the benign good spirits that seemed to emanate from those who, this evening, had left their warm homes to help build the church's nativity scene—an elaborate, detailed and life-size frieze that attracted fans from all over the upper part of the state. This was one of the most popular sights in Avalon this time of year, and the church, in cooperation with the Chamber of Commerce, went all out.

A number of volunteers were there already, organizing the components of the display—structures and figures, heavy-duty cables and lights, lumber and power tools. The boys approached their task with a cocky swagger that was lost on the church people. What was not lost was the boys' sagging jeans and oversize hoodies with tribal-looking symbols.

Ray Tolley came over to greet them. "Not your usual suspects," he murmured to Eddie. Ray was one of Eddie's closest friends, though they couldn't be more different. Ray came from a solid, stable background. He'd been born and raised right here in Avalon. He was a good keyboard player, mediocre at pool and big on practical jokes.

He was also Eddie's parole officer.

They'd met as boys at summer camp. They'd met again as adults, the night of the accident. Ray, a rookie back then, had been in charge of taking a statement from Eddie.

In his hospital bed, his injuries relatively minor after the fiery wreck, Eddie had not been able to offer much in the way of explanation. Ray hadn't wanted to hear about Eddie's romantic troubles that night or about Eddie's issues with the

Christmas holiday. Looking back on that time, it was surprising that they'd become friends at all, let alone bandmates.

Eddie introduced the Veltry boys to Noah Shepherd, a friend of his who played in the band. Noah was also a veterinarian who had access to large amounts of hay. Noah was with his stepson, Max Bellamy. The kid was growing like a weed, pushing his way awkwardly into adolescence. "These guys will help you with the truckload of hay bales," Eddie said, introducing Omar, Randy and Moby.

"Great," Noah replied. "Grab some work gloves out of the cab."

A dark, polished Maybach glided to a stop in the parking lot, and out stepped the pudgy kid Eddie had encountered the other night. The moment the elegant ride slipped away, some of the other teenagers present circled him like a school of sharks, taunting him, one of them tugging at his hoodie.

"That's Cecil Byrne," said Omar, who'd noticed Eddie's interest. "He just moved here and he's, like, the richest kid in town. Everybody hates him."

"Because he's new? Or rich?"

Omar shrugged. "He's pretty much of a geek. People can't stand that."

"Do me a favor," Eddie said to Randy, the eldest of the Veltrys. "Go see if he can help with some transformers."

Randy nodded, clearly grasping his task. He waded through the shark tank. The other kids gave way without hesitation, some of them greeting him and confirming Eddie's instinct that the Veltry boys were considered cool. Randy, with his Jay-Zstyle good looks and attitude, simply said, "Yo, Cecil, we could use some help with some electrical transformers over here."

Cecil nodded and followed Randy with unconcealed relief. He still had that outcast look, the look of a kid who wasn't comfortable in his own skin. High school was a bumpy ride for kids like that.

Guys were setting up power tools, plugging them into long orange extension cords. One of the volunteers, a local business owner who'd never liked Eddie for reasons Eddie didn't quite understand, leaned over to his friend and said, "Look who's back in town. Mr. Runaway Reindeer."

Eddie made a kissing sound with his mouth. "Always a pleasure to see you again, Lyall."

The guy jerked a thumb at the Veltry boys. "Check out the baby outlaws," he told his buddies. "Better keep track of your tools."

"Come on, Lyall," Eddie said, grinning through his temper. "Don't be an ass." The two of them went back way too far, all the way back to their summer camp days, when Eddie had stolen a girl from Lyall.

"Then quit bringing your trashy kids around and we won't have a problem," Lyall said.

Eddie stared down at the ground. Counted to ten. Silently recited the serenity prayer. Forced his fists to unfurl. "Let's not do this, Lyall."

"Fine. We won't do this. Just keep an eye on those kids."

Damn, thought Eddie, counting again. Why do I do this to myself? I could be back in the city, playing my guitar, or—

A car door slammed. "Hello," sang a female voice. "We brought hot chocolate."

He looked over to see Maureen Davenport with a hugely pregnant woman. They started pouring drinks from a thermos and handing them out. The blond, pregnant woman was pretty enough, but it was Maureen who held his attention. Dour little Maureen, wrapped up like a cannoli in a muffler, peering out at the world from behind her thick glasses.

He sidled over to her. "Didn't know I'd see you here. I guess you can't get enough of me."

She pulled the muffler down and offered a tight little smile. "Right. You are so irresistible. What are you doing here, Mr. I-Can't-Stand-Christmas?" Without waiting for an answer, she turned to the other woman. "This is my friend, Olivia Davis."

"Hey, Lolly." A big guy in a parka showed up, bending to give her a peck on the cheek. "Connor Davis," he said. "This is my brother, Julian Gastineaux. He's a Cornell student, just visiting for the weekend."

They didn't look like brothers; Connor resembled a lumberjack while Julian was clearly of mixed race, long-limbed and slender as a marathon runner. He wore a fleece-lined bomber cap but despite the dorky headgear, nearly every teenage girl present seemed to be swooning over him.

"I'm Eddie Haven." Eddie turned to the blond woman again. "Lolly. Have we met?"

"Lolly Bellamy," she said. "We both went to Camp Kioga, a hundred years ago."

"I didn't know you went to Camp Kioga," said Maureen.

"Five summers," Eddie said. "Best summers of my life."

"Olivia and Connor turned it into a year-round resort," Maureen said.

"Good to know," Julian said, aiming a teasing grin at Olivia. "I'm ordering room service breakfast in the morning."

"Huh," she said, "that's for paying guests only." She held out an insulated paper cup to Eddie. "Hot chocolate?"

He thanked her, and she went off with her husband and brother-in-law. Eddie turned to Maureen. "I'm here for the drinks. What about you?"

"I wanted to help out."

"Let's both be honest and say we didn't want to be alone tonight, and neither of us had a better offer."

She frowned as though unsure whether she believed him or not. "Who says I didn't have a better offer?"

"Yeah? What did you turn down in order to build a manger?"

"That's none of your business."

"You're trying to psych me out," he accused.

"Sure. Of course that's what I'm doing. Now, if you'll excuse me, I'm going to go uncrate a sheep."

The air came alive with the sound of hammering. Eddie worked on the lighting and sound for the display, because these were things he knew. And in spite of himself, he kept an eye on the Veltry brothers—not because he thought they might steal something, but because they had wandering attention spans. He commandeered Max and Omar to aim the floodlights at the display from all angles, with the most powerful beam installed above, streaming down into the middle of the manger. There were also yards of light strings that would outline the structure and the church, as well.

Maureen was hovering nearby. "It's not coming together," she said, her head tipped back as she critically surveyed the display.

"People are freezing their asses off," he pointed out. "Hard to do your best work when you're freezing your ass off."

"That's because it's twenty degrees out. Let's try putting on some Christmas music," she said.

"Oh, please."

"Not everyone feels the way you do about Christmas," she said.

"And not everyone feels the way *you* do about Christmas," he replied.

"Music," she said.

"Whatever you say." He stalked over to his van and fired up the sound system, selecting a mix tape that was sure to annoy her. A moment later, Rick James singing "Superfreak (U Can't Touch This)" blasted from the speakers.

It was worth the trouble just to witness outrage on Maureen's face. She didn't say anything, though, because everyone else had a different reaction. The suggestive thump of rhythm and ridiculous lyrics immediately took hold, as he'd known it would. One thing he was good at was music selection—matching songs to occasions.

"Superfreak" was one of those pieces no one could resist. Even the Veltry brothers, whose taste ran to hip-hop, stepped up their pace.

As she tilted back her head and regarded the night sky, Maureen looked skeptical.

"Now what?" he asked her.

She indicated a guy on a ladder. "Something's missing," she

said. "I can't quite put my finger on it." Her face changed—softened—as she tilted her gaze at the roof of the main structure. "That's Jabez," she said. "Have you met him yet?"

"Briefly," he said. Something about the kid kept niggling at him. Maybe it was just Jabez himself. He exuded a kind of subtle magnetism. The other high-school kids were drawn to him, handing over light spools and cords as he climbed the ladder. Perched on the roof of the flimsy structure, he appeared to be in a precarious position. Yet he seemed all but weightless as he hoisted the Star of Bethlehem, which was easily as tall as he was, and hung it in place at the peak of the roof.

"Ready for the lights," someone called.

Eddie hit a master switch and the scene came to life. A few moments later, the music changed to Leonard Cohen's "Hallelujah." Bathed in the glow of the lights, Jabez looked even more striking. Maureen's face changed. Softened, as though overcome by some kind of magic. He'd never known anyone quite like her. There was something about her that moved him; not just her earnest devotion to Christmas, but her air of...he wasn't quite sure. Optimism, maybe. And earnestness. There was a deep appeal in Maureen that made no sense to Eddie, yet he couldn't deny it. When he was a kid, he used to dream about a kind of Christmas that simply didn't exist. Maybe that was the thing about Maureen. She reminded him of the kind of girl who didn't really exist—not for him, anyway.

Then the lights flickered out. She shaded her eyes and looked around. Volunteers were putting away the tools and crates. "Where'd Jabez go?"

"Don't know. Do you need him for something?"

"I was going to give him a flyer about auditions. Maybe he'd like to join in."

"Hate to break it to you, but being in the Christmas pageant is not exactly a hot ticket for kids his age."

"That's why I made the flyer." She handed him a few. "Feel free to give these out."

He glanced at the sheet, angling it toward the false starlight. "'Featuring an original composition by Eddie Haven'?" he read aloud. "Since when?"

"Since you said the music I picked was stale, I thought a piece by you would freshen things up."

"And it never occurred to you to ask?"

"I'm asking. Will you?"

"I mean *before* you advertise my services."

"If you turn me down now, you'll feel like a heel."

"Christ, and here I was, starting to like you," he said. "Turning you down is not going to make me feel like a heel."

"I know. It's the kids and everyone counting on an amazing pageant this year," she said. "They're the ones who will make you feel like a heel." She went around collecting empty cups, moving through the crowd with brisk efficiency.

"I just got screwed," Eddie said to Ray. "But I don't remember getting kissed."

"By Maureen? Don't be sore. She does that to everybody."

"Does what?"

"Gets her way. I've known her for years, and that's just the way she operates. No biggie." Ray headed toward his truck.

"She's into you," Randy Veltry remarked as they reeled in the stereo speakers.

"What?"

"That woman. The one you were talking to. Totally into you."

"Right." Eddie gave a derisive laugh. He tried to dismiss the notion. Into him? Maureen Davenport? No way. She made it clear she couldn't stand him. Her being into him—that was the last thing he wanted or needed.

And yet…he liked her, bossy attitude, librarian bun and all. It was crazy.

"You ought to ask her out," Moby suggested.

"Nope. No way. We have to work together on this Christmas production so I can't be getting personal with her."

"Chicken." Omar flapped his wings.

"I'm not. It's just…I don't have such good luck with women around this time of year. You know what I call Christmas? Ex-mas. With an *E-X.* I've been dumped three times at the holidays." It was true; he hadn't learned his lesson with Natalie. He'd never tried proposing again, but his next two girlfriends both dropped him at Christmastime, too.

"Oh, let me get out my tiny finger-violin." Randy pantomimed the action.

"I'm just saying."

"You're looking for excuses."

Eddie regarded the three brothers. Thinking about their background and current troubles, he was amazed they even spared a thought for his love life. "Yeah, you're a bunch of wiseguys," he said. "That's what you are."

"Hear that?" Omar said. "We're wiseguys, all three of us."

"Which reminds me, you're going to try out for the pageant."

"Ha. That's a good one."

"You think I'm kidding? I wouldn't kid about something that's going to get you released from school an hour early, three times a week."

That clinched the deal for them. The Veltry boys caught a ride home with Noah and Max, leaving Eddie to finish up with the other volunteers. People trickled away, heading home, nagging their kids about weekend chores, checking their e-mail and seeing what was on TV. Eddie didn't have to worry about any of those things, so he lingered to finish up with the lighting. After a while, he realized only he and Maureen Davenport remained.

"Pretty cold tonight," he said, just to fill the silence.

"I hope the snow comes soon," she said. "It's always so lovely to have snow at Christmas. It never officially feels like the season has started until it snows."

"Not a fan. But don't worry. You'll get your snow any minute now."

"No, the weather report earlier said there's no snow in the forecast."

"Maybe not, but it's still going to snow. Tonight," he said.

She shook her head. "I've been checking the weather report regularly. There's not a hint of snow."

"Have a little faith, Miss Davenport."

"I have plenty of faith," she retorted.

"Right."

She studied him for a few minutes, her gaze both probing and compassionate. "What is it with you and Christmas? Did it start that night?"

Eddie studied her keen-eyed expression. So she'd heard the

story. Maybe she'd been at the church when his van had gone flying into the nativity scene. He wondered how much she knew. "Wasn't my best night."

"People said it was a miracle you survived the wreck," she said.

"That's me. A Christmas miracle. Yeah, people can believe whatever they want," said Eddie.

He was found lying in a snowbank some twenty feet from the van. Panicked worshipers exiting the church found him that way—dazed, reeking of alcohol.

"Maybe it wasn't a miracle, but incredibly good luck," she suggested. "I heard you weren't wearing a seat belt, and that was what saved you."

"That's what you heard, eh?"

"Am I wrong?"

The accident report had been exhaustive because there was an entire congregation to draw from. Witnesses reported seeing the van careen around the bend in the road and, "at a high rate of speed," it left the icy pavement, plowed down a slope, mowed over the nativity scene and burst into flames, all in a matter of seconds.

There could be no disputing these facts. Too many unrelated witnesses reported seeing the same thing. What no one had witnessed—what no one could explain—was how Eddie had survived. Without serious injuries.

Investigators theorized that the impact of the vehicle hitting the building had caused him to be thrown clear of the van and that the deep snow had cushioned his fall. Experts on such things said that this was one of those rare occasions when the victim had benefited from not wearing a seat belt.

The report went on for pages, recounting the statements of witnesses, police and investigators. It was very thorough in presenting the facts.

One key fact had been neglected, however.

Eddie had been wearing his seat belt that night. A lap belt with a shoulder harness.

He had explained as much to the investigators, and they instantly dismissed that part of his statement. For some crazy reason, he decided to test his theory out on Maureen. "Yeah," he said. "You're wrong. I had my seat belt on."

A soft gasp escaped her, and she pressed a mitten-clad hand to her mouth. "The paper said the only reason you survived was that you were flung from the vehicle before it exploded."

"I know what I know," he insisted. "And don't look at me like that—I read what the reports said. And I know I was in shock from a dislocated shoulder. I also read what the paper said about my blood alcohol level. It's not so unique for someone on Christmas Eve. Haven't you ever knocked back a few on Christmas Eve?"

"No," she said bluntly.

"Well, you might, if you'd had the kind of evening I'd had. My memory is not impaired. I wish it was, because there are things about that night I'd like to forget."

"What kind of things?"

"It'd take all night to explain. I don't want us to turn into a couple of Popsicles. Doesn't matter, because I do remember, and one thing I remember was clipping on my seat belt."

"Why would you remember that so specifically?"

"Because just like everybody else, it's a habit ingrained in me from a young age. I spent half my childhood being schlepped around in cars. The reason I remember the situation that night specifically is that I sat in the car for a few minutes, and I considered not fastening it. This was something I deliberated."

"Why would you deliberate?" she asked.

"Long story short, a girl broke up with me that night. I was still young enough to think it was the end of the world. I felt like shit and I kind of did want to die, but if I did, I'd miss out on the rest of my life, you know?"

Her lips twitched a little at the corners. "Funny how that works."

"Yeah, it's kind of a career decision. One you can't take back. So I buckled up." He could still feel the cold metal of the buckle in his hand. He could still feel and hear the decisive *click* as he latched it home. There was no way, no possible way he was mistaken.

Except the accident report contradicted him entirely.

"Have you ever felt that way?" he asked Maureen. "Have you ever been that hurt by another person, so hurt you didn't care if you lived or died?" That was how he'd felt that night, with Natalie. Later, with the clarity of hindsight, he realized the act of proposing had been more important than the woman herself.

He expected Maureen to say something utterly practical, like what nonsense it was to give a person that much power over you. Instead, she surprised him. She nodded slowly and said, "I have."

"You have."

"That's what I just said."

"When?"

"It's private." She looked away, busied herself picking up a stray spool of speaker wire. "No wonder you're jaded on love," she commented in a clear attempt to deflect his next obvious question.

"Who says I'm jaded on love?" he asked.

"You nearly lost your life. That must have been the last time you trusted your heart to anyone."

"Maybe I'm a slow learner. Getting dumped at Christmas kind of became a thing with me."

"You know what I think?" she asked, then went on without waiting for his answer. "I think you keep trying to sabotage Christmas for yourself."

"Hey—"

"And guess what? This year, you're not going to get away with it. This year, you're going to have a *great* Christmas."

"Because I get to spend it with you?" Oops, he thought, watching her face go stiff with humiliation. Wrong thing to say. "I'm teasing," he said.

"No, you're being mean. There's a difference."

"I'm sorry, okay? I really didn't mean to hurt your feelings."

The frames of her glasses were probably made of titanium; they looked tough as armor. "All right," she said.

He wasn't sure what she meant by all right. "Listen, I promise—"

"What?" she asked, every pore of her body exuding skepticism.

Good question, he thought. It had been so long since he'd promised anything to anyone. "That it'll snow," he said, noticing the barely detectable early flurries. "Now, there's something I can promise."

"The weather report said—"

"Forget the weather report. Look up, Maureen. Look at the sky."

Maureen was about to march off to her car, eager to escape him, when she felt a shimmer of magic in the air. No, not magic. Snow. Contrary to the weather reports, the first snow of the year arrived when Eddie Haven said it would. It started with tiny, sparse crystals that thickened fast. Soon the night was filled with flakes as big as flower petals.

"Glad the snow held off until we finished," said Eddie.

"No 'I told you so'?" she asked him.

"Nah, you're already annoyed at me."

She scowled at him. "I'm not annoyed."

"Right. Hand me that package of zip ties, will you?" He was still tweaking the light display. For someone who couldn't stand Christmas, he sure had worked hard on the display. She wondered if he considered it a kind of redemption.

She gave him a hand, in no hurry to get home. Franklin and Eloise, her cats, had each other for company. She wondered if Eddie had any pets. Or a roommate, back in New York. She also wondered if he'd really gone dashing off for a date the other night, or if that was just her overactive imagination. She warned herself that she was far too inquisitive about this man, but couldn't manage to stop herself from speculating about him.

As the minutes passed, the snowstorm kicked into higher

gear. Thick flakes bombarded them. It was a classic lake effect storm, a sudden unleashing of pent-up precipitation. The church parking lot, empty now except for their cars, was soon completely covered. The landscape became a sculpture of soft ridges, sparkling in the amber glow of the parking lot lights.

They walked toward their cars, sounds now muffled by the snow. She slowed her steps, then stopped. "I love the first snow of the year," she said. "Everything is so quiet and clean." Taking off her glasses, she tilted back her head to feel the weightless flakes on her face. Snow always reminded her of fun and exhilaration, safety and laughter. When she and her brother and sisters were little, their father used to be very quick to urge the school district to declare a snow day when the first big snow of the season came. The whole family would go to Oak Hill Cemetery, where they would make snow angels, engage in snowball fights or go sledding if there was enough of a base on the ground. No one ever remarked that celebrating the first snow in a graveyard might not be appropriate. It was Stan Davenport's way of bringing his five kids closer to their late mother. People tended not to argue with him.

Having lost her mother at age five, Maureen was considered too young to remember, but she did. Sometimes, like when the snow was coming down in a thick and silent fury, a perfect moment would come over her. In a flash of clarity, she could remember everything—the warmth of her mother's hands, and the way they smelled of flowery soap, the sound of her laughter, the way she liked to collapse like a rag doll in the middle of the bed Maureen shared with Renée, where she would lie with them reading *Horton Hatches the Egg* and *The*

Poky Little Puppy and *Each Peach Pear Plum,* always letting them beg for one more story before snuggling them under the covers and kissing them softly.

Maureen shook off the memory to find Eddie staring at her. And although it was entirely possible that she was mistaken, she sensed a new interest in the way he was looking at her, through half-lidded eyes, with what appeared to be desire. It was the way a man regarded a woman just before he kissed her. Which either meant she was a wildly poor reader of facial expressions, or he had unexpected taste in women.

"You okay?" he asked.

She hoped the amber parking lot lights concealed her blush. "I'm weird about snow," she said. "So sue me."

"I don't think you're weird," he said. "Just...you look different without your glasses."

"Everyone looks different without glasses," she said, and put hers back on. "I'll see you at auditions."

"I can hardly wait," he said.

He was speaking ironically, of course. She'd read him wrong a moment ago; she wouldn't make that mistake again.

"Same here," she said brightly.

"Be careful going home," he said.

"Of course." She got into her car and turned it on, letting the engine warm up and the defroster blow the windshield while the wipers did their work, clearing the window for a glimpse of the swirling sky. The beauty of the snow coming down never failed to take her breath away. She loved the first snow. She loved Christmas with all her heart, and she always had. It was a time of year that brought her together with friends and family, a time that filled her with hope, with the sense that anything was possible. She refused to let Eddie Haven ruin it.

He didn't seem to know what her role was on the night he'd told her about, the night of his accident. Apparently he didn't even realize she'd been present. It was remarkable how different her memory of that night was from Eddie's.

Maureen had attended Heart of the Mountains Church all her life, and that year, it had been more important to her than ever. Her long-awaited, dreamed-of college semester abroad had come to a premature and devastating end. If her family hadn't been there for her, she had no idea whether or not she would have survived. Yet that year, and in all the years since, no one had ever asked her what Eddie had tonight: *Have you ever been that hurt by another person, so hurt you didn't care if you lived or died?*

Singing in the choir at the church that night, Maureen had lifted her voice up to the rafters and beyond. She'd known it then—there was nothing so powerful as the healing she'd found in coming home to her family. She'd always believed Christmas to be a season of miracles. The year they'd lost her mother, the miracle had happened for her father. He'd started to smile again, to live again. At a Christmas Eve potluck, he'd met Hannah, the woman he would eventually marry, the woman who would make their family whole again.

That year, it was Maureen's turn.

She had dragged herself up from the depths of despair, and though she would never be free of the memories of her time overseas—the adventure, the romance, the heartache—she knew she would survive. That was something. When you learned you could survive the unbearable, you could take on the world.

Fortunately, taking on the world wasn't required of Maureen. All she had to do was rethink her dreams and remake her own life.

In this, she'd had help. She wasn't much of a believer in cosmic signs, but the world in general did seem to be sending her certain signals. Her heart broken and bleeding, she'd spent the remainder of her money on a last-minute ticket home. She'd reached the airport with only a few euro in her money belt. There, a kiosk crammed with books caught her eye. *Yes.* Her physical escape was one thing. But her mind had needed a refuge, too. And that refuge was the most reliable place of all—between the pages of a book.

She saw nothing ironic in the notion that a mystery novel rescued her from having a psychotic break. Some people needed a prescription from a doctor. Maureen needed a trip to the bookstore. At the airport, she'd bought a mystery novel by a popular author, opened it and immediately sank into the story. While she was reading, everything else fell away and she became part of a dark and dangerous world, vicariously experiencing a fantastic series of events. When she arrived home in Avalon, she read a fantasy novel about a quest to save a forgotten world. Then she read an Edith Wharton novel because someone had once told her that when you had a broken heart, you should always read an Edith Wharton novel just to see that your heartache was not nearly as bad as it might have been. After that, she read an international spy thriller about an ancient piece of art tainted by a curse.

During the post-breakdown period, she read books the way an addict swallowed pills. She devoured stories one after the other, trying not to let reality intrude too deeply. At the end of it all, when she knew she had to reclaim her life and remake it according to a new vision, she emerged with a strong, clear goal for herself.

"You're changing your major to library science?" asked her sister Renée.

"That's right."

Her father had beamed at her. "We've never had a librarian in the family."

It turned out to be the perfect fit for Maureen, so perfect that she was surprised she'd never considered a career as a librarian before.

And that Christmas Eve, surrounded by family, friends and fellow worshipers, she'd blended her voice with the others, and her heart filled up. Yes, she'd been hurt—devastated. But her spirit refused to break. Life was just too precious, and Christmas too wonderful, to be spent wallowing in misery.

From that moment onward, Maureen vowed, she was going to be all right. She was going to be—

On that night of reverence and healing, a terrific crash had exploded into her moment of revelation. All the lights in the church had gone out. Panic erupted from every quarter of the sanctuary. Women screamed and children cried. Parents gathered their families close and led them to safety. People took cover or fled through emergency exits, because at that point, no one knew what had happened.

Everyone rushed outside and saw that a fireball had smashed through the Christmas display and slammed into the building. It was not immediately apparent what had happened. Had a meteor hit?

As a blast of icy wind roared at the conflagration, Maureen could see what everyone else saw—the flaming, twisted, skeletal remains of a panel van. It was a red-hot shell, a torch, setting fire to the timber beams of the portico at the main entrance.

There was a hiss and whir as the sprinkler system engaged.

A few people leaped into action, yelling into mobile phones. A guy dressed like a shepherd used his staff to break open the fire extinguisher case, and an alarm shrieked into the night.

Kids in their angel and livestock costumes gathered in an intermingling flock.

Several people tried to get to the van, but the deadly flames held them back.

"Good Lord have mercy," someone said. "Have mercy on those poor souls in the van, whoever they are."

"No one could have survived that crash," someone else commented. "The thing must have burst into flames on impact."

Maureen's heart lurched. To see people killed on Christmas Eve only compounded the cruelty of the tragedy.

Within minutes, sirens sounded and the emergency vehicles started to arrive. Unnatural blue and red light swept the area, smearing color across the snow.

Maureen felt drawn to the scene, although she was of little use when it came to rescuing people. Someone—a firefighter—said it was a recovery situation, not a rescue. "It'd take a miracle to survive that fireball," said one of the EMTs.

As the meaning of that sank in, Maureen felt sick. She turned from the scene, lifting her feet high through the drifted snow. She felt oddly guilty, remembering how happy, how peaceful she'd been feeling only moments before. It was horrible to realize that while she was quietly exulting in the new direction of her dreams, someone else's life was ending. She felt horribly connected to the event. In the sanctuary, she had wept tears of relief upon realizing she had a home to return to, a family to comfort her. She was surprised that only moments had passed since then. It felt like so much longer. She automatically did a head count of her family, finding them all present and accounted for—her dad and stepmom, somber and holding each other close. Her sisters, her brother and his family—everyone safe and sound.

Drawing her choir robe more snugly around her, she wandered through the crowd. Kids were still crying. Some people prayed. Others looked desperate to do something, anything. Two guys were arguing about letting people back into the building. Everything had been left there—coats and purses, street clothes, car keys. Pastor Hogarth was inviting people into the reflection chapel, an annex to the church that had not been saturated by the sprinklers, which had been tripped on when someone pulled a fire alarm. He wanted to hold an impromptu prayer vigil for the unknown victims of the crash. The voices all sounded distant and hollow to Maureen, and no one spoke to her. It was as if she were invisible. Was her choir robe an invisibility cloak? The silvery fabric had been chosen by Mrs. Bickham years ago; she insisted the metallic look added a festive touch. Maureen had always thought they added a Vegas showgirl touch, but maybe that was just her. She detached herself from the crowd, heading away from the smoke and the noise.

Bloodred flashes fell from the revolving light of an emergency vehicle. This was crisscrossed by the glaring beams of searchers' flashlights and the bluish lightning bolts of police squad cars, flooding the area and turning the snow to an eerie shifting field of color. Here and there, she could see items from the nativity scene—piles of straw and broken weathered wood, unidentifiable bits of plaster statuary and shattered floodlights.

Weirdly, there was one string of lights still burning, unscathed by the accident. The string crossed the churned-up snow, clearly delineating the path of the out-of-control van.

The poor driver. Had he been scared? Had he panicked or had it all happened so fast that there was no time to feel anything?

She hoped that was the case. Hoped it had not been excruciating. She stopped for a moment, said a little prayer to that effect. To her surprise, her cheeks felt damp with tears.

She found baby Jesus, head down in the snow. She picked it up by one plaster arm. It was the same plaster baby on display year after year, forever frozen in a beatific pose, reclining with arms spread, palms out, a gold leaf coronet circling the head. The back of the statue was stamped with HECHO EN MEXICO.

It felt vaguely irreverent to abandon the plaster infant, but she wasn't helping anything by dragging it around. She set it right side up in a snowbank.

Maureen was shivering now, the snow and cold penetrating her thin silver choir robe.

She nearly tripped over one of the wise men. At least, she

thought it was one of the magi, or maybe it was a shepherd, or poor long-suffering Joseph. Bending to have a closer look, she let out a little scream and jumped back. Her heart nearly leaped from her chest.

Then she called herself a fool and approached more cautiously, leaning forward and removing her glasses.

She gasped loudly, realizing her eyes had not deceived her earlier. This was no wise man. This is no plaster saint at all. It was a man. A dazed and broken man, lying half-hidden in the snow, his eyes softly shut. A thin dark line marred his forehead. He looked young; he had longish, light-colored hair and a face she vaguely recognized.

"Hey," she said, her voice cracking. "Hey—hello?" She dared to touch him, nudging his arm. "I need some help over here!" she called, not looking away from the stranger. Without thinking, she reached out and stroked his cheek.

Warm. He was warm.

"Hallelujah," she murmured. "Please be who I think you are," she said. "Please be the car's only occupant."

His eyes fluttered open. In the artificial light flooding the area, she couldn't make out the color. But she could make out his faint smile. Why on earth was he smiling? At her?

"Another angel?" he murmured. "This place is crawling with angels."

"What?" She looked around, saw no one; apparently no one had heard her call out a moment ago. "What?" she said again, and then: "Where?"

He shifted, gingerly pulled himself up by bracing one arm behind him. The other arm didn't look so good, hanging at an awkward angle. Aside from that, he had a couple of cuts on his forehead and chin, one on his right cheekbone just below the rim of his eye. But he was alive, and talking. Considering the state of his vehicle, that was a miracle.

He frowned at her. "Sorry. For a second, you looked like an angel to me."

Despite the circumstances, Maureen felt a beat of warmth. She could safely say no man had ever mistaken her for an angel. Then she snapped herself back to reality. "You were driving the van," she said. "A white van?"

"Yeah." He frowned. "I was."

"Were you by yourself?" she asked. *Please say yes. Please say yes.* "Was anyone else in the car with you?"

"I was alone," he said. His teeth were chattering now. "All by my lonesome." Then he looked panicked. "Did I hurt anyone? Oh, Christ, did I hit—"

"No," she quickly assured him. "Everyone's fine. And you're going to be fine, too."

Thank heaven, she thought, allowing herself to smile weakly with relief. She remembered hearing the grim voice of the EMT…"It'd take a miracle to survive that fireball."

"You got a real nice smile," said the miracle.

Part Two

CREDO AT CHRISTMAS

At Christmastime I believe the things that children do.

I believe with English children that holly placed in windows will protect our homes from evil.

I believe with Swiss children that the touch of edelweiss will charm a person with love.

I believe with Italian children that La Befana is not an ugly doll but a good fairy who will gladden the heart of all.

I believe with Greek children that coins concealed in freshly baked loaves of bread will bring good luck to anyone who finds them.

I believe with German children that the sight of a Christmas tree will lessen hostility among adults.

I believe with French children that lentils soaked and planted in a bowl will rekindle life in people who have lost hope.

I believe with Dutch children that the horse Sleipner will fly through the sky and fill the earth with joy.

I believe with Swedish children that Jultomte will come and deliver gifts to the poor as well as to the rich.

I believe with Finnish children that parties held on St. Stephen's Day will erase sorrow.

I believe with Danish children that the music of a band playing from a church tower will strengthen humankind.

I believe with Bulgarian children that sparks from a Christmas log will create warmth in human souls.

I believe with American children that the sending of Christmas cards will build friendships.

I believe with all children that there will be peace on earth.

—attributed to Daniel Roselle, co-founder,
Safe Passage Foundation

6

Daisy Bellamy set her two-year-old in Santa's lap and stepped back, holding her breath and hoping for the best. The setting looked beautiful this year—a skating hut that had been turned into a gingerbread house, with Santa ensconced on his wingback throne, giving dreamy-faced kids a "Ho Ho Ho" and promising them the moon. She offered up the prayer known to parents of toddlers everywhere—*Please let him sit still long enough to get the shot.*

Hurry up, she silently urged the helper dressed like an elf. Take the shot. Take it. Now. In photography, timing was everything.

The elf held up a squeaky toy in one hand and the shutter release in the other. "Look at the birdie," he said in a light, singsong voice.

Charlie's eyes, usually twin emerald buttons of merriment, widened with horror. He looked from the red-clad, bearded stranger upon whose knee he sat, to the goggle-eyed elf holding up the squeaking thing. Charlie sucked in a breath, and there was a moment of perfect, stunned silence.

Take it, take it, take it, Daisy thought.

The elf pressed the shutter a split second too late. By that moment, Charlie's face had contorted into a mask of abject terror. His tiny T-shirt read Santa Loves Me but his expression said, "Who's the freak?" He let out a tortured wail that could probably be heard by everyone standing in line outside the gingerbread-bedecked cottage.

Daisy swooped in and rescued him. He clung to her, a shuddering mass of sobs, his wet face pushed into her chest, his tiny fists digging into her sweater. He refused to let go even long enough for her to get his parka on him, so she settled for merely draping it around his shoulders. "You'll probably catch pneumonia," she muttered.

"'Monia," he echoed with a tragic sniffle.

She made her way toward the exit, which obliged her to parade the tormented child past the other waiting children and parents. At a glance, they appeared to be well-groomed, calm children, accompanied by their soccer moms and commuter dads. Daisy could imagine them critiquing her parenting, speculating that she'd given her toddler too much candy or skipped his nap. (Guilty on both counts, but still.) That was the trouble with teenage mothers, they'd probably say. They just aren't ready to be parents.

Daisy wasn't a teenager anymore, but she still looked it, having rushed from class in her worn jeans and old snowboard parka to pick Charlie up from the sitter. She'd been pregnant at eighteen, a mother at nineteen. In just a short time, she'd gone from being a student at a Manhattan prep school to being a single mother in a small town, where she'd moved to be close to her family. Now Charlie was two and a half, and she was pushing twenty-one, which sounded young, yet there were times when being a single mom made her feel older than rock itself.

She sneaked a glance at a woman in heeled boots and a fashionable houndstooth jacket, bending down to put the finishing touches on her silky-haired daughter's bow. The two of them looked as if they'd stepped out of the pages of a magazine. How did they do it? Daisy wondered. How did they look so pulled-together and calm, instead of rushing from place to place, always forgetting something?

Deep breath, she told herself. She was blessed many times over with plenty of friends and family for support. She did acknowledge that she struggled because living on her own was her choice. Though her family had money, Daisy possessed a streak of independence and pride that made her want to succeed on her own. Charlie was healthy, she was making her way toward a college degree (albeit slowly) and getting occasional work in photography, her area of discipline at the State University at New Paltz. The holidays were on their way, the first big snow of the year had arrived, and life was good enough. She reminded herself to find and savor the moments of sweetness.

"Okay," she said to Charlie. "I'm relaxed. So what if we didn't get a shot with Santa?"

"Santa!" Charlie said, rearing back to regard her with shining eyes. "Lub him."

"Right. We got a picture of just how much you love him."
They walked by a path marked by human-size lollipops. She
stopped and made him put on his parka then, because it was a
bit of a hike across the park to the car. "I'll do your Christmas
picture myself," she said. "We don't need no stinkin' Santa."

"Santa!" He clapped his hands, clearly still in love with the
idea of Santa. Plunking him on the lap of a fat, bearded
stranger—now, that was another story.

"We'll try the real thing again next year," she said. "This
year, it'll be Photoshop Santa."

"Okay, Mom," he said.

"No problem." Manipulating a shot of Charlie with Santa
would be simply an evening's work. Daisy had been obsessed
with photography from a young age, as long as she could
remember. She commuted to the college three days a week
for classes, and spent the rest of the time doing freelance work
and looking after Charlie.

She zipped him up snugly and pushed open the door,
stepping out into the brisk day.

Every year, a section of Blanchard Park was transformed
into Santaland, and opening day had arrived, which was a big
deal around town. The weather was cold and bright; it was
the sort of weather the Chamber of Commerce prayed for
every year but rarely got. Santaland was the signature holiday
centerpiece of a town trying to make the best of the long, dark
winter, and volunteers went all out with the decorations. According to the *Avalon Troubadour,* the Chamber of Commerce
anticipated record numbers of tourists this year.

Children who were normally grumpy and reluctant to stir

from their beds on cold, dark school days had probably bounded downstairs today, tearing through breakfast, eager to get in line for Santa. People who usually looked out their windows and groaned at the sight of fresh snow perked up at the view today. The season had kicked off with a pancake breakfast at the fire hall. Kiosks lined the streets, offering everything from funnel cakes to balls of suet for the winter birds. Galahad's Gallery, a co-op of local artists, had a booth that featured glass sculpture, wind chimes and a selection of prints by local artists—Daisy Bellamy included. Her seasonal nature photographs were gaining in popularity. She stopped at the booth to learn that within minutes of opening, they'd sold two of her pieces—a panoramic shot of the Nordic ski trails winding through the winter woods, and a long-shutter-speed shot of the Schuyler River coursing beneath the town's covered wooden bridge.

It was heady stuff, knowing people were actually paying money for her photographs. The idea that someone liked her art enough to buy it improved her mood immeasurably.

"Charlie, Charlie, Charlie," she said as she prepared to drive away from Santaland.

"Mommy, Mommy, Mommy," he answered cheerfully from his car seat in the back. He knew how to charm her, that was a fact.

He was a lot like his father.

She pulled into the town library to check out some fresh books for Charlie. He adored being read to, and she liked having new material on hand at all times. Daisy and Maureen Davenport, the librarian, had become friends, thanks to all the hours of story time Charlie had attended.

"Books," he stated with satisfaction when he saw where they were headed.

"You got it. Anything you want—Dr. Seuss, *Clifford the Big Red Dog,* Olivia—you name it."

"Six books," he said. He had no idea how many that was, but he knew the number six.

"That's right. We're allowed to check out six books at a time on a single topic." When she got out of the car, she saw a guy hiking across the library grounds, a backpack slung over his shoulder. It was his army-surplus jacket that caught her eye, and his easy, loose-limbed gait. He didn't walk the way people usually did in the snow, hunched over with hands jammed in their pockets. He was walking lightly and easily, with a spring in his step and his posture as straight as the trees all around, as though the cold didn't bother him at all. The jacket, the trees and the snow made a striking palette, so she pulled out her camera. She was taking a class on editorial images, and this might be a good shot.

Charlie made an impatient sound in the back of the car. "Hang on," she said, taking two more shots. Then she put her camera away and freed him from his car seat. Holding his arms out like airplane wings, he headed for the door to the library.

There was a large placard at the entryway of the building with an urgent appeal for donations. Help Us Save Our Library, it read. We Can't Do It Without You. Daisy dug in her pocket and forked over ten bucks. She'd saved more than that by not buying the deluxe Santa package. And way more than that by borrowing all the books she wanted.

She brought Charlie straight to the children's room and

peeled off his jacket. At the moment, they were the only ones in the section. This was lucky, because around other kids, Charlie tended to be loud and friendly, another legacy from his father and the Irish side of the family. She constantly had to shush him in places like the library and church.

He was a lot like his father in that way, too.

Maureen came by, rolling a cart of books to reshelve. There was no separate children's librarian at the Avalon Free Library. Judging by the call for donations at the entryway, Daisy suspected it was a budget issue.

"Hey, Maureen," Daisy whispered. "How's everything?"

"Great, thanks." Maureen offered a cheerful smile, though she seemed a little tired. Worried, maybe. Maureen could be anywhere from twenty-five to thirty-five; it was hard to tell based on the way she dressed. Sweater sets and A-line skirts tended to make all their wearers look the same age. Maureen was actually an extremely pretty woman who didn't make much of her looks. This was a quality Daisy admired. Before Charlie, Daisy had been a teenage train wreck of insecurities. She used to spend hours playing up her looks by dressing in the perfect outfit, making sure her hair was just right, her makeup worthy of a cover girl. Maybe if she'd just left herself alone, pulled her hair back and worn a sweater set, her life would have turned out differently.

Well, of course it would have. For sure, she would be Charlie-less. Logan never would have given her a second glance if she hadn't thrown herself at him that one crazy weekend.

Since the thought of life without Charlie was completely unbearable, she did not allow herself to go there.

"There's a new Jan Brett that just came in," Maureen said, pulling it off the cart. "Beautiful scenes of snow."

"Thanks." Daisy took the book, admiring the intricate drawings. Charlie was pushing a copy of *Thomas the Tank Engine* along the floor, making putt-putt noises with his mouth.

"I see Charlie is in the heavy equipment phase," Maureen observed.

"Deeply."

"How are you doing?" Maureen asked.

"Fine, thanks," Daisy said. "I survived midterms. This is when I always regret signing up for too many classes."

"Do you have plans for the holidays?"

Daisy hesitated. Between her family and Logan's, things were always a little complicated around this time of year. When Charlie was first born, the O'Donnells didn't want to have a thing to do with him, so decisions about the holidays were easy.

On the other hand, Logan, against all expectations, had embraced fatherhood with gusto. He was respectful of Daisy's role as the main parent, but insisted on seeing Charlie on a regular basis. This amazed everyone who'd known him as an edgy, undisciplined teenager, getting by on looks and charm, fueling his personality with booze and prescription drugs. By the time Charlie came along, Logan was clean and sober—and serious about being a father. Before long, the O'Donnells were as crazy about Charlie as the Bellamys.

This was great for Charlie—fantastic, in fact, but often tricky to manage.

And awkward for Daisy. Because as much as the O'Donnells were in love with Charlie, they were less enthusiastic about

Daisy. As the mother of an adored grandson, she was tolerated. But as the girl who, as far as they were concerned, took away their son's future, she didn't exactly own their hearts. They were a family with high-flown hopes for their only son. They'd dreamed of a topflight education for him. He was expected to take charge of the family shipping business, enjoying a country-club lifestyle with a family of his own.

Instead, their golden boy knocked up some girl, went to rehab and became a teenage father.

She studied her son—red-haired, merry-eyed, apple-cheeked and innocent. That'll never happen to you, she silently vowed.

And she knew, of course, that the O'Donnells had probably said the same thing to their own red-haired son, years ago. It was kind of understandable that they weren't all that thrilled with Daisy. She used to resent their skepticism of her, but now that she had a beautiful red-haired boy of her own, she knew where they were coming from. The thought of some girl— any girl—being involved with Charlie one day made Daisy nuts. It was completely irrational but she couldn't help herself. When you loved someone the way she loved Charlie, there was no room for reason. She imagined that was how the O'Donnells felt about Logan.

"Still kind of up in the air with plans for the holidays," she told Maureen. "How about yourself? What are you up to this year?"

"We always have a big family celebration. This year, I'm going to be super busy. I'm directing the Christmas pageant at Heart of the Mountains Church."

"Wow, sounds like a big project."

"Huge. But I'm excited. It's something I've always wanted to do. I was in the pageant every year, growing up, and in the choir as an adult. When Mrs. Bickham retired from the job, I was first in line to volunteer."

Daisy thought directing a Christmas pageant ranked right up there with going to traffic ticket school, but she didn't say anything. To each his own.

"I guess you'll be busy saving the library, too," Daisy said.

Maureen cast her eyes down. "We're not doing so hot on that front. The library's scheduled to close at the end of the year."

"Close? No way." Daisy could scarcely get her mind around the idea of a town without a library. "I'm sorry. That's just wrong."

"Everyone I talk to feels that way, but it's an economic reality."

"I'm going to ask everybody in my family to pitch in."

"Thanks. I have to be prepared for the worst, though."

"The worst being…?"

"We really do have to close, and I'm out of a job."

"What will you do?"

Maureen offered a tight smile. "I could land a position with the bookmobile, but I get carsick. I've put my credentials up online. We'll see if anything comes of it. In the meantime, I'll try to focus on the pageant and the holidays. Christmas has never let me down."

"I know you'll do a great job," Daisy said, trying to sound reassuring. "If I can help out—behind the scenes—let me know. I'm a photography student and I do freelance work on the side. What about a poster?"

"Really? Gosh, that's so nice of you. I'd love to have some pictures of the event. And a poster or flyer would be wonderful."

"I can help you out with that," said Daisy. She dug in her messenger bag for a card and handed it to Maureen.

"Great. And I'll make sure you and Charlie get VIP seats at the pageant."

Daisy's stomach lurched. "It'll just be me," she said. "Charlie is going to be with his dad this Christmas." It hurt just to say it aloud.

"Oh. I imagine that will mean a lot to both Charlie and his dad," Maureen said diplomatically. She regarded Charlie, who was now applying his motor-mouth sounds to *The Little Engine That Could.* "He's one of my favorite patrons, you know."

As though sensing he was the topic of conversation, Charlie looked up at her, raised his arms, and offered his future-heartthrob grin.

"You had me at hello," Maureen said.

He held up the book as if it were the holy grail. "Read it," he said.

Daisy moved toward him. "We'll check the book out and take it home, okay?"

His expression turned tragic. "Read it."

"I've got a few minutes," Maureen assured her, pushing aside the book cart. "There's always time for a story. It's one of my main rules as a librarian."

"You're sure?"

"Trust me. I'm a professional." She hoisted him onto her lap.

There was something wistful in her eyes as she settled down

with Charlie and the book. A sadness, almost. Daisy wondered briefly about the source.

"Then he's all yours," Daisy said. Her mobile phone vibrated, signaling an incoming text message.

A moment later, Charlie was blissfully ensconced in Maureen's lap, chanting, "I think I can, I think I can," along with the little engine.

Daisy headed outside and pulled out her phone to check messages. There was a text from Logan: HEY YOU. HOWS MY BOY?

ON SANTA'S NAUGHTY LIST, she sent back. HE DIDN'T LIKE THE LAP.

THAT'S MY BOY. I WAS ALWAYS CREEPED OUT BY THE FATMAN. WANTED 2 TALK 2 U ABOUT XMAS. WHEN?

2-NITE WORKS. 7-ISH AND YOU CAN GIVE HIM HIS BATH.

She put her phone away, feeling a thrum of apprehension. She and Logan had no formal custody arrangement. Theirs was based on mutual love for their son. Logan lived in New Paltz, where he was a student, within commuting distance of Avalon. Ignoring his parents' wishes, he'd chosen the state college in order to be close to Charlie.

And despite a rocky start as grandparents, the O'Donnells had stepped up, as well. And this year, for the first time, they'd asked if Logan could bring Charlie down to their place on Long Island for Christmas Eve, and bring him back Christmas Day.

Daisy had agonized over the decision. Surrender Charlie on Christmas Eve? Give up her two-year-old on the most magical night of the year? Could she do that?

Ultimately it was Charlie who'd made up her mind. He completely adored his father, and he deserved to be a part of the O'Donnell family as well as the Bellamys.

Still, it hurt to imagine spending Christmas Eve without him. Daisy reminded herself that she had a great family she could lean on. Her parents and stepparents were the best. But earlier today, she'd been hit by bad news. Sonnet, her best friend, who had been studying abroad in Germany, had opted to stay overseas another semester and planned to spend the season with her host family.

Daisy's phone sounded again, this time with a ring tone that made her heart flip over—"You've Got to Hide Your Love Away," the Eddie Vedder version. It was the tone she'd assigned to only one person in her life—Julian Gastineaux.

Julian was *that* guy.

The one she'd been thinking about since tenth grade, the one she could never quite get out of her mind.

She hit the button. "Hey."

"Hey, yourself. I'm in Avalon. Got in last night. Did Olivia or Connor tell you?"

She leaned back against the building, a smile spreading slowly across her face. "I haven't talked to my cousin. God, I can't believe she didn't tell me. I can't believe *you* didn't tell me."

"I have to go back tonight. When can I see you? It's a four-hour drive to Cornell, so the sooner the better."

Daisy hugged herself. The words were a song, soaring through her. *Julian.* One summer, before the craziness, before Charlie, before everything, Julian had been the best thing about her life. Sure, they'd both been young, only high-schoolers, but every time they were together, she found herself thinking of forever. There had been a glimmer between them of…something powerful and rare. A passion. Even a future, maybe.

But when you're sixteen, you do stupid things. Daisy did, anyway. At summer's end they parted, she for her oh-so-exclusive prep school in Manhattan, and he for a life he refused to describe in Chino, California. Despite a sweeping but unacknowledged yearning between them, she and Julian followed separate paths that rarely crossed.

But, oh, when they did… Thank God his half brother, Connor Davis, and Daisy's cousin, Olivia, were married. That meant she and Julian were family, no matter what. And he didn't realize it yet, but he was going to save Christmas for her.

He had a habit of showing up unexpectedly, often when she needed him the most. The glimmer that had sparked between them never quite disappeared. She told herself to snap out of it. To snap out of *him*. He was a student at Cornell, financing his education through the Air Force ROTC. Every spare moment, it seemed, was spent in training.

Daisy decided not to worry about any of that. Julian was in town. "Where are you?" she asked. "How soon can we—"

"Turn around, Daze."

Her heart nearly leaped out of her chest. She dropped her bag with a thud and ran to him, suddenly so desperate to feel his arms around her that she practically flung herself at him.

"Hey," he said, laughing, his breath warm in her hair as he clasped her against him. "Hey, you."

She pulled back. There was that moment, awkward and ponderous, that always seemed to occur between them. Do we keep hugging? Let go and step back? Kiss each other's faces off? She was never sure what to do, because she was never sure what they were to each other. She stepped back, feeling the cold wind snaking between them. No need to be seen making out with him in a public place. People probably gossiped about her enough, anyway. *That poor Bellamy girl, such a disappointment to her family....*

"How did you find me?" she asked.

"Spotted your car in the parking lot." He grinned. "It's kind of hard to miss."

When she'd launched her wedding photography business, her dad had given her magnetic signs with her logo to put on the sides of her car. Daisy wasn't sure about the logo, but since her dad had given her the car, she didn't criticize.

"So, can you go for coffee?" Julian asked. "Or..."

She wanted the coffee. She wanted the *or....* But neither one was an option at the moment. "I wish," she said, gesturing toward the library. "Charlie's inside, having story time."

"Tonight, then," Julian said. "Are you free tonight? I don't care how late it is when I drive back."

She thought of Logan's text just a few minutes ago, and her heart sank. "Unfortunately, I'm not free." Damn, she thought. *Damn.* There never seemed to be a good time for her and Julian. "And I don't want you driving in the snow late at night. Still, I wish we had more time together."

"Like more than five minutes?" he said. "Yeah, me, too."

He had the most magical smile. He had the most magical

everything, come to think of it. He was tall, stunningly good-looking, even after he'd sheared off his dreadlocks for ROTC. She was drawn to him by more than looks, though. He was fascinating to her and always had been fiercely loyal and protective, sometimes to the point of recklessness.

"So...at least I'll see you at Christmas," said Daisy. Thank God, she thought. With Charlie at the O'Donnells' on Christmas Eve, the holiday had been shaping up as a disaster. But with Julian around... She pictured them cozying up alone together, listening to soft music, finally getting some uninterrupted time to talk, or just to hold each other and grow closer. She couldn't stifle herself—she simply told him so. "You have no idea how much I'm going to need you on Christmas Eve, Julian. I was afraid I'd be spending it by myself."

"Daisy—"

"I've been dreading it," she went on in a rush. "Logan's taking Charlie to spend the night at his folks' on Long Island, and it was totally going to suck for me, you know, with him being gone, even for one night. To not be able to get up with him on Christmas morning."

"Daisy, I can't fix that." Julian's expression was soft with pain.

"I know, but with you around, at least it'll be bearable."

"I'm trying to tell you, I won't be around. I have training in Florida over Christmas break."

It took her a moment to assimilate this. "Training. You're training at Christmas."

"It's mandatory," he said.

"Over *Christmas?*"

"That's the ROTC for you," he said. "I'll get a forty-eight-hour liberty, but that's not enough time to make it home and back. Look, it's what you sign up for. I'm getting an education out of the deal. That's a fair trade. I'd love to be here for Christmas, but I can't. I need to stay in this for my future. I started with nothing, no way to pay for Cornell, without this. It's the only ticket I have to a decent life. You know that. It's important."

When will I be important? Daisy wondered. Or will I ever?

She stared at the ground, unwilling to burden him with her insecurities. "You're right," she said quietly, using all her self-control to hide her yearning and regrets. "You do what you have to do. And I'll do the same."

"I'm sorry," he said.

"Don't apologize. It's nobody's fault. I'll see you…when I see you, right?" She pasted on a bright smile. Then she glanced at her watch. "So, listen, I don't want the librarian to think I've abandoned Charlie. I'd better get inside."

"All right." He took her hand and pressed it briefly to his chest, next to his heart. His eyes told her things she knew he'd never say. Then he swiftly bent to touch his lips to hers. "Bye, Daisy. I hope you and Charlie have a nice Christmas."

Again, she thought. Kiss me again.

He didn't, though, so she stepped back. "You, too, Julian. Call me, okay?"

"Of course."

Better yet, she thought, ask me to spend more time with you right now. He didn't, though. She tried not to hurry too fast into the building, didn't want to seem as though she was fleeing. In the foyer, she paused to compose herself. She shut her eyes and stifled a sigh. *I hope you and Charlie have a nice Christmas.* She was sending her son to be with his other family this Christmas. Sonnet wasn't coming home. Julian wasn't coming home. How good could it be?

Oh, and Logan wanted to talk about Christmas tonight. She wondered what *that* could be about.

Daisy had given up trying to plan things past the next few hours. With a little kid, it was impossible to do much more than that. She was at an age when her friends were seeing the world, meeting new people, heading toward dreams held dear since they were very small.

Daisy's life was different. It revolved around Charlie, and everything else came in a distant second. Her dreams were still there, though, deeply held, yet distant. She still wanted to follow her passion for photography and art.

And she wanted to be in love. She wanted the kind of love so strong it reminded her of pain. She wanted the feeling she got when Julian pressed her hand against his heart and let everything show in his eyes. But it was a fine line to walk, between love and pain.

People liked to say when the right kind of love came along, you knew it.

But did you?

One thing Charlie had taught her was that there were a lot of different kinds of love. There was the love she had for her child, which was composed of bubbling-over joy so bright it seemed to shine with a light of its own. And in the blink of an eye, it could morph into icy terror, when Charlie got sick, or it could turn into a fierce protectiveness that gave her the strength of an Olympian, willing to fight to the death for him if need be.

And then there was the emotion she felt for Logan. Though he was the father of her child, he'd never been her boyfriend. They had come together out of hormones and confusion and teen angst, high on pot and pills. A few weeks after that, Daisy was shuddering with morning sickness and Logan was in rehab.

No one, least of all Daisy, had expected him to step up and be a dad. Logan had surprised everyone by doing just that. She had to give him props for his commitment and devotion. But was it the same as love? Having made Charlie together, both adoring him so much, was a powerful bond. It was a kind of love. What she didn't know was whether or not it was the kind of love that felt as necessary as breathing, that lasted as long as life.

They had never talked about it. Not directly, anyway. Weirdly, she approached Julian the same way. There was a tacit agreement to leave their relationship undefined. If you didn't know what something was, if you didn't admit to a feeling, then it couldn't hurt you.

Right?

7

After Daisy and her little boy left, Maureen was covered in *essence de bébé,* from holding Charlie in her lap. The scent of tearless shampoo and the powdery smell of disposable diapers lingered in her sweater and skirt.

Maureen didn't mind. She loved babies, probably more than anyone suspected. That was because no one really knew Maureen; she didn't let them into the locked-up past she never talked about. It wasn't a calculated move on her part, just the way she was. And unlike some people around town, she didn't regard Daisy as someone to be pitied or scorned. Maureen had heard the whispers. And the criticisms spoken aloud. What a shame, some people said, such a bright girl from a good family got herself in trouble like that. She made a life-changing choice before she even had a life.

Maureen didn't see it that way at all. To her, it looked as if Daisy was doing quite all right. There were moments when

Maureen found herself envying women like Daisy, even though life as a single mom couldn't be easy. She knew that there were some unwritten categories for unmarried women. A woman in her twenties was simply known as single. Unattached. There was no stigma; people in their twenties were *expected* to be single and unattached. It was interesting, she mused, the way attitudes about dating shifted depending on a person's age. People who were in their twenties, and single, were regarded as normal. However, this was understood to be a temporary state. Maureen was still in her twenties. For a few more months, anyway.

Singles in their thirties were regarded as quirky, but in a good way, and their friends often felt obliged to fix them up. Pressure mounted to get married, or at least to be part of a couple. If a woman stayed single in her thirties, people started to worry about her. Maureen was not looking forward to this phase.

Nor did she look forward to her forties. Once a person hit her forties, she came under suspicion. Not that there was anything wrong with being forty, but singles in their forties were categorized either as spinsters or closeted gays. Fifty-something singles inspired pity—had life passed her by?—but if you could make it to your sixties and still be single, you were suddenly respected again, regarded as independent and enjoying life's freedom. You didn't have a boring spouse or bitter ex, or boomeranging adult children. You simply had your own life on your own terms, and probably a clutch of adoring nieces and nephews. There was always an element of pity, though; a never-married woman was all alone except maybe for her cats.

Men operated under a different set of rules. Nobody seemed

bothered by a single guy at any age. If you were George Clooney, you got a free pass. If you were Eddie Haven... Maureen reeled in the errant thought.

In addition to a stack of picture books, Daisy had selected some self-help titles on making a relationship work. Maureen hadn't commented or judged, of course, and she tried not to speculate. Her patrons' privacy was of tantamount importance to her. Yet she admired Daisy's determination. In many ways, self-help was one of the most important sections of the library. Even the name—*self-help*—implied its importance. The entire library was about people helping themselves, improving their lives, striving to get better. Yet another reason the library closure was so unthinkable.

One of her favorite volunteers was currently emptying the return bin. Maureen went over to lend her a hand. "How are you this evening, Mrs. Carminucci?" she asked the older lady. Penelope Carminucci ran an old-school boardinghouse called Fairfield House, yet she always managed to give the library a few hours of her time. "Started your shopping yet?"

"Goodness, no," Mrs. Carminucci declared. "I haven't even begun to think about the holidays just yet. I'll probably go into panic mode a week before. That's my usual routine. How about yourself?"

Maureen added some books to the return cart, a series of thrillers and a book on empowerment through yoga. "I think about Christmas all the time," she said, scanning a book of cookie recipes.

Mrs. Carminucci paused, touched her arm. "I'm so sorry about the library, Miss Davenport. We're all just devastated."

"Thanks." Maureen hadn't realized she was wearing her feelings on her sleeve.

"I have half a mind to donate my entire shopping budget to the cause," Mrs. Carminucci said.

"I wish more people thought the way you do."

"What way?" asked the next patron, stepping up to the desk.

"Hey, you guys," Maureen said, her face lighting with a smile at the sight of her sister Renée, and Renée's three kids.

"Aunt Maureen! Hi, Aunt Maureen!" crowed Wendy, her five-year-old niece.

"Hush," Renée cautioned. "Remember your inside voice."

"Hi, Aunt Maureen," Wendy said in a stage whisper.

"Hi, yourself," Maureen whispered. "Hi, John, hi, Michael. How are the best niece and nephews in the world?"

"We're good," her nephews—six-year-old twin boys—said solemnly, without looking up from their Matchbook cars, currently making their way along the edge of the counter.

"I got a book about angels, see?" Wendy showed off an oversize picture book. "I saw an angel in the reading room."

"You did? That's fantastic." Maureen exchanged a glance with her sister, who was rummaging in her purse for her library card. "How did you know it was an angel?"

Wendy shrugged. "Eyelashes." She flipped open the book to a close-up illustration of a serene face with enormous eyes, beautifully fringed with perfect lashes. So cheesy, Maureen thought. Like a Maybelline ad.

"Did you talk to the angel?" she asked, stamping the pocket of the picture book with the date.

"Yep." Wendy grabbed the book and stampeded for the exit. "I talk to everybody."

"What can I say, I have a kid who sees angels." Renée checked out car books—what else?—for the boys and one on time management for herself.

"She is a big fat liar," Michael declared.

"Hush." Renée gave him a nudge. "If your sister says she saw an angel, then she did."

"I want to see the angel," John said.

"Go ask your sister," Renée said. She grinned at Maureen. "So…touched by an angel, or touched in the head? You decide."

"Are you kidding? I have a niece who sees angels. You think I want to mess with that?"

"Thanks, Maureen." Renée put away her library card. "See you at Dad and Hannah's on Sunday?"

"Of course." Sunday dinner with the family was a routine that almost never varied. It expanded and contracted to include various family members and guests who happened to be around. Sunday afternoons had always been a special, quiet time, away from the bustle of work and school. There were no elaborate productions; the Davenports simply took time to hang out together. Depending on the weather, they might take a long walk, play with the kids, organize a game of touch football or organize a Scrabble tournament. Then everyone pitched in to fix an early dinner. The only rule was that no one was allowed to think or talk about work or school during the time they spent together. For most of the Davenports, this made it the most cherished time of the week. Maureen was looking forward to not thinking about the library disaster, at least for an afternoon.

At the end of each business day, the library closed in the same fashion. Five minutes prior to closing, the lights blinked to signal to people to finish up what they were doing—print their school papers, check out their books, finish up their computer games, fold away newspapers and magazines.

Maureen liked being around at closing time. There was a sense of control in supervising the orderly exodus and then surveying the building one last time at the end of the day. She and the volunteers finished up and bid the last of the patrons goodnight, even though it was hardly night. It was a six o'clock closing today. Maureen would have preferred that the facility stay open much later, but the budget wouldn't allow it, and hadn't for a long time. She should have seen the closure coming, but hadn't wanted to.

Feeling a press of anxiety on her shoulders, she thought about taking one of those heavy-duty headache pills her doctor had prescribed long ago. She suffered from infrequent but intense migraines, and they tended to come over her when she was fretful and stressed.

First she needed to lock up for the day. She had her keys in hand when a shadow loomed behind her.

"Jabez! I didn't realize someone was still here," she said, standing aside to let the stray patron pass.

"Sorry. I guess the time got away from me. I kind of got lost in something, in the reading room."

"Did you need to check something out?" she offered, unconsciously rubbing her temple.

"No," he said, "but thank you." He paused. "How are you, Miss Davenport?"

"Bit of a headache, but I'll be all right. Nice of you to ask. How is Avalon treating you?"

"Just fine," he assured her. "See you around." He offered a nod of farewell as he passed through the door. He had such a pleasant face—olive-toned skin and the most enormous eyes, fringed by dark lashes.

"Good-night," said Maureen, watching after him thoughtfully as he took off into the twilight. He was barely adequately dressed for the weather, in an army surplus jacket and high-top canvas sneakers. He seemed perfectly comfortable though, strolling at an unhurried pace.

"Hey, you dropped something," she called, stooping to pick up some object. It was a key on a small bit of string.

He returned and took the key. His hand was surprisingly warm as it brushed against hers. "Great, thanks," he said, then headed off into the night.

Maureen went to her desk and opened the drawer, grabbing the bottle of pills. She hesitated before opening it. Funny, the gathering storm clouds of the headache had disappeared. Grateful, she put away the pills and straightened up her desk. The space was little more than a work cubicle. In her dreams, she had a proper office, maybe an airy space high up in the building, where the light flooded in and she could see down into the atrium as well as across the grounds outside. She'd designed that office over and over again in her head. Now she wished she'd spent the time and energy doing something else.

"Enough's enough," she muttered under her breath. "It's not as if somebody died." Yet she recognized the feeling of mourning that made her heart ache. "Think of something else," she commanded herself. "I could spend my pension money on a really decadent vacation. Yes, a vacation, that's just the thing."

She hadn't really gone anywhere since her college semester abroad, which she now thought of as a disaster abroad. She needed to go someplace, to replace the harsh memories with fresh, pleasant ones. Yes, that was what she'd do, right after the first of the year. She'd find a place where she could lie on a white sand beach beneath a nodding palm tree. Basking in a warm breeze, she would while away the hours, reading big, juicy novels and ordering drinks with tiny paper umbrellas in them. *Yes.*

"You will not," she fussed, knowing she'd probably chicken out. She rationalized her fear the way she always did—what good was a vacation if it meant leaving her family behind? How could she have a good time all by herself? How could she rationalize squandering money when she was unemployed? She knew she'd spend the whole time wishing her family could be with her, phoning them and writing e-mails. That was no way to spend a vacation.

She did a final lockup and headed for her car. As she was crossing the parking lot, a dark sedan swung in beside her. A man got out, his long, elegant overcoat swirling on the wind as he approached her. "Miss Davenport?"

"Hello, Mr. Byrne. I'm afraid the library is closed for the day."

"So I see," he said. For a moment, his attention seemed caught by a retreating figure, halfway down the block, walking with shoulders hunched against the cold. "Who was that?" he asked.

"A boy named Jabez Cantor. He's new around here."

Mr. Byrne frowned. "He struck me as familiar...." Then he shook his head slightly. "No matter. I came to speak to you. Do you have a moment?"

She wondered what he could possibly want from her or what she might say to him, and still remain civil. Gee, I'm a little busy now, she might say, but once you sell the town library down the river, I'll have nothing but time on my hands. "I was just leaving for the day," she said, hedging.

"I won't keep you long," he said. "It's about the library."

"Has something changed?" She allowed herself to feel a flutter of hope.

"I'm told you're in charge of this year's Christmas pageant."

She nodded, startled. What did that have to do with anything?

"My son recently moved to Avalon with his wife and son. This pleased Mrs. Byrne and me immensely, because we only have the one son, and one grandson—Cecil. He goes to the high school. Perhaps you've met him?" He softened when he spoke of his family.

"Perhaps. Most of the high school students are regulars at the library." She couldn't help but add, "It's a key part of their education."

He didn't take the bait. "I'll be as frank as you seem to be, Miss Davenport. Cecil has been having trouble settling in at school. He hasn't quite found his place. But he's a talented performer. I believe if he's given the lead role in the pageant, it will help with his self-confidence. Give him a chance to make some friends."

Maureen had to break it to him—performing in plays and pageants was not exactly a way for a boy to prove his coolness in high school. "Believe me, sir, giving him the lead part is not going to rock his world," she said, remembering her own high school days. She had been active in drama, something that surprised people who hadn't known her back then. She'd left her dramatic self behind long ago.

"I think I know my own grandson," said the older man.

"Then I hope he'll come to the auditions."

"Oh, there's no question of that. He'll be there."

"Very good." She moved toward her car, feeling mystified by the encounter. "Er, good night, Mr. Byrne."

"We understand each other, then. Cecil will play the lead role."

She stopped, turned back to him. "I can't say at this point. The role will go to the student who can do the best job."

"Exactly. And that student is Cecil."

Maureen could understand a man who was devoted to his grandson. But this was over the top. "As I said—"

"Miss Davenport, you understand I'm in a position to help you," he said.

"Sir, we have all the volunteers we need for the pageant."

"Not like that." He cleared his throat. He emphasized each word.

She lifted her shoulders as a gust of wind scurried through the parking lot. "Mr. Byrne, I'm sorry for seeming dense, but maybe you should explain what you mean."

"Certainly," he said. "Miss Davenport, the library is closing due to a budget shortfall."

"Allow me to correct you," she said, surprising herself with her own audacity. "It's going to close because you won't renew the lease without a guarantee of the annual budget."

"And now I'm telling you there might be some flexibility in that. So you see, we each have something to offer the other."

"Let me make sure I understand this. All I have to do is promise Cecil the main role, and the library gets a second chance at life. That's insane," she blurted out, then covered her mouth with her hand. "I mean—"

"Quirky. People with my kind of money are considered quirky. There is simply no price to be put on the happiness of people you love."

"And yet you've done exactly that. Mr. Byrne, would you listen to what you're saying? You're offering to *buy* a role in a Christmas pageant, of all things. It's so…unethical."

"More unethical than closing the doors of the library? It's a simple equation. My grandson wants to be chosen for the main role. You need to save the library."

The idea seemed strange and uncomfortable to her—and far too tantalizing. "That doesn't make it right."

"And doing the right thing means letting the library close?"

"Doing the right thing, in this case, means you'll put the needs of the community above the needs of your grandson."

"It boils down to family loyalty."

A simple transaction. It wasn't so bizarre, was it? Bit parts in ballets and operas went to the children of benefactors all the time. She'd do anything to keep the library open. Anything. Still… "Mr. Byrne, if your grandson auditions like any other student, I'm sure he'll get a role—"

"The lead role."

"How do you know Cecil even wants this? Have you asked him?"

"I think I know my own grandson."

"Then you should know you're not sending him a healthy message."

"He doesn't know. And he never will unless you tell him."

8

Arriving at the church for the auditions, Maureen parked her Prius in the spot marked "reserved." Even though, as the pageant director, she had every right to park there, she felt as though she were getting away with something. This was a new sensation for Maureen, a woman who got away with absolutely nothing. Ever.

Perhaps this was a sign. Things were about to change. She sat for a moment, contemplating the sensation of raw power. Mr. Byrne had handed her an opportunity, that was exactly what he'd done. Could he really mean it? Or was he just playing her in order to get special consideration for his grandson? The whole thing was just too bizarre. And yet the possibility dangled before her. If she did his bidding, the library could be saved, after all. And as for directing the pageant—another opportunity. Here was a chance to create something from nothing, the power to make dreams come true. She intended to do the best job she knew how.

To some people, this was simply a Christmas pageant, a night of drama, music and entertainment. To Maureen, it was so much more—a celebration of all that was kind and good and holy in the world, a chance to remind people to step out of themselves and sink into the sweet mystery of a deep and abiding faith.

Rummaging through her bag, she took a swift inventory—script, check. Clipboard, check. Music folio, check. Extra pencils and steno pads, check. Everything was in place. Of course she had all the supplies she needed. Her involvement in the pageant was a lifelong affair. At six months of age, Maureen had portrayed the baby Jesus, swaddled in a fringed shawl that had been woven by her great aunt. Every year after that, she played a role. In fact, it was the pageant that had given her the acting bug. And the bug had hung on all the way through her junior year of college. The year her world had imploded.

She was about to exit the car when she paused, wondering if she should repark. The forecast promised clear weather, but it was always good to hedge one's bets. The night of the nativity-building was a perfect example. Not a breath of snow in the forecast, yet she'd driven home in a blizzard. She started the engine. It was bad enough that the weatherman had called it wrong. Worse, Eddie Haven had gotten it right.

After reparking the car facing out, she buttoned her coat snugly, wound a handknit muffler around her neck, and pulled on her hat and gloves.

Just for a few seconds, she bowed her head, thankful for this day, this glorious opportunity to play a key role in the celebration of the season. It made all other problems—and yes, she most definitely had them—seem to shrink, at least for a while. She felt the world around her with heightened awareness. There was a still, breath-held quality to the winter evening, a quiet that pervaded the soul. The air smelled of the crisp sweetness of the cold season. Everything had an air of waiting, edged by the sense of things about to begin.

Thank you for this day, she thought. She'd waited so long for it.

Eddie Haven's white van careened into the parking lot, strains of a Black Sabbath tune shrieking and thumping from its speakers.

He jumped out, stuffing a wad of keys in his pocket. He wore only a dark T-shirt and skinny jeans, jacket flapping open, no hat or gloves. Black motorcycle boots with chains around the heels. "Hey, Maureen."

"Hello, Eddie. Ready to get to work?"

"Sure." He'd brought nothing with him, she observed. Nothing at all. He probably traveled with nothing but his guitar and an ice chest of beer.

"You might want to repark," she commented, "in case it snows."

"Forecast said clear to the weekend. It's not going to snow." He spoke with complete conviction.

"Last time we argued about the weather, you disputed the forecast," she reminded him.

"Last time we argued about the weather," he said, "I won."

Maureen dropped the subject. The two of them seemed inclined to argue about everything, and it was silly. "Don't you need to lock your van?" she asked.

"This place isn't exactly known for its crime," he pointed

out. "And no self-respecting thief will go near my wheels. The stereo is fifteen years old, at least. Plays cassette tapes."

Loudly, she thought. It plays them loudly.

He lengthened his strides toward the building. "Jesus Christ, it's cold. I'm freezing my nuts off," he said.

She scowled at his language. "You could always zip up your jacket. And wear a hat. Maybe a muffler, too."

"Yeah, good idea. Thanks, *Mom.*"

Maureen knew he was trying to tease her.

He was succeeding admirably.

"Can you give me a hand with some of these things?" she asked. Maybe if she put him to work right away, he'd be too busy to annoy her. She went around and opened the trunk of her Prius, which held several boxes of supplies.

"Damn, you got enough stuff here to put on a Broadway show," Eddie commented.

"I like to be prepared." She flicked a glance at his bare arms. "I asked the building steward to leave the heat on inside," she said. "Let's go get things ready."

"I can hardly wait."

She felt a lash of resentment from him, though his comment wasn't directed at her. And then worry set in. She was supposed to put on a pageant with this guy? Determined to make the best of it, she headed for the sanctuary. They walked under the portico—the one that had been rebuilt after he had crashed into it. She wondered if he thought about that every time he came here.

She unlocked the sanctuary, and he held the door for her with a gallant flourish. "After you."

Glancing up at him was a mistake. Though she'd resolved to avoid letting his looks affect her, she was struck by the dazzling blue of his eyes, and that slight smile lifting the corners of his mouth. Good grief. For a second, she flashed on an image of the face that had captured the hearts of America all those years ago. He'd changed, though, perhaps losing some of his teen-idol perfection to true character. Nearly hidden at the edge of his hairline was a faint, thin scar, a remnant of the night their lives had collided, a night he remembered so differently than she did.

Flustered, she tore her eyes away and stepped into the church. At this time of day, it was deserted. The large, airy space was laid out in perfect symmetry, the long aisle forming a gleaming path to the front, pews fanning out on either side.

And in that moment, Maureen forgot her irritation with Eddie Haven, forgot her troubles and the quiet discontent with which she usually lived her life. She forgot everything. This was where it would happen—the voices lifted in song, the hearts soaring with joy.

"So here we are." Eddie started down the aisle, his boots ringing on the polished floor. "What time do auditions start?"

"In about thirty minutes. It's on the schedule I gave you."

"Didn't really have a chance to check it out. You're pretty organized."

Of course she was. A person couldn't take on a production like this without being organized. Her goal was to put on the kind of pageant that embodied everything joyous and bright about the season.

She set down her things and unbuttoned her coat. He was hardly the first to question her ability to fill Mrs. B's shoes.

Members of the church council had raised their eyebrows, as well. Maureen didn't understand all the admiration of Mrs. Bickham's productions. It was true, she'd done a fine job for at least three decades. A perfectly adequate job. She'd been a new-school-type of pageant director, jumping on trends each year. She had subscribed to the belief that people would better relate to a show with elements that were recognizable and relevant in their lives. Over the years, the pageant had featured prominent pop culture icons such as Care Bears and Barney. Depending on the year, Shrek might be one of the wise men and marching penguins could be seen in the stable. The angel's call had been delivered in any number of ways, from Western swing to hip-hop, and "Joy to the World" might be sung by characters from *Harry Potter.* Under Mrs. B, the pageant had been produced with every theme imaginable, and some unimaginable—Camelot, the Old West, the Age of Aquarius, disco. Maureen's father used to joke that he was waiting for the "Christmas in Hell" theme.

Maureen had her own ideas. She believed deeply in tradition and ceremony. Bringing the greatest story ever told to life was a sacred duty to her, and she didn't want to mess it up or lose the message by trying to be trendy. And this year, she was going to prove that tradition, not trendiness, was the most powerful way to deliver the message of Christmas. She wanted to revive the old ways, yet make them fresh and relevant. Were she and Eddie Haven going to succeed?

He had to buy into her vision.

She went to shrug out of her coat when she felt the gentle embrace of a pair of hands on her shoulders.

"Here, I'll help you with that," Eddie said, lifting the coat away from her.

Barely able to stifle a gasp, she surrendered the garment, murmuring, "Thank you." The cavernous room suddenly felt hot.

The documentary crew showed up—a cameraman named Chet and his assistant Garth, and an associate producer named Josie. "Try to forget we're even here," she said. "Ninety percent of what we shoot won't make it into the piece. The more we shoot, the more we have to work with."

"That's fine. Pretty soon we'll be too busy to notice," Maureen said, indicating the students who had started to arrive. She saw that Eddie had turned away, busying himself with some sound equipment by the stage. "Camera shy?" she asked.

"Yeah, that's me."

"Do you know how to work the sound system?"

"I can give it a try."

"Can I help?" she offered. "I'm pretty good with A/V equipment."

"You librarians," he said. "Second only to superheroes." He laughed at her expression. "Don't worry, I'll get it all set up."

Maureen hoped the camera wasn't turned on her, documenting her blush. He was a trained musician, so he ought to know what he was doing. She left him alone while he assembled and tested the sound system. Already she could tell their styles were radically different. He plunged right in, figuring things out by trial and error. In this case, it was a good division of labor. She would have still been reading the table of contents of the user's manual.

She clipped an evaluation form onto her clipboard and

prepared one for him, as well. "I made a column for each person's name and phone number, one for potential roles, and one for us to make notes."

He nodded, but didn't take a clipboard. "Okay. I don't need that."

"I expect to have several people trying out for each role. How are you going to remember?"

"You've got that covered," he pointed out.

"I value your opinion," she stated.

"My opinion is, I don't need to rate people on a sheet of paper."

"Do you have a real issue with this, or are you trying to get on my nerves?"

"Issue," he said without hesitation. "Nerves, that's just a bonus."

His admission surprised her. "So what's the issue?"

"It's hard enough performing on stage. Having a couple of geeks with clipboards judging you only makes it worse."

"You're speaking from experience, aren't you?" she said.

"So what if I am? Listen, how about you do things your way and I'll do things mine, and then we'll compare notes?"

She would have argued with him further, but Ray Tolley showed up to help with the auditions. Ray, who played piano, showed up straight from work to help out, still in his uniform. The kids' eyes bugged out at the sight of his police uniform. Some of the high schoolers looked uncomfortable. Maureen wondered if Eddie felt uncomfortable around Ray, too. But they seemed like friends; Eddie went to help him set up his keyboard.

A few minutes later, she stood at the door, greeting people

as they arrived for auditions—parents and their little ones, who would populate Bethlehem, and older students from middle school and high school who would fill the speaking roles and sing solos. She was gratified by the large number of older students, even though she knew many were there because they would earn release time from school and a half credit in drama and choir. She tried to figure out if Cecil Byrne was among the high school students. Was he the quiet-looking boy in the Argyle sweater? The husky one in the hockey jersey? The cutup with the faux-hawk? She hoped he'd be the heart-throb boy who sat surrounded by adoring girls, but given what Mr. Byrne had told her, that was unlikely.

It was chaotic at first, getting organized for tryouts, but eventually she had the parents situated in the back and the children in the front pews in order by age, so the youngest ones could finish early. True to their word, the film crew stayed discreetly in the background, though the camera stayed on the whole time.

Maureen stood up in front of the group and tapped on the microphone. "I'm excited for everyone to be here. Each person who wants to take part will get that chance. The auditions will determine where each of you fits in." She had rehearsed that tidbit quite exhaustively. Her main goal was to include every student in some way. This, she knew, was a departure from traditions established by Mrs. Bickham, who had limited the cast each year.

"Do you mean that?" asked Eddie when she shut off the mic. "About including everybody?"

"If I didn't mean it, I wouldn't have said it."

The auditions would start with the youngest, who would go in groups of three. Maureen thought it might be less intimidating than having to do a solo. She recognized most of the kids from the library. Not vice versa, though. Children tended not to recognize her out of context. When she was behind her long pickled oak desk at the library or seated in the big Kennedy rocker for story hour, yes. In the grocery store or elsewhere in the community, doubtful.

She spent several minutes organizing the little ones, making a game of putting them in rows at the back of the stage area. She enlisted a parent—Mrs. Andrea Hubbell—to assist her. "You're so wonderful with children," Mrs. Hubbell commented. "Are you planning to have your own one day?"

Maureen laughed to cover her reaction to the woman's audacity. People tended to ask this of single, unattached women her age—as if being twenty-nine placed her personal life in the public domain. She considered ignoring Mrs. Hubbell's question, but decided that would be rude. Being from a large, close family only strengthened the assumption that she was moments from popping out babies.

"Every child who comes through the library doors is mine for a little while," Maureen said, her stock answer to the too-frequently-posed question. "It's one of the best things about being a librarian."

"Kids without the commitment," said Eddie. "You get all the cuteness with none of the mess."

"Very funny," Maureen said, surprised he'd caught the exchange. Why did people never bug guys about starting families? It was a double standard. People should be nagged on an equal-opportunity basis. She clapped her hands to get everyone's attention. "We're ready to start."

Ray played the familiar opening chords of "Away in a Manger."

The first three children stood shoulder to shoulder, looking very small in the empty setting. Maureen gave them a smile of encouragement. Emily, Ginger and Darla were their names.

"All right then, girls," she said. "You're up." She nodded at Ray.

According to her schedule, this should take three minutes. The children merely stood there, white-faced and frozen.

"Is everything all right?" Maureen asked.

No response. The girls looked at each other as the piano repeated the opening notes. There was not a sound from the stage, though. The middle girl, Emily McDaniel, leaned over and whispered to the one on the end.

"Is something the matter?" Maureen asked.

Emily scurried down from the stage. Leaning in close and cupping her hands around Maureen's ear, she whispered, "Darla has to pee."

"Oh." Maureen looked at Darla. "Do you?"

Eyes wide, Ginger shook her head. "Not anymore."

"Oh, man. She peed," yelled a little boy. "Check it out, she peed!"

"She totally peed," another kid chimed in.

Darla burst into tears. The other two girls joined in, weeping in sympathy. Chaos erupted—some kids crying, others laughing, some chasing each other. Darla's mother cleaned up her child and the puddle on the stage which, Maureen couldn't help thinking, was where Sunday worship took place. As Chet's camera panned across the scene, Maureen was tempted to join in with the bawling children.

"What's next?" she whispered to Eddie. "Fainting? These kids are scared to death. Am I that scary?" She studied his face. "Don't answer that."

"I was going to plead the fifth. No offense, Maureen, but you've got them lined up like prisoners in front of a firing squad." Before she could reply, he got up and grabbed his guitar. As he exited the pew, he passed so closely in front of her that their bodies brushed together. She felt the warmth of him, caught his scent, and for a second, she was the one nearly fainting.

He smiled down at her, his blue eyes full of knowledge. "Excuse me," he said. He made his way to the stage, looking like a giant amid a sea of little people. Then three big electronically-enhanced chords sounded. It was as if Elvis himself had entered the building. Everybody froze for about three seconds. That was all it took for Eddie to stride onto the stage, handing out tambourines, triangles and marachas from a box. Then he launched into "Joy to the World"—not the traditional version, but the one by Three Dog Night. Within minutes, the youngsters were singing "Jeremiah was a bullfrog" and leaping around the stage. Maureen felt torn between outrage and amusement. She didn't dare look back at the parents. They would think she'd lost control of the situation the very first day.

The final "joy to you and me" resounded, and then Eddie took his seat in their midst, strumming a few chords. Something happened—his face and demeanor changed as though he went somewhere else, or maybe the music took over, and he turned into a different person as he started to sing softly.

The children joined in, and the magic of Christmas seemed to move through them. Their faces glowed, their voices floated in the rafters. He was masterful with them, coaxing the song from their hearts. He had them take turns, each singing a line or two by themselves.

Maureen was so mesmerized that she forgot to take notes. It didn't matter, though. She knew the children's chorus would be just fine with Eddie's help. It was such a singular moment that she set aside the schedule and sat back to listen.

She'd known he could sing. Everyone knew Eddie Haven could sing. But she hadn't seen him in action up close before, and she'd never seen him play in person. Ray Tolley took a seat beside her. She'd known Ray all her life, though only in passing. He was a few years older than her. And apparently, he was friends with Eddie Haven.

"You look gobsmacked," he remarked.

"I didn't know he…" Her voice trailed off. She couldn't quite get her head around the idea of this new Eddie.

"Yeah, he's good with kids. Works with teenagers in some music program in the city. Did you know that?"

"He sounds too good to be true."

"Nah, don't get me wrong, he knows how to be a jerk, same as the next guy. But I give him credit for his work with kids."

"It's going to be a great pageant," she murmured to Ray.

"Word. There was never any doubt."

Oh, yes there was, she thought. She had totally doubted Eddie.

He finished with the little ones, then returned to her side to listen while Ray took over.

"Thank you," she said.

"Just doing my job." By the end of the first hour, Maureen's spirits were high. She was finding talent and enthusiasm among the students, and it was giving her high hopes for the show. She grabbed her clipboard again and started writing. Her notes were dotted with stars and happy faces. A clear game plan took shape, involving little angels, shepherds and chorus members. She noticed Eddie still wasn't making any notes at all. He sat back, ankle crossed over his knee, hands clasped behind his head, and listened with polite attentiveness. At one point, she leaned over to him and asked, "Are you sure you don't want to make any notes?"

"I don't have to make notes," he said. "The ones I like, I'll remember. Mrs. Bickham always kept the cast really small."

"I'm aware of that."

"Made for easier rehearsals."

"My purpose is not to make things easier on myself," she declared. "It's to celebrate an event that changed the world."

He grinned and propped his knees on the pew in front of them. "Yeah, good luck with that."

The next auditions would be crucial, more than anyone could know. They were charged with choosing students to play the principal roles. She had no pop culture trends to hide behind, only the enduring message for the ages. She listened to the girls' auditions with the highest of hopes. Fortunately, there were no tears and plenty of talent.

The male roles, of course, she expected to be more challenging. And Maureen couldn't stop thinking about what Warren Byrne had proposed. He wanted to see his grandson, Cecil, as the angel who announced to the world that the Savior had been born.

It was a pivotal role, of course, and if young Cecil was a disaster, it could ruin the whole show. If, on the other hand, he was merely adequate, or even quite good, she could choose him and give the library a fighting chance for survival. It still felt as though she was making a deal with the devil, but was she? What harm in making a choice for the library?

Three large boys jostled their way onto the stage. Eddie sat forward. "Oh, good," he said. "These are the Veltry brothers. I asked them to audition."

They looked like cutups, the kind of kids who hid out in the library and bugged each other with their snickering and noise. Two of the three were in need of haircuts and the third had a broken front tooth. As they jostled their way onto the stage, Ray murmured, "They're in foster care right now. Eddie and I will keep an eye on them."

Maureen's heart softened and she offered a smile of encouragement.

"Can we sing together?" asked one of the boys. "We sing in harmony."

"Sure, go for it," Eddie said before Maureen could object.

They snapped their fingers to the beat, and went right into a doo-wop version of "We Three Kings."

The smile on Eddie's face expressed exactly what Maureen was thinking. The boys were natural and engaging. When they finished, she asked them each to read a passage. That was where the trouble started. They were poor readers, stumbling over words, hesitating and mumbling.

"Thanks, guys," Eddie said. "Good job."

A stocky boy with earnest eyes and bad skin stepped up. "Cecil Byrne," he said, standing stiff and upright.

All right, thought Maureen, moment of truth. "Whenever you're ready."

The boy cleared his throat. He was blushing furiously, holding his hands in white-knuckled fists at his side.

Uh-oh, thought Maureen. It was not looking good for Cecil. Who named their child Cecil, anyway? There was nothing specifically wrong with the name, but it was precisely the kind of thing other kids would make fun of.

He took a deep breath, then let it out and finally began. The first few notes wobbled tentatively from his lips.

Maureen's heart sank. She wanted him to be wonderful and he wasn't. He—

A large hand covered hers. Eddie was not trying to hold her hand but to keep her from drumming with her pencil on the clipboard.

She forced herself to be still and fixed her face into what she hoped was an expression of mild encouragement.

Although the notes were uncertain, they were on key. That was something, at least. On the next couple of lines, his voice gathered strength.

Maureen sat forward in her seat. All right, he wasn't half bad. He was…extremely adequate. He was quite good, actually. Yes, he was. *Yes.* He read his lines without incident and hurried away.

He turned out to be just what she needed—a deserving kid who could adequately fill the role. He didn't need to be brilliant, because he came with an added bonus—his grandfather just happened to be in a position to save the library.

Merry Christmas to me, she thought.

"Thank you, Cecil. The cast list will be posted tomorrow."
And you're going to be one happy boy.

There were a few more tryouts and she was gratified to
know she had good choices for all the roles. With enough
practice and hard work, they could create a meaningful, mem-
orable Christmas pageant. If the Angel of the Lord was
mediocre, perhaps other elements in the production would
overshadow it. Flaws could be edited out of the PBS show. At
least she hoped they could.

As she gathered up her things, Maureen realized they had
not stuck to her schedule at all. From the very first audition,
they had been derailed. It didn't matter, though. "Productive
evening," she said to Eddie as the last student left the floor.
She was about to ask him if he wanted to help her assign the
roles. Then one more student showed up.

"Sorry I'm late," said Jabez Cantor.

It was the boy from the library. The boy with the eyes. He
wasn't on her list, but it didn't matter. From the first moment
she'd met him, she'd felt drawn to Jabez, and she was interested to see if he had talent.

"Whenever you're ready," she said. "The floor is yours."

"I'll start with the reading if that's all right." Unlike most
of the students, he didn't seem nervous or bashful in the
least. Quite the opposite. He behaved as if he was supposed
to be there.

And as it turned out, he didn't read from the sheet she
provided, with a passage from Luke. Instead, he spoke the
words simply and directly:

"…And there were in the same country shepherds abiding in the field, keeping watch over their flock by night…"

The recitation had the most curious effect on Maureen. The boy had such a presence with his oddly old-fashioned longish hair and straightforward manner. He was a natural storyteller. The age-old words became new again. It was as if she was hearing the passage for the first time. She was riveted, yearning to hear the rest of the story. Which made no sense at all, since she knew the rest of the story by heart. Some things, she reminded herself, simply defied logic.

She glanced over to Eddie to see if the recitation had the same effect on him. But his face was in shadow and he held himself statue-still.

Jabez finished with a tiny smile that reminded her that he was just a kid. Then he started to sing, and that was when, for Maureen, the world shifted.

The moment the boy named Jabez started to sing, Eddie felt a rare shimmer of awareness, the feeling of being in the presence of a singular talent. People who had been gathering their things to go stopped what they were doing to listen. Even restless little kids turned their faces toward the stage and paid attention. The guy was great. He didn't even know how great he was. He was enough to carry a whole show, for sure. That was it, then. The casting was done. Put this kid front and center, and everything else would fall into place.

Chet's camera stayed on after Jabez's performance was done and people trickled away. Ray Tolley offered the Veltry boys a lift home, and they found the prospect of a ride in a squad car too interesting to resist. Eddie started gathering up cords and equipment and putting things away.

The camera crew, though fairly discreet—for a camera crew—bugged Eddie. Just having them around reminded him of his very public childhood. He didn't make a big deal of it, though. The more you resisted, the more intrusive they got. He'd figured that out a long time ago.

"Don't mind us," said Josie, the producer, with a casual wave of her hand. "We're just getting some footage of the casting process."

Eddie figured that would have all the drama of watching paint dry. Glancing over at Maureen, he expected to see satisfaction on her face. After all, it wasn't every day you met a kid with a voice and presence like Jabez. Yet her brow was furrowed and she appeared to be chewing the eraser off her pencil. Eddie wondered what the hell had her so worried, anyway. Clearly, she was just a worrier.

Mrs. Bickham hadn't been a worrier at all. Back when she was in charge, casting decisions had been made with ease. "Who do you think for this role?" she used to ask. Then he'd tell her, and that would be that.

Something told him this was not going to be the case with Maureen.

Also, Mrs. Bickham didn't mind letting him laze around plinking on his guitar while she took charge. Now here was Maureen Davenport who actually expected something of him. What a concept.

They talked about the casting as they put up the sound

system and folded away chairs. Or rather, she talked and made notes on a rolling white board while he put things away.

He didn't have much to say, anyhow. He was still blown away after listening to Jabez. That boy was nothing short of spell-binding. Hearing him made Eddie glad, for the first time this season, to be on this project. He was no fan of Christmas per se, though he did believe in trying to be a part of something larger than himself. And frankly, anything beat sitting around with his folks, reminiscing about Christmases past, the good times they'd all had, such fun, such adventure. Did they really think so, or was that just something they said? People told themselves all kinds of stories to make their lives bearable.

"...just right in that role, don't you think?" Maureen was asking him.

"Sorry," he said. "I didn't catch that."

"Chelsea Nash," she said, "in the role of Mary."

Crazy hair, braces, glasses, nice tone to her voice, Eddie recalled. "Okay," he said, and went back to coiling up the power cords.

"Do you have any thoughts about the Magi?" she asked.

"Yeah, historically they didn't actually show up until a week and a half after the fact."

She regarded him with eyebrows raised in surprise.

"Just because I'm not a librarian doesn't mean I don't know anything," he said.

"What I meant was, who do you see in those roles?"

"I know what you meant. Just wanted to show off."

She flushed, then shifted her gaze uncomfortably to the camera. "Anyway, what about those roles, then?"

"The Veltry boys. A no-brainer," Eddie said immediately.

She plucked a pencil from the bun in her hair and drummed it on her clipboard. "I liked their singing. Their reading was…problematic."

"They'll be great, you'll see." He hoped like hell he wasn't lying. Ray had said the kids had it rough, but Eddie sensed they'd rise to the occasion. He'd make sure of it.

"And then I thought…"

He wouldn't have noticed anything if she hadn't hesitated. But she did hesitate, and he noticed.

"You thought what?"

"Jabez could have the part of Joseph and Cecil could be the angel of the lord."

Eddie resumed his dismantling of the sound system. "You mean the other way around. Jabez is the angel and—what's his name? Yeah, Cecil. Poor kid, he was such a cipher. He can be Joseph." Placing the speakers on a hand truck, Eddie wheeled them to a storage closet. By the time he emerged, she still hadn't said anything. The look on her face was one of physical pain.

"I didn't mean it the other way around," she said.

He frowned. No way she could be that out of touch. "Sure you did. Joseph only has, what, the one line and a duet with Mary. The Byrne kid can handle the part. The angel is the whole production—you know that. We all heard him. He's a showstopper. He'll bring down the house."

"We don't know anything about this boy. Suppose we give him the main role and he disappears?"

"He won't. I have a feeling about Jabez," Eddie said.

"A feeling. And we should hang the whole production on your feeling."

"Why are you being so bullheaded about this? You heard him, Maureen. You know I'm right. He'll blow the doors off."

"That's not the only consideration here. There are lots of other things to consider."

"Like what?"

She opened her mouth. Closed it again. For a minute, he thought she was going to tell him something. Then she shut down. He could see it, like a curtain going down over her eyes, and in its place he saw nothing but distrust. What was up with that?

"It's a community event," she said. "I have to do what's best for the community."

"What's better than a kick-ass production? Everybody wins."

She flinched, and he didn't know why.

"Tell you what—you put him in that role and I'll make sure he doesn't let you down."

Another beat of hesitation. Then worry again.

"Come on, Maureen. Have a little faith."

She looked affronted. "I have plenty of faith."

"That's what you said about the first snow, too. Seems to me you're hedging your bets."

She looked even more affronted. "Just suppose I go along with you and I do it your way."

"Suppose you do." He gently took the clipboard from her and scribbled Jabez's name on the cast list. "There. It's done. You can go post it for everyone to see tomorrow."

For a second, he thought she was going to...he wasn't sure

what. Faint, maybe. For the first time, she looked straight into the unblinking lens of Chet's camera. Then, still a little green around the gills, she walked purposefully to the church vestibule, Chet dogging her footsteps, and hung the list on the bulletin board, stabbing a tack into the top. Finally, she turned to Eddie, eyes narrowed. He could almost see her calculating. "Don't forget about writing that original song for the program," she said.

"What?" He'd heard her, though. So had the camera crew. They were hungry for any little bit of conflict they could record; it made for more interesting TV.

"Just like I said on the flyer. Original song, written and performed by Eddie Haven."

"Yeah, about that. I don't think so."

She folded her arms in front of her. "You expect me to do things your way, but you won't even perform a song? You know what I think? I think you're afraid."

"Oh, now you're trying to psychoanalyze me."

"For your information, I don't give a hoot about your psyche. Or any other part of you except your musical talent." She looked him square in the eye. "I think you're afraid to show that part of yourself."

"Number one, what makes you think there's that part of me to show? And number two, what makes you think people would be interested?"

"Those women in the bakery the other day were certainly interested."

"You're not going to see folks like that at your damn Christmas pageant."

"They'd come if they knew you were performing."

Eddie couldn't help himself. He laughed aloud. "You crack me up, Maureen. You really do. Do people call you Moe?"

"Not to my face."

"Come on, it's a nickname."

"I've never had a nickname."

"You do now. I'm calling you Moe."

Her face turned red, though he couldn't tell if it was anger or a blush. "You're trying to change the subject," she accused, as if she hadn't just done exactly that. "I just want to make sure I have your cooperation about the original song. Will you do it?"

"I'd do anything for you, Moe."

"Now you're mocking me."

"I'm giving you what you want. How is that mocking you?"

She didn't answer, but pursed her lips and stared at him for a long, drawn-out moment. She stared at him so hard it was almost sexy.

The subtle thrum of excitement took him by surprise. It was a surprise because she was not his type, not in the least. His type tended to be girls with big tits and outgoing person-alities, girls with names ending in *i,* who drew little hearts in place of the dot over the *i.* Girls who didn't constantly question and challenge him.

Now here was this Maureen, this librarian, all buttoned into her matching sweater set, checking him out. Challenging him while the whole exchange was recorded for a documentary. And against all common sense, he felt turned on.

9

"*Score.* He's sleeping like a log." Logan O'Donnell came out of Daisy's bedroom, his face wearing that peaceful expression of bliss that comes from having rocked a child to sleep. "Took three books, including two readings of *Babar and the Wully-Wully.*"

Daisy couldn't help smiling at him. Not only did his every expression and nuance remind her of Charlie, but Logan had a peculiar boyish appeal that was impossible to resist. People talked about "Irish charm." Logan O'Donnell embodied it, and in him, the attribute seemed to be both a blessing and a curse. Making friends and getting girls had always been easy for him. Keeping promises and staying sober—not so easy. Yet for Charlie's sake, Logan was succeeding at both. Now a junior in college, he lived in a sub-free frat where drinking and drugs were absolutely forbidden.

But it was still a frat. That meant they were just as crazy, but they stayed up later and partied longer. Logan was as popular as ever with girls, and even as a commuter student, Daisy was aware of this. She tried not to mind, but these things did matter in a very big way. Suppose, she'd think, during her crazy times when she couldn't help herself, suppose he got serious about someone. That someone would be a part of Charlie's life, and Daisy would have no say whatsoever in who she was or what influence she'd have over their little boy.

When Daisy confessed things like this to Sonnet, her best friend, Sonnet would tell her to quit obsessing. Easier said than done. Daisy knew the cause of her obsession lay within her, not in Logan or some sorority sister he was dating. The truth was, Daisy ached for things she couldn't have. The encounter with Julian only underscored that fact. Sometimes she woke up at night feeling so lonely she thought she would disappear. Even though her life was filled with abundance—family, friends and most especially, Charlie—there was a huge, missing gap of something. In her heart of hearts, she knew what would fill that gap.

"There's something I want to ask you," Logan said, taking a seat on the sofa beside her.

"What?" She turned, pulling her knee up to her chest, hoping the turmoil didn't show on her face. "Have I been a good girl this year?"

"Sure," he said with a teasing grin. "That's exactly what I'm wondering."

"Let's see. I finished twenty-one credit hours at school, and I can officially count myself a sophomore. Oh, and my GPA? A three-point-six. Not too shabby, eh?"

"You are a star. I always knew it."

She wasn't a star. She was someone who stayed home with her baby every night, so she tended to use the time to study. The rest of the time, she hung out with Charlie, and she worked. She'd shot several weddings that year, earning enough to pay the rent and keep Charlie in Cheerios. With respect to money, she knew she was beyond lucky. Her tuition was covered by family money. Charlie's expenses were covered by Logan.

Not having to worry about money was a priceless gift. But it was also an obligation.

"Seriously, I do want to ask you something," Logan said. "I feel bad, taking Charlie away on Christmas Eve."

You feel bad, she thought, biting her tongue.

"Not being together as a family at Christmas feels all wrong to me," he continued.

Welcome to the club.

"So I wanted to invite you to spend Christmas on Long Island with my family," he said.

Crap. Holy crap, she thought.

"You're looking at me funny," he said.

"Have you mentioned this to your parents?" she asked, thinking about the O'Donnells, and how slow they'd been to accept her.

"I did mention it, and they said you'd be welcome. You're Charlie's mother. That makes you part of the family."

She narrowed her eyes in suspicion. "What's the catch?"

"No catch. We want you with us."

Ever since she'd decided to allow Logan to have Charlie on Christmas Eve, she had faced the holiday with dread. She'd never been separated from Charlie for more than a few hours.

An entire night would be torture for her, certainly. And maybe for Charlie, as well. Logan's offer addressed her deepest fear, offering her a way to be with her little boy on Christmas Eve.

There was a catch, however. And that catch was having to leave her own family—her parents and brother—behind in Avalon. That was going to hurt. She loved Christmas Eve with her family—her two families, now. Her dad's and her mom's. Somehow, it all worked. There would be a dinner at the Inn at Willow Lake, which her dad and stepmom ran, and then the pageant with her mom and Noah and their kids, at Heart of the Mountains Church. Afterward, they'd take a slow drive through town, admiring the light displays and feeling the pervasive, quiet magic of the holiday.

Daisy told herself she wasn't a kid anymore. She had a kid of her own, and her decisions were governed by what was best for him. And going to the O'Donnells' place was the best choice for Charlie.

A fleeting thought about Julian Gastineaux crossed her mind. The quick visit at the library wasn't enough. He'd been in Avalon last Christmas, and they'd managed to steal a few hours together, talking nonstop, both of them feeling the exquisite tension of unacknowledged attraction. If she knew Julian was coming home this year, would that color her decision? Bluntly honest with herself, she knew she wouldn't budge from Avalon.

The notion shocked her. Could she care about someone that much? Was she that selfish?

The point was moot, however. Julian had already told her he wouldn't be coming home for the holidays. What Daisy really needed to do was put him from her mind. And out of her life. Things were never going to work out for the two of them, and the smart thing would be to move on, to find a way to live her life without constantly looking back over her shoulder and wondering, *what if?*

She considered the present situation, and realized without the promise of seeing Julian, nothing was holding her back. It would be the first Christmas Eve away from her parents and brother. They were her family. But Charlie was her future. Besides, she would come back to Avalon on Christmas day in time for not one but two feasts—a kid-centered midday meal with her mom and Noah and their two little ones, then dinner with her dad and Nina at the oh-so-elegant Inn at Willow Lake.

She smiled at Logan, who had no idea what was going on in her mind. And she said, "I'd love to spend Christmas Eve with you."

His face lit with a smile. "Cool. I was hoping you'd say so. I know you got off to a rocky start with my folks, but that's over. They love you as much as Charlie and I do."

She tried not to read too much into his words. Logan tossed around the word *love,* but she wasn't certain he knew what it meant on the deepest level. "I hope you're right about your folks," she said.

"It's going to be great. The beach at Christmas—it's awesome there. The deck has a view of the lighthouse, and the beach goes on for miles."

"I know."

"Oh. Uh, yeah."

They'd made Charlie at the beach house at the very farthest

tip of Long Island, a forgotten place swept by wind and sea. Their senior year in high school, when Daisy had been stupid with emotional pain over her parents' divorce, she went to an unchaperoned party there, never knowing that one illicit weekend would change the direction of her life for good.

Feeling awkward, she got up and headed for the kitchen. "Hey, can I get you something to eat or drink? I can make coffee, or—"

"Thanks, but I need to head back. I've got an early class tomorrow."

She envied him, living on campus. Being able to sleep until ten minutes before class was a luxury she'd never experienced. Her mornings were an intricate and lengthy ordeal, getting Charlie dressed and fed, his diaper bag packed for the sitter, hugs and kisses doled out, then a commute to campus. "I'll see you around, then," she said, and walked him to the door.

"I'm glad you said yes," he told her. "To Christmas, I mean."

"It was easy to say yes. Thanks for asking me, Logan."

"No problem." He took hold of her shoulders. Before she realized what was happening, he kissed her. Really kissed her, in a way she hadn't been kissed in a very long time. For a few seconds, she forgot everything; she felt completely filled up by the kind of passion and heat that kept loneliness at bay.

She felt slightly breathless, her senses heightened by his touch. It scared her, this kind of wanting. Could it be she was so lonely that she would cling to anyone? Did it matter that this was Logan? Or was she just desperate?

She pulled away in confusion. "Bad idea, Logan," she said. "You shouldn't kiss me like that. You shouldn't kiss me at all."

"Why not? I liked it. I think you liked it, too."

"The last time you kissed me like that, we made Charlie."

He stuck his hand in his back pocket, took out his wallet. "Don't worry, this time I came prepared—"

"Logan," she said, and to her dismay, her voice broke in the middle of his name. It was just that his touch brought all her loneliness to the surface. "Logan, I—"

"You what?" he asked, taking her hand, carrying it to his mouth.

Why did he have to be so cute? Why was she such a sucker for those Irish looks—boyish face, red hair and green eyes? Because he had that physique, of course—the shoulders and strength of a rugby player, and gentle hands that knew more about her body than she dared admit.

"I think we should keep this about Charlie," she whispered, not trusting herself to speak louder, past the thick emotion in her throat. Yes, she was alone to the point of pain. Yes, she ached to be touched and held. She ached to make love, something that hadn't happened for her since Charlie was conceived. But not like this, not out of loneliness and desperation.

"It's okay for it to be about you sometimes," Logan said.

"Which is why we'd better say good-night."

He didn't get mad. He didn't sulk. Instead, he cradled her cheek in his hand, gently skimmed his thumb across the ridge of her cheekbone. "Sure," he said, leaning down to place the lightest of kisses on her forehead. "That's what we'll do."

He took off into the night, hurrying away in a swirl of snowflakes. She stood at the door, watching his taillights disappear. She sighed against the glass pane, touched her lips and wondered how her life had become so complicated.

10

Maureen woke with the worst what-have-I-done headache of her life. It was the kind of headache she imagined women suffered after a night of partying, maybe even after wild sex with someone slightly dangerous.

Not that Maureen would know. But she read a lot of books.

Her current headache had to do with the choice she'd made last night. She had allowed herself to be persuaded by Eddie Haven to put a stranger in the role that was supposed to belong to Cecil Byrne. What was she thinking? She hadn't been thinking. She'd been so caught up in Jabez's performance, and then in Eddie's simple, persuasive argument that she'd simply caved. The documentary film crew had recorded everything and somehow she hadn't been able to choose anyone but Jabez.

She scrambled into her clothes. There was still time to change what she'd done. Surely no one had seen the list yet. She could simply change the original. No, she thought, giving Franklin and Eloise a cup of kibbles. The list was written in indelible, unforgiving ink. She would have to redo the whole thing.

The air was crisp and cold on her face as she got in the car and drove to the church. For a split second, she considered exceeding the speed limit. But no. Going too fast often ended up costing more time, particularly when the roads were slippery with snow and ice. The town was just waking up, with the first wave of commuters heading to the station, the brigade of fitness fanatics out jogging in skintight warm-ups, lights winking on at the bakery and newsstand. It was interesting to see this whole world of activity that took place in the semidark of the early-morning hours.

No, it wasn't interesting. It was nervewracking. She didn't understand all these early risers. Didn't any of them stay up late into the night, absorbed in a novel they couldn't put down? Maureen did so every night. In order to wake up in the morning, she required two alarms and three cups of coffee. One of her favorite things about being a librarian was that the place didn't open until nine-thirty in the morning, a very civilized hour, in her estimation.

At this time of day, there were no other cars at the church. No tracks marked the freshly fallen snow, she saw with relief. She hurried to the main door and used the key she'd been given. Even so, she felt...furtive. Sneaky. As though she was doing something wrong.

"Good morning," said a friendly voice behind her.

She gasped and dropped the keys as she spun around. "Jabez, you startled me."

"Sorry, didn't mean to."

"What are you doing here at this hour?"

"Hoping to get a look at your list," he said. "You said it would be posted in the lobby today."

"Yes," she heard herself say, "but it's not quite final..." Her voice trailed off. She was in a pickle now. She regarded Jabez's unusual face—mild, with unexpected flashes of intensity. Even in the stark morning light he appeared beautiful and somewhat exotic. She could still hear inside her head every single gorgeous note he'd sung at the audition, and she knew deep down that Eddie was right. This boy was born to sing. Having him do so for all of Avalon would be a priceless gift to the community.

The headache that had been building all morning reached a crescendo. Then again, so would the library. She hated having to choose. How did one compare the ineffable lifting up of the spirit with the priceless treasure of the library?

You didn't, she realized. And the decision had already been made the night before, the moment her pen touched the paper. Changing it now would mean that once again, she was second-guessing herself, just like Eddie accused her of doing. It would mean she'd caved in to Mr. Byrne's bullying. She led the way into the vestibule.

"It's done," she said stoutly. "You'll have the most important role, so I hope you're up to it."

His eyes lit, and his amazing smile seemed to warm the whole room. "I'm definitely up for it."

They shook hands, sealing the deal. "With all the rehearsals in the coming weeks, we'll be seeing a lot of one another. I'm looking forward to getting to know you."

His smile turned a little bashful. "Okay."

"You have an incredible voice."

"Thank you."

"Have you had professional training?"

He gave a soft laugh. "No, ma'am." He shouldered his backpack and headed for the door. "See you around."

"Yes," she said. "Have a good day, Jabez. Hey, can you use a ride?"

He must not have heard her, because he was gone in an instant. After he left, she took one final look at the list. Her stomach tightened into a knot of nerves. She had better make this a kick-ass program, as Eddie would say.

No pressure. No headache, either, she realized. One minute it was coming on like a freight train, yet now it was gone.

With a feeling of well-being she wasn't sure she'd earned, she headed for the door. As long as she was up this early, she might as well make the most of it.

Because now, in addition to putting on a kick-ass program, she had to kick some ass in the library fund-raising department.

She was so not good at ass-kicking, but realized it was all up to her. Having created this mess, she was the one who needed to figure a way out of it. The library's budget was tapped out. What on earth made her think she'd find a way? Because she had no choice. She had to fix this. She stepped outside, into the gray early-morning chill. It was a new day. Every new day was an opportunity, she reminded herself.

As she walked across the parking lot to her car, something struck her as odd. She frowned, not knowing what it was, and stopped in her tracks.

Her tracks, that was it. She saw, in the snow, a line of footprints from her car to the portico of the building. But those were the only tracks she could make out. Where were Jabez's footprints?

She looked left and right, wondering if there was a different exit she didn't know about that he could've taken. But no. There was none visible. There must be a simple explanation, but for the life of her, she couldn't fathom what it was.

The day had turned colder with the coming of the light, and snow flurries started up, chasing her and her overactive imagination to the car. She jumped in, blasted the heat and turned on the radio, which was set to her favorite local station, WKSM.

"And here's hoping this fine day is off to a great start for you," said Eddie Haven.

If she hadn't been wearing her seat belt, she would have jumped right out of her seat. "Eddie?"

"So take it from me, Eddie Haven. Get your shopping done early, and buy local this year. Your community will thank you."

Maureen was hyperventilating. "What on earth—"

"...and thanks to Zuzu's Petals boutique for sponsoring this part of our program," Eddie continued. "Remember, Zuzu's Petals, your neighborhood fashion-forward boutique."

"Oh." Maureen slumped back against the seat. "Good grief, you're on the radio." She carefully pressed the accelerator and eased out of the parking lot. "I'm an idiot," she said to an imaginary Eddie. "I thought I was hearing things." She snatched up her phone and dialed her friend Olivia Davis, who was always up at oh-dark-thirty. "Eddie Haven's on the radio," she said.

"Good morning to you, too," Olivia said.

"Are you listening to WKSM?"

"Sure, every morning. The regular host is Jillian Snipe. She's on hiatus and Eddie's her substitute. He's doing a good job, too."

"I never listen because it comes on at such an ungodly early hour," Maureen confessed.

"What are you doing up?" Olivia asked.

"Long story," Maureen said.

"Meet me for coffee and we'll have a chat."

Maureen smiled; Olivia was the best sort of friend, the kind who would drop everything if she sensed she was needed. Soon, Olivia would go the way of new mothers. This was what her married friends did. They moved on, retreating to that quiet place where new mothers dwelled, removed from everyday matters as they went about the hard but vital work of loving their newborns. Maureen understood this completely, but each time one of her close friends or sisters had a big life change, it left a void.

"I'll call you later, okay?" She rang off and sat with the car's heater gently blowing while she thought about the idea that Eddie had a radio show. She knew it was broadcast from the Fillmore on the town square, a vintage brick building that housed the local cable and Internet company, as well. The show was called "Catskills Morning," and it was a combination of NPR, talk and music. Other than that, she didn't know much about it.

Then Maureen had a brainstorm. She was about to find out a lot more about "Catskills Morning." She turned up the volume as she drove a short distance from the church to the town square. "… and now, here's one for all you fans of quirky love affairs that only last a little while. This is Courtney Swaine singing 'Temporary Insanity,' off her album *You Should Know Better.*"

"Ah, yes," Maureen muttered as she leaned forward over the steering wheel. "Big fan of quirky love affairs that only last a little while. Huge fan."

The song was excellent, though, she had to admit. The female vocalist performed solo, accompanied by an acoustic guitar played by the lightest of touches and plenty of unsentimental honesty. Maureen listened to two more selections while she drove, both also good. Eddie seem to favor new artists and unmixed music. She didn't mind admitting to herself that she liked his taste.

"...sponsored by Pluggit MIDI Controllers, the musician's choice," Eddie was saying in another promo. "Now bands can record for the price of a laptop and release albums all around the world. A fantastic gift for musicians and music lovers."

"I'll put that on my list," Maureen said to herself. "'Dear Santa, I want a Pluggit.'"

The station had a shop front window with a painted logo of a microphone emitting lightning bolts, and the slogan, "You're in good company with WKSM."

"I certainly hope so," she said, getting out of the car.

She could see Eddie in the window. He was wearing a headset and speaking into a microphone equipped with a diffuser the size of a dinner plate, smiling as he talked. He spotted her and gestured at the door, motioning her inside. Two young women sat in the tiny reception area inside the door. Their desk signs identified them as Brandi, the producer, and Heidi, the engineer. Brandi wore a pleated plaid miniskirt and cropped sweater that showed off a navel ring. Heidi, with pink-tipped hair, looked as though she was about to head out for a day of snowboarding. They both had porn-star names and looked like Hooters waitresses. If a thirteen-year-old boy was allowed to design the ideal coworkers, he would probably come up with these two. In her wool slacks and sweater, Maureen felt old and dowdy.

"I stopped in to see Eddie," Maureen said after introducing herself. "Can you tell me when he'll be available?"

"You can go on in now," Heidi said, gesturing toward the broadcast booth. "We're live on the air, but he's got seven-and-a-half minutes of music going."

"Thanks."

Eddie motioned again, and she squeezed into a small room crammed with equipment, including a console with a padded stool on rollers. She took a seat on the stool. He flipped some switches, moved the mic out of the way and turned to her.

"Stalking me this morning, Moe?"

Moe. Why did that sound sexy to her? "Yes, I have nothing better to do."

He laughed, his blue eyes twinkling. Good grief, the guy had twinkling eyes. He shouldn't hide on the radio.

"Okay," he said, "what can I do for you?" He leaned back in his chair. A tight Radiohead T-shirt accentuated his chest.

She reminded herself not to stare. "I—we—need to do a fund-raiser for the library."

"Sure, you got it."

"I love the fact you didn't hesitate."

"It's the library, not the NRA. Who doesn't like the library?"

"See, that's the thing. Everybody loves the library. But when it comes to funding, only a few carry the load."

"Sort of like public radio." He gestured at the rows of mugs and totebags given out to subscribers. "Seems to be human nature to want something for nothing, and then gripe when it gets taken away. So tell me what you have in mind."

"It's an emergency appeal. A life-or-death matter for the library, and that's no exaggeration. It's slated to close if we don't make our target by the end of the year."

"No shit."

"Um, right. I wish I was kidding. Unfortunately, I'm not."

"That sucks. So what do you need? What's the goal here?"

She explained about the need to raise a year's operating budget in an impossibly short amount of time, and he gave a low whistle. "By the end of the year? In a community this size, you'll need a year, minimum. Maybe two years."

"We don't have that kind of time." Maureen was surprised to find herself on the verge of tears. This mattered so much. Couldn't he see how much it mattered?

"Hate to burst your bubble, but I don't think it can be done. Even rich people don't give away chunks of money like that."

"You're probably right. But some guy once told me I had to have a little faith. Maybe I heard him wrong."

"Touché," he said.

"You understand, I have to try. I could never live with myself if I didn't give this everything I've got."

He looked at her for a long time. In the soundproof broadcast booth, she could hear the beating of her own heart. She could hear it speed up.

"Same here," he said. "Let's do it."

11

Eddie was dreaming of the angel again. At least, he—the Eddie in his dream—assumed he was in the presence of an angel. It wasn't a person, but a vision of light, a breath of warmth in his soul, a feeling of comfort surrounding him, a sense of safety. Sometimes Eddie's sleep yielded disturbing matters, yet whenever he dreamed of the angel, a peaceful calm settled over him like a fresh blanket. The light pulsed gently with an unarticulated promise to resolve into the face of someone he knew, but it never quite went there. That was where the dream always left him, wondering what more lay beyond the light.

He hovered between slumber and full wakefulness, reluctant to acknowledge the insistent buzz of the alarm. Just a few more minutes, he told the angel. Just a few. He wasn't eager to leave the golden presence. Maybe other people dreamed of angels all the time, but for Eddie, it was a rare occurrence. Like the opening sequence of a movie, the dream had started…he could actually pinpoint exactly where it had started—the night of his wreck. The moment everything had changed. His mind went back to that night, and he observed himself from a distance, as if watching a stranger. His life had been spinning out of control like the van on black ice, gathering speed until some obstacle stopped him. In the case of the van, the obstacle was an elaborate nativity scene. He'd first seen the angel then—more than one if he was being honest with himself. But it was crazy enough to have even one vision, so he never told anyone.

He lingered inside the dream until finally, it evaporated along with the last of his sleep, shrilled to wakefulness by another series of rings. He blinked and sat up, scowling at the clock, only to realize the noise wasn't coming from the clock. He grabbed his mobile phone, hitting the button to silence it.

Then he glanced at the screen, rubbed his eyes and looked again. Flipped the thing open.

"Hey, Barb," he said. He called his mother Barb because in the commune where he'd been raised, there were no moms and dads, no terms of authority or rank. Back in the commune days, she'd gone by the name Moonbeam, but even as a little kid, he couldn't bring himself to go there. It had felt false, and forced, particularly to a boy who wanted to call her Mom.

"There you are, you handsome thing."

"You're up early."

"My new regimen. I've taken up hotbox yoga, five-thirty in the morning."

"Oh. Um, okay." He pictured her in her yellow Long Island kitchen, wearing the latest trend in yoga outfits.

"Did I wake you?"

He shook off the last of the angel. "I'm up. I'm going in to the station."

"For your morning show."

"Yeah, I'm filling in for the regular host."

"We listen to you on the Internet, you know."

"Actually, I didn't know. Thanks."

"You're very good. We're proud of you, son."

"Thanks," he said again. Eddie's relationship with his parents was functional. Just not real deep. As a recovering alcoholic, he knew he needed to make amends with them, and make peace with a past he couldn't change. He simply…hadn't tackled the issue yet, though he often promised himself he would. It was a painful business, though, so he kept putting it off. Easier just to maintain a polite distance. Yet he knew he carried around a burden of unacknowledged rancor for his peripatetic childhood. He tried to be philosophical regarding the past. His parents, like everybody else, were products of their own upbringing. They both came from show business families, thrust into the spotlight before they were old enough to know whether or not it was the life they wanted. Their marriage as kids of just eighteen and nineteen was more pub- licity stunt than lifelong commitment, yet here they were thirty-five years later, still together. As newlyweds, they'd starred in a short-lived but popular variety show, and afterward they'd done their best with Eddie, more or less. More when they took responsibility for him, less when they abdicated their parental duties in favor of the backwoods commune they'd shared with a crazy hodgepodge of old hippies, young idealists, tax dodgers, earnest environmentalists and misfits determined to live off the grid.

"How're you doing, Barb?" he asked. "How's Larry?"

"We're both fine," she said. "Great. Your dad's in the city three days a week, working on voice-overs. He's doing intimate reads for a series of fragrance commercials."

Eddie's father had a whole stable of voices, from graveltoned cowboy to continental lover. The "intimate read" was an industry standard. It was also, to Eddie's embarrassment, one of Larry's specialties. It was always startling—and a bit disconcerting—to turn on the radio or TV and hear him voice a car commercial or political attack ad. But that—as both parents would say—was showbiz. You never knew what was around the next corner.

"So I wanted to talk to you about holiday plans this year," his mother said.

Correction, he thought. Sometimes you knew exactly what was coming next. "I'm all ears, Barb."

"We're planning our usual Christmas Eve get-together—old friends and neighbors." She spoke in the light, sweet voice that had endeared her to America, decades ago. She still sounded endearing. "Oh, and we're having the Sheltons up from Florida. You remember the Sheltons."

"They had the annoying dog act, years ago."

"I don't know about annoying—"

"I do."

"Well, they're a nice family, and they've got a lovely daughter—"

"Evelyn," he filled in for her, remembering a girl about his age, with red hair and a child-star smile, the kind that blazed like a spotlight, turning on five thousand watts of pure, blinding artifice, on command. He went to the window and raised the shade. It was still dark out. Street lamps cast a yellowish glow through the neighborhood, an eclectic mix of lakeside cottages. From his window, he could see the lake in one direction, the town in the other. A few cars lumbered along the snow-covered streets.

"Yes," his mother declared. "She's been abroad, and now she's back. I thought maybe—"

"Abroad as in rehab?" Eddie asked. "Or abroad as in overseas, in another country?"

"Don't be silly," Barb said. "Abroad simply means abroad. We've got such fun times planned. There's going to be a caroling party and then a Christmas Eve visit to the Village Family Shelter. You know, to bring them a little holiday cheer. Lord knows, battered homeless women and their children could use a little of that."

"Lord knows," he echoed, focusing on the blinking neon of Hilltop Tavern in the distance.

"And of course, afterward, we'll have everyone back here for a party. And we'll screen your movie, same as we do every year. It just wouldn't be Christmas without a viewing of *The Christmas Caper.* That's always my favorite part. Everyone always has such fun watching it."

"Don't they, though." He dragged himself to the kitchen and started making coffee.

"This year more than ever, because the remastered edition is just so fantastic. We're hoping you'll come. It'd be such a special treat if you could be here. We always have such fun—party games, eggnog, a fabulous potluck. And of course, you shouldn't worry about your, ah, problem."

Her lowered tone irritated him. "You can say it, Barb. I'm an alcoholic."

She didn't say it, of course. She never did. Giving his disease a name might mean she'd have to acknowledge it, and maybe even see herself in an unflattering light. "I've found a recipe for a delicious fizzy punch, made strictly from soft drinks and lime sherbet. Doesn't that sound divine?"

"I'm salivating."

"And I had all our old photos scanned, so they're digital, and this year, I made a computer slide show, complete with music to go along with the images. The photos start with a vintage circus shot of your dad's great-grandfather and go right up to the present day. Most of them are of you, of course. People are going to die when they see how cute you were. They'll just die. Having you there would be the icing on the cake."

It beats a sharp stick in the eye, he thought.

He pictured his parents and their friends, settling attractively into middle age, sitting around and toasting the crazy times of their youth. These days, the Havens and the others from the commune lived in modest Long Island houses, listened to NPR and collected heart-healthy recipes. And, apparently, attended hotbox yoga classes.

"I might even start a Web site to show them off to the world," his mother continued. "A 'Meet the Havens' official Web site. Maybe that will be my project for the new year."

That sharp stick was beginning to look a little better to him. Christmastime was something Eddie wished he could erase from the hard drive.

There were no misty memories for him of carols around the piano, family feasts, stockings stuffed with goodies and a tree surrounded with gifts. For most people, the sights, sounds and scents of the holiday were all wrapped up in warm, loving feelings. For the Havens, Christmastime meant hitting the road. His parents claimed that in addition to being the most lucrative season for an act like theirs, it was also the ideal way to avoid the crass commercialism of the holidays. In the process, they managed to avoid anything that might predispose Eddie to actually liking the holidays. His Christmas memories consisted of long days at train and bus stations, or riding in a borrowed VW microbus. Paper-wrapped meals eaten on the fly. Funky-smelling hotel rooms. Not knowing what day it was—even when it was Christmas Day.

And the funny thing was, his parents didn't have a clue about how lousy that was for a kid.

He vividly recalled staring dull-eyed out the window of the van, watching the gray sky race by like a river through towns where he was a stranger. He and his parents generally played a different venue every night, wending their way through small towns where their act was a big deal.

"Meet the Havens" was built around Eddie himself. Ever since the movie hit had rocketed him to fame at the age of six, he'd been a recognizable figure. Unfortunately, the laws of physics and showbiz both dictated that a meteoric rise was followed by a swift fall. He'd been too young to understand the concept, which was probably a good thing.

His mother called it "super-fun," and often sang and composed in the car between homeschooling sessions, which entailed a lot of spelling. To this day, Eddie could spell pretty much anything.

On a typical day on the road, he'd wake up in a motel room with bad carpeting, the tables littered with empty bottles and torn packets of headache powders. Breakfast usually consisted of a row of powdered doughnuts purchased at a gas station or convenience store, always the first stop of the day. This was before the days of mobile phones, so his mother would use a pay phone to call ahead to confirm the next booking.

His father would check the van's oil and tires, gas the thing up. Eddie would consume the doughnuts and maybe a tube of salted peanuts, washed down with milk or juice from a paper carton.

"We get a different Christmas every day," his mother would declare, returning from her phone call to beam at him. "How much fun is that?"

He figured out pretty quickly that she didn't expect an answer. The three of them would sing together as they drove from place to place, practicing the numbers they would perform in Scranton, Saranac or Stamford or any of the dozens of towns on their itinerary. His mom would do her hair, using some kind of goop and big rollers and plugging in a blow-dryer at a gas station as showtime approached.

Their venues ran the gamut from high school stages to Knights of Columbus halls to community playhouses to country clubs. Their repertoire consisted of the usual Christmas fare, interspersed with his parents' banter, which for some reason never seemed to grow stale.

"So tonight we invite you to step back, take a deep breath and remember the simple joys of the season," his father would say, underscoring his words with a gentle stroke of guitar strings.

And every time he uttered those words, Eddie's dad would sound as warmhearted and calm as a Zen master. No one in the audience would know they'd nearly been late to the show because of a flat tire. Or that they'd missed their exit or gotten lost or that Larry had spilled half a can of Utica Club on his shirt. All the preceding chaos fell away when the three of them hit the stage.

Sometimes the lighting masked the audience from Eddie, and as he performed, he went away in his head somewhere, picturing himself in a different world. Other times, he might have a full view of their listeners, and he'd imagine what it was like to belong to a different family, to have siblings, to attend public school, to go home to the same house every night. His parents assured him that he'd be bored in an instant. They said siblings took your stuff and blamed you for everything.

The Havens were on the road through New Year's Day each year, but the highlight of the season, financially speaking, was always Christmas Eve. His parents told him so, anyway. That was when people were feeling particularly generous and kind. Sometimes when he performed, he would look out into the audience to see if he could recognize kindness in people's faces. It always gave him a pang, seeing kids who would sleep in their own bed that night and wake up to the sort of Christmas morning Eddie knew only from the movies. It was amazing to him that there were children who actually experienced the brightly lit tree, a stocking stuffed to overflowing, cinnamon rolls baking in the oven, and the longed-for, yearned-for, wished-for Santa gift hidden beneath the pine boughs.

Eddie had grown up wanting to believe Christmas wishes could come true. Everyone's favorite line in his movie was "Miracles can happen, if only you believe." And indeed, in *The Christmas Caper,* little Jimmy Kringle was reunited with his long-lost family. Eddie had tried hard to be a true believer, even though his parents dismissed Santa as an agent of materialistic greed. Eddie used to write letters in secret and post them on his own, asking Santa for the kind of things any boy might want—a new bike, a model rocket, a puppy, an aquarium full of neon-colored fish. He never got anything he asked for. On Christmas day, he'd wake up in some nondescript hotel room or motor court unit. His parents would sleep in while he watched church on TV and ate whatever he could find—often a tin of brightly frosted cookies given to them by a producer or stagehand. After a while, Larry and Barb would get up and fish a dripping bottle out of the slush in the ice chest and crack it open, and sip the fizzy stuff until they were in a good mood. The drink was called Cold Duck and it smelled weird and tasted worse.

Eddie never said anything to them about Santa. He knew they didn't believe and wouldn't approve. The lack of gifts under the tree—not that there was a tree—merely proved their point.

"Sorry to have to disappoint you," he told his mother on the phone, "but I'm stuck here in Avalon, same as I am every Christmas, working on the pageant."

A pause. "Surely by now you've fulfilled your community service."

"Still at it," he said. What nobody knew, what he kept from everybody, was that his community service sentence had been fulfilled a long time ago. He kept coming back, year after year, because in spite of everything, he stupidly wanted to believe in Christmas.

"My goodness. You've done more than your share. I can't imagine what that judge was thinking."

Eddie and his mother had, more or less, the same conversation, year in and year out. She wanted him to spend Christmas with them, while he would resort to anything—including a lie—to get out of it. The reason he worked on the pageant year after year was simple. It saved him from having to deal with something he liked even less.

He offered the same line he always gave her. "I'll come down for a visit after."

"The Sheltons will be so disappointed. They specifically said how much they were looking forward to seeing you."

He felt his jaw tighten. Did she think, after all this time, that he would change his mind? That he would suddenly want to make merry with the people who had ruined the holiday for him? "Tell them I'm sorry to miss them, too," he said. "Tell them I had to go abroad."

A beat of silence tripped by. "Well. That *is* disappointing. We'll miss you," she said. "Christmas just isn't the same without you, son."

"I'll miss you too, Barb," he said. "Tell Larry I said hi."

He set down his phone, wishing he could dive under the

covers and go back to the angel again. He couldn't, though. He was haunted by echoes of the wistful note in his mother's voice as he dressed for the day and headed to the station. He didn't like to disappoint her, hell no. But he could not fathom a way to survive Christmas Eve, complete with a screening of *Caper* and—good God—a musical slide show, all accompanied by the requisite cocktails and spiked eggnog. He was confident in his sobriety, but if anything could drive him back to drinking, it would be a night like that.

Later that day, Eddie pulled into the gym parking lot and headed for the handball court. Athletics weren't really his bag, but he liked the game well enough, and he was meeting his friend Bo Crutcher here. A major league pitcher, Bo had a strict winter training regimen which he stuck to with the devotion of a fanatic. For Eddie, a handball game with a baseball pitcher was kind of a mismatch, but it was a good workout.

He found Bo in the weight room. "Ready to get your ass kicked?" Eddie asked him.

"Yeah, I'm shaking."

"Let's get going, then. I got a lot I have to do later. Christmas pageant stuff," he added. "With my new boss, Maureen Davenport."

"Maureen Davenport." Bo tried out the name. "What's she like?"

An interesting question and one Eddie had been contemplating a lot lately. What was she like? "Bossy," he said. "A take-charge kind of woman."

"She single?" asked Bo. Up until recently, Crutcher had been the womanizer of the group. These days he was a happily married man, so he transferred his flirtatious ways to his unattached friends.

"Sorry to disappoint you, but I didn't ask," he said. *I didn't have to.*

"Bet she is. So what's she like?" Bo persisted.

"She's a librarian, okay? She's like…a librarian."

"What's a librarian like?" Crutcher asked.

"You know, all smart and stuff. Know-it-all attitude, hair pulled back with chopsticks or knitting needles sticking through it, glasses." A couple of times during auditions, he had glanced at Maureen and caught a glimpse of an attractive woman. When she smiled, when she listened to music, she looked incredibly pretty. And—he couldn't be sure because he didn't want to be rude—he thought maybe under the sweater, she might have a figure. Not that it should matter, but he looked for things like that in a woman.

Bo wiggled his eyebrows. "Sounds like just your type."

"I'm working on the Christmas program with her. And helping her put on a big fund-raiser for the library."

"You're going to a lot of trouble for a chick you don't even like," said Bo.

"I didn't say I don't like her," Eddie pointed out. "I do like her. Just not, you know, in that way."

"What way?" Bo asked, playing dumb. He did that a lot.

"You know what way," Eddie said.

"The way I don't like *that* chick?" Bo paused in his workout to indicate a statuesque redhead coming toward them as though on a catwalk. She was drop-dead gorgeous in a tight yoga top and formfitting pants folded down to reveal a glimpse of skin and a belly button ring.

She aimed a cool glance at Bo, her gaze heating up as it progressed from his head to his feet and back again. Then with unhurried leisure, she went to him and planted a lingering kiss on his mouth.

Eddie wasn't shocked or surprised, just envious. The redhead was Bo's wife, Kimberly.

"Sure," he said under his breath, "that way. That's the way I don't like Maureen Davenport."

"Hi, Eddie," said Kim. "Did you say something?"

"Yeah, I got roped into helping organize a library fund-raiser."

"Good for you. Count on us for a donation. A big one. Everybody loves the library."

"So I hear. But do we love it enough to hand over a wad of cash the size of Poughkeepsie? Hey, maybe you guys have that wad of cash. A major league player? You could save me a lot of trouble—"

"How much?" asked Bo.

Eddie dug a pledge form out of his gym bag and indicated the target amount at the top.

"I'm not *that* major," Bo said. "Dang, that is a wad. I don't have that kind of money. The ink's barely dry on my contract."

"I thought baseball players were loaded," Eddie pointed out.

"Like movie stars," Bo countered.

"We should both be swimming in dough," Eddie said. But neither was swimming in anything. Bo's career in the majors was too new, and Eddie's in the movies too old.

"That's the reason for the fund-raiser," he said. "One person can't get it done. But if everybody contributes, we can pull it off."

Kim's expression lit with a bright smile. "We'll do what we can. Just tell us where and when."

"Thanks. As soon as there's a plan, I'll let you know. I'll announce it on the radio, too."

"You're doing a lot for a woman you don't like in *that* way," Bo said.

Maureen was busy helping a group of volunteers and children decorate the library's Christmas tree. Each year, a tall noble fir was donated by Gail and Adam Wright, owners of a plant nursery on the Lakeshore Road. A team of off-duty firefighters had helped stand the twenty-foot tree in the central atrium of the library, a big airy space illuminated by a white winter glow through the skylight two stories above.

Renée was there with her three kids. Daisy Bellamy managed to keep tabs on little Charlie as she snapped picture after picture. After the lights were strung, each child present created a hand-made ornament to hang on the tree. Volunteers on ladders adorned the upper branches while the little ones looked on in wonder.

Gail Wright had three school-age kids. The youngest was George, who went by the nickname Bear. His ornament was a crude angel made of a toilet-paper tube, with wings constructed of Popsicle sticks. "I made this for my dad," he told Maureen. "He's on deployment. He won't be home for Christmas."

"Let's get a picture of you with it," Maureen said, taking him by the hand. "Then you can send him the picture, all right?"

He glowered at her, not fooled for an instant. His father was gone, and just having a picture wasn't the same. Her heart ached for the little boy, his mother and siblings. Adam Wright had joined the state's National Guard in order to supplement the farm's income during the lean years. He'd expected to be called to help his community during floods or forest fires, or to be in the first line of defense in domestic disasters. Instead, he found himself amid a frontline fighting force in a dangerous foreign land.

"You don't have to smile," Daisy said, squatting down to Bear's level. "Your dad'll understand. I've got a friend in the military, and he understands when I feel scared for him."

"My dad says I got the best smile," Bear said.

"You want to give it a try, then?" asked Daisy.

The little boy's attempt was a sad trembling of the chin, a grimace of his lips, but Maureen knew the photo would be precious to his father, checking his e-mail from some remote outpost.

The Christmas tree grew steadily more beautiful as more ornaments were added. "It's time for the treetop angel," said Maureen's niece, Wendy. "Who's gonna put up the angel?"

"Maureen should do it," said Daisy, ready with her camera.

Maureen recoiled. "No, I couldn't—"

"We insist," said Mr. Shannon, the president of the board. He took the elaborate ornament, made of silk and blown glass, from its box. "You should do the honor of placing the angel on the treetop. I assure you, the ladder is quite sturdy." What he didn't say, what he didn't have to say, was that this could well be the last time for the library's tree.

"Here," said Renée. "I'll hold the ladder steady while you climb up."

Maureen was too proud to admit she was afraid of heights. She took the angel and climbed the first few steps of the ladder. About halfway up, she made the mistake of glancing at the floor, which suddenly appeared distant and forbiddingly hard. Yikes. She needed to hang on with both hands. She grabbed the angel's hanging loop in her teeth, which probably didn't look very attractive, but it was better than turning back. As she climbed each level of the tree, she tried to distract herself from her fear of heights by focusing on all the beautiful homemade ornaments. They had been created by children through the years, with such love and hope. Some depicted smiling faces superimposed on books. Others had brief, scrawled messages: I ♥ *the library. Reading is fun.* There were even a couple of portraits of Maureen herself. Seen through children's eyes, she was all heavy-rimmed glasses and a giant hair bun, yet they always drew her smiling, so that was something. Nearly there, she recognized an ancient ornament, one she herself had made as a schoolgirl. It was a small ceramic reindeer with *Christmas is Magic* written on the side. It was the runaway reindeer from Eddie's movie. Even then, she thought.

She reached the upper steps of the ladder without incident, and was now close enough to place the angel on the treetop. The trouble was, she'd made the mistake of looking down and was now too scared to let go of the ladder.

Renée said something, but Maureen wasn't listening. Everything was drowned out by the whir of panic in her ears. Vertigo made the world seem to tilt.

"Everything all right up there?"

The sound of the familiar voice made her stomach drop. *Eddie Haven.* When had he shown up? With the angel still dangling by its loop in her teeth, she dared to glance down again—and immediately wished she hadn't. Eddie stood at the base of the ladder where Renée had been. He appeared to be staring straight up her skirt.

"Fine," she said through gritted teeth. How many people, she wondered, insisted they were fine a split second before disaster struck? She tried to console herself that her skirt was long enough, her tights dark enough, to preserve her modesty. Now she was frozen, not just with fear but with embarrassment.

"Need some help?" he asked.

She could swear she heard laughter in his voice. "I've got it," she said. Her fear of heights was easily overpowered by the embarrassment of having Eddie Haven at the base of the ladder, looking up her skirt. She reached out and set the cone-shaped angel on the topmost point of the tree.

The trouble with a just-cut noble fir was that its slender limbs tended to be too flexible. The top branch nodded under the weight of the angel. It instantly tumbled downward, bouncing off the lower branches and then smashing on the marble and black tile floor of the foyer.

For a moment, no one said anything. Then Wendy stated, "You broke the angel."

A ripple swept through the children present: "Miss Davenport broke the angel." One of the girls started to cry, and that set off a chain reaction—murmurs of dismay, calls for a broom and dustpan, admonitions to kids not to touch the broken glass.

Maureen—the klutz, the breaker of angels—climbed down the ladder in defeat.

"I can't believe I did that," she said to her sister.

"It was an accident," Renée said loyally. According to family legend, this was the sister whose first words uttered were "I'm telling." Now she merely shooed her kids away from the glass and patted Maureen on the arm.

"We need another angel, stat," said Eddie. He was speaking to Bear, who still hadn't placed his ornament on the tree. "Mind if I borrow yours?"

Eyes wide, mouth agape, Bear surrendered the toilet-tube angel. Eddie quickly climbed the ladder, showing none of Maureen's hesitation. Maureen and her sister didn't even try not to stare at his butt, so perfect in perfectly faded jeans.

"Real quick," Renée whispered, nudging Maureen. "Remind me I'm a happily married woman."

"You're a happily married woman," Maureen whispered.

"You're not. You should—"

"I'm happily single," Maureen snapped, forgetting to whisper. Feeling dozens of eyes on her, she wanted to sink into the marble floor. Had Eddie heard? He probably already thought she was ridiculous. This would only reinforce that notion.

Eddie appeared to be busy placing the new angel securely at the top of the tree. He threaded a light string through and around it, then climbed back down the ladder. "Somebody flip the switch," he said, turning to Bear. "How about you do the honors?"

Someone showed the little boy the master switch. He flipped it on, and the tall tree came to life. People burst into spontaneous applause. Bear's switch turned on, too, powered by the pride of accomplishment. Daisy took another photo of him.

"Thank you. That's his first real smile in weeks," said his mother to Eddie.

"You did your good deed for the day, then," he told Maureen.

"What?" She still felt impossibly flustered around him.

"Breaking the angel. It wasn't such a disaster after all."

"Oh. Um, I guess." She would not allow herself to make eye contact with her sister. Renée was gesticulating, trying to get Maureen to…to what? Come on to him? To Eddie Haven? Right. "What are you doing here?" she asked him.

He hesitated. "I brought you an on-air schedule for the launch of your fund-raiser. We can put you on the air during the Monday commuter hour."

"Thank you." She took the printed sheet from him. "So, Monday at the station, then."

"It's a date," he said.

"Swear to God," said Renée, watching him go, "you are TSTL."

"I beg your pardon."

"Too stupid to live. He totally wanted to see you. He probably would have asked you out if you'd given him half a chance."

"Nonsense. He just brought me this schedule."

"He could have e-mailed that, you complete ninny. But he didn't. He came in person. And you all but ran him off."

"I was polite."

"'What are you doing here?'" Renée mimicked her. "That's what you said. You call that polite?"

"Now you're just being silly. Eddie Haven and I are working on a project together. You're reading too much into it."

"Uh-huh."

"He's Eddie Haven, for goodness' sake."

"And you're Maureen Davenport. So what?"

12

Maureen walked into the radio station and said hello to Brandi and Heidi, the producer and engineer. The last-ditch effort to save the library would be launched with a live interview today. Though she didn't want to admit it, she was nervous about going on the air. This was definitely outside her comfort zone, but the library needed all the help it could get. She let herself into the broadcast booth, where she took a seat across from Eddie at a bank of controls. He showed her how to put on headphones and positioned a furry-looking mic in front of her.

"It's another cold, cold morning in Avalon," he announced in his buttery voice. "The current temperature is a brisk sixteen degrees, so bundle up before you go out today. Better yet, pour yourself another cup of coffee and stay home a while longer. We've got a very special guest in the studio today. Please join me in welcoming Maureen Davenport, Avalon's own librarian on a mission. She's the branch manager of our library, and she's here to share some news. Welcome, Maureen."

"Hello, thank you for having me." She sounded stiff and awkward. Long ago, she had taken drama classes in high school and college. She should know how to do this, how to relax and let go. Instead, her throat felt tight and her brain emptied itself of anything resembling coherent thought.

Eddie regarded her with compassionate professionalism— the host attempting to set the guest at ease. "Tell us a little about the library. What's the story and what can our listeners do to help?"

His killer blue eyes did not put her at ease. Fortunately, she'd brought along a cheat sheet of notes. He winced at the loud crinkling sound the paper made as she unfolded it. "Um, sorry," she said, then mentally kicked herself. The listeners were probably reaching for their dials right now, changing the station. Maureen told herself sternly not to blow this. The library shouldn't suffer just because Eddie Haven's eyes disabled her brain cells.

Glancing down at her notes, she explained about the loss of the grant, the 99-year lease and its imminent expiration. She emphasized that the library's only hope of survival was to raise a year's operating budget and a guarantee of funding in the future. She mentioned the failure at the ballot of the extra penny of sales tax and the industrial utility tax that would have funded library operations.

As she talked, Eddie pantomimed an enormous yawn. "To make a long story short," she said, switching gears, "our library will be closed for good unless we come up with the funds. And *fast*."

He gave her a thumbs-up sign. She got it. Keep it simple.

"Tell us what impact losing the library would have on the community," he suggested.

"You know, it's a subtle impact compared to other public services and institutions. No one's electricity is going to be cut off. People's houses won't burn down. The snowplows will still do their work every morning. In other words, life will go on. But it's still a loss. The community loses a source of cultural richness and learning. It's not as immediate as road and bridge maintenance, but its impact is far-reaching. A community without a library is a community in danger of unraveling."

"Can you explain what you mean by unraveling?" asked Eddie. "In what way?"

"Well, to my mind, a community is measured by the kind of sanctuary it offers people. A church or temple—that's a sanctuary for the spirit. A hospital or shelter—for the body. A library is a sanctuary for the mind." She glanced down at her notes. "Each year, our schools are given a mandate to raise reading test scores. How is that going to happen without a library?"

He scribbled something, passed her a slip of paper with one word on it: *story.*

All right, she thought. Deep breath. Tell a story.

"Our town library exists because the people of Avalon built it. Back in 1909, the original building burned to the ground. A boy died in the fire, too. No one ever knew his name. It was assumed he was a vagrant. Sadly, it happened on Christmas Eve, and it was believed he'd been secretly sheltering in the basement of the building, and he'd made a fire to keep warm. The loss must have been horrible, but everyone came together and gave the boy a proper burial. A community-spirited man, Mr. Jeremiah Byrne, funded the building of a new library, and that's how our current structure came into being."

Eddie made a wavering motion with his hand. She was starting to bore him again. Good grief, the man was a demanding listener.

"In a small town like this, the library is so much more than a place to get books. We hold town meetings here. It's a place for kids to come after school. We provide Internet access. A free art gallery for local artists. And losing libraries is a precursor to losing businesses. No business wants to set up shop in a city without a library." Warming to her topic, she added, "Just to give you an example of the human element in this—one of our adult literacy clients is another example of the vital role the library plays," she said.

Eddie's stare intensified.

"He didn't want to go through life as a nonreader, but he was embarrassed by his situation. Thanks to the library, I'm able to work with him directly. He's keeping his privacy, *and* he's learning to read."

"Some of that credit goes to you," Eddie interjected.

She flushed. "The point is, without the library, this patron might not have approached me in the first place." Switching gears again, she said, "Every Wednesday morning, we have children's hour. People bring their kids to sit on a braided rug around a Kennedy rocker that's been in the building for fifty years. And someone reads them a story. That's when the magic takes over. A kid who might squirm every waking hour is suddenly sitting there, spellbound. The children sink into the story and it takes them to another place. Without the library, kids will probably still have story time at preschool or home or the bookstore. But there's something about gathering around that old rocking chair at the library. You can't deny it."

Eddie gave her another thumbs-up.

"The other day, a woman brought her granddaughter Katy to story hour," Maureen recalled, abandoning her cheat sheet. "She requested an old favorite—*Mike Mulligan and his Steam Shovel,* a book that's never been out of print since it was first published in 1939. Not a word of the narrative has ever been changed, and not a line of the drawings has been altered. Yet that story is brand-new every time a child opens the book. Later, the grandmother told me she remembered that book from her own childhood. She used to come to story hour when she was little, to the same building, in the same children's room, and it was a joy to bring her granddaughter into the tradition."

"There," said Eddie, "you nailed it right there. Anybody can go to the Web site and learn about the many services the library provides, free of charge. But to really understand what the library's about, all you have to do is think about what Maureen Davenport just told us. So this holiday season, please be generous. You can pledge or make donations by phone, by mail, on the web, or better yet, show up in person. See for yourself why the library is worth saving."

"Thanks for listening," Maureen said.

Eddie smoothly added, "Thanks for joining us. And I hope everyone will mark their calendar right now for all the up-coming library fund-raisers. Let's finish out the hour with some songs related to this morning's theme. Here's 'Who Wrote the

Book of Love' by Monotones, from 1962. We'll follow that with the Beatles' 'Paperback Writer' from 1966."

"Great job," he said after switching off the microphones. "Think it'll work?"

"It can't hurt. Every single donation helps. Thanks, Eddie." She was in a quandary now. Every time she made up her mind not to like him, he did something like this. And she would get a crush on him all over again.

As she stepped out of the booth, Brandi and Heidi abruptly stopped their conversation and broke apart. Maureen flashed on a feeling she hadn't had since high school—being a joke to the cool girls, the pretty girls. Being whispered about.

It wasn't the same, of course, and their whispering probably had nothing to do with her, but it served as a reminder—*You don't belong here.*

After a full day at the library, Maureen's workday wasn't over. Her mobile phone rang, and the name that came up on the screen made her smile—H. Lonigan. "Lonnie," she said, picking up.

"How's my favorite librarian?" His deep, masculine voice sounded like melted chocolate.

"Anxious to see you," she said. "I've missed you."

"Just got back. I did a mining run up in northern Canada. First of the season."

Maureen winced, picturing Lonnie in his huge rig, lumbering over narrow, icy mountain roads to bring diesel to mines in remote locations. "I'm glad you're back safe," she said, knowing it was futile to point out the hazards of his job. He was a dangerous-load trucker who laughed at danger—all the way to the bank. "When can we meet?" she asked.

"How about right now?"

She checked the clock on her desk. "Perfect. I'm just finishing at work. Where?"

"How about your place?" he suggested.

Something about the quality of his voice tipped her off. She looked up, and there he was, filling the entire doorway with his bulk.

"Lonnie!" she said, and a moment later she was folded in his embrace. "I didn't know when you'd be back. I have something for you."

He stepped back, beaming at her. "Yeah?"

She rolled a stool toward a high shelf. He beat her to it, easily reaching up and grabbing a stack of books. "This what you're after?"

Maureen nodded, leading the way to a long table in the adult reading area. "It must be handy, being as tall as a giant redwood."

"Sometimes," he said. "Are we…all alone?"

"Of course," she assured him. "Have a seat, Lonnie." She opened one of the books. "I think you're going to like this."

He took off his Mackinac jacket, sat down and studied the title page. "Are…" He glanced at her, and she nodded. "Area. T-tan…go. Tango. Delta. *Area Tango Delta.*"

"Good job. It's the first of a series. It's set in the future, about a guy who's an expert in military transport. He gets into all kinds of dangerous situations."

Lonnie nodded. "Sounds like my kind of book."

Maureen hoped so. The low-reading-level, high-interest

material was designed to appeal to guys like Lonnie—emerging readers whose skills would improve with practice. She glanced at the clock. "Let's get started. Did you bring your notebook?"

He put it on the table, a three-ring binder filled with sample forms he was learning to fill out, everything from a voter's survey to a loan application. As Maureen browsed through the pages, his big shoulders hunched. "I didn't get much of a chance to work on stuff while I was on the road."

"That's okay. We're taking this at your pace. Always."

He nodded, but still appeared tense. Built like a linebacker with the heart of a lion, he was more comfortable blowing methyl hydrate into his transmission than he was being surrounded by books.

"I wish you'd relax," Maureen said. "It's an adult literacy program, not a secret society." But it was a secret, which she'd alluded to in her radio interview. Lonnie's troubles had come to a head when he was pulled over for a traffic violation and couldn't read the citation. The officer—Ray Tolley—was the only one besides Maureen who knew the real problem. "You'd make faster progress if you could take some of the classes at the community college—"

"I'm not going to classes," Lonnie said. "I went all the way through the tenth grade and never learned a damn thing."

"You're a different person now," she said. "What are you really afraid of?"

"Used to be, I was scared of kids teasing me, you know. Looking a fool. Now I'm scared I'll never get good at reading and writing, and I'll let people down."

"You're already getting good at it," she assured him. They'd been working together for a year, sneaking around like a couple of adulterers because he was so self-conscious about his inability to read. "But Lonnie, I don't know how much longer I'll be able to do this with you."

"What's the matter?"

"The library's scheduled to close at the end of the year. I'll have to get another job, and I don't know where that'll leave us."

"Whaddya mean, closing? The library can't close."

She explained about the financial crisis. "We're still trying to raise funds, but it's not looking good," she said.

"The library can't close," he repeated. He pushed aside the Tango Delta novel and took a sheet of lined paper from the binder. "I'm gonna need help with this. I want to write a letter."

"What kind of letter?"

"You know, to the newspaper. And…I guess we can send copies to the city and county and state. Wherever you think it'll do some good."

"Sure, Lonnie," she said. "What would you like to say in the letter?"

He paused. Picked up a mechanical pencil, his big, blunt fingers all but swallowing it. "I'm gonna say that when I first came to the library a year ago, I couldn't read or write well enough to even fill out a form to get a library card. I'm gonna tell how you helped me, staying late some nights or coming in early, and how I can read a lot better now, and I'm studying to take the GED test. And that none of that would have happened if it wasn't for the library."

"That would be a very powerful letter," Maureen said. "But I have to tell you, no one will read it or print it if you don't sign your real name to it. The paper will withhold your name if you tell them to, but you still have to sign the letter."

"In other words, I'm gonna have to blow my cover." He twiddled the pencil in his thick fingers.

"If you want anyone to take the letter seriously, yes."

"Shoot."

"Lonnie, you don't have to—"

"Let's do it. I'll sign my name. Heck, a year ago, I could barely *write* my name."

"What about keeping your secret?"

"I'm done with that," he said. "Starting now. You asked me what I was afraid of, and I didn't really have an answer for you. I was afraid of people seeing who I am, but guess what? I'm not a bad guy. Just a bad reader."

She smiled. "You're getting better every day." As he carefully wrote, "To the Editor" on the paper, she got a lump in her throat. "Thank you, Lonnie," she whispered.

He paused and offered a slightly bashful smile. "No prob."

Seized by impulse, she leaned over and kissed his cheek. "You're the best."

Eddie decided to stop by the library to give Maureen the fund-raising report from the station after their interview. He figured she'd be pleased by the numbers. It was a good start. Truth be told, he could have e-mailed the results to her, but he wanted to see her in person. He wanted to see her face when he showed her the results.

It made no sense that he would want to see her. Or that he wanted to be the bearer of good news. She was prickly, cautious and bossy. Not to mention judgmental and obsessed with Christmas. Objectively speaking, she should be his own personal nightmare. Yet there was something about her, something he wasn't ready to define but definitely wanted to explore.

The girls he worked with at the station, Brandi and Heidi, had noticed right away that Maureen Davenport was not the usual morning chat guest. He'd caught the two of them whispering about it after Maureen left. "You're totally crushing on that girl," Brandi had said. "The mighty Eddie Haven, falling so hard you've been smashed to smithereens."

He hadn't bothered to deny it. "So?" he'd demanded.

"So what're you going to do about it?" Heidi had demanded.

The suggestion had haunted him all day long, and now it was nearly dinnertime. He needed to leave his van at the mechanic's to have the brakes done. Maybe Maureen would offer him a lift. Yeah, that might be a way to steal some time with her. He drove to the library, hoping to catch her before closing time. Her car was one of two in the parking lot; the other was a flatbed truck with Hugo Lonigan Trucking on the door. A moving truck? Were they already starting to vacate the building? Eddie hated the thought more than he'd expected. What the hell kind of town was this, giving up its library?

The front door was locked, but he figured she'd hear him if he pounded on it long enough. He raised his fist, then spotted movement in the main reading room. He could see Maureen sitting beside some guy—a very big guy—at a table.

Only a single green-shaded lamp illuminated their silhouettes. They sat together at a table with their shoulders touching, their heads inclined toward one another.

What the...?

She was whispering in the guy's ear. Eddie couldn't be sure, but he thought maybe she kissed the guy. Eddie salted the air with a word that would have blistered Maureen's ears if she could have heard it. He crammed the report into the book return slot and stalked back to his vehicle.

Part Three

When Christmas bells are swinging above the fields of
    snow,
We hear sweet voices ringing from lands of long ago,
And etched on vacant places
Are half-forgotten faces
Of friends we used to cherish, and loves we used to know.

—Ella Wheeler Wilcox (1860-1919),
American author and poet

13

With his van in the shop for repairs, Eddie walked to the Hilltop Tavern, his shoulders hunched against the blowing snow and his acoustic guitar in a weatherproof case on his back. People who knew his story sometimes asked if it was hard, hanging out in a bar as an alcoholic in recovery. He assured them it was not. What used to be hard was hanging out in a bar and drinking himself blind, facing the fear and confusion and shame of not knowing what he'd done during a blackout, how he'd disgraced himself. *That* was hard. Compared to that, staying sober was a walk in the park. He had his moments, of course, but for the most part, meetings and his friends in the fellowship kept him focused on recovery.

The reason for tonight's visit to the tavern was artistic. Eddie and three other guys were in a band together, calling themselves Inner Child. Whenever he was in town, Eddie played lead guitar and vocals. They had Noah Shepherd on drums,

Bo Crutcher on bass and Rayburn Tolley on keyboards. Eddie
and Ray had been making music together for a long time.
Over the years, a lot of people had given up on Eddie, but not
Ray. Not even when Eddie wanted him to.

Together with Noah and Bo, the foursome enjoyed an extremely low level of success but managed to have plenty of
fun, performing for a familiar, friendly bar audience or at
local festivals.

Eddie was the last to arrive, stepping into the warm, cave-
like bar. "Dudes," he said, and grabbed a bar towel to dust the
snow off his guitar and gig case. The place had a subtle yeasty
smell, mingling with woodsmoke from the fireplace.

Maggie Lynn, the owner of the Hilltop, had a fresh pot of
coffee on, knowing Eddie's beverage of choice. He offered her
his best smile. "You," he said, "are an angel."

"Yeah, sure," she said. "Just try convincing my ex of that."

"I'll pass," he said, and went to set up. There were only a
few patrons present so far—a couple in a booth, and two guys
at the bar, watching a hockey game on TV.

"How are things with Little Miss Sunshine?" Ray asked, un-
furling a power cord.

"Maureen Davenport, you mean," Eddie grumbled.

"I figured by now, you'd be trying to sweet-talk her into
the sack."

"Number one, she's not my type. And number two, she's
seeing somebody."

Ray lifted his eyebrows. "Yeah? Who?"

"I don't know him. I think he might work for Lonigan
Trucking."

"Lonnie?" Ray paused. "She's not seeing him. Not to date, anyway."

"How do you know that?"

He shrugged. "I just know."

"Come on. Don't go all Officer-Friendly on me. How?"

"Hey, if you don't believe me, ask *her*. Ask Maureen. Better yet, ask her out and quit bellyaching to us."

"I'm not—"

"Dude," said Ray, mimicking Eddie. "You totally are. Now, shut up and sing."

It bugged him that people thought he had a thing for the librarian. It ought to be obvious to anyone with half a brain that she wasn't his type at all. The earnest, smart, well-adjusted type didn't usually find much in common with Eddie Haven. "Let's get started, okay?"

They played for a while, warming up with some old standards, then playing around with newer material. Eddie had a written a song called "Ax to Grind" with some of his students recently, and this was the first time to try it in public. The applause from Maggie Lynn and her patrons was enthusiastic. A couple of women, standing around a bar-height table with their friends, tried to catch his eye. Ordinarily he'd go for it, but tonight he was preoccupied.

"That's a good tune," Ray said. "You ought to do this professionally."

"Ha ha," said Eddie.

They finished the set early, since the crowd was so light. Bo and Noah—both relative newlyweds—were in a hurry to leave. Eddie and Ray were shooting pool when Ray prodded him with a cue. "Don't look now, loverboy, but you got company."

Eddie turned toward the door. There, looking like she'd caught a whiff of something bad, was Maureen Davenport, bundled against the cold. In his head he heard a babble of voices, friends and coworkers: *You're totally crushing on her. You're into her…* And against all odds he was. She was vulnerable and sincere, and a little prickly. In every way, she was the antithesis of his kind of girl. But he couldn't help liking her. He motioned her over. "You're out late," he said. "Is everything all right?"

As she unwound her muffler and peeled off her coat, her gaze swept the bar as though it were an opium den. She glanced at the group of women in their tight jeans, and unconsciously tugged down the hem of her sweater. Clearly she didn't come here often. "It's not late. I'm a night owl," she said, pushing her glasses up the bridge of her nose.

Eddie started to feel flattered that she would step so far out of her comfort zone just to see him. It must mean she had a crush on him. She probably couldn't stop thinking about him. Ray had been right about the trucker guy, Lonigan, then.

"You just missed a set," Eddie told her. "You should get here earlier next time."

"I'm not here to be entertained. I've been thinking about the program," Maureen said. "I wanted to know how your song is coming along."

"You came here to see if I've been doing my homework?" Eddie laughed, though he wasn't amused. She hadn't come to hear him after all, which bugged him more than he wanted to admit.

"Is the song ready?" She turned to Ray. "He's going to perform an original song in this year's program."

"That's our Eddie. He's such a sweetie," Ray said.

"Piss off," Eddie grumbled.

"Hey, just because you have the red ass for Christmas doesn't mean the rest of the world feels the same way," Ray said.

"I don't have the red ass for Christmas," Eddie said.

"Just be careful around this guy," Ray warned Maureen. "He's got issues with Christmas."

"Bullshit," Eddie said. "It's like any other day."

Ray aimed a meaningful nod at Maureen. "See?"

"Christmas denial," she said.

"Exactly," Ray agreed.

"I thought you were my friend," Eddie complained.

"Didn't I just call you a sweetie?" He checked the clock. "Gotta bounce. I'm pulling a late shift at the station. Keeping the world safe from Christmas haters."

"Hey," said Eddie, "I need a ride, remember? My van is in the shop."

"I can give you a ride," Maureen offered. "You go on ahead, Ray."

Tolley was out of there before Eddie could say bah, humbug. He turned to Maureen. "I need to grab my guitar."

She was quiet as they walked outside together. He was her prisoner.

"What's bothering you now?" Eddie asked as he placed his guitar on the backseat of her car. Her little Prius was cluttered with language CDs, knitting stuff, canned goods packed in a food bank box and sacks of birdseed.

"Why do you assume something is bothering me?" Maureen waved a hand. "Never mind, don't answer that. I'd only be insulted by your answer."

"Ha, I knew it. Something *is* bothering you. I mean, something more than the usual stuff."

Maureen turned on the ignition, adjusting the heater to a high setting. Although they both buckled their seat belts, she didn't put the car in gear. Instead, she turned to him. "How are you going to write a tender, loving Christmas song if you hate Christmas?"

He had to laugh. So *that* was what was on her mind. "Same way I write any song, one note at a time. I don't need to buy into what I'm writing."

"You don't?"

"It's a song, okay? Music and lyrics. With a very specific topic."

She pulled out of the parking lot and started down the hill.

He gave her the address and wondered if he should invite her in once they got to his place. Ask her if she'd like to hang out, maybe fight with him some more. Yeah, that would be fun.

"So *have* you written it?" she asked him.

"No."

"We need it now, Eddie. Why haven't you written it?"

"Dammit, Maureen, I've been busy, okay? I need a little white space to throw something together."

"How much white space?"

She was the most annoying female he'd ever met.

"What, you want a number?"

"Yes. What do you need? Thirty minutes? An hour? A day?"

"Hell, I don't know."

"You don't know how long it takes to write a song?"

"It takes whatever it takes. I can't be any more specific than that."

At a stoplight, she turned to study him briefly. Then she clicked on her turn signal and headed away from Willow Street.

"Hey," he said, "I thought you were giving me a lift to my place."

"I changed my mind," she said evenly. "We're going to *my* place."

Maureen knew she was taking a huge risk, bringing Eddie here, the two of them all alone, at this hour. But she was desperate. She needed that song from him. She needed it to be wonderful.

"This is the library," Eddie said.

"I'm aware of that." She took his guitar from the backseat and handed it to him. Then she fished out a set of keys, led the way around to the side of the building and unlocked the staff entrance.

"It's eleven o'clock at night."

"I can tell time, too."

"I thought we were going to your place," he said.

"This is my place."

"And we're here because…"

"Because you need white space. The library is perfect for that." She disabled the alarm, then led the way through a darkened work area filled with littered desks and shelves of books, into the library proper.

"Me and my big mouth," muttered Eddie.

She stopped at a smallish room with a single high window, a table and a few chairs, an old upright piano and nothing else.

"We call this the piano room," she explained. "With the door shut, it's nearly soundproof. It's mostly used for study groups, and sometimes tutorials. And now songwriting. You'll be our first songwriter."

"It looks like the plasma center."

"I don't know what that is."

"It's a place where people sell their blood for money. Did you know your plasma is worth thirty bucks a pint?"

She shuddered. "I had no idea people could sell their blood. I thought you *gave* blood."

"You've led a sheltered life, clearly. Selling plasma is the kind of thing people do when they have nothing left."

"Hmm. I might be out of a job soon—" She gave a laugh. "Kidding. I suppose the overhead lights are a little harsh. Hang on a second." She went to the children's reading corner and returned with a floor lamp with an old-fashioned fringed shade. As she bent to plug it in, Eddie was very quiet. She straightened up, confused by the stricken expression on his face. "Is something the matter?" she asked.

"Not at all."

Suspicion slid through her. "Why are you looking at me like that?"

"Let's just say I've become quite a fan of yours."

"I beg your pardon."

"I was checking out your ass," he admitted.

If dying were an option, Maureen might choose it right about now. "That's obnoxious."

"Any woman who's going to get down on all fours in front of a guy is going to get checked out, simple as that. And in case you need to know, you have an amazing butt. Like, world class, seriously. I never noticed that about you before."

She glared at him. "You weren't meant to."

"You're a sexy woman, Maureen. Why are you trying to hide that?"

"I'm not hiding anything."

He took his time inspecting her thick cable-knit sweater and oversize jacket. "Right. So what about that guy I saw you with—are you hiding him?"

She frowned. "What guy?"

"Drives a truck?"

Oh, for Pete's sake, thought Maureen. "That's Lonnie. And I'm not going to talk to you about him."

"Damn. Ray said I should ask."

"You talked to Ray about me? About Lonnie?"

"Is that a crime?"

"It's nosy."

"So sue me. Are you dating him?"

"No."

"Are you dating anyone?" Eddie asked.

This was the last conversation she had expected to be having with him, and it caught her off guard. "I try not to date at all," she blurted out.

"Why? It's fun."

"Some people think so. Not me. To me, dating is less fun than…" She paused to think.

"Than what?"

Anything, she thought pathetically, but she didn't want to admit that to him. "Jury duty," she said. "I would rather serve jury duty than go on a date."

"Okay, what else? Church. Is church better than going on a date?"

"I like going to church."

"Then how about a root canal? Would you rather go on a date or have a root canal?"

She tried to stay serious. "At least they numb you up before a root canal, right? On a date, every nerve is exposed."

"You are one crazy girl, you know that? Who've you been dating, Attila the Hun?"

"I told you, I haven't been dating because I don't care for it. The last date I had was—" she thought for a moment, then remembered "—with a guy named Walter. A bad concert. And before that, Alvin Gourd took me to a philately exhibit."

Eddie burst out laughing. "No wonder you'd rather have a root canal. *Philately?* Is that even freaking legal?"

"Some people consider stamp collecting a high art."

"Good God." Tears streamed from his eyes. "And…I'm sorry…Alvin *Gourd?* Are people constantly asking him if he's out of his gourd? Who the hell is Alvin Gourd?"

The kind of guy who would date me, she thought. "You shouldn't make fun of a person's name," she said.

"True. I've got a weird name myself."

"Eddie? That's not weird."

"It's also not my given name. My original name is Doobie."

"Give me a break."

"Swear to God. It's on my birth certificate."

"What kind of people would name their baby Doobie?"

"People named Willow and Moonbeam."

"No way."

"Way."

"Your parents are Willow and Moonbeam?"

"They went through a psychedelic phase."

"Okay, time out." She made a *T* with her hands. "There's no way I can leave you alone to work until you tell me about Willow and Moonbeam and the psychedelic phase."

"Gee, Miz Davenport, I didn't know you cared."

She gave his arm a slug, comfortable with this teasing Eddie in a way she wasn't when he was checking out her... derriere. "Spill."

"Now who's the nosy one?"

"Me," she freely admitted, as unapologetic as he'd been earlier.

"Okay, so my folks raised me on a commune near Wood-stock. I was homeschooled, too."

"That's fascinating," she said. "What a remarkable child-hood you had."

"You think?"

"Of course. From the reading I've done, an upbringing like that results in children who are nurtured and balanced, deeply connected to their family members and to the others who helped raise them."

"I never read about it," Eddie said. "I just lived it. And honestly, my parents were young and naive, and they'd be the first to tell you, they had no notion of how to raise a child. They brought me up with guesswork and a little faith. They grew their own food and pot, and raised kids and livestock through communal efforts—with mixed results. I was born in a cabin without electricity. Through sheer luck alone, I was born to robust health but an unfortunate name—Doobie."

It all sounded bohemian and romantic to Maureen. "So you lived in a commune, and then you became a child star. What was that like?"

"I don't have anything to compare it to. Also—what people tend to forget about the child stars is that so few of them grow up to be *adult* stars. They remember the success stories—Jodie Foster, Shirley Temple, Brooke Shields. And the gossip magazines never let us forget the train wrecks, like Lindsay Lohan, McCauley Culkin. Danny Bona…whatever. And then there are those of us who achieved middling careers in film or TV or theater, and just as many who got out of the business altogether. People are surprised by that."

"Sure we are," she admitted. "I mean, when you create a character like Jimmy, we tend to think we're seeing a star being born."

He chuckled. "When you get into a career at age five, you're not exactly following your passion. It's more like you're following directions. One benefit of doing the movie—I got to change my name. And my folks went back to their given names—Barb and Larry."

Maureen could have sat there all night, listening to him talk about himself. He stopped and studied her for a long moment. She couldn't be sure, but—yes, she was sure of it. He was staring at her mouth.

"I don't usually talk about this stuff," he said.

"I won't tell a soul," she promised.

"It's no secret. Just…something in the past. But enough about me," he said softly.

"Right," she hastily agreed. "You're here to write. I'll let you get to work."

"I need inspiration." He flicked on the fringed lamp and flipped off the overhead switch, plunging the room into an amber glow.

"I can't give you that," she said.

"Oh, yes," he said, cupping his hands around her shoulders, "you can."

The touch nearly set her on fire. She tried to offer a casual, dismissive laugh, but what came out was a funny little helpless gasp.

"Seriously," he said, "you can."

"What on earth are you doing?"

"Trying to be a little more interesting than a stamp-collecting exhibit." Very gently but insistently he walked her backward, trapping her between himself and the table. "Making out at the library. I could write a song about that."

"So you're just using me for inspiration."

"No. I'm dying to make out with you."

Fighting the urge to let him, she shoved at his chest. "This isn't funny, Eddie." There was a sharpness in her voice. She knew the source, but to Eddie, it probably sounded childish and shrill.

He took a step back, holding his hands up, palms out. "Fine, whatever," he said. "I'll quit."

She nodded grimly. "You have work to do."

"Work…?"

"The Christmas song."

"I can't stand Christmas, remember?"

"So you've said—repeatedly. What I don't understand is why."

"And I don't understand why you like it so much."

"It's the season for miracles," she explained. "Everyone's at their best—their most kind and most generous. And here in this town, the season has a special beauty. And for me, a special significance. Being here at Christmas helped me get through a very difficult time in my life." The moment she said the words, she wished she'd kept them to herself.

Now he made the time-out sign. "This I gotta hear."

"No, you don't. And why do you care, anyway?"

"You don't look like the kind of person who's ever had a difficult time."

"Really? What sort of person do I look like?"

"The sort who gets along with her family, goes to church every Sunday, never thinks an impure thought. Somebody who likes to stay home at night, in her jammies with her cat and a good book."

Two cats, she thought, but refused to admit it. "You think you have me nailed, don't you?" She motioned at the piano bench. "Write."

He laughed. "It doesn't work that way."

"Then enlighten me. How does it work?"

"I have to feel the song first."

"And how are you going to do it?"

He paused. Then, before she could stop him, he bent and

placed a soft kiss on her mouth. "Like that. Which, by the way, was what I was trying to do earlier."

Maureen broke away, shocked beyond speech. She couldn't believe what he'd just done. It was one thing to imagine kissing Eddie Haven, quite another to actually do it. The real kiss was so much more intense than her imagination could ever allow. Good grief, *she* was the one who was about to burst into song, and she wasn't even terribly musical. It was all a bit overwhelming. She hated feeling overwhelmed almost as much as she loved kissing Eddie.

"That's the most fun I've ever had at the library," he said with a grin. "I feel smarter, just being here."

She stepped back, out of range. "Excuse me," she said, her face on fire. Was he toying with her? Seeing how far he could push the geeky librarian girl? "I'll leave you alone so you can get to work. I have some things to do in my office." She scurried away, wishing she didn't feel so mortified. There was plenty of work to be done, and she often stayed quite late, savoring the uninterrupted quiet of the library. Tonight, though, she couldn't concentrate.

She was so agitated that she reshelved every book from the return bin in record time, and even straightened her desk, parts of which had not seen the light since she'd been hired fresh out of college. She could hear the occasional piano note or guitar chord drifting from the study room, but she did her best to ignore the fact that not only was Elvis in the building—he had kissed her.

As of a few moments ago, Maureen had been kissed by a grand total of five guys, counting Eddie. How pathetic was that? She sometimes told herself it was because she was extremely picky—in a good way. The reality, of course, was that she tended to avoid kissing. She'd learned long ago that kissing led to all kinds of things and eventually culminated in heartache.

Sorting through the mail on her desk, she came across a correspondence she'd recently initiated. She didn't relish the idea of finding another job, but this was the reality she faced. A few other staff members had already given notice, having found other, more secure places to work. The IT manager was moving on to SUNY New Paltz. The reference librarian got a job at the local bookstore. The support services coordinator had decided to follow a lifelong dream—going to cooking school in Northern California. Maureen didn't want to be left at loose ends. Even if all the fund-raising efforts succeeded, it probably wouldn't be enough to keep the facility open. She'd tapped into her network of librarians, asking about job openings. Already, the request had yielded a lead—a corporate firm in Boston had requested her credentials.

The thought of moving far away was depressing in the extreme, so she finished straightening up her work space. It wasn't a proper office but a corner in the general staff area. Each year, the board tried to find the wherewithal in the budget to construct an actual office for her, but the money was never there. Now, it seemed, it never would be.

She closed up her desk and wandered out to the stacks. Maybe it was time to try her usual method of seeking wisdom. With eyes shut, she ran her index finger along the spines of the books, raising and lowering her arm as she progressed. Keeping her eyes closed, she stopped at random, pulled a book from the shelf and let it fall open, a fat, heavy, musty-smelling tome. Wrinkling her nose, she touched her finger to a page and opened her eyes.

"'Roman youth dashed in to carry off the maidens, who were the victims of impious perfidy,'" she read aloud. Oh, dear. "'The Sabine women, whose wrongs had led to war, went boldly into the midst of the flying missiles with dishevelled hair and rent garments…'"

"Wonderful," muttered Maureen. "I go looking for advice, and I get the Rape of the Sabines."

"Hey, come on, it was a kiss, that's all" said a voice behind her.

She was so startled that she dropped the book as she spun around. The heavy tome landed on her foot. "Ow!" she said. "You startled me."

"Did you hurt yourself?" asked Eddie, bending to pick up the book. He checked the title. "Livy's *History of Rome.* Move over, *Da Vinci Code.*"

"Give me that." She grabbed the book and reshelved it, feeling his stare like a physical touch. "What?" she demanded, turning back to face him.

"Nothing," he said. Heavens, but he had a sexy smile. "Just trying to figure you out, Moe."

"There's nothing to figure out. I am what I am." She wondered if he could tell she was lying. Clearing her throat, she changed the subject. "All right. So did you finish the song?"

"Yeah." Indeed, he had his parka on, his guitar zipped into its case.

"Well?"

"Well, what?"

"When am I going to hear this masterpiece?"

"I never said it would be a masterpiece. It's a song, okay? Just something I wrote."

"Then let's hear it."

He looked at her for a long time. The look turned to a glower. With slow deliberation, Eddie shrugged off his parka, unzipped the guitar case. "I swear, you are one stubborn woman."

She sniffed. "I'll take that as a compliment."

He propped his hip on the edge of a library table, flexed his hands and lightly strummed a few chords, hummed a melody. Even the casual tuning of his guitar and warm-up had a quality that seemed to reach for her. She could imagine his music as a gentle embrace. Oh, Maureen, she thought. You're in trouble.

"Did you study music in college?" she asked, hoping he couldn't tell what she was thinking.

He nodded. "Majored in theory and composition."

"And where was that?"

He didn't look up from his strumming. "Juilliard."

"Wow. I had no idea."

"I figured you knew all about me," he said. "Figured you looked it up on Google or Wikipedia or something."

She regarded him, appalled. "Why would you assume that?"

"You being a librarian at all."

"I would never. That's intrusive. And unprofessional. I would never use my skills as a librarian to intrude upon someone's private life."

"I wish more people felt that way."

She indicated his guitar, willing his fingers to pick out the notes. "The song."

He heaved a sigh of exasperation. "Fine." His hands gently drew a chord from the strings of the guitar, the sound burgeoning with rhythm and melody. He sang with a sense of sweet resignation, misted by emotion. The lyrics—a metaphor about trees in winter—were unassuming, telling a story of a journey from loneliness to connection. He picked the guitar with a clean precision that showcased his training. The music wove through the empty library, the melody circling around like swirls of warmth.

Maureen couldn't help herself. She was always moved by true talent, particularly at the moment of the muse taking over. Sometimes, like now, it was an identifiable event. One minute, he was a guy playing the guitar. The next, he was…gently, softly possessed. He didn't move, yet he seemed to shift into another realm or dimension. He was still here, yet gone away somewhere, and she felt herself following.

The lyrics of the musical bridge gave her chills. "You look like an angel to me…"

Maureen wasn't certain she'd heard right. The words transported her back in time to that night when she'd found him flung into a snowbank, dazed and wounded, yet able to speak. She would never forget the words he'd said to her that night: *Sorry. For a second, you looked like an angel to me.*

"Stop," she said sharply, interrupting the song. "Cut it out."

"Hey, you were the one who wanted to hear the song."

"Not *that* song."

"Oh, sorry. You should have been more specific."

"It's hard to specify something as yet unwritten," she said. "But you're a professional. You promised to write a Christmas song."

"This is a Christmas song." He glared at her. "What the hell did you think it was?"

"Sounded like a love song to me."

"Every Christmas song is a love song," he said.

She couldn't argue with his reasoning, but he was twisting her logic. "There are different kinds of love," she stated.

"Just what I need. A lecture on love from a woman who won't even go on a date."

"With you," she clarified. "I won't go on a date with you."

"Fine, who will you date?"

"That's none of your business."

"Why won't you go on a date with me?" he asked.

Because it will hurt too much when you walk away, she thought, but didn't say aloud. There was no doubt in her mind that if she went out with him, she would fall head over heels for him. But the outcome of anything between the two of them was inevitable. He would leave. It was what guys like Eddie Haven did. It was what happened to girls like Maureen Davenport.

"The song," she reminded him, trying to bring the conversation back on track. "It's not working for me."

"Because it's about love? Well, excuse the hell out of me."

"It's about romantic love," she said.

"That's your opinion. People bring their own meaning to a song. 'You look like an angel to me' is not inherently romantic."

Then why did the sound of him singing the words set her heart on fire?

"It's something a parent might say to a child," he explained. "Or a friend to a friend. It depends on the context you bring to it."

"I just don't think it's a good fit for the program."

"Nothing I write is ever going to make you happy," he said. "Maybe the key with you is that you don't want to be happy."

"Now you're being absurd," she said. "Of course I want to be happy. That's what everyone wants." She frowned, offended by what she thought he was saying about her.

"Fine, prove it," he said.

"What do you mean, prove it?"

"Prove to me that you want to be happy instead of stuck in the past somewhere, mired in something that happened a long time ago."

She studied his face. Good grief, did he know? Or was he guessing? "And just how do you propose I prove this to you, assuming I decide I should?"

He did it again—gave her that special smile. The one that crinkled the corners of his eyes and mocked her reserve. "Go out with me. Let me show you a good time. Loosen up a little, for Chrissake."

"I'm loose," she protested. "I know how to have a good time."

He threw back his head and laughed. "Excellent," he said. "Then this is going to be easier than I thought. What are you doing tomorrow night?"

"I'm busy." It wasn't a complete lie.

"Afternoon, then," he said, picking up his guitar. "Tomorrow after rehearsal? Yeah, that'll work. And if you argue with me, I'll invite the camera crew along."

14

Damn, thought Eddie as the kids filed out of the church after Saturday morning practice, that sucked.

"Was the practice really that bad?" asked Jabez, pausing at the door.

Eddie frowned. He didn't remember speaking aloud. "Pretty bad," he said. "We've got our work cut out for us. The program's in rough shape."

"Uh-huh."

"You rocked it out, though," Eddie told the boy. Jabez's singing was a bright spot in the program. His technique was effortless and straightforward, completely engaging. "Have you had formal training? Outside of school, I mean."

There was a very slight pause. Then Jabez said, "A little. It was a long time ago. Something the matter?" The kid had a way of seeing into his head.

"Nothing that won't get better once it's over," Eddie said

with a grin. "I asked a girl out and now I don't want to let her down."

Jabez grinned back. "You need dating advice, you're barking up the wrong tree."

"You don't have a girlfriend?"

He gave a little laugh. "Nah."

That was curious to Eddie. The kid had the shaggy-haired good looks teenage girls couldn't resist. Eddie had seen several of them making eyes at Jabez during rehearsals.

"One thing, though," Jabez said, "just figure out something new, something that'll make her happy, and do that. Simple."

"Right," Eddie agreed. "Simple. I'll figure out what she likes."

"Okay, then. See you around." Jabez zipped up his jacket and headed outside.

Eddie watched him go. Unlike some of the teenagers, Jabez didn't drive a car. He appeared to get around on foot exclusively. No one knew much about him, and Jabez didn't offer anything. Yet whenever he was around, he seemed intensely present, focused and interested in what was going on, particularly with people around him. He joined Cecil Byrne outside the church, a kid who couldn't be more different from him. Cecil was, it had to be said, a geek.

Despite Jabez's dating advice, Eddie felt no closer to a plan with Maureen. He'd asked her out on impulse. Now he had to figure out what to do. How to show her a good time. No, it was more than that. He had to make her happy.

The burden of someone else's happiness was not exactly his favorite thing to drag around.

It occurred to him that he didn't really know what would

make her happy. *Something new.* Eddie stepped aside as a speeding little kid whooshed past him. In the blur of speed, he recognized one of Maureen's nephews, who played Shepherd #4 in the pageant. The kid's mother was in pursuit. Maybe Maureen's sister would clue him in about Maureen's likes and dislikes.

"Do you have a minute?" he asked her before she disappeared. "Eddie Haven," he added, extending his hand.

"Renée Quinn," she said. "And I know who you are. Good grief, who doesn't?"

She had a nice smile. A pretty face. She was like a more relaxed, slightly disheveled version of Maureen.

"Does that mean my reputation precedes me?" he asked, herding her to the side in the church vestibule. Parents and kids swarmed the area, keyed up after a fairly routine rehearsal, and eager to head out to enjoy the day.

"Ha. As if you didn't know." She had Maureen's no-nonsense manner, too. "You're even cuter in person. Maureen's had a crush on you since she was a kid."

"Yeah?" He let a slow smile unfurl.

"Don't get cocky," Renée warned him. "I'm just saying."

"If I was feeling cocky, I wouldn't be asking for your advice," he pointed out.

"My advice about what?"

"I asked her out. Like, on a date."

Renée's eyes narrowed in suspicion. "Why?"

"Take it easy. I like Moe a lot—"

"Moe? Did you just call my sister *Moe?*"

Uh-oh. Now he'd put his foot in it.

Renée's suspicion softened. "That's so sweet. She's always secretly wanted a nickname."

He could see her across the room, swarmed by little kids. "Glad you approve."

"I approve of the nickname. The going-out—not so much."

"No offense, but it's not up to you," he pointed out.

"True. I'm protective of Maureen. I don't want to see her hurt."

"I like her," Eddie repeated. "Why would I hurt her?"

"I'm not saying you'd do it on purpose, but…my sister's not made of stone. She'd probably never tell you this, but she went through…a bad time. I think everyone in the family's been overprotective of her ever since."

He recalled something Maureen had said to him. She'd hinted at an old wound, but had completely shut him down— *It's private*. Now, though, he had the sister in his corner. "What do you mean, a bad time?" he asked her.

"Mo-om!" Renée's boy came tearing back into the vestibule. "Wendy just traded a box of Lucky Charms for a gerbil, and she's carrying it around in her pocket."

Renée blanched. "I have to go," she said, and rushed out the door after her son.

So, thought Eddie, weaving his way toward Maureen, his instincts had been right. The lady had a past. It only made her more interesting to him. "I met your sister," he said. "I told her we were going out."

Three of the angel-choir girls, who had been milling around nearby, snapped to attention. "You're going out with Miss Davenport?" asked Emily McDaniel.

"Sure am," Eddie said, "if it's okay with you."

The girls scurried away, whispering and giggling.

"I never said I'd go out with you," said Maureen, looking flustered. Her cheeks were pink, and wisps of hair escaped her hair clip.

"You have no choice. I just told our biggest busybody." Indeed, Emily was working her way through the angel choir like a hummingbird, spreading the news. "So we're still on for our date," he said, giving Maureen no chance to demur. "Wear something warm."

"Snowshoeing?" Filled with apprehension, Maureen regarded the footgear Eddie offered her after he'd parked at the trailhead.

"Yup," he said easily. "I take it you've never gone snowshoeing before."

"There's a reason for that."

"I don't mind being your first time, Maureen." He offered what she'd come to think of as his trademark Eddie smile, a crooked grin loaded with charm. "Here, I'll help you get them on."

"But—"

"Unless you'd rather wade through thigh-deep snow."

Expelling a martyrlike sigh, she stuck out her foot. He grasped her ankle, and in that instant, the insanity that was her attraction to this man surged through her like a wave. This was not good. She had no business being with him, out here in the wilderness. The best thing to do would be to play along with him, tromp through the snowy woods for a while and then get home to her warm living room and her cats and the oh-so-politically-incorrect sexy novel she was reading. Protesting would only prolong the wilderness ordeal.

"Let's go," he said, leading the way.

Maureen's feet immediately tangled in the unwieldy snowshoes. She pitched forward, doing a faceplant in the soft, new-fallen snow.

"Whoa, there." Eddie was at her side immediately, helping her up and brushing off the snow. "The shoes take some getting used to."

"Thanks for letting me know," she said, licking at the snow that trickled down her face.

"Easy now. One step at a time. You'll get into the rhythm of it."

She tried again, taking it slowly and keeping a wide stance as she lumbered along behind him. Her gait was probably unattractive in the extreme, but at least she stayed upright. Eddie moved with light-footed grace, though she could tell he was keeping the pace slow for her sake.

"What gave you the idea to go snowshoeing?" she asked.

"I wanted to do something new. Something that would make you happy. You don't look too happy."

"Give me time." She couldn't help smiling.

"My friend Noah Shepherd—he taught me a lot of this outdoor stuff. He's an iron-man athlete. Does that triathlon every year, with the dogsled, speed skating and snowshoeing. I like the great outdoors. Always have, ever since going to summer camp as a kid."

"Wasn't your commune like being at camp year-round?" she asked.

He laughed. "Pretty much. But in the summer, my folks went to a bunch of Renaissance festivals, and it was easier to send me to camp. My grandparents performed at Camp Kioga in the fifties, so they knew the Bellamy family."

"So the Havens are a true show business family," she said. "I'm picturing the von Trapps in *The Sound of Music*," she said. "Or something more modern—the Partridge Family?"

He groaned. "I'm thinking the Osbournes."

She couldn't tell whether or not he was kidding. "So the camp—that's your connection to Avalon?" she asked.

"That's part of it." He paused at a curve in the trail, took out a small flask and offered it to her.

"No, thank you," she said. "I'm clumsy enough on these snowshoes without drinking."

"It's water," he said with a laugh.

"Oh. In that case, thanks." She took a long drink, grateful for the pause. Walking on snowshoes was hard work. She handed the flask back to him. He drank from it without wiping off the spout, which she found insanely sexy. Of course, she found everything about him insanely sexy, so that was no surprise.

"Just so you know, I don't drink alcohol," he said as he put the flask away. "Anymore."

"Why not?"

He smiled. "I'm an alcoholic, Moe."

Yikes. She wasn't sure what to say. "I'm...sorry?"

The smile burgeoned into laughter. "The crisis is over. I've been sober for ten years. I took my last drink the night of my wreck at the church. I still feel bad about that, but not about getting into the program, with a golden ticket from Judge Wilhelm."

"I see." They started walking again, heading for the summit of Watch Hill, where the trail ended. Maureen was surprised by what he'd just told her, yet at the same time, she liked his honesty. He seemed more human and approachable, somehow. "What do you remember about that night?" she asked. "The night of the accident. That is, if you don't mind talking about it."

"I don't mind."

"You, um, said you broke up with a girl…" she prompted.

"Yep. I planned on getting engaged on Christmas Eve. Instead, she turned me down."

"That's horrible."

"No shit. It was for the best, I know that now. We were too young, and my head definitely wasn't in the same place as my heart, although at the time, getting dumped was the end of the world. I dropped her at the station to catch the last train to Albany, where her family lived. I planned to head back down to the city. I was driving toward the turnpike. And then there's a big gap in my recollection, until I was being loaded into an ambulance."

So he didn't remember the vehicle bursting into flames, the cries of the onlookers, the wash of emergency lights through the snowy night. He didn't remember being found in a snow-bank by Maureen herself. She hovered on the verge of telling him, but held back.

"I didn't realize it at the time," he said, "but that was the bottom I needed to hit in order to get my life on track. I'm grateful as hell I didn't hurt anybody in the wreck."

Though it made no sense at all, Maureen felt an affinity with Eddie after hearing his side of the story. Like her, he'd had his heart broken. And like her, he'd changed the direction of his future because of it. Their lives had intersected briefly that night and now, years later, they were at another intersection.

Maureen thought about this as they followed the trail through the woods. She was not usually one to rush out to embrace the lavish beauty of nature, but here in the pristine wilderness, it was hard to ignore. The quality of light was dazzling, the colors starkly delineated. The eye-smarting blue of the sky outlined the clean contours of the snow and the sharply towering bare maples. Evergreens—noble firs and tall pines—sparkled with natural icicles dripping from the tips of their branches. The occasional fisher or snowshoe hare darted through the forest, leaving a dimpled trail.

At the summit, she shaded her eyes to survey the scenery. Eddie donned a pair of Bono-style shades. "Nice view," he remarked.

"I'd say so." It was, if such a thing could be, almost *too* nice—so beautiful, she felt a thick ache of nostalgia in her throat. The snow lay upon the mountains like a bridal gown, overlaid by the intricate lace of the bare trees. Far in the distance, Willow Lake was a vast, blank field, the town of Avalon hugging the shore. Maureen felt caught up in the magnificence of the day. "It's incredible," she said softly. "Thank you for bringing me here."

Moving close, he slipped his arm around her. With his free hand, he took off the sunglasses. "Thanks for coming along, and for being a good sport about it."

Maureen didn't dare move. She even refused to breathe. She

was consumed by the urge to turn to him, to lift herself up on tiptoe, grab his parka by the lapels and kiss him long and hard, in broad daylight. It was the scenery, she told herself. It was making her insane, all this beauty impairing her judgment.

But ultimately, reason intervened. This was Eddie Haven, of all people. Sure, he was flirting madly with her and had been for days, but that was all it could be—an elaborate flirtation. And Maureen knew better than to sacrifice her hard-won balance and emotional stability for a mere flirtation.

"Hey, Moe," he said, a suggestion plain in his voice. His arm tightened around her.

Oh, no. This was it. If she didn't do something, he was going to kiss her in broad daylight. "Look," she said, "I don't want to go all Sabine on you, but we should probably head back down."

"What's your hurry?" asked Eddie. "Never mind. What I'm really wondering is what hurt you so bad that you can't conceive of letting someone get close to you?"

"I have no idea what you're talking about," she said, terrified of the tears that had inexplicably gathered in her eyes.

"Right," he said, putting the sunglasses back on. He seemed agreeable enough, but she sensed a sharpness about him that hadn't been there before. Good grief, had she hurt his feelings? Impossible.

"Going down is going to be a lot easier than climbing up was," she declared, forcing a chipper note into her tone as she returned to the wilderness trail.

"That depends," said Eddie.

"On what?"

"On what we talk about on the way down."

She slipped a glance at him, but the sunglasses concealed everything. "What would you like to talk about?" she asked.

"You, for a change. Your sister said you have a past."

Maureen felt a flurry of panic in her chest. "She said what?"

"She told me you'd had a bad time in the past, and she didn't want to see you getting hurt again."

The mouth, thought Maureen. I'll kill her.

"So is it true?" Eddie asked.

"Everybody has a past," she hedged. Too cryptic, she decided. Maybe if she told him a little of the background, he'd be satisfied and quit asking questions. "Renée was referring to my junior year of college. I spent my life savings to study abroad, in Paris. I was a theater major. I lived and breathed drama, and after college I planned to move to New York, live as a starving artist, eventually take the world by storm. When that didn't work out, I gave up on that, finished college and moved back to Avalon to become a librarian."

"I can think of worse things."

"I'm not saying it's bad. It was just such a change, from theater to library science."

"So what turned you from an out-there theater major into a librarian? And why are the two incompatible?"

"They're not, necessarily. Just for me. It's a long story." She hunched her shoulders, tucked her chin down into her muffler. She'd already said too much. What had happened to her was not so much a long story as an extremely personal story. A painful one. A story she had never told anyone in its entirety. Ever.

They returned to the van, and Eddie put away the snow-shoes. She gazed out the window during the drive home, knowing she would never forget this day, the beautiful scenery, the cold, the unearned intimacy she'd felt with Eddie.

At the edge of town, he pulled over at a latte stand. "Tell you what. I'll go get us some hot chocolate. And when I come back, we'll talk. You'll talk."

"I never agreed—"

"Sure you did, Moe. I'll be back in a few." They were pulled off to the side of the river road as it wended its way back to town.

The man had the most infuriating way of putting words in her mouth. She tried to picture herself opening up to him, showing him a glimpse of her past. In her younger days, she used to be easy and open, sharing herself freely with people. She'd started college as a theater major, of all things. The most flamboyant, emotionally risky major she could pick. In her theater classes, she remembered having to do exercises involving trust and personal confessions, and she had loved those things. Then something happened to change all that.

Maybe she could tell her secrets to Eddie. He was neither family nor friend. Just...an associate. Eddie Haven was someone she'd met when their lives had intersected a time or two. He had no power or influence over her. Telling him about her past would be akin to confessing to a benign stranger. He was someone who might lift the emotional burden and carry it away. In that sense, perhaps opening up to him could be like going to a therapist, only cheaper.

But it was not a therapist who had kissed her in the library. She was counting on them both to forget about that, and about the moment at the top of the hill, when they'd nearly kissed again.

But, oh, where to begin? Maybe she'd start with the physical manifestation of her secret, the one that could only be seen when she bathed or wore the skimpiest of bikinis. Years ago she'd gotten a tattoo on impulse, at the urging of her French lover.

Part Four

Paris, a city of gaieties and pleasures, where four-fifths of the inhabitants die of grief.

—Nicolas de Chamfort, 1741-1794

15

"It should be drawn just here, where I like to kiss you," Jean-Luc had said, and he'd marked the spot with his tongue.

As a college girl experiencing Paris for the first time, Maureen had been dizzy with excitement to have the attention of a man who was so handsome, so sophisticated, so very French. They had met at the Musée Rodin, in the sculpture garden. It had happened on one of those crisp days in early fall, a day of gorgeous weather, the kind people associated with feel-good movies set in Paris. There was the slightest nip in the air, the leaves just beginning to turn gold as they fluttered to the cut stone walkways and manicured greenswards around the historic building.

There were almost no visitors at the museum, a white plaster wonderland of a house in a quiet neighborhood, tucked away from the hectic boulevards of the city. Maureen had been completely taken by Rodin's work. Unlike the polished precision

of the Renaissance sculptures, Rodin's power was in his por-
trayal of raw emotion, be it in the collective pain of the *Burghers
of Calais,* or *The Thinker,* lost in concentration. Her favorite,
of course, was *The Kiss,* the most romantic piece of art she'd
ever seen. She was spellbound by the deep, oblivious passion
of the entwined lovers.

Gazing at the larger-than-life bronze, she wondered if she
would ever be loved like that, with such complete abandon.
Could two people truly be so absorbed in one another? And—
this was the part that was such a cliché, the part that should
have warned her off—that was the moment Jean-Luc had
stepped into her life.

"You have found my favorite place," he said, his English
shaded by only a hint of an accent. "This is where I come to
escape the world."

"Why do you need to escape the world?" she asked, immediately intrigued by him.

"It will take me a long time to explain," he'd said, and that
was the moment she had known they'd be together.

The affair began the way it ended, with a shocking body-
slam of emotion. She was swept away, a willing victim, desperate for the very newness of him. He was every fantasy
come to life for her. Paris donned its autumn finery and they
rushed out to embrace it, racing along in the dry leaves that
littered the city's boulevards and jardins and collected on the
sidewalks where they sat sipping cold Ricard at out-of-the-way
zinc bars in Montmartre. They took long walks together,
stopping on street corners to kiss, lost in each other in the way
only new lovers could be. They stood on the Pont Neuf and

rode the Bateaux Mouches, and each kiss was like a postcard snapshot. Except Maureen didn't feel as though she were acting. This was life, this was passion, and she was grasping it with both hands.

Looking back, she realized she'd been a goner from the very start. He had incredible looks and charm. He was dark-eyed and slender, with an amazing ageless face that reminded her of a cologne ad in a high-end magazine. He was the most glorious man she'd ever met. There was no question that she would fall in love with him.

The question was, why would he fall in love with her?

She dared to ask him one day, after they'd been lovers for about two weeks. They were in her tiny studio in the 17th arrondissement, a bohemian neighborhood of students and artists. She had a walk-up in an old stone building that used to house monks. To counter the ascetic chill of the building, the room was furnished with overstuffed furniture, including a bed with an eiderdown comforter they used to luxuriate on when he stole time from his lunch hour at work.

She had never been in love before, and she was unprepared for the crush of emotion she felt for Jean-Luc. It was wonderful in the way of rainbows and shooting stars, comets and heat lightning—a natural phenomenon she could not control but could only sit back and wonder at.

Hunched over a computer in a little Internet café in her neighborhood, she'd tried to compose an e-mail to her sister: *Dear Renée, I'm in love.*

She deleted that and every other attempt to explain what was happening. There were simply no words to explain what it was like, living a fantasy—she was swept away, over the moon. Her classes—conversational French, aspects of Samuel Beckett's *En Attendant Godot,* and the world of Collette—barely registered with her. Not a single word or concept penetrated the rainbow-glazed bubble of her happiness, the result being that her heretofore perfect grade point average plummeted.

She didn't care. There was no way to care about something as mundane as grades when faced with a monumental, once-in-a-lifetime love like the one she had found with Jean-Luc.

In fact, they used to talk about such things while lying naked in one another's arms. It was invariably afternoon and they always went to her place because it was just one metro stop from the bank where he worked.

Yes, he worked at a bank but he had an artist's soul. Every once in a while he would attend one of her readings or performances. He declared that she made him the proudest of men.

They used to lie together with the afternoon sun slanting across the floor, their bodies sweetly drowsy from lovemaking. They would talk in true earnest fashion about the miracle of their love and the kindly fate that had led them to find one another. Every time she gazed into his eyes, she could see forever. There was no question of where they would live. Right here in Paris, where a single afternoon at a museum garden had blossomed into the love of a lifetime.

Though she hadn't told her family, she knew they would understand. She had a wonderful family, loving and supportive of everything she did. She could already picture them coming to visit her. In her mind, she mapped all the places she would take them—to the Tuileries and the Jeu de Paume, the Musée de Cluny and the Beaux Arts.

Jean-Luc had transformed her from a mere student of life to someone who lived every moment with gusto. She learned to eat raw oysters and drink pastis and say things like "You are my everything" with a straight face.

In the dizzying whirlwind of those early weeks, she forgot everything. She forgot, for example, to question him about his family. She told him everything about her parents and siblings. He told her nothing about his, and it didn't occur to her to wonder why. She didn't question why he never brought her home and why their trysts were always in the afternoon.

None of that was important. Only Jean-Luc, and loving him, and Paris in the autumn, mattered.

Even when she chanced to see him on the street one day, with a pleasant-looking woman and two small children, Maureen did not immediately absorb the situation. She thought they might be relatives, or customers of the bank where he worked.

It wasn't until he kissed the pleasant-looking woman on the lips and was told, "Adieu, Papa," by the older child that Maureen finally forced herself to see the obvious.

Love fell away in broken shards as she crossed the street to confront him. At first he didn't see Maureen as he helped his family into a waiting Peugeot station wagon, then waved while his wife and children lurched away through the traffic. Maureen felt each moment as distinctly as a physical blow.

By the time she stood before him, there on the sidewalk in front of the Crédit Lyonnais, she was as exposed and raw as an accident victim.

Jean-Luc was impassive. He had the sangfroid of a robot. He briefly studied her face, then offered a charming smile. "Maureen. What a surprise."

"Yes," she agreed, "a surprise."

He showed not a hint of remorse when he said, "I take it you saw them."

For a wild moment, she imagined him falling to pieces, sinking to his knees, declaring that he couldn't bear to be without Maureen, that he would walk away from everything in order to be with her. She imagined him telling her that their love was too powerful to be denied.

But instead, he said, "I want to keep seeing you."

She was filled with revulsion—at him, at herself for even considering the ruination of his children's lives. But a part of herself—and no small part of herself—yearned to carry on, as he was suggesting. Though it filled her with shame, she cried, and cried. And, to her eternal shame, she made one last pathetic attempt to rescue the fantasy. "Does that mean you'll leave her?"

He didn't answer. He didn't have to. It was written all over his face.

He turned and started to walk away.

"Wait," she said. "Wait."

He stopped, turned back.

She held up her hand so he wouldn't say anything more. Then she walked away, leaving him standing on the rain-wet sidewalk. It was a small thing, insignificant. But she wanted to be the one to walk away, not him.

She thought she'd hit the very bedrock of heartbreak that day. She couldn't imagine anything worse.

She was wrong. The true bottom, the deepest hurt of all, came later.

A week after leaving him, she dragged herself out of bed on an unseasonably hot, muggy morning to panic. She'd missed her period.

A frenzied count of the weeks sent her rushing to a drug store. A home pregnancy test confirmed her worst fear. They'd been careful, she thought. They'd used protection. But somehow, they'd made a mistake.

She called home—her sisters, her stepmother—but always hung up before the phone rang. She couldn't figure out a way to tell them what had happened. She could barely explain to herself. Spoken aloud, the story sounded so monumentally lurid and pathetic: *I had an affair with a man I didn't know was married. And now I'm pregnant.*

She started to cry and didn't know how to make herself stop. Perhaps that had triggered what happened next. Maybe the gallons of bitter tears instigated what the doctor later called an incomplete embedment—a common cause of miscarriage. Still crying—it seemed she hadn't stopped for days—she went to a clinic with bleeding and cramps. The new life, scarcely more than a secret division of cells, had flowed away on a current of bitter tears, gone before she could even make sense of what had happened.

Several hours later a doctor gave her something for the bleeding and pain, and a shot of antibiotic. He regarded her not unkindly, and said, *"Il n'était pas destiné."*

No, she agreed. It wasn't meant to be.

After that, she was a dead woman, haunting the streets of Paris. Here she was, in the most beautiful, most vibrant city on earth, and she was nothing but a wreck. She couldn't bear to go near the places she'd gone with Jean-Luc. And they'd gone everywhere together. She couldn't bear to do anything.

She felt herself detaching from reality. It was probably some kind of psychotic break. And so, leaving word with the program's registrar, she packed up her things and went home. She had spent her life savings to go to Paris to study. She left with scarcely a penny to her name, but that was not her greatest loss. Not by a long shot.

She never told her family. All she said to them was, "Paris wasn't what I thought it would be. This is where I belong." Renée had guessed that there had been a failed love affair. Maureen told her as little as possible; it was simply too painful to talk about.

Back at school, she changed her major and she changed her dreams. She had to find a dream that fit into the shape of her life—not the life she used to envision for herself, but the new life of a mature person whose youthful illusions had been shattered. This new life was one that gave Maureen control, in which her validation didn't depend on others. She no longer wanted to perform and be judged—heavens, what had she been thinking? She wasn't an actor. Why would she ever want a profession that required her to strip herself bare in front of an audience? Acting was all about making yourself feel things—love, rage, euphoria, agony. She had to unlearn those things now. She had to teach herself not to feel. Refusing to feel hurt also meant she numbed herself to joy, but the sacrifice was worth it.

Dreams could change, she told herself. They had to change as she gained the wisdom of painful experience. Her love of books and stories turned out to be a perfect match for the new Maureen. A story that unfolded in the mind was less emotionally risky than one acted out on a stage. Once she realized that, the decision was easy. She never looked back.

In the darkest depths of despair, she never thought she would smile again. She never thought she would reclaim her heart.

And then Christmas came. She faced the holiday with dread that year, bracing herself for relatives who would ask her about the trip to Paris. She had no idea what she would say to them.

Then Stella Romano, the church choir director, asked Maureen if she'd sing with the choir at Christmas.

No, Maureen wanted to say. No, I'll never sing again. But for some strange reason she was compelled to agree.

"Sure," she'd said. "I'm flattered to be asked."

She did what her father had raised her to do—found solace in helping others. At holiday time, this was easy to do. It seemed self-indulgent in the extreme to moon about a heartache when she was helping a family whose house had been foreclosed, or when she met a woman escaping an abusive relationship, or encountered a teen struggling to overcome addiction. Helping others with their troubles put her own problems into perspective.

For her, salvation was not some dramatic, musical-comedy moment. She didn't wake up one day and decide she was over him. It was the cumulative effect of stepping outside herself and her pain, and giving to others. Simple as that. Although it had seemed impossible at the time, the pain eventually faded, bit by bit. She made the biggest strides at Christmas, when she threw herself into focusing on others.

She learned to be grateful for the profound yet simple things in her life. Her family, which rallied around her, understood that something had happened to her in Paris but didn't press her to tell them anything she didn't want to.

Her father always said, "Be part of something bigger than you." And finally, that year, Maureen discovered how right he was. It was impossible to dwell on some failed love affair when you were serving coffee to a woman whose child was being treated for cancer.

And that, then, was the true gift of the season. That was why Maureen loved it and why she believed so deeply in its power. If the annual pageant could convey even some of that, she would be satisfied.

This was how the miracle occurred. It was a silent, secret miracle. No one could see or hear it, but Maureen felt it in her heart, a deep sense of healing and peace.

The light came back into her life, flickering on like an ember fanned by the smallest breath.

Christmas truly was a season of miracles. And each year, she only grew to love the holiday more.

16

"Hey, Moe." Eddie snapped his fingers in front of Maureen's face. "Wake up and smell the hot chocolate."

He handed her a cup of frothy cocoa. "Thanks," she said, trying to shake off the old, aching memories.

He didn't say anything more, just waited.

Could she tell him? He had been so open about everything—his own past, the accident, going to AA. And he was none the worse for it. Maureen had a need to tell someone, finally. Why not him? He'd given up a huge secret about himself. If she did the same, they'd have mutually assured destruction. No, she corrected herself. Mutual trust.

She took a tiny sip of hot chocolate, then said, "I'm trying to figure out if there's any possible way to explain what happened and not seem like a complete moron."

"You have to not care about looking like a moron," he pointed out.

"It's just so…predictable."

"Nothing about you is predictable," he said. "You're constantly surprising me."

"Really?" She thought about this while sipping her hot chocolate. He seemed to be in no hurry to get anywhere; he sat there with the engine running and the warm breath of the heater wafting from the vents. She felt pleasantly exhausted from the exertion of snowshoeing, and strangely relaxed under the circumstances.

In the yard across the way, Invisible Fence flags sprouted from the snow, warning that a dog was in training. Or, dogs, as she soon saw. Two mutts. One resembled a large poodle, its coat natural rather than groomed. The other was a giant shepherd mix, scary-looking. The only thing standing between him and a busy road was this unseen force field of radio waves, which would deliver a buzz of shock to the poor creature's neck if he ventured too close to the boundary. The shepherd patrolled up and down the perimeter of the yard, and each time a car went past, he gave a little *yip* as he ventured too close to the fence. The dog kept testing, as though it might get a different result with each new attempt.

The poodle, on the other hand, was nobody's fool. Maureen could tell the caramel-colored dog knew exactly where the boundaries lay and was not about to stray beyond them. Even when the shepherd charged a pair of joggers with a sleek Doberman on a leash, the poodle felt the sting only once, then held back. Maureen could tell the dog was tempted almost beyond bearing; it pranced and feinted behind the invisible boundary. Once the joggers with their dog passed by, the shepherd settled down, content to sniff and sprinkle the snow in its yard. The poodle meandered away. Disaster averted.

She realized Eddie was still sitting there, patiently waiting. "Believe me," she said, "I'm very predictable. Pathetically so." And then, almost against her will, she talked, and he listened. It was remarkably easy to level with him. She wondered why that was so. His good opinion of her mattered, yet he was so nonjudgmental and relaxed that she found herself trusting him. She told him about her girlhood dreams of being in the theater, and spending her life savings to study in Paris. She thought her explanation of meeting Jean-Luc and falling in love with him would seem trite to Eddie, but if it did, he gave no indication.

It felt remarkably good to unburden herself of something old and hurtful. She explained about Jean-Luc, and what an idiot she'd been, and how much the betrayal had hurt.

"So that's it?" Eddie asked, polishing off his hot chocolate. The shepherd dog was on patrol again, jogging up and down the length of the invisible fence.

"Essentially, yes." She didn't mention the miscarriage. She might, one day, but that was for another time, if that time ever came for her and Eddie. "I still feel horrible about it," she said. "I never want to feel that way again."

"I hate that you were hurt by some jerk. But honestly, you think you're the first person to have a failed romance?" asked Eddie. "People cheat on their lovers all the time. You're in good company. I mean, Anna Karenina, Hester Prynne, Major Scobie. Or hell, Yuri Zhivago. Literature is full of examples, and so is life."

She was startled to hear him rattle off literary references.

And the fact that he knew Dr. Zhivago's first name made her fall a little bit in love with him, an occurrence she knew she must absolutely keep to herself. "In other words, I shouldn't think I'm so special. Or immune."

"Come on, Moe. What I mean is, people get their hearts broken every day."

"People get their arms broken every day, too. Just because it's a common occurrence doesn't mean it can't hurt. And for good reason, they take care not to let it happen more than once."

"It's not the same thing, and you know it," he said.

She disagreed. They had each been broken in the past and each had survived, but the way they dealt with the aftermath only underscored their differences. Eddie went on with his life and lived as though each day were his last. Maureen turned in on herself, wearing emotional body armor forged by fear. That was proof they were incompatible. Wasn't it?

The shepherd dog retreated again, perching on a high spot in the yard.

"This was fun," he said, oblivious to her thoughts as he put the van in gear and eased onto the road. "We'll have to do it again sometime."

"Fun?" she asked. "Sitting here and opening a vein?"

He laughed. "Hey, it wasn't that bad. The date part, anyway. We should do it again sometime."

"Not such a good idea. This once was enough."

"Fine, we won't call it dating, then. Tomorrow night, after play practice."

"But—"

"But nothing. We're going out again. Deal with it."

17

"Are you ready for our next date?" Eddie asked, falling in step with Maureen as they left the church after rehearsal.

"I never agreed to go out with you," she reminded him. "The snowshoeing—you bullied me into that. I never agreed." Then again, she thought, she hadn't refused.

"Fine, let's not call it a date. I thought of something you'll like better, anyway."

"What's that?"

"Shopping."

Maureen thought she'd heard wrong. "You want to go shopping?"

"That's overstating it a little. I have to go. I have to buy gifts for my parents." He shook his head. "Just one more thing to love about Christmas." He held open the door of his van.

She paused, then climbed into the passenger seat. "What's not to love about buying gifts for your family?" she asked, in-

trigued in spite of herself. There was something inherently re-
vealing—and maybe romantic—about shopping for gifts with
a man. "It's one of my favorite things about the holiday."

"The rampant consumerism?"

"The gestures of love. Giving someone a gift doesn't always
have to be about spending money. I have a big family and a
small salary. But I always try to pick a gift the recipient will
appreciate. Sometimes I don't buy anything at all. I simply give
my time. For example, last New Year's Eve, I babysat my
sister's kids overnight so she and her husband could have an
evening out together."

"That's a hell of a gift, giving up New Year's Eve."

"I loved doing it. And I know what you're thinking. You're
thinking I'm pathetic for not having a better offer on New Year's."

"Actually, I was thinking I'd like to be that better offer."

She tamped down a flutter of excitement. New Year's Eve
with Eddie Haven. "Right."

"Why are you such a skeptic all the time?"

"I'm not a skeptic all the time," she said. "Only when it
comes to you."

"You mind telling me why?"

"Because I don't trust you. I'm trying to guess your ulterior
motive."

"And you're so convinced I have one."

"People like you don't go out with people like me," she said.
"Especially on New Year's Eve."

"Yeah?" He chuckled, nosing the van into a parking spot
in the town square, swarming this evening with shoppers. "So
what kind of *people* am I?"

Great. He was going to make her say it. "The kind who goes out New Year's Eve and stays out all night long," she said. "The one everybody wants to be friends with. The life of the party."

"And you're not?"

That made her laugh. "I'm a librarian."

"Don't pigeonhole yourself. The world is full of hot librarians. And I like the way you laugh. You should do it more often."

"It feels good to laugh," she admitted. *It feels good to be around you.* "But you just changed the subject. We're supposed to be figuring out what you're giving your parents for Christmas."

The town square was resplendent, decked out for the Christmas season. Back when Nina Romano was the town mayor, she'd introduced measures to encourage local businesses to coordinate their decorating efforts. The result was a winter wonderland designed to highlight the beauty of the season. Swags of twinkling lights festooned the streets and shop fronts. Music drifted from speakers and shoppers bundled against the cold hurried from place to place. It was the sort of bustling scene Maureen loved this time of year. They passed Santaland, snow-sparkled and lit for business, a line of kids waiting to get in to see him and tell him their secret wishes. She glanced over at Eddie, who looked about as happy as someone about to have his teeth drilled.

"There they are," Maureen said, gesturing at the excited children, a sight that was sure to cheer him up. "True believers. I dare you to tell me you didn't believe in Santa when you were little."

"I didn't believe in Santa when I was little. No, actually I stopped believing when I went to ask him for a puppy for Christmas, and Santa asked for my autograph."

"He didn't." Maureen bristled with indignation.

"You think I'd make that up?"

All right, so enough about Santa, she decided. "Let's talk about your folks. What do they like?" she asked him, heading into a gift shop.

"Happy hour," he suggested. "Starting at about three o'clock every day."

Oh, dear. "All right," she continued gamely. "What else do they like? Board games? Collecting things? Music?" She paused. "Old movies?"

"One in particular." His tone flattened with ill humor.

"Not helpful," she said. "Do they like books? What about hobbies, like cooking? Golf? Needlework—"

"I don't know, okay?" he snapped. "So quit asking."

She frowned. "I don't understand. How can you not know these things?"

"Back off, Maureen," he warned her.

Clearly he'd forgotten his insistence that this was a date. The closer she came to figuring him out, the madder he got. People turned defensive…when? She thought about this for a moment. When they were cornered. Guilty. Fearful. Of course, it made perfect sense. But what in heaven's name was Eddie Haven afraid of?

Deeply intrigued, she said, "Let's try this a different way. Picture your mom on Christmas day. You've just handed her a wrapped package. What is she hoping the package contains?"

"That's ridiculous. How the hell would I know what she's thinking?"

"Because she's your mother. You've known her all your life.

Same with your dad. When you walk into their house on Christmas morning—"

"Okay, I guess I didn't explain this very well. The idea is to pick up something for my folks, take it to the wrap-and-mail, and send it off, end of story. The idea is not to resolve my family's issues."

"So you do have issues with your family," she said.

"We all do," he replied.

"Imagine what might happen if you reach out to them. That's the magic of Christmas."

"Excuse me while I go into a diabetic coma here."

"Eddie—"

"Is he serious?" asked a familiar voice. "He's diabetic? Oh, Maureen, and here I was counting on him taking part in the cookie exchange."

"This is a surprise," Maureen said, giving her stepmother a hug.

"I came to do a little shopping, then I'm meeting your father for dinner. Hannah Davenport," she said, plucking off a hand-knit mitten and shaking hands with him. "And you're Eddie Haven. I've been dying to meet you."

"It's a pleasure. And I'm not a diabetic. Just giving Moe here a bad time."

"*Moe.* Renée told me you'd given her a nickname. I love that." Hannah beamed at them both.

Wonderful, Maureen thought. She's got the matchmaker gleam in her eye.

"I'm counting on seeing you at the library Saturday," Hannah continued. "For the cookie exchange."

"Wouldn't miss it," he said.

Maureen was fairly certain he had no idea what a cookie exchange was.

"In fact, I've just had a brainstorm," Hannah declared. "You can go around with the sample tray. Oh, my stars and little catfish, yes. That's exactly what you'll do. Sales will go through the roof! Eddie, thank you so much for stepping up. You're a prince, you honestly are." She beamed at him, then said, "I am unforgivably late. Maureen, your father will murder me."

"I'll look for you on the evening news," Maureen said, giving her a hug. As Hannah rushed away, Maureen turned to Eddie. "Congratulations. You've just been Hannahed. That's what we call it in our family. Getting Hannahed means getting roped into something before you've figured out what you're agreeing to and whether or not you really want to do it."

"I see. So what did I just agree to? Sample tray of *what?* Cookies?"

"Ha. You'll have to show up to find out. People who allow themselves to be Hannahed are on their own. Come to the library Saturday morning and you'll be surprised."

"I don't want to be surprised."

"I didn't want to go snowshoeing, so we're even. And speaking of things we don't want to do, you still haven't bought anything for your parents." She perused a display of luxury gifts in the window of Zuzu's Petals, the town's most interesting shop. The boutique had the added appeal of a sign in the window, announcing that a percentage of each sale would go toward saving the library. "Cashmere bedroom slippers?" Maureen suggested, leading the way into the shop. "A Foucoult's Pendulum clock? What do you think of that signed print by

Daisy Bellamy?" She indicated a dramatic, lavishly-framed shot of Meerskill Falls, cascading down a wooded gorge.

"Now you're talking. How about all of the above?" He made his purchases, then headed for the shop door, his strides quickened by impatience.

A few minutes later, they left with a sack of wrapped parcels. "You're no fun at all," she said. "This is not shopping. This is…order-taking."

"It's efficient. I'm glad you came along, Moe."

She felt slightly deflated. "You're such a guy. Don't you know that half the fun of shopping is the thrill of the hunt?"

"What's the other half?"

She smiled up at him. "Walking through the door on Christmas, with your arms laden with gifts. Seeing people's faces when they open their packages."

He stepped outside. "Yeah, that's not going to happen."

"What do you mean?"

"Walking through their door. On Christmas Eve, I'll be busy with the pageant, so there's no way I can pay them a visit."

"Yes, but on Christmas day—"

"Not happening," he said, scowling at her. "What?"

"Why won't you go see them at Christmas?"

"Let's just say my parents have a different view of the holidays than I do."

"Is there something you're not telling me? Were they horrible to you? Did they force you to make that movie?"

"Hell, no. I don't blame them. They had a kid who was good at performing, and they saw it as a way to earn a living."

"Then why not go home to them?" she asked, truly baffled.

"It's such a lovely time to be together, to relax and celebrate the joys of the holiday."

"Moe, I'm happy for your family. Mine's different."

"That's sad, Eddie," she blurted out. "It makes me sad for you."

"Don't be." He leaned against the building, shoved his hands in his pockets and stared off into the distance, across the plaza with its swags of twinkling lights. He let out a long sigh of frustration, and frosted air bloomed from his mouth. "You want to know why I don't head home for Christmas? Because I can't stand sitting around hearing them reminisce about how great it all was, back in the day. I can't stand suffering through another showing of that movie and I don't want to sign the deluxe edition DVD for their friends."

"What about just seeing your parents? Just being with them?"

"They don't need that from me. We can't all be as freakishly functional as the Davenports, Moe."

"We're not freaks."

"Okay, sorry. I'm just saying there's a huge difference between the way our families deal with the holiday. For us, getting together on that particular day is not that crucial."

"Yes, it is," Maureen insisted. "Every day matters, but especially Christmas." She hesitated, braced herself and steadied her nerves, because explaining her family dynamic to people was always hard. "Hannah is my stepmother," she said. "I'm crazy about her, and she's been with me through the hardest times of my life." She watched Eddie's face, knowing he was remembering what she'd told him about her ordeal in Paris.

"I didn't realize she wasn't your birth mother," he said.

"Hannah and my dad have been married for twenty years,

and they've been together even longer. We all love her, and we're incredibly lucky to have her in our lives."

"Is your mom…?" He clearly didn't want to ask.

"She died when I was five. One of us kids came home with a virus—you know how kids are always getting sick—and she caught it, and the virus attacked her heart muscle. She was dead within weeks. The only thing that could have saved her was a transplant, and…well, that isn't really something you can plan for and time perfectly. At the age of five, I barely understood this. All I knew was that like any kid, I adored my mother, and when she died, we *all* lost our hearts, the whole family. It's been more than twenty years, and I still miss her every day."

"Man, I'm sorry. That's just—shit. I'm so sorry." In a motion that was both completely natural, but wholly unexpected, he drew her close, gently pressing his warm lips against her forehead.

She hadn't expected to feel so touched by his sympathy. It nearly made her forget the point she was trying to make. Pulling back to look up at him, she said, "You know what? My mother wasn't perfect. I bet, like your mom, she had her flaws and made mistakes. So what? I'd give anything to have one more day with her."

"And you wouldn't care whether that day was Christmas or some other time," Eddie pointed out. "Don't get me wrong. I visit my parents often enough."

"Christmas is special."

"For you, maybe. For me, it's just another day. And for my folks, it's an excuse to crack open the Cold Duck and reminisce about things I didn't think were so hot the first time around."

She was completely intrigued by his aversion. "And you'll

do anything—even spend years doing community service—to avoid being with them on this particular day."

"You missed your calling, Maureen. You should have been a psychiatrist."

"Family counselor."

"Whatever."

"Daisy, this is incredible," Maureen said, holding up the glossy poster.

Daisy never quite knew how her work would strike someone until she got their unfiltered reaction. Then she saw that Maureen's eyes were wet. "Incredible good, or incredible bad?" she asked, her confidence faltering.

"It's perfect," Maureen assured her. "Don't mind me. I get emotional over everything this time of year. Thank you so much. Everyone who sees this is going to want to come to the pageant. It's so evocative."

The poster bore a striking image of the night sky in winter. Far below, so tiny it resembled a toy, was the church with its glowing nativity scene. The image was dreamy and brushed with magic, as though painted rather than photographed.

"I'm glad you like how it turned out." Daisy had come to the church straight from the printer's. "I hiked halfway up Watch Hill to get the shot."

"At night?" Maureen shuddered. "In the snow?"

"I had a friend with me," Daisy said quickly. She'd talked her friend Zach into it. A fellow student at SUNY New Paltz, he sometimes helped out as her assistant on challenging shoots.

Zach was also, to his great chagrin, her favorite photographer's model. With his straight, white-blond hair and strong, Nordic features, he was a compelling subject. Daisy liked being around Zach, because unlike the other guys in her life, she wasn't confused about him.

"Well, it's gorgeous." Maureen touched a finger to her name. In the corner of the printed poster, it said Codirected by Maureen Davenport and Eddie Haven.

"I thought I'd get some more candid shots today, during rehearsal," Daisy said, taking out her favorite camera, a good digital SLR. "That is, if you don't mind."

"I don't mind." Yet Maureen's expression was uncertain as she looked around the stage area of the church. "I'm afraid it's pretty chaotic around here."

"That's her polite way of saying things aren't going her way," said Eddie Haven, coming in through a side door. He was carrying a guitar in a case and some kind of sound equipment. "Right, Moe?"

Daisy aimed the lens barrel at Maureen just in time to catch a completely spontaneous and attractive blush. Okay, I get it, thought Daisy. And when Eddie grinned at Maureen, Daisy shot that, too. I *really* get it, she thought. This was something she enjoyed, capturing people's emotions, particularly the honest, unscripted ones. She was a good wedding photographer, and maybe this was why. She loved what the camera revealed about people when they were in the moment, not thinking about what they looked like. In the spring and summer, weddings were fast becoming Daisy's bread and butter. A lot of photographers shied away from weddings, but

Daisy loved them. She was inspired by the sweep of drama and the intensity of emotion that tinged the air, the over-the-top happiness and even the nerves. Maybe she enjoyed weddings so much because she didn't ever expect to have one of her own, not a traditional one, anyway. Her past was too complicated. Her present, too full of Charlie. So the chances of her future including a traditional wedding were slim. It gave her a keen eye for others, though. Take Maureen and Eddie. They had excellent chemistry. They'd make a great bride and groom, not that they seemed to know it.

"No, you're not right," Maureen said to Eddie. "It's not just me. Everybody knows this program is in trouble."

Eddie turned to Daisy. "See what I have to put up with?"

"Where are the three wise men?" Maureen asked. "They've missed the past two rehearsals."

"Ray's working with them," Eddie said. "They'll be fine."

"And what about Cecil Byrne? Who's going to work with him?" She sent Daisy a look of desperation. "He's a nice boy, but he can't carry a tune in a basket with training wheels."

"You think that's going to matter?" Eddie asked.

"We're here!" The broad double doors of the sanctuary burst open, and in flowed the after-school crowd of little ones. "We're ready for play practice," announced one of the girls.

"And play practice is ready for you," Eddie said. "Come on in and let's get started." He touched Maureen's arm. "I've got this. Good to see you, Daisy."

"You go right ahead with your pictures," Maureen said, blowing a wisp of hair off her brow. "The kids are cute no matter what."

"I know what you mean," Daisy said. "Listen, Maureen, I wanted to let you know I won't be around for the Christmas Eve performance."

"Other plans?" asked Maureen.

"Charlie and I are going down to Long Island. We're spending Christmas Eve with Charlie's dad's family." Daisy had cried when she'd told her parents, but they'd been incredibly understanding.

"Eddie's parents live on Long Island," Maureen said, her gaze drawn to him as if by a magnet.

You've got it bad, Daisy thought, hiding a smile. "Here are some outtakes from the poster shoot." Daisy handed over her portfolio. "If you want, we can use something more traditional."

"I love the one you picked." Maureen paged through the large pages. "You're so good," she said. "This is an impressive portfolio."

"Other than Charlie, it's pretty much been my life since high school. I'm glad I found photography. It's a way to connect with the world."

Maureen lingered over studies of Daisy's two best friends, Zach and Sonnet.

"I recognize these two from the library."

"Sonnet's my stepsister, doing an internship abroad this year. I miss her a lot. And Zach... It's Zach Alger. He used to live in Avalon, but he had to move away."

"I'm familiar with what happened. I always felt sorry for him in that situation."

"He's doing all right," Daisy assured her. "He's in New Paltz, working and going to school."

Maureen turned a page, stared at a portrait of Julian Gastineaux. "Oh."

Her tone of voice said it all. Everyone said "Oh" like that when they saw Julian.

"So this is a cookie exchange." Eddie stepped into the foyer of the library, which was crowded with people and lined with tables that appeared to be set up for a bake sale.

Maureen greeted him at the entrance. "That's right. We're so glad you came to help out."

"Not familiar with the concept." He stepped back and regarded Maureen. She had a sprig of holly in her hair, and she was wearing a frilly bib apron covered in little kids' handprints and embroidered along the hem: *To Miss Davenport with love.* Most women would be too fashionable to wear the handmade apron, but on Maureen, it looked cute. In fact, he found everything about her cute, but every time he tried to convey his opinion to her, she turned wary. Given what she'd told him about her first love affair, he could understand that—sort of. What he couldn't understand was her reluctance to give love another shot. He'd never met a woman so afraid of getting her heart broken. He wanted to prove to her that every relationship didn't have to end like that. He wanted her to believe that some didn't end at all. Why he wanted to be the one to prove it to her was a matter that had been in his heart ever since that night at the library.

"Come on and check it out," she said, grabbing his hand and towing him into the big, open room. It appeared to be the quintessential community event. She introduced him to Jane and Charles Bellamy, who had recently returned to Avalon to spend their golden years in the small town. He recognized dozens of other people—Noah and Sophie and their two younger kids. Maureen's friend Olivia, and Olivia's sister, Jenny, from the bakery. Bo Crutcher's mother-in-law, Mrs. Carminucci, with a giant box of cookies. Greg and Nina Bellamy—Nina had been the town mayor at the time of Eddie's accident, and she'd applauded the judge's sentence of community service. And in a way, so did Eddie. Without that, he wouldn't have a place to return to every Christmas, and he'd probably end up doing something crazy.

He noticed Maureen studying him. "It just occurred to me," he said, "I seem to know more people in Avalon than I do in my own neighborhood in New York."

"Maybe you're in the wrong place," she said, then quickly turned away before he could tell whether or not she was kidding.

At the center of the room was the Christmas tree in all its glory. Kids of all sizes crowded around it, munching on cookies and regarding the lights and decorations with shining eyes. He thought about what Maureen believed about kids and magic and Christmas. She wanted him to get over his holiday hang-ups as much as he wanted her to get over her romantic hang-ups. Maybe they could make a deal.

"We've held a cookie exchange every year as a library fund-raiser," Maureen said. "This year, it matters more than ever."

"Chin up, Moe."

"I did the math," she said, indicating the fund-raising graph on display, "and—short of grand larceny—I just can't see a way to raise enough money."

"There's another way to look at your chart." He indicated the list of usage and circulation statistics. "If everyone who used the library in the past year would contribute, you'd be in the clear."

"You're talking about a lot of people," Maureen said. "Thousands."

"I rest my case."

"That's not the way it works. In a perfect world, maybe. But the world is not perfect."

"Man," said Eddie, "you need to eat more cookies."

She offered a tremulous smile, one that made him want to hug her close. "I'll work on my attitude. Today was not a good day," she admitted. "Our operations manager left with no notice. Got a job in Green Bay."

"Hey, about those cookies," Eddie said.

"You're right. I'm sorry." She stood a little straighter, smoothed the colorful apron. "Come take a look."

He stepped into the main atrium of the building and was assaulted by sweetness. The air was thick with the aroma of home-baked cookies—butter and sugar, cinnamon, chocolate. Everything was displayed on long tables, and volunteers circulated with trays, offering samples—gingerbread angels, lemon bars, chocolate mint patties, pecan balls. Daisy Bellamy was present, taking pictures of the festivities—close-ups of fancy plates loaded with goodies, photos of wide-eyed kids and laughing adults. This was what Christmas was supposed to be, thought Eddie. But all the good spirits in the world were not going to rescue the library.

"I'm dying here, Maureen," Eddie said. "Do you now how good it smells?"

"Hard to resist, isn't it?" she said. "The Davenports' table is this way."

It had been a hell of a long time since a woman had introduced him to her family. He usually screwed things up with a girl long before the intros were in order. That was the beauty of doing the pageant with Maureen. She was stuck with him, at least until Christmas Eve. So even if he screwed things up with her, he had a few more weeks to make things right.

The Davenport family manned a long table at the back wall of the library. Maureen's father, Stan, was the silver-haired patriarch in a red plaid shirt with the sleeves rolled back. His wife, Hannah, beamed like Mrs. Santa Claus as she passed out samples of nut chewies and iced raisin bars. The sisters— Renée, whom he'd met briefly, and Janet and Meredith were outgoing and funny, and the brother, Guy, good-natured as his wife, Mindy, bossed him around.

"Try this," Meredith said. "It's our grandma's recipe."

Eddie bit into a bar cookie crammed with white and dark chocolate. His eyes rolled back in his head. "My God," he said. "I think that might be the best thing I ever ate. *Ever.*"

"Oh, we're just getting started," said Janet. "Rumball?"

"Thanks, but I stay away from rum," he said. "How about one of those? What is it?"

"A soft molasses cookie that'll change your life," said Mindy.

Eddie tasted one. "If this doesn't earn you a fortune, nothing will."

"Here's hoping."

"I mean it. These cookies could definitely save the library. Maybe they could save the world."

"People drag out their best recipes for the cookie exchange," Janet explained. "It gets pretty competitive."

Maureen took him aside. "So, what do you think of my whole 'freakishly functional' family?"

"I didn't mean anything bad, calling them that," Eddie said with a grin. "Kind of the opposite. I haven't met that many families where everybody gets along."

"Meaning yours doesn't?" she asked.

"We're okay," he said. "It's complicated."

She studied him for a moment, her eyes soft with touching sympathy. "You should do something about it, then," she told him quietly. "Sooner rather than later."

He lifted his hand, brushed her cheek. The brief touch lit a blush there. "Don't hold your breath, Moe."

"But—"

"We're all looking forward to knowing you better, Eddie," said Hannah, sidling over. "Maureen's told us so much about you."

"She has? You don't say." He was intrigued.

"Whoa, not so fast. You know that's not so," Maureen protested, blushing even deeper.

"Nonsense, of course it is." Hannah turned to beam at Eddie. "You've been all she talks about since before Thanksgiving."

"Shoot me now," Maureen said to no one in particular.

"With Cupid's arrow," Hannah declared, thrusting out a silver tray laden with a dizzying variety of cookies. "Have a nut cake, Eddie."

"Thanks. Don't mind if I do." He savored the tidbit, closing his eyes in ecstasy, pleased with both the cookie and the disclosure from Hannah. "Now, about the things Maureen told you…"

★ ★ ★

Maureen stood back and watched in dismay as Eddie effortlessly fit himself into her family. His natural charm served him well. They surrounded him in a cocoon of welcome—Hannah, the sisters, the various nieces and nephews. Even Maureen's dad and brother warmed right up to him. What an ideal setup, she thought. Between Eddie's charm and her family's openness, it was a match made in heaven. The only misfit…was her. She simply didn't feel comfortable around him, for reasons she almost couldn't bear to face. It was because she was half in love with the man. More than half, probably, and her feelings were getting harder and harder to hide. She had to, though. It was too risky to simply let this…this whatever-it-was-between-them sweep her away.

She regarded her family with both affection and exasperation. Hannah was the ringleader, as always. Maureen's stepmother was blissfully happy in her marriage, and she firmly believed everyone in the world was meant to find someone.

Furthermore, Hannah saw interfering in her stepchildren's lives as not just her right, but her duty. "In my younger days, I was a confirmed bachelorette," she told Eddie, always happy to have someone new to tell her story to. "I didn't want anything to do with marriage. And kids? Forget it. Then I met this guy." She beamed at Maureen's father. "A widower with five young kids. What were the chances?"

"Pretty good," Maureen's dad said, "since I'd been stalking you for about a year." He winked at Eddie. "Seriously, she took a leap of faith. Thought I might be damaged goods, you know, losing my wife all of a sudden. To be honest, we were all damaged. And then Hannah came along, and she rebuilt our family."

"It's a work-in-progress," Hannah said. "Especially you, young lady. I'm glad to see you having a little fun with Eddie. He's a keeper."

Maureen's cheeks flamed. "Don't you ever get tired of saying things like this? How do you get away with it?" She turned to Eddie. "Sorry about her."

"Are you kidding? I'm dying to hear more."

Maureen aimed a pointed glare at Hannah. "She has cookies to sell. And you're supposed to be circulating and getting people to make huge donations."

"Hand me a sample platter," he said, then snaked through the crowd like a skilled waiter. Within minutes, people flocked to him. Women, mainly, Maureen couldn't help but notice. Nor could she blame them. Eddie had a kind of magnetism that went beyond looks. Photos were snapped, and his smile never faltered. That was the trouble with a guy who could act. You were never sure what was an act and what was genuine. His vociferous claims about the cookies caused a run on Hannah's table, and they quickly disappeared.

The president of the board approached Eddie, and they talked for a bit. Then Mr. Shannon went to the podium, tapping the microphone to get everyone's attention. He offered a brief opening address, explaining the dire situation faced by the library. Then he said, "And now, with a short tribute to the library, please welcome Mr. Eddie Haven."

Eddie went to the podium and adjusted the microphone, offering his trademark smile, all white teeth and blue eyes.

"Thanks for the welcome," he said. "I have to confess, this is my first cookie exchange, and now that I've figured out what it is, you may never get rid of me. When I was a kid, we moved around a lot. At the holidays, we played in a different town every night."

Maureen pictured this, and it made her immeasurably sad. She glanced around the room to see if she was the only one, and was surprised to see an unlikely group of visitors—the Veltry brothers, Jabez and Cecil Byrne. An unexpected friendship had sprung up between them, different as they were. She went to welcome them, offering a flyer about the cookie exchange.

"We didn't bring any cookies to exchange," Randy Veltry said, his voice low, as Eddie was still talking.

"They'll take cash in exchange," Cecil whispered, pulling out his wallet.

Maureen felt a welling of guilt, wondering if she truly had made a mistake in not complying with Cecil's grandfather and making him the star of the play. It was done, though, and Cecil was a nice kid who seemed perfectly happy with his role. She only hoped he could convey that to his grandfather.

Jabez was quiet, paying close attention to Eddie. As if feeling her attention on him, he turned and nodded his head in greeting. "Kind of makes you sad, doesn't it?" he remarked. "You know, the stuff about his family."

"It does," she agreed, and studied Jabez. He had fast become one of her favorites, though she didn't now him well. "How about your family, Jabez?" she asked, trying not to seem nosy.

His face softened, though he kept his eyes on Eddie. "Everyone should be with family at Christmas," he said.

"People who think they want to be alone during the holidays are the ones who need family the most."

This was Jabez's way, she'd noticed, saying things that didn't really reveal much about himself. The way he'd spoken just now, she suspected it was more about Eddie than about Jabez himself. He seemed centered and wise, which was surprising in someone so young. Hannah would say he was an old soul, with that soothing air and quiet certainty, a peaceful quality that seeped into those around him. Worldly cares seemed less important to Jabez than making someone smile.

"But in every town we visited," Eddie went on, "I could always find a library. It's a place where a kid's imagination can take flight, and where a person's intellectual freedom goes unchallenged. There's no price you can put on something like that, but there are costs. The library is scheduled to be shut down the first of the year. The only hope of keeping it open is for every person in this community to contribute. That's what today is about. That, and cookies. Enjoy, everybody. And when you think about giving this year, think about this library."

"Yikes, Hannah was right for once," her sister Janet whispered in Maureen's ear. "I totally love him."

Me, too, thought Maureen before she caught herself.

Pulling back from the Cliffs of Insanity, she watched a grown woman bat her eyes at him while selecting a morsel from his tray.

Maureen shook her head. "I wonder what it's like, being that popular."

"Ask him," Janet suggested with a shrug.

"Ask him what?" Meredith joined them.

"I was just thinking how hard it would be to actually be with someone like that," Maureen admitted, "someone so attractive and popular. When would he have time for anyone else? I'd always feel as if I were in competition with the rest of the world."

"Are you writing him off because he's too popular?"

"No, because we're not a match."

Someone tugged at her skirt, and she looked down to see one of her youngest patrons, a kindergartner named Toby. "Hello, Ms. Davenport," he said, regarding her with worshipful eyes. "This is for you." He offered a cookie slathered with neon-colored frosting and pocked by sprinkles.

"Thank you, Toby." Maureen gave him a hug. "You have a Merry Christmas, okay?"

"See, you're looking at this all wrong," Meredith pointed out as the little boy scampered off. "You're just as popular as he is, only your fans are shorter."

"Gotcha." Maureen couldn't suppress a smile.

"That's another thing Hannah's right about," Janet said. "You're going to be a great mother someday."

"Whoa, slow down. How did I go from selling cookies to imminent motherhood?"

"Don't you want to be a mother?"

"Sure. I want to be a millionaire, too, but that doesn't mean it's going to happen."

Maureen kept her tone light, pulling her mind away from the past. Her sisters didn't know. No one did. She'd been strangely tempted to tell Eddie, of all people, the day of the snowshoeing. For some crazy reason, he'd felt like a best friend that day.

"You're too young to be so cynical," Meredith said.

"I'm too young to think about having kids."

"And you're so good with kids," Janet said.

"I'm good at playing Chopin's nocturnes, too, but I'm not ready to be a concert pianist," Maureen said, not liking the direction of the conversation. "Why can't anyone concede that you don't need marriage and motherhood in order to have a fulfilling life?"

"You absolutely can," Janet said loyally. "Is that what you're doing?" The look Janet and Meredith exchanged was weighted by doubts.

"I have friends," said Maureen. "I have my book group. A weekly game of mah-jongg and all the time I want with my nieces and nephews. I'm active in my church, and I have a subscription to the Met. There's plenty going on in my life. I'm giving a speech at a library meeting this weekend, down on Long Island." She didn't dare tell them the meeting was in Seaview, the same town where Eddie Haven's parents lived. She couldn't help herself; she was dying to meet them. She had a feeling they were completely clueless as to why Eddie avoided them at Christmas. It would probably only take a word of explanation.

"It's liberating, isn't it?" Meredith said, nibbling on a polvorone, which showered her with powdered sugar. "Knowing you don't need a man in your life? It lets you get on with the things that are important."

Like cardiology, Maureen thought. That was Meredith's passion. Meredith, the eldest of the Davenports, was wonderful, but she had her issues, too. Although they'd never talked about it directly, Meredith could never forget that she was the one who had come home sick one day years ago, bringing with her the virus that took their mother.

"Yes, but she doesn't want to be liberated from Eddie Haven," Janet said.

Joining them, Renée chimed in. "There's something kind of sad about him, don't you think?"

"He doesn't go home for Christmas," Maureen said.

The sisters looked appalled. "That's horrible," Renée said.

"It's…complicated." Maureen felt a twist of pain as she thought about what Eddie had told her.

"That's just wrong," Janet said. "You've got to do something."

"I tried talking to him, but he didn't want to hear it."

"No, I mean *do* something," Janet said.

"Like what?" Maureen regarded her three sisters, already regretting having told them about Eddie. They all had that woman-on-a-mission gleam in their eyes.

18

One thing Maureen liked about winter was that it got dark so early in the day. This drove some people crazy, literally. Deprived of sunlight, they started acting weird.

Not Maureen. She welcomed the darkness because it meant she would get to relax and start the evening that much sooner. She arrived home just as twilight descended hard. Sometimes she ran into Carolyn, the mail carrier, as her street was the last on Carolyn's route. The building was a 1920s brownstone that housed four apartments—Mr. and Mrs. Greer, who had the distinction of being the longest-married couple in Avalon, as far as anyone knew—67 years. Then there were Chip and his partner Gordon, a different sort of couple. They were fire-fighters at the local station and both gourmet cooks. The third apartment was occupied by Trent and Dee, newlyweds so inseparable that people gave them a couple's nickname—Trendy.

Finally there was Maureen, sharing her apartment with

Franklin and Eloise, who, as it happened, were also a couple. Maureen had adopted Franklin as a stray, naming him after Benjamin Franklin, founder of the first subscription library in the U.S. She felt guilty leaving him alone while she went to work, so she visited the local shelter and found an adorable gray tabby. For both Eloise and Franklin, it was love at first sight. The three of them lived quite happily in the vintage walk-up.

Maureen wasn't at all clever about decorating, but her place didn't need much. It exuded old-fashioned charm all on its own. Bookcases of dark polished oak lined nearly every wall. The front window framed a view of Rotary Park and Willow Lake, and had a built-in window seat with comfy cushions. It was the cats' favorite place in the house. They sat there for hours, shoulder to shoulder, watching out the window.

The library had closed early today, as it did every Friday. Kids had games and swim meets to go to so there was no play practice. Maureen was happy to have the extra time. She was giving her presentation on Long Island tomorrow, and had to catch an early train. The free evening also gave her an opportunity to explore the new books she'd brought home from work. Having a whole stack of books to choose from excited her. She felt like a child with a supply of brand-new toys. She loved the deliciously indulgent feeling of having to decide which to tackle first. A dark thriller that was bound to keep her up all night? The latest Oprah pick? A memoir of a woman who had escaped a cult? A critically panned but hugely popular novel about a woman's sexual adventures in a far-off land? They all looked enticing.

So enticing, in fact, that Maureen decided dinner wasn't

important. She indulged in one of her favorite reading getaways—the bathtub. Her apartment was equipped with an old-fashioned claw-footed tub, extra deep. She loved to sink into a sea of frothy vanilla-scented bubbles and lose herself in a good book. She spent a luxurious hour with the Oprah book, reading a dark, emotionally wrenching story that made Maureen's life look like a trip to Disneyland. Maybe, she speculated, that was the appeal of the quintessential Oprah pick. It gave the reader a glimpse of struggle and survival much harder than most people ever had to face. As Maureen raced through the pages, the water turned lukewarm and the bubbles disappeared, so she got out, wrapped her head in a towel and grabbed a robe. It was just 7:30, too early for bed, but she saw no point in getting dressed again, so she put on her favorite flannel pajamas—the ones with the cats on them—and her fuzzy slippers. Though she rarely resorted to pathetic frozen dinners, tonight she broke her own rule and popped a Lean Cuisine into the microwave.

Barely looking up from the novel, she poured herself a glass of milk and retrieved the dinner from the microwave. It was some kind of pasta that had looked good to her in the grocery store, but was, upon closer inspection, just mac and cheese.

She propped the book open on the kitchen table to keep reading while she ate, glancing up occasionally to watch the cats. They were in their usual spot in the window seat, looking adorable in a halo of bright strings of fairy lights with which Maureen had festooned the window. Next to that, she'd placed a small, living Christmas tree in a red enameled bucket, and covered it with lights and a few dainty ornaments.

"If I was any good with the camera, I'd take your picture for my annual Christmas card," she said to them. "It's probably better I don't, though, because people would die of your cuteness."

She sighed and picked at her food and tried to focus on the book again, but she'd hit a slow spot and her attention wandered. "I don't know what it is with me lately," she confessed to the cats, "but I'm just feeling so *single*. It seems like everybody is part of a couple. What's up with that? Even Meredith's dating that thoracic surgeon. The only other single I know is—"

The doorbell interrupted her. Probably one of the neighbors, needing to borrow something. She opened the door, and there stood Eddie Haven.

"Oh," she said. It was the only sound she could manage at the moment. She just gaped like a nitwit.

"Hey, Maureen," he said. "Mind if I come in?"

It wouldn't matter if she minded, since she'd recently lost the ability to speak.

He strode inside, looking wonderful; the cold air had whipped the color high in his cheeks and his eyes were lit with a smile. "So," he said, "this is your place."

She forced herself to inventory what he was seeing—the two cats and too many books, the TV dinner in its cardboard box still on the table, next to the glass of milk and the propped-open novel.

Finally, Eddie's eyes came to rest on Maureen's faded flannel pajamas, fuzzy slippers and damp, stringy hair. Every cell in her body felt as though it was melting in mortification.

Somehow, she managed to find her voice. "I, uh, wasn't expecting you."

"Just dropped by kind of spur of the moment. I would have called first, but you probably would have told me to scram."

Deep breath, she told herself. It doesn't matter what he thinks of you. Yet there was no denying what she felt—busted. He was seeing her alone in her apartment, completely unprepared for company on a Friday night. She might as well be waving a sign that read Loser.

"What, um, what can I do for you?" she asked lamely. It was loser-speak for *Please go away.*

"I'm stuck," he said bluntly. "You're making me rewrite that song for the pageant and I'm stuck."

"And you're here because…"

"Because I can't give you what you want." He handed her the CD she'd loaned him to inspire him. "If I'm going to write something, it's got to come from somewhere else."

And you had to barge in here and tell me that in person? she wondered. "What do you want from me, Eddie?"

He indicated the CD in her hand. "I listened to your kind of music. How about you listen to mine?"

"All right," she said, "I will."

"Tonight," he added.

"Agreed." She waited, then picked up the CD. "Did you put it on here?"

"I'm talking about live music." In his exaggerated DJ voice, he said, "Live, for one night only, it's Inner Child at the Hilltop Tavern."

Her last trip to the Hilltop had been uncomfortable in the extreme. She'd felt like a total misfit among the regulars—the women in their tight sweaters, the guys eased back with beers in longneck bottles. It just wasn't her scene. What did people *do* in bars anyway?

She folded her arms in front of her. "I'm busy."

He glanced at the propped-open book on the table, the half-eaten TV dinner. "You're choosing a book over listening to my music? Now I'm getting a complex."

"It won the Orange Prize," she pointed out.

"Oh, in that case," he said, full of irony. "Come on, Maureen. What are you afraid of?"

You, she thought. Everything. But she was out of excuses, and standing here arguing would only keep him in her apartment longer, prolonging her humiliation.

"Fine," she said. "I'll meet you there."

"Cool. We'll probably start around nine."

"I can hardly wait." She closed the door behind him, leaning against it as though to hold it shut. Then she sank slowly to the floor, drawing her knees to her chest and dropping her head, filled with humiliation. Finally, deeming the writhing unproductive, she burst into action, racing to her bedroom to find something to wear. She whipped clothes out of her closet, frustration mounting with each drab, out-of-date garment she threw onto the bed. Good grief, when was the last time she'd gone shopping? Her wardrobe was seriously boring.

Fifteen minutes later, she stood at the front door of her friend Olivia's house, driven there by desperation. Olivia was the most stylish person Maureen knew. She hated to disrupt the couple on a Friday night, but she was desperate. She could see Olivia and Connor through the porch window, seated across from each other at the coffee table, deep into a game of

Scrabble. Connor said something to make Olivia laugh, and her eyes seemed to brim with warmth.

Maureen hesitated as a pang hit her in a soft place, the way it sometimes did when she observed a happy couple. It wasn't an ugly feeling, like envy. Just…a brief emptiness.

Get over yourself, she thought. Tonight is about *not* being alone. She knocked at the door. Connor let her in. She greeted them with a flustered smile, then focused desperately on Olivia. "Sorry to interrupt your evening," she said, "but I need your help."

"Sure, anything," Olivia said easily. Connor took her by the hand and helped her to her feet.

"I need a great outfit," Maureen said.

"Sure, I'll get right on that," Connor said.

Olivia gave his arm a smack. "Smart aleck."

He stepped back, holding his palms out in surrender. "Okay, I'm out of here."

"Connor, I'm sorry," Maureen said. "Honestly, if I could do this on my own, I would."

"No problem, Maureen," he said good-naturedly, bending to place a kiss on Olivia's cheek. "I'll go soothe myself with a beer and a hockey game."

"Thanks for being a good sport," she said, and he headed to the basement and his big-screen TV. Maureen glanced at the Scrabble board. Most of the words there were sexual in nature, or laden with innuendo.

Noticing her startled look, Olivia gave a laugh. "Honey, I'm eight months pregnant. This is about as much sex as we're having these days. And speaking of sex, I'm going to go out on a limb here and guess that you need the great outfit to impress a great guy."

Maureen nodded. "That, and redeem myself." Because Olivia was her friend, she told her honestly about Eddie Haven, and about the pajamas, the cats, the TV dinner. The fuzzy slippers. "And yet I feel so shallow, trying to doll myself up to impress some guy."

"That's not shallow. It means you have a healthy sense of self-esteem." Olivia grabbed her by the arm and took her to the master bedroom. "This is going to be fun," Olivia said, flipping on the lights in her walk-in closet. "I haven't seen some of my clothes since I started showing."

Prior to moving to Avalon, Olivia had run a real estate staging business in Manhattan. Her inimitable style was also evident in her wardrobe, and before long, she'd put together an outfit of snug-fitting high-fashion jeans, an equally snug cashmere sweater and boots with stiletto heels.

Maureen felt exposed but daring in the sweater and jeans. The boots, however, she regarded with horror. "I can't wear those. I'll kill myself."

"Nonsense. It's just for this evening. Put them on and you can get used to them while I work on your hair and makeup. Do it. Resistance is futile. Oh, and you did bring your contacts, right?"

"Reluctantly," Maureen admitted.

Olivia went to work on Maureen's hair with the electric flat-iron and shine products. She applied an array of makeup products, taking her task as seriously as a plastic surgeon.

"I really appreciate this," Maureen said. She normally wasn't much for primping, but for some reason, this felt indulgent and good.

"It's fun for me," Olivia assured her. "It's going to be even more fun for you, when you get a load of yourself." She refused to let Maureen see herself until the look was complete. Finally, she took her by the hand and led her to the full-length mirror. "Ready?" she said. "Turn around."

Maureen turned. Blinked her glasses-free eyes in astonishment, and finally found her voice. *"Whoa."*

As he set up in the corner of the Hilltop Tavern, Eddie conceded that he should have called Maureen instead of showing up unannounced at her place earlier. She had looked embarrassed, although she tried not to let it show.

What she probably hadn't realized was that he'd found her inadvertently sexy, alone in her dimly lit apartment, fresh from the bath, smelling delicious.

"What are you looking so happy about?" asked Ray, flipping switches on his keyboard. "You get laid, or something?"

"Nope. Can't a guy look happy?"

"Not like that, not without getting laid. Who's the girl? Come on, spill."

Ray was one of the few people who knew Eddie's sentence of community service had ended a long time ago. He probably didn't quite understand why Eddie continued to volunteer for the pageant year after year, but he never said anything. So much of friendship was just that. Keeping your mouth shut.

So this current line of questioning was very un-Ray-like. "Who is she?" he persisted.

Eddie shook his head. "You wouldn't believe me if I told you."

"Try me."

"I bet it's that librarian, Maureen Davenport," Bo Crutcher stated loudly, plugging in his bass.

Ray played an ominous minor chord on his keyboard. "No way you're banging Miss Hair-in-a-bun-librarian."

"It's not like that." Eddie couldn't describe what it was like, because this kind of attraction had never happened to him before. "I mean, that's where I hope it's going."

"Of course you do. Every guy wants every relationship to end up there. Tell me something I don't know."

"You don't—" Eddie stopped talking as a woman walked into the bar. She paused in the doorway, and for a moment, the blue-white neon of the marquis outlined her in a bright glow. She was a knockout in tight jeans and a sweater that showed off every curve, high-heeled boots and long, loose hair. The guys at the pool table forgot their game, and a few of those lined up at the bar checked her out. A sense of surprise and recognition caused Eddie's brain to shut down.

Ray played a riff of "Good Golly Miss Molly."

Eddie grabbed his water glass and took a gulp, then went to greet her. "Maureen."

Her ankles wobbled a little in the high-heeled boots as she lurched forward. He slid his arm around her to steady her.

"Sorry," she said, seeming flustered as she untangled herself from him. "Between the heels and contact lenses, I'm setting myself up for a big fall. But what the heck. A girl can live dangerously, right?"

Eddie couldn't help staring. The contrast between the

bathrobe-clad woman in her apartment and the one in front of him made him wonder just what was going on in her head. That was the thing about Maureen. She went layers deep, and just when he thought he had her all figured out, she showed him something new.

"I liked you fine in fuzzy slippers," he said.

"Just so you know, they're going right back on when I get home."

Ah, the old Maureen was alive and kicking. "Well, I really appreciate you coming, Moe."

"I'm here to listen to you play," she reminded him. "Isn't that what you wanted?"

He grinned. "It's a start. Come and say hi to everyone." Following her to the corner table, he couldn't keep his eyes off her. She really ought to wear tight jeans more often.

She greeted Kim Crutcher and Noah's wife, Sophie, who was enjoying a rare night out while her older kids watched the younger ones. Kim and Sophie took to her instantly, drawing her into their girl talk. It was interesting, the way Maureen's personality shifted with the change of clothes. The shy librarian persona stepped aside, and this new Maureen was social. Almost confident. Bo set aside his bass and sidled over to the table and slid in next to his wife, who turned to him with her eyes brimming with love.

"What would you give to have somebody look at you like that?" Ray asked him, indicating Bo and Kim. Still relative newlyweds, they couldn't stay away from each other. "Your eyeteeth?"

"Yeah. Sure. Who needs eyeteeth?"

"Left nut?"

"Ouch. Shut up and play, Tolley."

They pried Bo away from his wife and did a thirty-minute set for the small but enthusiastic crowd at the Hilltop, covering a few popular songs and performing a couple of their own. While he played, Eddie watched Maureen without seeming to be too obvious about it. Some guy, tanked up with a few beers, approached her, bent and said something in her ear. Eddie was poised to leap to her defense, but she seemed composed enough as she gave the guy the brush-off with a puzzled frown, leaning away and saying something that looked like "No, thank you." It didn't seem to register with her that the guy was hitting on her. Man, she was an odd duck.

And he was crazy about her. What a world.

At the break, he ordered a cup of coffee and took a seat next to her. "Well?"

"You and your friends are great. And your original songs… You're a wonderful songwriter. I mean, I already knew that, but listening to you just now, well…now I feel bad about asking you to write a song for the pageant." She shifted uncomfortably in her seat.

"I don't get it. Why would you feel bad?"

"I didn't realize what I was asking. Your songs are your heart."

"Yeah? You think?"

She nodded. "The one you sang at the library—it was wrong of me to criticize it."

"It's all right," he said. "Seriously. That song was about you, not the Christmas program. I decided to work on something else for that."

She glanced around, a trapped expression on her face. "About me?"

"Yep. Maureen—"

"Eddie—" She looked as if she was about to bolt.

He smiled at her, trying to put her at ease. "We don't have to talk about this right now."

She slumped against the back of her seat. "Thank you." Then she leaned forward and took a nervous sip of her drink.

He raised his coffee mug in salute. "Cheers, then. To music and lyrics."

She clinked her glass against his mug. Her drink was something girly-looking, with a cherry in it. "Can I ask you something...kind of personal?"

"You can ask. I can't promise I'll answer."

"Oh. Well, then—"

"Kidding, Maureen." He loved how earnest she was about everything. "Ask away. I got nothing to hide."

"I was just wondering if it bothers you to come into a bar, you know, since you're a nondrinker."

"An alcoholic in recovery," he clarified. "That's a particular kind of nondrinker. And no, I don't mind talking about it." Staying sober had once felt like a daily battle to him, long ago. Not anymore, though. Now it felt like a daily gift—to wake up clearheaded and stay that way. Some people might take sobriety for granted, but not Eddie. He'd come too close to losing everything to put it all at risk again. "Hell, there's a whole page about it online."

"I told you, I don't look at things like that," she said.

Another thing to like about her. She was loyal. She had integrity. "Thanks, Moe. I wish the bozos who wrote the online article were more like you." The Internet offered a compilation of bare facts and tabloidlike material that skirted the edge of truth. There were links to articles of questionable veracity, pictures of him, past girlfriends and his family. As Maureen put it, the existence of such a resource on the Internet felt intrusive. Seeing the stark facts spelled out on a computer screen robbed the humanity from a person's story. *Haven was involved in a drunk driving incident that resulted in court-ordered community service....* It made him cringe to read stuff out of context in a way that made him seem like a total loser.

"After all this time," he told Maureen, "it's simply a nonissue. It's like walking into a store that doesn't sell a single thing I'm tempted to buy."

"Seriously?"

"Seriously."

She subjected him to a long, searching look.

"What?" he asked.

"You should be proud of yourself, Eddie."

"For saving my own life? Not such a feat, considering the alternative."

"I think you're making it sound easier than it was. I bet your parents are proud of you, too."

At that, he gave a shrug. "They never seemed to want to talk about it. I suspect because it hits a little too close to home. They partied hard in their day, and having a son in recovery is probably an unwelcome reminder."

Maureen regarded him aghast. "Did they tell you that?"

"Nope, just a guess."

"Well. Clearly you need to talk to them about it."

He couldn't help smiling. "Everything's so simple to you, Moe."

"Talk to them. You'll have a better sense of where you're going if you know where you've been."

"You're a philosopher tonight."

She swirled the cherry in her drink around by its stem. "I read that in a book somewhere. There's this thing I sometimes do with books—" She stopped and waved her hand. "Never mind. You'll think I'm silly."

"I could use a little silly right about now," he said, happy to dispense with the topic of his family.

"Okay, sometimes I close my eyes and randomly pick out a line in a book, and I let it guide me. It's a little game, is all." Her cheeks flushed, and she lifted her cherry to her lips, nibbling at it, then finally drawing it into her mouth. When she noticed him staring, her cheeks flushed even deeper.

"Another drink?" he offered.

"Sure."

"What are you having?"

"It's, um, a Shirley Temple."

"Shirley Temple," Eddie called to Maggie Lynn. "Two cherries."

"Thank you," said Maureen. There was something both guileless and charming about the way she regarded him. No, not just charming. Undeniably sexy.

Damn. He hadn't felt this way about a woman since…

ever. He'd never felt this way about anyone. Not even girls he'd said *I love you* to, not even the woman he'd proposed to.

What were the chances? he wondered. The town librarian, of all people.

He was falling in love with the town librarian, and he had no idea why.

"I can't imagine that it's easy," she said, "yet you make it look easy."

Eddie corrected himself. He did know why he was falling in love with her.

Maureen stood at the door to her building, wishing she'd had something stronger than Shirley Temples to drink at the bar. No, she didn't wish that. It didn't feel right, having a stiff drink when Eddie worked so hard to stay sober. Still, she felt horrendously nervous. At the end of the evening, he'd insisted on following her home, overriding her protests.

"I don't need anyone to see me home," she'd insisted.

"I know that. I *want* to," he'd said.

And now they faced each other on the top step of the brownstone, and she was a bundle of nerves. "Well," she said, "thanks."

"Invite me up," he said.

"Oh, I don't think—"

"Good plan. Let's not think. Just invite me up and we'll see what happens."

She wanted to. It made no sense, it was foolish in the extreme, but she wanted to more than she wanted another breath of air. Before she lost her nerve, she stabbed her key into the lock and led the way to her apartment. The cats swirled around their ankles in greeting. Everything was just as she'd left it, dashing out for her speed-makeover on the way to the Hilltop. There was her book, still propped open on the kitchen table. Dishes in the sink, TV dinner in the trash. She'd left with no notion that the apartment would soon be a scene for seduction.

"I like your place," Eddie said, shrugging out of his parka and slinging it over a chair. He helped her off with her coat. "I like you. I think I'm starting to love you."

Her breath stopped, until she realized she was holding it and forced herself to exhale. Somehow, she found her voice. "Really?"

"Yeah," he said, turning her in his arms and bending down to kiss her. "Really."

She tried to tell herself it was foolish to believe him, and yet she did. He took her by the hand, and like a ninny, she let him lead her to the bedroom. The reading lamp was on, and he frowned at its glare. "Too bright," he muttered.

"I read myself to sleep every night," she explained.

"Not tonight, you don't."

The tone of his voice filled her with a yearning heat. "Eddie—"

"Wait there," he said. "Don't move." He went and got a string of Christmas lights from the front window, and returned to the bedroom. "Stand back," he instructed her. "I'm a professional." He plugged in the light string and draped it across the headboard, plunging the room into a dim, multicolored glow. "Better," he said, and slipped out of his jeans as if it were the most natural thing in the world.

She stared at him. "Are those…*Santa* boxers?" She started to giggle until his kisses turned humor to passion, a passion that burned through the last of her apprehension, turning her pliant with need. Then he undressed her with a leisurely eroticism that drained every brain cell from her head. He laid her back on the bed, the Christmas lights bathing them in a rainbow glimmer. She reached for him in a moment of delicious, willing surrender. He was everything she'd imagined in her most secret dreams—gentle and slow, considerate, utterly comfortable, as if making love to her was his greatest goal in life.

Oh, he showed her things—the power of a perfectly placed kiss, the irresistible warm pressure of his hands skimming down her body, the intoxicating suggestion of a whisper in her ear. The explosive joy of pent-up wanting, finally and exuberantly released. He asked nothing of her, yet she gave him everything, the passion that hid inside her in a place no one but Eddie had ever bothered to find. And she was good. She knew it, because he told her again and again as the moments drifted by, turning into an hour…two hours, longer….

"A tattoo," he said with a chuckle, bending to trace his fingers over the small of her back. "The librarian has a tattoo. God, Maureen, that's…*God.*"

"Well, if I'd known it was called a 'tramp stamp,' I never would have gotten it," she said. She couldn't believe what they'd just done, couldn't believe she'd left the Hilltop and brought him home with her, couldn't believe they'd just made love until she nearly wept.

Wait, she could believe it, because they were about to do it again.

★ ★ ★

They both had to get up at the crack of dawn the next morning, Eddie to go on the radio and Maureen to catch an early train. There was that morning-after awkwardness—on Maureen's part, anyway. She tried to behave as if waking up next to a warm, attractive man was something she could take in stride. Eddie seemed completely natural, stretching luxuriously, groaning with reluctance as she slipped from the bed and grabbed her bathrobe.

"I have to go," she said. "It's our annual holiday meeting." She briefly contemplated unplugging the Christmas lights around the bed, but decided to leave them burning. Heck, why not?

"Can't you skip it?" he asked.

"No, especially not this year. I might be looking for a job soon, so I need to stay in touch with people."

"Still hedging your bets." He stood there in his Santa boxers, looking so appealing she actually thought about canceling everything and staying right here with him.

"I need to be realistic," she told him. "I know we're doing everything we can for the library, but time's running out, and we're not even close to raising the money we need."

"Yeah, well, it's not over 'til it's over. Stay here." He grabbed her and gently pressed her against the wall, bending to nibble her neck. "I'll tell the girls at the station to play a canned show this morning."

She nearly succumbed, getting the hot shivers from his beard stubble. "I have to go," she repeated, ducking down and slipping from his grasp. "It's being held in Seaview this year." She regarded him with knowing eyes.

"Home of the Havens," he said in a radio-announcer voice. "I don't really think my folks are library patrons."

"Maybe I'll drop in and see them, invite them up for Christmas."

He laughed. "Right. They'd love that. Nope, trust me, honey, they have other plans."

"Have you ever invited them?"

"I think their Christmas program days are over and they like it that way."

"But you've never invited them."

"I know what they'd say."

"They might surprise you."

"Moe, I hear what you're saying," he said, pulling her into his arms. "And I appreciate your concern. But believe me, I don't need to be with my folks at Christmas, and they sure as hell don't need to be with me. We tried that when I was a kid, and it didn't work out so hot."

He gave her a delicious kiss, sweet as candy. "In case you haven't noticed, I got something better to do at Christmas."

Part Five

Christmas Eve was a night of song that wrapped itself about you like a shawl. But it warmed more than your body. It warmed your heart...filled it, too, with a melody that would last forever.

—Bess Streeter Aldrich (1881-1954),
American author, in "Song of Years"

19

Eddie was dreaming of the angel…yet again. This time was different, though. Unlike all the other dreams, made up of half-formed memories and wishful thinking, the images in his head, teasing him awake, were as clear as a cloudless winter night. The first part of the dream was the same as ever—he lay nearly buried in a snowbank after the crash, mute with pain and shock, about to freeze to death, unnoticed by the people who had poured out of the church…until the angel showed up. The thing that was different about this dream was that he saw the angel's face.

He sat up, fully awake, walked straight to his guitar and wrote his song for the Christmas program. Just like that—no hesitation, no groping around for meaning or melody. In his life, he'd composed hundreds of songs for all kinds of reasons, but never had he written with such clarity and conviction. He couldn't wait to sing it for Maureen, offering it to her like a gift. A promise.

Unfortunately, he'd have to wait. She'd gone away overnight for some library meeting on Long Island. The twenty-four hours without her dragged. When she returned, he promised himself he'd devote every free minute to her. He'd embark on a campaign to get her to fall in love with him. Maybe he'd take her to the Apple Tree Inn and…no. The place still had some bad associations for him. Okay, maybe he'd bring her home, then, to his place by the lake. Hell, maybe he'd even make dinner. He'd definitely make love to her again. From the very start, she had surprised him, but never more than when he took her to bed. She was sweet and not afraid to be vulnerable, and she drew from him a tenderness he didn't know he had.

In other areas of his life, she challenged him, too, never making things easy. She wasn't after his surface charm like an autograph seeker, but what lay beneath. And for the first time in a long time, that didn't scare him.

He burst into action, straightening up. The place wasn't a disaster, but he wanted her to like it here. He wanted to play her a song on his Gibson guitar, the one his grandfather had given him, signed by Les Paul. He wanted to tell her stuff that was sappy but true, stuff that would make her smile. He wanted to give her a gift, but the only thing she wished for was something he couldn't give her—a way for the library to survive. Damn. If he could make that happen, if he could give her that….

He turned the problem over and over in his mind. Made a call to his entertainment lawyer. If the silver anniversary DVD was selling as well as the trades said, maybe Eddie could at least buy the library some time. Or hell, according to the lawyer, the clips on the Internet were getting a zillion views per hour; surely he could parlay the renewed popularity into something. Eddie didn't want to be famous again, but maybe he could use his popularity to help out the library. Maureen would love that.

He listened to the new Drive-By Truckers album and sang along while putting clean sheets on the bed. No harm in being optimistic.

In the pause between songs, he heard the insistent sound of a doorbell.

"Sorry," he yelled. "Coming." He wasn't expecting anyone. Maybe it was Maureen. Maybe she was thinking the same thing he was.

He halfway believed it would be her as he swung the door open with a big smile on his face.

"Surprise!" his parents said in unison.

Oh, boy. "Barb. Larry. What are you doing here?" he asked.

"We wanted to see you. And it's been so long since we've visited Avalon. I'd forgotten how *Christmasy* this place is." She was beautiful as ever, his mother, with her hair in a stylish cut, wearing an expensive-looking dress coat and leather boots that matched her narrow belt. Yet when she looked up at him, he was tempted to believe the tears pooling in her eyes and the slight trembling of her mouth. His father, looking younger than a guy in his fifties, offered a hearty hug and then a handshake.

"Your mother's right, son," he declared. "Too damn long."

"Impulse decision," Barb added. "We've come to spend Christmas with you."

Nonononono. "Uh…yeah. About that—"

"Don't worry, we won't be any trouble at all." His parents blustered inside, bringing a gust of cold air with them. "We're staying at the Inn at Willow Lake—adorable place, do you know it? Maureen set it all up for us."

"Maureen? How do you know Maureen? What's she got to do with this?"

"She came by and introduced herself. She had a library meeting in Seaview, and took the time to call and introduce herself. We think she's wonderful, Eddie, so sincere and full of ideas."

Eddie tried to be as false as they were. He tried to say, "Thanks for coming" or "I'm glad you're here." But when he opened his mouth, the words that came out were, "Calling you—the invitation—that was all Maureen Davenport's idea? I had no idea what she was planning."

His mother gave his arm a squeeze. "I'll remember to thank her again after the performance Christmas Eve," she said. "She seems like a wonderful girl."

"Everybody thinks so," Eddie said, wondering what the hell she could have been thinking.

"Did you know she was one of the original Christmas Belles?" asked Barb.

"What?"

She handed him a cellophane-wrapped CD. "We brought this for you. Her name's right there on the list of singers—Maureen Davenport. Isn't it wonderful that she was in the group that did such a beautiful rendition of your signature song?"

"That's not my—good God. That is not my signature song. I don't have a signature song, but if I did, that wouldn't be it."

"Well. No need to get huffy," his mother said. "Anyway, back to Maureen. As I was saying, we think she's wonderful. The three of us put our heads together right then and there, and arranged the whole thing. As a surprise for you. Are you surprised?"

He forced his mouth into a smile. "You bet. Totally surprised."

"It's wonderful to be back in Avalon after all these years," his mother said. She aimed a fond look at his father. "Do you remember the first time we came here, Larry? We were just kids, and our families came to spend time at Camp Kioga."

Larry's eyes glowed as he looked at her. "How could I forget? Back in the day, it was a camp for whole families to get away from the city heat in summer. Your grandma and grandpa Haven performed at camps all over the area, but Camp Kioga was their favorite." His expression warmed as he gazed at his wife. "Ours, too."

His parents were each other's best friend. Married at eighteen, they'd practically raised each other. It was kind of incredible that they were still together, but in spite of their lives, which seemed to change completely every decade without fail, there was a steadfastness about them. Sure, they'd been clueless about the real world, both of them having come of age in the murky chaos of show business. They hadn't always made the best choices, particularly when it came to their son. But there was never any question that they loved each other.

"We're so pleased you changed your mind about Christmas," his mother said. "And that Maureen. I can't praise her enough. What a lovely young lady."

"Yeah," Eddie said, "she's lovely, all right."

★ ★ ★

He was seething as he drove to the church for rehearsal, but in the press of activities, he had no chance to confront her. Two days before the performance, a zillion things went wrong—sick kids, a snowstorm, and the pièce de résistance, the discovery that all the costumes had been destroyed in storage—sprayed with a toxic chemical or insecticide—and were now unwearable. Maureen looked like she was on the verge of a meltdown. After a completely lame run-through, most everyone had cleared out for the night.

Eddie spotted her in the sanctuary, sitting and staring at the half-completed stage set. She looked up at him, and for a moment he wanted to forget what she'd done. Or better yet, he wanted to pretend it didn't hurt. She was so damned... nice. Sincere. But she'd shown a new side of herself, a side he couldn't trust. His anger must have been apparent, because she immediately shifted away from him, a question in her eyes.

"You brought my parents here." He leaned his hip on a seat back and glared down at her.

"I invited them," she clarified. "They came on their own."

"They came because of you," he snapped.

"No," she told him quietly. "Because of you."

"Jesus, Maureen, I told you the way it was for me. There's a reason I don't spend Christmas with my folks. I thought you'd figured that out."

"Families should be together at Christmas," she said, her expression turning mutinous, reminding him of the uptight, judgmental woman he'd locked horns with at the beginning of the season.

"Every family can't be as perfect as yours for the holidays," he said.

"Perfect?" She looked incredulous. "Is that what you think of my family?"

Pretty much, he thought, picturing Hannah and Maureen's dad, the siblings, nieces and nephews. "You had no right to interfere."

"I just thought—"

"No, Maureen, you didn't think. You had this idealized vision in your head about the way you want Christmas to be, and the rest of the world is supposed to conform to that vision. Well, guess what? It doesn't work that way."

"It will never work if you don't try."

"Don't you have enough on your plate, with this program tomorrow night and the library?" he demanded. "Tell you what. Let's just get through the show, and after that, you won't have to deal with me anymore, or try to fix my family. Will that make you happy?"

"You don't care about making me happy," she stated simply. "I don't expect you to. That's not your job. Just like it's not my job to fix whatever's going on with you and your family. I simply invited them. Everyone is welcome on Christmas Eve." She slid out of her seat, taking care not to brush against him as she passed by, and walked away with a curious dignity.

Eddie clenched his jaw to keep from calling out to her. It was better this way, he thought. Better not to take this any further than it had already gone, because it wasn't going to end up anywhere good. He was an idiot for thinking he could have something with a woman like Maureen, a woman who was so grounded, so enmeshed in the life of her community and family. They'd never make it, the two of them. Why the hell would he want to be with someone who held up a mirror to his flaws?

He stalked to his van and jumped in, and drove home too fast, the rear tires fishtailing on the snowy road. On his doorstep, a parcel was waiting for him, marked Special Delivery. He took it inside and opened the box. A small envelope with a card in it indicated the gift was from Your friends at Silver Creek Productions, the company that had produced the original *Christmas Caper* movie and the new DVD. Apparently, it was the top-selling DVD in the country, earning him a hefty bonus. Fishing through a sea of packing foam, he pulled out a magnum of champagne, already pre-chilled from having sat on the stoop.

All of his senses leaped. He remembered champagne. Did he ever. Like drinking the stars, as Dom Perignon had termed it.

20

On the day before Christmas, Daisy was ready for the train trip downstate, to spend the night at the O'Donnells'. For little Charlie's sake, she needed to cultivate a good relationship with his paternal grandparents, and what better way to do that than to share the holidays with them? She'd told her own family farewell, getting a strange lump in her throat even though the trip with Logan and Charlie was only going to be an overnight affair. "It's just that this particular night is special," she said to Charlie as she double-checked the inventory of his massive diaper bag. "I've never been away from my family on Christmas before. It feels like kind of a big deal, if you want to know the truth."

"Yep," said the toddler, eliciting a smile from her.

"It's a rite of passage, I suppose you could say. This marks a transition for me, from being a kid with a kid to being an adult on my own. Spending the holidays *away* from my family means I'm truly on my own, right?"

"Yep," Charlie said again.

"And that's not such a bad thing," she added, folding the stroller and leaning it by the front door. Sometimes she had the strangest sensation that she was living a make-believe life, a life that was in a holding pattern until…until what?

She reminded herself of her blessings—that always helped. She was blessed by the support of her family, both material and emotional, and blessed, especially by Charlie himself. Although she had nothing to compare him to, she considered him to be an easy baby. What that meant, as far as she could tell, was a baby who ate well and slept a lot and rarely got sick.

Charlie had always been a pretty good eater, and he didn't usually put up a fuss about sleeping. Actually, he did at night, except when it was with Daisy, snuggled up against her like a warm puppy. And that, of course, was controversial. One school of thought declared that a baby should never be allowed in his mother's bed or he'd never learn to be independent. Another school insisted just the opposite—that a baby was designed for sleeping with his mother. The security he derived from the closeness would make him a well-adjusted person later in life. Daisy found herself subscribing to both schools, depending on her mood.

At the moment, he was using foam blocks to build some kind of structure. There was a knock at the door, and his face bloomed with a smile.

"Daddeee!" Charlie abandoned his blocks and lunged for the door.

Daisy swept the room with a glance, which was the only sweeping she would do today. As usual the house was littered with toys, schoolbooks, unopened mail, clutter. How did people with little kids keep their houses picked up? she wondered. How did they have time to do anything else?

She went and unlocked the door, having learned the hard way to keep it bolted at all times. When Charlie had first started walking a year ago, he'd let himself out in subzero temperatures. She'd turned her back for like two seconds, and off he went. Her only indication that something was amiss had been an icy gust of winter air. That was the thing about a baby. When things went wrong, they went wrong fast. There was very little room for error.

For a supposedly smart person, she'd done plenty of crazy things. And the craziest of all was walking through the door right now.

"Hey, Logan," she said.

He entered the house on a blast of fresh, cold air. "Hey, yourself."

"Dad. Dad. Dad." Exhibiting pure elation, Charlie clung to Logan's leg, looking pleadingly upward, his head lolling back like an angel gazing up at heaven.

"Charlie, Charlie, Charlie." Logan peeled off his gloves, then picked him up. "How are you, little guy?"

"'Kay, big guy."

Logan beamed at him, then got busy zipping him into his snowsuit.

Daisy stood back, warmed by their mutual admiration. It was hard to believe just three years before, she and Logan had been a couple of rebel teens, parking caution at the door and having careless sex one crazy weekend.

Now here they were, a family.

And that, thought Daisy, was enough. She had no reason to complain and no business wishing for something else.

Every once in a while, she felt a twinge of *what-if.*

She'd look at her best friend and stepsister, Sonnet, a brainiac preparing for a career in international relations, and think, *What if I'd done better in school?* Or she'd look at her cousins, Olivia and Jenny, now both blissfully married, and she'd think, *What if I'd let myself fall in love before having a baby?* She knew regrets were a slow poison, but sometimes they sneaked in, particularly with regard to her love life. Or lack thereof.

Her heart had been captured but that didn't mean she was free to follow it. She'd given up that option in one wild weekend with Logan O'Donnell. Still, she couldn't quite manage to shield herself from all the *what-ifs* that bombarded her at vulnerable moments. And at the center of every what-if question was Julian Gastineaux.

Daisy forced herself to shake off the thought which struck her, as such thoughts always seemed to do, when she was with Logan. What was up with that? She had to figure out a way to quit yearning for something out of her reach.

"All set?" asked Logan, scooping up the baby. "Let's roll."

"Yeah," said Charlie.

Daisy shouldered the diaper bag, which had expanded to the size of a Winnebago. She went around making sure all the windows were locked tight. Even though she'd only be gone overnight, it felt as though she was leaving forever. Silly, she thought, swallowing another twinge of regret. Then she grabbed the folded stroller and followed Logan outside, double-locking the door behind her.

Charlie would be in heaven, she reminded herself on the way to the train station. And when he was happy, so was she. That was really what governed her choices as a mother. They drove to the station and reversed the packing-up process. Traveling with a toddler was labor intensive, to say the least. "This is how the pioneers must've felt, loading up to head west," she said, brushing crumbs out of the stroller seat.

"He's just a guy with a lot of gear," Logan said good-naturedly. He strapped the baby in the stroller, hooked their other bags onto the back of the apparatus and pushed it toward the terminal. Daisy ducked into the ladies' room. She stood in front of a mirror for several minutes, trying not to panic. Tonight was going to be fine, she told herself. Absolutely fine. Thanks to Charlie, the O'Donnells had warmed up to her. They'd gone from refusing to see or acknowledge the baby to sincere, gooey grandparenthood. Logan's sisters doted on Charlie, too. Daisy was simply going to have a different kind of Christmas this year, surrounded by a different family—one she didn't belong to except through the most haphazard of ties. Still, this evening was going to be all right. She'd be so busy with the festivities, she wouldn't let herself wish she could be at the Christmas pageant at Heart of the Mountains Church. She'd be going to midnight mass with the O'Donnells, a first for her. She'd feel like an anthropologist studying an exotic culture.

All right, she thought. Deep breath.

She dabbed at her face with a damp paper towel and headed up to the platform. It was harder than she had anticipated to climb the stairs to the southbound platform, away from Avalon and her family on Christmas Eve. At the head of the steps, she spotted a girl in raspberry-colored tights, trendy boots and a short plaid skirt, flirting with Logan and ogling Charlie. Yes, she was totally flirting. Although Daisy herself was out of practice, she still remembered the body language. You leaned in, tilted your head adorably, maybe even touched a finger to your lips. If there was a baby present, as there was in this case, you appealed to its cuteness, knowing it would only enhance your own charm. The flirting girl was gorgeous and made the most of it. She looked the way most girls only dreamed about—as if she'd stepped from the pages of a magazine.

Daisy felt a twinge of—okay, here it was—pure, green-hot jealousy. Although she tried telling herself not to be jealous of some girl flirting with Logan, she couldn't deny the feeling. Maybe—rationalizing here—her discomfiture grew out of concern for Charlie. Suppose Logan took up with someone who didn't like kids? That would be totally unacceptable.

Oh, Daisy, she thought. Quit being a control freak.

She sauntered over to Logan. "Hey, guys," she said. Okay, maybe she leaned a little closer to Logan than she normally would. Maybe the smile she aimed at the girl on the platform was vaguely territorial, but she couldn't help herself.

"Have a good Christmas," the girl said, taking a step back.

"Sure, same to you," Logan replied, affable as ever. After the girl left, he explained, "Somebody from my poli-sci class." Then he studied Daisy's face. "Something wrong?"

She felt her cheeks flush. "No. Why do you ask?"

"You were giving that girl the stinkeye."

"Is that what it looked like?"

"That's what it was."

"She was totally hitting on you," Daisy said.

He seemed genuinely surprised. "Nah. It was Charlie she liked. The kid's a babe magnet." Apparently done with the subject, he unbuckled Charlie and freed him from the stroller. Daisy allowed it because, number one, she was trying to be less of a control freak and number two, it was a long trip to the city and the kid needed to work off his excess energy.

Logan and Charlie played their signature game on the platform, which Daisy had termed their running-around game. Basically it consisted of Charlie running in circles, giggling hysterically, with Logan in hot pursuit, making the occasional threatening growl. It had absolutely no point other than to amuse Charlie. Daisy took it as yet another sign she was doing the right thing this Christmas. Charlie, playing so joyously with his father, was having the time of his life, and that was what mattered. Since he'd had no nap so far today, he tired quickly. Within a few minutes, Logan had buckled him back into the stroller and tucked a blanket around him, and Charlie had nodded off.

"Score," said Daisy. "Good job, Logan."

He squinted into the distance. "The train's coming."

"It probably won't even wake him up. Noise doesn't seem to bother him," she said. Her mobile phone emitted a beep, signaling a text message. Glancing at the screen, she saw that it was from Julian. Her heart stumbled in her chest, and she quickly put the phone away.

"Everything okay?" asked Logan.

"Fine." She figured she'd read it and respond to Julian later when she had a moment to herself.

Logan bent and tucked a blanket more snugly around Charlie, who was completely zoned out by now. In the distance, the train slowed and then stopped. "Switching tracks, it looks like," Logan said. "The northbound train's just arriving, too."

"Is all your shopping done?" she asked Logan, talking to fill the silence rather than out of any true curiosity.

To her surprise, he slipped his arm around her waist. "Yeah," he said. "I got everything I need."

He said something else, but it was drowned out by the gnashing of brakes from the train arriving on the opposite track.

"That's good," she said, somewhat bemused by his arm around her. Ever since he'd kissed her that one time, she kept catching herself wondering, playing a slightly different version of *What if…?* As in, *What if Logan and I…?*

Unperturbed by the noise in the station, Charlie slept on.

Across the way, the train from the city closed its doors and pulled away. At the same time, the southbound train rode a surge of steam into the station. One going, one coming, Charlie drowsing in his stroller.

At that moment, the departing train and blowing steam left her a clear view of the just-arrived passengers on the opposite track, twelve feet across the way. She saw people carrying luggage and shopping bags stuffed with brightly-wrapped packages, filled with surprises.

Then her gaze was caught by a tall young man standing alone on the platform, an olive-drab duffel bag at his feet and a glossy blue shopping bag in hand. Broad shoulders and a proud bearing. A service cap barely covering impossibly short hair. His beautiful mahogany-colored face matching the one she dreamed about far too frequently.

She didn't—couldn't—speak. Surprise took her voice away. Her lips formed his name:

Julian.

It was impossible, but there he was, a look of puzzlement, then confusion, on his face. Suddenly Logan's arm around Daisy felt like a dead weight. And then, just as quickly, Julian was gone, obliterated by the arriving southbound train.

"Here we go," Logan said cheerfully, having completely missed the unexpected arrival. He took his arm from around her. "All aboard. Can you give me a hand here?"

Daisy's limbs felt sluggish, her mind on fire. There was a line at the nearest train car, so they had to wait. She kept craning her neck, wondering if she was seeing things. No way. That was Julian. What was he doing here after he'd sworn he wasn't coming, apologizing all over the place? And more, what was he thinking?

She stood next to Logan on the platform, waiting their turn to board the train with their overnight bags and Charlie and the stroller. When a delay was announced over the PA system, Daisy stepped to the area between cars and looked across at the now empty platform. Where had he gone?

Grabbing the mobile phone from her pocket, she opened it to read his message—Surprise, coming for Xmas after all. Noon train. See you soon. Love, J.

She sent a wild look at the clock. Oh, no. Oh, God. Oh, no. Then, as though conjured up by her yearning and confusion, Julian emerged onto the platform, his cap gone, his chest heaving with exertion. "Daisy," he said.

"I thought you weren't coming for Christmas."

"I'm using up every minute of a forty-eight-hour leave," he said. "But…where are you going?"

"None of your business," Logan snapped, striding across the platform. "Later, pal. She's with me."

"Hey," Daisy said sharply. "You can't just leave Charlie parked in the stroller like that!" Exasperated with both of them, she hurried over and grabbed the stroller, maneuvering it around. She returned in time to see them facing off, drawing the curiosity of onlookers. Great, she thought. Just great. They each looked menacing in their own way, Julian in his ROTC uniform, handsome as a recruiting poster, and Logan assuming a protective stance, the weak afternoon light glinting off his fiery red hair. They seemed oblivious to everything around them, even Daisy.

"…had a problem with you since day one," Julian was saying.

"You think I care about that?" Logan demanded.

It was hard to tell who pushed first. They clashed like a pair of freight trains, the steam of the engine swirling around them, a small crowd gathering. Daisy shoved herself directly between them, narrowly missing a flying punch. "Cut it out," she yelled. "Quit acting like a pair of jerks."

"'Top it!" yelled Charlie, now awake in his stroller.

Logan barely slowed down as he neatly went around Daisy, intent on another attack. Julian stepped aside at the last possible second, causing Logan to lurch to the edge of the platform. He teetered there, arms windmilling at empty air. Daisy screamed, flashing on an image of Logan dying under the train's wheels. Just as quickly, Julian grabbed a fistful of Logan's jacket and hauled him back. Momentum from the quick save propelled them backward, and they fell in a heap. The fight didn't end, though. Logan muscled his way out of Julian's grasp and turned toward him, fists flying. Clothing ripped and things erupted from their pockets—coins, keys, a pocket knife, a subway token, a single leather glove.

"That's it," Daisy said, bodily inserting herself between them again, so pumped with adrenaline that she was able to stop a flailing fist. Both guys stepped back, breathing hard, sweating despite the cold.

At some point during the shoving match, a small velvet box had hit the platform and popped open. The glare from a fluorescent overhead light struck the contents—a diamond solitaire, winking at her.

"Oh," Daisy said, looking from one guy to the other, her head abuzz with confusion. "Oh," she said again. "You dropped something."

21

There was something almost ritualistic in the way a champagne bottle was opened—the quick peel of the metallic foil, the unwinding of the wire basket and the slow, inevitable twisting of the cork. You never quite knew when the cork was going to blow, but the wise drinker took care to keep the neck of the bottle angled away from his face. The entire ritual lasted about twenty-three seconds, Eddie reckoned, because for some reason he didn't understand, he was counting the twists of the cork. Twenty-three seconds to wash away years of hard-won sobriety.

The cork blew with a satisfying *thwok,* and thumped against the ceiling of the kitchen. He didn't have a champagne flute, so he poured the dancing liquid into a juice glass from the cabinet over the sink. He watched the tiny bubbles surge upward in the glass, each one a celestial bead of promise.

At times like this, he was supposed to call Terry Davis, the guy who was his sponsor here in Avalon. But the holidays were here and Eddie didn't want to be a pest. This year in particular, Terry was preoccupied, with his first grandchild on the way; his son Connor and daughter-in-law Olivia were expecting. Eddie knew damned well that wasn't how the program worked. When you were about to take a drink, you called your sponsor, end of story. Do not pass go, do not pick up that cold, delicious glass of oblivion and carry it to your lips, do not—

A sharp knock at the door broke into the moment. Eddie set down the glass and went to answer it, glancing at the clock as he crossed the room. Still hours to go before it was time for the pageant.

"Hey, Mr. Haven," said Omar Veltry, pushing inside without waiting to be invited. "Check this out. We got something to show you." He was followed inside by his two brothers, then Jabez and Cecil.

"Check what out?" Eddie said.

"You online over here?" Randy demanded, barging toward Eddie's laptop, which was set up at the dining room table.

Eddie's laptop was a musician/composer's dream, tricked out with all the bells and whistles needed for music production. He planted himself protectively in front of it. "Whoa, slow down. What do you want with my laptop?"

"You gotta hear this," said Moby. "Cecil made it from our session with you the other day."

"Cecil, man, you're a freakin' genius, that's what you are," Omar said, typing in an address.

"Hey," Eddie started to object.

"Just listen," Jabez said.

A moment later, his original song came through the

speakers, the one he'd written for Maureen. No, for the program, he corrected himself. A video appeared, showing a montage of shots from the PBS filming—the crew had been covering rehearsals all week. The images were interspersed with still-life winter scenes by Daisy Bellamy. There were live-action studio shots of Eddie himself, recording the song. It was a surprisingly professional production, mixed in a way that was curiously mesmerizing.

"You did this?" he asked Cecil.

"Yep," he said with a shy grin.

"He's a mad geek," Omar added. "A genius."

"Look at the stats," Randy said. "Look at all those hits. It went viral, man."

"You're gonna be famous all over again," Omar added.

Eddie felt queasy. He didn't want to be famous. "Take it down," he said to Cecil. "Seriously—"

"Wait, check this out," Moby said. "He set it up to enable downloads."

"For the library," Cecil interjected. "Every download sends a donation to the library."

"No way," Eddie said. "That's insane."

"That's the Internet, man," Omar said.

Eddie stepped back, incredulous. "You're sure that's how it works?"

"That's exactly how it works," said Jabez.

"Wait till Miss Davenport sees this," Randy said. "She's going to love you for it, man."

"Doubtful," said Eddie.

"They're fighting," said Omar.

"How do you know we're fighting?" Eddie demanded.

"That's what Jabez said."

"And how do *you* know?" Eddie asked the boy.

He shrugged. "Lucky guess?"

Eddie furrowed his fingers through his hair. "I screwed up," he admitted.

"You did," the brothers agreed.

"I've got a lot of work to do."

They nodded in unison. "What are you going to do about it?" asked Randy.

"Me?" Eddie asked. "Nothing I can do."

Jabez chuckled. "Right. We have to go get ready for tonight. See you later, Eddie."

They left in a jostling whirlwind. Eddie stood listening to the music on the computer. Those kids were amazing, producing this practically out of nothing. A totally unlikely friendship had sprung up between the ultracool Veltry brothers, Jabez and geeky Cecil Byrne. Without the pageant, they never would have become friends. Thrown together, they'd made this…this thing people all over the world were downloading at a furious rate.

Eddie dared to scroll down to read some of the comments, which already numbered in the thousands. Damn. He was famous all over again. Not exactly what he wanted, but if the boys were right, this might be exactly what the library needed. Holy crap, thought Eddie. It was his own personal Christmas miracle.

He went back into the kitchen. There was no hesitation. He took the champagne bottle in one hand and the glass in the other, clinking them together in a toast. "Cheers," he said, and poured everything down the drain.

22

Maureen was proud of herself for not falling apart over Eddie Haven. She'd known from the start that he was a mistake, but she'd been swept away. She'd allowed herself to forget the pain and shame and risk that came from handing her heart over to another person. Ignoring the lessons of the past, she had dared to dream of a future. Where had that foolishness come from? She should have known better. Eddie had blinded her. He was like that, as dazzling as the sun.

Her doorbell rang, causing her heart to leap, proving that even though she'd resigned herself to the end of her and Eddie, some foolish part of her still dared to hope. She fixed her hair and straightened her sweater, then opened the door.

"Oh," she said. "Mr. Shannon." One look at his face, and she knew something was wrong.

"I wanted to tell you in person." The president of the library board took off his knitted cap. "It's about the library fund."

Her spirits sank. "We didn't make our goal," she said.

He nodded, his face bleak. "I'm sorry to tell you this on Christmas Eve. I'm going on vacation tomorrow night and won't be seeing you until…until the closure is done, and I wanted to tell you in person."

"So what you're saying is, the library will be closed for good."

"Maureen, I'm so sorry. I don't know what else to say."

There was nothing left to say. She simply nodded her head, accepting the inevitable. The emotional one-two punch of Eddie, followed by the library failure, left her reeling. Somehow, she managed to keep a brave face as she insisted on making up a plate of cookies for him, then bade him a merry Christmas.

Just get through tonight's performance, she told herself. After that, she'd throw herself into finding a new job. And she'd never have to deal with Eddie Haven again. For the time being, the best therapy was to stay busy. For pity's sake, stay busy.

It was easy enough to do. She still had a few last-minute gifts to put together. She took special care with her mail carrier's annual assortment of Christmas cookies. Maureen's street was at the end of Carolyn's route. On Christmas Eve, it would be one of the final deliveries before the holiday kicked into high gear. A sweet treat at the end of the day would be just right for Carolyn. Maureen chose a selection of iced lemon bars, chocolate mint gems, soft molasses cookies and gingerbread men.

She nestled each morsel in wax paper in a pretty basket and found a CD with her favorite Christmas songs to tuck in, as well. The cats deemed her tears boring and padded away to nap by the radiator. Tears? Good heavens, she was working with tears pouring down her face; she was falling apart at the seams. Pull it together, she admonished herself. She turned on the TV for company while she worked.

When she heard the familiar opening strains of *The Christmas Caper,* she hurried to change the channel…and then stopped herself. Just because she and Eddie were over didn't mean she had to go cold turkey. She still had to live in a world where this movie played, where his photo ran in the occasional magazine and his voice came over the radio. There was no point in hiding.

She had to prove she could survive the hurt. This meant letting herself feel the pain, acknowledge the terrible lash across her heart and carry on in spite of it.

Almost defiantly, she turned up the volume just in time to hear little Jimmy Kringle deliver a line: "I'm not giving up hope, I swear I'm not."

"You go right on hoping, little fella. See where it gets you," said the cynical Beasley, who played the head of the orphanage.

There was no reason a cringe-inducing line like that should work, yet in the context of the heart-touching movie, it did. For a moment, Maureen just stared at the boy's face on the screen. He was every child who had ever been scared and lonely. That was his magic. The naked yearning in his enormous eyes was palpable. He showed the kind of vulnerability most people kept inside, buried beneath layers of protective armor. Eddie left it all out there, as a small child and all his life. Even in this performance, he was emotionally fearless. She knew now that this talent had led him to highs and lows, to falling in love repeatedly, to feeling pain so deeply he tried to numb it by drinking, and finally to have the courage to change.

He claimed she never truly took a leap of faith, that she was always hedging her bets. Was she? Perhaps so, but flinging herself into things—into passion, music, love—was just not her way of conducting herself. She couldn't turn into someone else. She did believe there was a way to live her life without fear, to bring meaning into every moment. It was up to her to find optimism and faith, even in the midst of heartbreak. That would be her project, then, she thought, her way of getting over him.

He'd grown into a remarkable man, she thought, but she was not so starry-eyed about him that she considered him perfect. He was flawed and human. His issues with his parents ran deep. She should know better than to fall for a guy who didn't want to be around his own parents. A guy like that couldn't be right for her. Could he?

She put the finishing touches on the mail carrier's gift, dangling the last of the curly ribbon to Franklin and Eloise to play with. The cats leaped upon it as though it was the treasure of Sierra Madre. She stared at the face filling the screen now. No wonder she'd fallen in love with Eddie. She thought about the pain he was actually feeling at that age and the unhappy times he'd had with his family at Christmas. "I'm sorry," she said. "I didn't realize how much it would hurt you. I didn't know it would ruin us."

These were things she needed to say to the real Eddie. And she would. Maybe. Just not…not now. He made her care too much, feel too much. Maybe that had been what had driven her to contact his parents. Perhaps she'd felt a secret need to throw an obstacle in the way and she'd found the perfect

thing—his parents. Meddling where she had no business—
what better way to sabotage their relationship? No. That wasn't
her motivation and she knew it. The reason she'd contacted
his parents, the reason she wanted him to reconnect, was that
she loved him. Against all good sense, she loved him and
wanted him to be happy.

Her immediate concern was to put on a Christmas pageant
that would not be a complete disaster. That, and get her emotional body armor back in place, praying the hairline cracks
would not become a gaping wound.

In the falling twilight, the streetlights diffused by snow
flurries, she saw the mail carrier approaching and hurried
down with her basket of homemade cookies. Despite the
snow, Carolyn had a spring in her step, probably because the
workday was nearly over.

"I'll trade you," said Maureen, holding out the gift basket.

Carolyn's face lit up. "From the cookie exchange?"

"That's right."

"You're an angel." She handed Maureen a batch of mail.

"Ditto," said Maureen, sifting through the stack. Plenty of
junk mail, ads for sexy garments she would never wear, places
she would never go. There were also Christmas cards—a few
stragglers from people in far-off places. And, at the bottom of
the stack, an official-looking business envelope. "Oh," she said.

"Everything all right?"

"Yes." Maureen turned the envelope over, touched her
thumb to the return address. "This is the kind of thing you
both expect and dread. I believe it's a contract for another job."

"You're leaving?"

"I might not have a choice. Everyone's worked so hard to keep the library from closing, but we fell short. There's no way to reach the goal in time."

"Change is always hard," Carolyn observed. "But it's usually for the best, right?"

"Right."

"Merry Christmas," Carolyn said. "Thanks again for the cookies. See you at the pageant tonight."

Maureen managed a wobbly smile. Then she fled upstairs and ripped open the envelope. There it was in black and white. An offer from the securities firm in Boston. She would be a corporate librarian, in charge of company documents and archives. It was for a bigger salary than she had ever dreamed of. And it couldn't have come at a better time. A securities firm. Even the name sounded—well, secure. Safe. She ought to be feeling a sense of relief, not defeat.

She dressed for the evening in clothes she believed suited a pageant director—a charcoal-gray wool jumper, dark leggings and knee boots with low heels and soft soles. The outfit suited someone who was meant to be behind the scenes, in the background. Invisible.

Her one concession to whimsy was to don the Christmas earrings the little ones had given her. For a moment she was tempted to wear her hair long and loose, the way she had the night of the tavern. No. She didn't want to send the wrong message and besides, her hair would only get in the way.

"I need to quit fussing over myself," she told the cats, expertly clipping her hair into a bun. "You two wish me luck. It's showtime."

23

The Inn at Willow Lake was festooned with twinkling lights strung from the trees along the driveway. Gaslights glowed along the railed porch and electric candles lit the windows of the large historic building. A grand Christmas tree dominated the bay window in the front. There was something achingly pretty about the place, a warm quality that filled Eddie with a peculiar nostalgia. Peculiar, because he wasn't looking back and remembering times past. Instead he was remembering the past he'd never had. It was the kind of scene that would make Maureen exclaim with delight. If she were speaking to him, anyway.

He parked and walked up to the front door, lifting his collar high to protect his neck from the knife blades of wind blowing off the frozen lake. He hurried inside to the Christmas tree room—a large Victorian parlor with a roaring fire in the white marble fireplace.

Several guests milled around, listening to music or playing

board games at the occasional tables around the room. Two women immediately leaned toward each other, whispering. He took care not to make eye contact. His parents were waiting by the big central hearth, their faces wreathed in smiles. Their cheery expressions were so well practiced that Eddie was probably the only one around who understood there was nothing behind the smiles and words of welcome.

"Oh, Eddie," said his mother, folding her arms around him. "Let's sit." She drew him to a dainty-looking sofa and chairs by the fireplace. He could feel some of the other guests in the lobby looking on. To outsiders, the three Havens probably resembled the all-American family—Mom and Pop and their strapping son, having a reunion just in time for Christmas.

"We were just having a cup of coffee," his father said. "You want some?"

"I'm good, thanks." Eddie was surprised. Finally it struck him. Something was different about his parents. They seemed... more present. And they lacked that powerful sharp perfume of early-afternoon cocktails, a smell forever associated with his childhood.

"I can't wait to get to know Maureen Davenport better. It was so kind of her to pay us a visit. She certainly seems taken with you. We've been hoping for a long time that you'd meet someone special," his mother said.

Eddie wondered how to explain his and Maureen's relationship. Up until recently, he thought they were something—until Maureen went behind his back and drew aside the curtain of his past. What the hell did she expect to accomplish? Now he didn't know what to think, or what to tell his folks.

"She's pretty special, but—"

"And she thinks you hung the moon," his mother finished for him. "Finally, Eddie."

"She doesn't actually think that anymore," he admitted. "I kind of blew it with her."

"Why, because she invited us here?" Larry asked.

Eddie stared at his father. Shit. Had Maureen—

"She didn't say a word," his mother said, correctly reading Eddie's expression.

"Don't look so shocked," Larry said with a hint of a smile. "We know more than you think we know."

His mother's smile was less assured. "We understand why this isn't your favorite time of year, and we wanted to talk to you about it, try to explain."

"I'm not asking for an explanation, Barb," he said. "I've figured out a way to spend the holiday that works for me."

"We're hoping to find a way that works for *us*. As a family. Ah, Eddie. We did our best. Granted, our best wasn't always so hot. Those years we spent Christmas on the road—we did it for you."

Right, he thought, that was always a real picnic for me. He said nothing.

"We believed it was a good way to distract you from thinking about all the things we didn't have and couldn't give you. We were broke, Eddie, and didn't want you to know."

"What the hell—" He stopped himself, realizing he'd raised his voice. "What do you mean, broke?"

His parents exchanged a glance. "Your grandparents both got sick and their union coverage wasn't enough," his father explained. "That assisted-living place, the one we visited so often, wasn't covered at all. Keeping up with their expenses took nearly everything we had. Most years, that meant skipping the big holiday extravaganza. We thought it would be less painful to do something entirely out of the main-stream. You were such a quiet boy, never complaining. When you hit the stage every night, you lit up like a Christmas tree, literally. We had no idea it was bothering you."

Eddie sank down onto a chair. "You should have said some-thing. I would have understood." He wondered if his life would have been different if they'd simply leveled with him. Maybe he wouldn't have grown to resent the holidays. Maybe he wouldn't have been so angry in college and so desperate to fit in that he drank himself into oblivion every chance he got. No, he thought, dropping the maybes and what-ifs. You don't get to look back. You look ahead.

He kept his mouth shut, stared down at his hands, carefully lining up his fingers in the shape of a steeple. Deep inside him, something unfurled and flew free—old resentments, the last of them, the ones he never talked about at meetings because he didn't want to admit they were there. Then he lifted his head and regarded his parents, who weren't perfect but who loved him, and a kind of pleasant resignation settled over him. A kind of peace. "It's okay," he said quietly. "It's okay."

"Son," said Larry, "I had my pride. Too much of it. And FYI, you're never going to have to deal with something like that. Your mother and I took out a policy."

"You didn't have to do that."

"We did it for you. Are we good, son?" Larry asked.

"Yeah," said Eddie. "We're good." It was a good start, anyway. They all knew they weren't going to resolve a lifetime of issues over one holiday, but the door had cracked open.

A small sigh of relief escaped his mother. "Well, then. Tell us more about this Maureen Davenport. She said you've composed an original work for the Christmas program."

"It's good to see you showing your talent," Larry interjected, "instead of hiding who you really are."

"I'm sure the program is going to be one for the ages," his mother said, clasping her hands in delight.

Eddie looked from one parent to the other, feeling all the years of his childhood weirdly compressed into this moment in time. The three of had been an unconventional family in many ways, but they'd been a *family*. They'd looked out for each other and made music together, and fought and laughed and lived their lives in each other's company. He remembered a childhood of moving from place to place, wishing he belonged somewhere. Maureen had made him remember the laughter and affection, and the fact that he always felt safe and loved, even when he was in the back of the van eating HoHos and staring out the window at strangers in unfamiliar places. When he looked at his parents, he no longer saw everything he did not want to be. He saw people who were flawed but who wanted him to be happy.

He could be happy with Maureen. He knew it, and that was why, like an idiot, he'd pushed her away. Something in him didn't think he deserved her.

"Yeah," Eddie said, "about that. I have a favor to ask."

* * *

Maureen had one stop to make on the way to the performance. It would only take a few minutes, and she was neurotically early for the pageant, anyway, so there was no need to hurry. She stopped by the library. After hours, it was eerily deserted, a quiet and somber place. She thought about one of her favorite novels, *Children of the Book,* about some kids who get locked in the library after closing time. At first frightened, they gained wisdom and ultimately salvation from the books they read.

Performing her lifelong ritual, Maureen turned down a random aisle. Eyes shut, she ran her hand along the spines of the book, stopping when she felt just the right one. She pulled it out, let it drop open and placed her finger on a page. Then she opened her eyes.

"Launder garments in the shape in which they are to be worn: zipped, velcroed, and buttoned up, with pockets emptied and cuffs unrolled. The simplest nontoxic stain removal method is cold water and ice.—Martha Stewart." So that was what the library had to say to her. After reading the snippet aloud, she shut the book, muttering, "Good to know."

There were no revelations here or anywhere else, no easy answers. Just an old, venerable and doomed institution. She saw the latest *Troubadour*—true to his word, Lonnie had written a letter to the editor.

To the editor and people of Avalon: This is the first time I ever wrote a letter like this so excuse me if I screw something up. Two years ago I couldn't write hardly anything except my name. This was embarrassing. but also it made me stop dreaming about doing anything with my life. I didn't learn to read in first grade like most people. I learned at age twenty-four, from Miss Maureen Davenport at the library, in the adult literacy program. Last year I earned a GED and started my own trucking company. Without the library, I never would of learned. If the library closes, how many people like me will miss out? I can't give you a number because most are like me, afraid they might seem dumb or weak. She didn't just teach me to read. She gave me back my dream. Don't let the library close. Or you will close the doors on someone's dream. Hugo Lonigan.

"I'm so sorry," she whispered to the ghosts and echoes that haunted the marble halls. "It's going to be hard to say goodbye." It was probably a good thing she'd be moving away. Living in Boston, she wouldn't have to watch the building and its surroundings transformed into a commercial center of shops and boutique hotels.

On the way out, she noticed the collection cart under the book return slot was filled to overflowing, likely from people returning materials after a last-minute holiday cleaning. Several books littered the floor. Out of habit, she picked them up. The last one flopped open, and a phrase on the page caught her eye: "Unless you change direction, you'll wind up where you're headed."

24

Outside, the snow flurries had abated, giving way to a cold, crystalline twilight sky, pierced by early stars. As far as she could tell, Maureen was the first to arrive at the church. She'd cautioned the parents of the little ones against arriving too early. The kids would be keyed up and rambunctious, and they'd end up running off their energy and ruining their costumes. Not that there were any costumes to ruin. That had already been done at the storage unit. So late in the game, all she'd been able to do was tell the parents to try something creative.

She paused in the parking lot, tilting her head back to look up. She must remember to always look up, to keep the world around her in perspective. The endless bowl of night reminded her of the vastness of the unknown, shrinking her troubles to the size of a pinprick.

Focus, she thought, letting herself in and turning on a few lights. Don't try to think about the fact that we're not ready,

that the pageant is a disaster in the making. She'd set out with
such a grand vision. She had imagined the spectacle filling
everyone with a sense of reverence and wonder. Instead, the
costumes weren't ready, the little ones barely knew the words
to their songs and the program was full of stumbling blocks.
The final dress rehearsal had been a nightmare. She didn't even
want to think about the voice mail that had been waiting for
her this morning. Two of the four musicians in the ensemble
were sick. She'd called Ray Tolley in a panic. He'd tried to
reassure her, but he hadn't sounded happy. And—icing on the
cake—the entire debacle was being recorded for national TV.
The film crew had reassured her that editing would make the
production look fine, but she took no comfort in that, not
with the live performance looming in front of her.

She stepped inside and turned on the lights. At least the stage
was in readiness, fragrant with the scent of the pine bough swags
that decorated the sanctuary. Brass urns of holly branches and
potted poinsettias lined the aisles. The musicians' area to the side
was crammed with Ray's keyboard and an array of amps, speakers
and a multichannel powered mixer with tiny stand-by lights
flickering. To her surprise, a drum set had been added to the mix.

Deep breath, she told herself. Take a deep, calming breath.
She searched inside herself for a glimmer of hope. Christmas
had always had a magical effect on Maureen and her life. No
matter how bad things got for her, she always managed to find
hope and healing at Christmas. There was something about the
holiday spirit of kindness and generosity that nurtured the soul.

This was supposed to be her moment—a night of song and
celebration, something she'd always wanted to do.

Then again, maybe Eddie was onto something, she thought with a twinge of cynicism. Despite everything she'd hoped the pageant would be, she felt glum about its prospects. She was preoccupied by the library closure, by her aching heart and haunted by the most singularly bad final rehearsal she had ever witnessed. Maybe, just like Eddie had said, she was wrong about the magic. At the moment, it certainly seemed that way.

"Thanks for being here," Maureen said to Olivia, who was serving as her assistant backstage. "It's now or never."

"Relax," Olivia said. "It's going to be fine."

"How many disasters have been preceded by that statement?" Maureen wondered aloud. "I bet that's what people said right before the *Titanic* hit the iceberg." She leaned forward to peek out through a gap in the curtain. Nearly every single seat was filled. The film crew was set up, cables snaking along the side aisles. Excitement crackled in the air, and in spite of her misgivings, Maureen felt herself getting caught up. Even the usually dour Mr. Byrne was there, seated with his wife, his son and daughter-in-law. Maureen wondered if things might have worked out differently for the library if she'd complied with his request and given his grandson, Cecil, the angel's role. Doubtful, she thought. If she'd gone along with him, she'd be feeling even worse right now for having given a bully what he wanted.

"Five minutes," she said to Ray Tolley, who was about to go out and start tuning up. "Can you do it?"

He grinned. "No worries. Help is on the way."

"I need the help to be here right now," she said.

"Like I told you, no worries. It'll be fine." He studied her for a moment. "You okay?"

Maureen laughed, because she couldn't do anything else.

"Maybe after the program, you and Eddie might want to—"

"Eddie and I don't want to do anything together," she said, cutting him off. "Sorry, but it's not like that for us. In fact, when this is all over tonight, I'm going to ask the court to declare that his community service is fulfilled."

Ray smiled. "Didn't you know? That ended for Eddie years ago." He headed for his keyboard.

It took a moment for the words to sink in. Eddie had let her believe he was court ordered to work on the Christmas pageant. In reality, he was doing it…why? Why on earth would Mr. I-Can't-Stand-Christmas subject himself to weeks of the holiday, year in and year out?

She spotted him on the opposite side of the stage and caught his eye. He shot her a look that was unreadable, but gave her a thumbs-up sign as though everything was all right.

All right?

She found Jabez, getting into position. "You're wearing *that?*" she asked.

He shrugged, seeming unconcerned by his jeans and hooded sweatshirt. "I'm an existential angel," he said simply. "Don't worry. It'll be fine."

There was no time to argue. The music started with a few uncertain notes. Then the overture took off, the melody soaring to the rafters, mingling with the subtle aroma of frankincense. Startled by the majestic sound, she leaned forward to see not just Ray on the keyboards, but his bandmates Noah on drums and Bo Crutcher playing the bass. In addition, there were—she did a double take—Eddie Haven's father on guitar, his mother with a tambourine, warbling backup vocals as the first number commenced. The little shepherds and angels had indeed improvised, all of them in pajamas. *Pajamas.* It should have looked ridiculous, but instead was adorable. And that was only the start. Nothing was as she'd envisioned. Then the Angel of the Lord appeared, and magic took over.

Jabez's voice transcended everything, holding the entire audience in its thrall. The holy family showed up in ordinary street clothes, though Cecil Byrne's Joseph added a touch of humor with a T-shirt that said Eat at Joe's. Maureen was so busy orchestrating everything behind the scenes she didn't see Eddie take the stage with his acoustic guitar. Seated on a stool in the middle, a single candle burning nearby, he offered his song like a benediction. The melody alone was beautiful, enhanced by lovely backup vocals from his own parents. Maureen felt their emotions mingling together, and the performance seemed at once intimate and expansive, a song that spoke to everyone in different ways.

Somewhere, somehow, between the first "And it came to pass" to the final "Hallelujah," the magic did its best work. Maureen felt tears in her eyes. She was as enraptured as everyone in the congregation, faces aglow, voices raised, joined in a rousing "Joy to the World," filling the sanctuary with the special grace Maureen had been looking for all season long. It was a beautiful program, and the applause at the end of it all was thunderous. She never should have doubted it.

During the final ovation, she spied Jabez, grinning from ear to ear. She touched his arm.

"It's a miracle we pulled it off."

His grin softened into a sweet, shy smile. "Nah, I wouldn't say that."

"Good point. A lot of work went into that miracle."

He nodded. "A lot of things would be lost or undone if people sat around, waiting for a miracle."

She studied him for a moment, such a singular boy, so open but at the same time hard to know. "Are they here tonight?" she asked him. "Your family?"

He looked around at the surging crowd, ducked his head a little bashfully. "Yeah, they're all here."

She wanted to ask who he meant, but they were both soon swept and separated by the crush of people everywhere. Maureen found herself swimming in accolades. People brought her flowers and cards, homemade candies and shiny-bright gift bags. "That was so wonderful," someone told her. "It made my heart soar," declared somebody else.

"Mine, too," she said, regarding the milling crowd with apprehension. The place emptied out quickly, as people were eager to head off into the night. Maureen didn't want to ruin the buoyant feeling in her heart with a confrontation with Eddie. Inviting his family to Avalon had been a mistake; she was well aware of the blunders she'd made. But it was done, and so were she and Eddie. There was no point in mooning about it. She ought to be grateful she'd ended their relationship sooner rather than later.

Suddenly the urge to flee overtook her. She had to get out

of here before she lost it. She needed to be alone right now. And tomorrow, she wanted to celebrate Christmas with her family as she'd always done, and then move on.

Moving furtively through the crowd, she headed for the back door. She paused on her way out, looked around at the luminous decorations and gave thanks for all the blessings that were hers. She had an adored and adoring family, her friends, her cats and her good health. And she had a future, perhaps not the one she'd expected, but one she would grow into cautiously, getting used to her new life bit by bit.

Then she left the sanctuary through the back, shutting the door firmly behind her.

Part Six

Christmas gift suggestions:

> *To your enemy, forgiveness.*
> *To an opponent, tolerance.*
> *To a friend, your heart.*
> *To a customer, service.*
> *To all, charity.*
> *To every child, a good example.*
> *To yourself, respect.*

—Oren Arnold (1900-1980)
American writer and editor

25

Maureen didn't sleep well that night. The headboard of her bed was still decked with the colored lights Eddie had laughingly hung there, just before he'd made love to her. She curled herself into a ball and tried not to think about it, but the memories of that night wouldn't leave her alone. She could still remember every touch, every kiss, every whispered promise.

Let it go, she tried to tell herself. Let it go. It never would have worked, anyway. They were too different, she had to accept that. But she couldn't. He'd brought laughter and love into her life, and now it was gone. She felt completely emptied out, and she wondered if, in fact, Eddie was right about Christmas after all.

No, she thought, drawing the covers over her head. She wouldn't let him be right. Just because she'd let him break her heart didn't mean he got to ruin Christmas for her, too. Somewhere in the distance, she could hear the sound of carols and loud chatter, and she decided it was a sign that someone, somewhere, agreed with her.

In the morning, she woke up slowly and cuddled with the cats, sipping hot tea and watching out the window. The world always looked different on Christmas morning. It was a quality of the light, a tingle in the air, that singular sensation that all was new. Merry and bright, as the old song went.

Kids were trying out their toys from Santa—sleds and ice skates, cross-country skis, snowshoes. Maureen loaded the car with all her carefully wrapped presents and headed to her parents' house, which by midday would be filled with family. Surrounded by them, she'd share in the laughter and love, watch the faces of her niece and nephews when they opened their presents, help prepare a sumptuous feast. She drove slowly and carefully, past strolling couples and families, rollicking children, the faint ringing of bells in the distance.

Her family swarmed her when she walked in the door. The niece and nephews were eager to show off their Santa gifts and then get down to the unwrapping. In the midst of the festivities, the doorbell rang.

"Maureen, would you mind getting that?" Hannah trilled.

She opened the door, and there was Eddie, looking tired but happy. "Merry Christmas, Moe," he said.

This man was bad for her heart. One simple greeting, and it was once again trying to leap out of her chest. "Um, same to you."

"I brought you something." His smile could melt icicles.

"Oh! I didn't get you anything, Eddie, I—"

"Hush. I'm not worried about a gift from you." He stepped aside and held the door wide open.

There, on the street in front of the house, was Lonnie's big flatbed truck, hastily swagged with pine boughs and jammed with passengers—library patrons she recognized, kids and adults alike. Others congregated on the snowy lawn. What appeared to be the whole town had shown up. Christmas music streamed from speakers.

"Now hear this." Mr. Shannon's voice spoke over the music. "The Avalon Free Library is staying open. Just after midnight, the funding goal was reached."

Maureen walked out onto the porch, her family crowding around behind her, and a cheer went up. "We're keeping the library!" people shouted.

She turned back to Eddie. "What did you do?"

He told her that like a parade float, Lonnie's truck had lumbered through the streets of Avalon all night long, exhorting people to save the library. Others had gone door to door, soliciting donations and pledges. Kids and their parents had pitched in. Emergency e-mails had gone out, and a phone tree of volunteers had worked tirelessly. The boys in the pageant, with Cecil Byrne taking the lead—had hastily produced a version of his Christmas song and offered it up on the Internet, with each download adding to the library fund. The combined effort pushed them over the top. The library would be safe.

Maureen was speechless for quite a while. She hugged everyone, she cried, she laughed. "We got our library back," she told anyone who would listen. There was a spontaneous songfest right there on the frozen front lawn.

Eddie took Maureen by the hand and drew her inside, to a quiet corner by the fireplace. She wanted to beg him not to touch her, not to remind her that there were some things that couldn't be fixed, not even by an entire community. Still another part of her wanted to hold on to him and never let go. Very carefully, she extracted her hand from his.

"What you did—what everyone did—it's just so huge, Eddie. How do I say thank you for something like this?"

He smiled down at her, then gently cupped her cheek in his hand and caught an errant tear with his thumb. "You just did."

Her gratitude was one thing, but it didn't begin to cover their troubles. She remembered how furious he was at her for inviting the Havens to the pageant. "And your parents?"

"I was pissed as hell that you told them to come here for Christmas."

"I shouldn't have interfered. It was wrong of me, and I'm sorry."

"Was it wrong if it worked out right?"

"What do you mean?"

Taking her by the shoulders, he turned her toward the kitchen, where her father and Hannah were serving coffee to the Havens. "There's nothing to forgive," he said gently in her ear. "I was a jerk, and you were right about them. I've never been with someone who made me want to be better than I am. I guess that's why I panicked and pushed you away."

She held hope at bay, not trusting what her heart kept telling her. She kept thinking about the previous night and how lonely she'd felt, how empty. She couldn't survive another night like that. "I'm happy for you, Eddie. And for your family. But the two of us...I just don't see it."

"Bullshit," he said. "Sorry. Baloney. You're hiding behind that old hurt, or using it as an excuse, I'm not sure which. And don't tell me you can't fall in love again because you might get your heart broken. Well, guess what, Maureen? You might. You wouldn't be the first, or the last. And guess what else? You might not get hurt at all—this could be exactly what you've been waiting for. But you're equally scared of both outcomes."

"Who made you such an expert?" she asked.

"I've been in love before," he said. "I just didn't stay that way. This time is different."

"How do you know?"

"I don't have any guarantees. Nobody does. But I have faith in us. Take a leap of faith with me, Moe. We can do this."

His words wrapped around her heart, and she stopped trying to tally up all the ways she might get hurt. Eddie had come through for her in so many ways. He'd saved the pageant, bringing in band members at the last minute. He'd had Lonnie drive a truck all over town to raise money for the library. She could trust Eddie with her heart; she finally knew this with a certainty that took her breath away. Slipping her arms around him, she pressed her cheek against his chest. "It was an amazing Christmas, wasn't it?"

"Uh-huh."

"I'll always wonder about Jabez, though. The mystery kid."

"Something tells me he's going to be just fine. And so are we, Moe." He lifted a sprig of mistletoe over her head and kissed her. "So are we."

Epilogue

One year later

"Hold it right there," Eddie said. "Smile." He snapped a picture of her as she hung a sign on her new office door: *M. Davenport—Branch Manager.*

These days, Maureen had a lot to smile about. Thanks to the now healthy library fund, she was able to expand her office beyond the little space she'd occupied previously. She and Eddie were cleaning out a big, unused space on the upper floor. It was going to be converted into a sleek new office, just for her.

She had a lot more to be thankful for, and a lot more to smile about, than just the library. In the aftermath of the most surprising and triumphant Christmas of her life, she'd had a glorious year. Her personal life had been turned upside down, and she couldn't be happier.

Well, she could. But the next step was up to Eddie, and she

wasn't going to push it. He lived in Avalon now, and for the past year, they had been nearly inseparable. They told each other more of their secrets, laughed together, sometimes fought, and always forgave each other. She greeted each day like a gift, soaring with love.

She used to think she knew what romantic love was. She thought she'd experienced true passion in her youth, and decided it was too risky and overwhelming. And then Eddie had come along, and everything changed. His presence in her life was like a love song in her heart—powerful and compelling, its gentle rhythm unending. With Eddie, she felt the expected giddiness, but there was something deeper. It was brand-new, and yet as old as time and familiar, although she'd never felt it before. She could not imagine spending any part of her life without him.

The notion made her smile even wider, because only a year ago, she hadn't been able to imagine spending even one moment with this man.

He surprised her at every turn, proving himself to be a man of his word who cared deeply for others, even burying his own hurt rather than bringing those around him down. He'd become her best, most intimate friend, entrusted with her deepest secrets. When she'd told him about the miscarriage, he'd held her while she cried, and then whispered that he wanted her to have his baby one day. Sometimes she thought she'd dreamed him. With his shaggy beach-boy hair, soulful eyes and athletic body, he was unbelievably sexy.

Just how sexy was something she had discovered this past year. And there was still a lot more to find out.

"All right, enough of that," he told her sharply, setting down a crate of old files.

"Enough of what?" she asked.

"Checking me out like that." He caught her against him, drew her close. "If you keep staring at me, we'll never get any work done."

She smiled up at him. "I think we earned a little break."

"Good plan," he murmured, and lightly kissed her, drawing a sigh from her lips.

The only thing that could have made her happiness more perfect would be to know they would be together forever, that this never had to end. Her stepmother was completely out of patience with the situation. "Cripes, Maureen, if you don't marry him, then *I* will," Hannah had said recently, all but stamping her foot in frustration.

Maureen refused to feel frustrated. He hadn't asked. He wasn't ready. She wasn't going to push. She tucked away a tiny snippet of disappointment and told herself not to be greedy. Still smiling, she kept her thoughts to herself; if he realized what was on her mind, he would probably go screaming into the hills.

"Hey, look outside," he whispered, turning her toward the window.

Snow had begun to fall in big flakes, settling softly on the sloping roof and turning the library grounds and gardens into a winter wonderland.

"The first snow of the year," she said. "I know I'll be sick of it by March, but the first snow always makes me happy."

"You know what always makes me happy?" he asked. "You do. And you always have."

Reaching up, she flung her arms around him. She couldn't believe she used to be afraid of this, afraid of feeling this much. There would be no more hiding in books to avoid making herself vulnerable. Now she wanted to feel everything, life in all its richness and depth. She never doubted she would stumble and fall, tripped up by hurt. Yet Eddie made her see that life was not about avoiding pain. It was about living every moment, good and bad.

So simple, she thought. That was the miracle of loving Eddie. That was—

A gust of Arctic air slipped through the window caulking, rattling the brittle glass panes and rustling through old papers stacked on the floor. Her gaze fell on an ancient yellowing newspaper. The *Avalon Troubadour* had been in publication for more than a century. The headline was spelled out in old-fashioned type: **UNIDENTIFIED BOY PERISHES IN LIBRARY FIRE.**

"Look," she said, "it's an article about the first library. I knew it burned to the ground a hundred years ago, but I've never seen an original account of the disaster." She stooped and picked up the yellowed paper, dry as leaves in autumn. She cradled the section carefully as she angled it toward the light.

It was front-page news, with a grainy photograph of the burned-out building. The article reported that apparently a vagrant had sought shelter at the library, hiding away after hours. A Mr. Jeremiah Byrne was quoted as saying, "I have the most profound of regrets over the life that was lost. Constructing the new library is an act of contrition for me."

Her attention was caught by one of the photographs that

accompanied the article. The caption read, *His life was cut short when he died in the fire.* Her heart skipped a beat, and she glanced up at Eddie.

"Is that…?" She didn't quite know how to ask it. "Do you see what I see?"

"Yeah," he said. "That's a ringer for Jabez."

"It's like some kind of miracle." She had the oddest feeling, looking at a photo from a hundred years ago and recognizing the features of the boy they'd once known, a boy who had slipped away after the performance last Christmas Eve and hadn't been seen since. *Truly* hadn't been seen. In going through Daisy Bellamy's photographs of last year's pageant, Maureen had not found a single shot of Jabez. The PBS documentary, *Small Town Christmas,* had recently aired, but there was no footage of him there, either. Josie, the producer, reported that some of the digital files of the filming had been corrupted.

"I knew there was something about Jabez," said Maureen. "He was…do you believe in angels?"

Eddie smiled at her. "Oh, hell, yeah."

"I'm not kidding. I—"

He pulled her close. "They come in all shapes and sizes. You were there the night I wrecked my van," he said.

She didn't say anything. They'd never talked about it.

"I thought you were an angel," Eddie said. "And I was right."

"That's impossible," she said. "Completely and utterly impossible."

"Sounds funny, coming from a girl who saved the library."

"You are giving me way too much credit. It was you, Eddie—"

"Nope. People didn't pitch in because of me. They did it because of you."

"I don't want to be that important," she insisted.

"Moe." He gently touched her cheek, caught a tear she didn't realize she'd shed. "You don't get to choose."

"The real miracle is what Christmas did to this town," she said, "and what it does to people's hearts, year in and year out, all over the world. You know I'm right."

"Fine, you're right. Now, back to what I was saying a few minutes ago…"

Her breath caught. Somehow she knew. But she was afraid to think it consciously, afraid she might be wrong. Yet she couldn't stop the hopes and prayers from leaping up in her heart. Please, she thought. Oh, please, ask me.

He laughed softly, bent down and brushed a kiss against her forehead. "I'm getting to that."

Oh. She hadn't realized she'd spoken aloud. In the past year, she'd grown much less guarded and prone to blurting things out. Still, she flushed deeply, though she couldn't suppress a goofy, crazy-in-love grin. "Getting to what?"

"You're going to make me say it, aren't you?"

"Every word."

"This could take a while, then. Because, see, I've been wanting to ask you for a long time. I spoke with your father, and he's good with this. Not that it would stop me if he disapproved."

"My father would never disapprove of something he knows I want with all my heart."

"You're getting ahead of me," Eddie said. "I had this long speech all planned out, and I wrote you a song, too, just for you."

"You what? You wrote me a song?"

"Just for you. I think you're gonna like it, too."

"Boy, I hope you know CPR," she said. "Because I am dying. Right here, right now."

"Okay, in that case, here's the short version." He sank down on one knee. "I love you, Maureen Davenport. I first fell in love with you when you locked me in the library to write that song. It was...you were amazing, Moe. You were the first person to make me show you who I really am. And then I knew it was forever when you brought my family here. I couldn't figure out why the hell you'd do that, except that you care so much. You cared enough to challenge me and piss me off and make me be better than I am. And that's how I always want it to be. So what do you say?"

Her voice was gone, washed away by wonderment and drenched in tears.

"A simple yes will do," he urged her, standing up and pulling her into his arms.

"Yes," she managed to whisper. "Yes, forever."

Appendix

*The Avalon Free Library Cookie Exchange
Recipe Book and Sing-Along*

Table of Contents

Jane Bellamy's Mint Meltaways

My old family recipe was a secret, until we realized everybody else knew about this perfect pairing of chocolate and mint.

Ingredients *(48 cookies)*

¾ cup butter

1 ½ cups brown sugar

2 tablespoons crème de menthe liqueur or water

12 ounces bittersweet chocolate chips

2 eggs

2 ¾ cups flour

½ teaspoon salt

1 ¼ teaspoons baking soda

24 Andes Mints

Directions

1. Preheat oven to 350°F.

2. In a saucepan, melt together the butter, brown sugar, and crème de menthe liqueur (or water), stirring occasionally.

3. Add the chocolate chips and stir until melted. Let stand 10 minutes to cool. Add the remaining ingredients and combine with a spatula to form a soft dough.

4. Wrap the dough and chill at least 1 hour.

5. Roll the dough into 1½-inch balls and place on a lightly greased cookie sheet, leaving ample space between the dough balls. Bake 8 to 9 minutes.

6. Remove the cookies from the oven, and on top of each cookie, place half of an Andes Mint. Allow the mint to melt and then swirl with the back of a spoon.

Song Suggestion:

"Silver Bells," performed by The Supremes

Eddie's "Shut Up and Sing" Blues Bars

Even a nonbeliever knows better than to refuse a Christmas cookie. Nobody ever said a skeptic has to be stupid. However, these are even better when baked by a true believer.

Ingredients *(28 bars)*

Crust

2 cups (approx. 8oz.) salted pretzels, finely crushed

¼ cup sugar

½ cup butter, melted

Filling

4 eggs

1 ½ cups sugar

¼ cup flour

½ teaspoon baking powder

4 teaspoons plus 1 tablespoon fresh lime zest

⅓ cup frozen margarita mix concentrate, thawed

4 tablespoons powdered sugar

Directions

1. Preheat the oven to 350°F.

2. Line a 9x13 inch baking dish with foil, allowing the foil to hang over the short sides. Lightly butter the top of the foil.

3. In a mixing bowl, combine the pretzels, sugar, and butter. Firmly press into the prepared dish. Bake until the crust is firm, about 10 minutes; remove from the oven.

4. Beat the eggs, then add sugar, flour, baking powder, and 4 teaspoons lime zest. Slowly add margarita mix.

5. Pour filling over the crust; bake 18-22 minutes or until the top is golden brown and the filling is set.

6. Let cool at least 1 hour. Just before serving, combine remaining lime zest and powdered sugar. Sprinkle over the top; cut into bars.

Song Suggestion:

"Hallelujah," performed by Jeff Buckley

Fairfield House Eggnog Cookies

It's every man for himself at the boardinghouse.
Best to make things in big batches.

Ingredients *(72 cookies)*

Cookies

2 ½ cups flour	1 ¼ cups sugar
1 teaspoon baking powder	½ cup eggnog
½ teaspoon ground cinnamon	1 teaspoon vanilla
1 tablespoon freshly grated nutmeg	2 egg yolks
	1-2 teaspoons rum extract
¾ cup butter, softened	or rum (optional)

Glaze

2 cups powdered sugar	around 1 teaspoon grated nutmeg
4 tablespoons eggnog	

Directions

1. Preheat oven to 325°F.

2. Combine flour, baking powder, cinnamon and nutmeg.

3. Beat together sugar and butter until creamy. Add eggnog, vanilla, egg yolks, and rum (if using); beat until smooth. Add flour mixture and beat to combine. Drop by teaspoonfuls 1 inch apart onto ungreased cookie sheet.

4. Bake 20 to 23 minutes until bottoms turn light brown.

5. Combine powdered sugar and eggnog. Drizzle over cookies. Before glaze dries, grate a pinch of fresh nutmeg over each cookie.

Song Suggestion:

"Christmas Song" by Jethro Tull

Inn at Willow Lake Snow Day Cookies

When snowed in, rummage around in the back of the pantry and dig out all the one-time-use ingredients, like cream of tartar and almond extract. This recipe will help polish them off.

Ingredients *(48 cookies)*

2 ¼ cups flour

1 teaspoon baking soda

1 teaspoon cream of tartar

1 cup butter, softened

1 ½ cups powdered sugar

1 egg

4 teaspoons orange zest

1 tablespoon orange juice

1 teaspoon almond extract

1 ½ cups dried cherries, chopped

½ cup chopped pistachios

4 ounces white baker's chocolate, melted

Directions

1. Preheat oven to 375°F.

2. In a medium bowl, stir together all-purpose flour, baking soda, and cream of tartar.

3. In a large bowl, beat butter with electric mixer for 30 seconds. Slowly add powdered sugar. Beat constantly until combined, scraping sides of bowl occasionally. Beat in egg, orange peel, orange juice, and almond extract. Mix in flour. Fold in cherries and pistachios.

4. Form dough into two rolls about 12 inches long. Chill in the refrigerator until firm enough to slice, about 1 hour.

5. Cut rolls into ½-inch slices, placing 2 inches apart on greased cookie sheets or ungreased parchment paper. Bake for 8 to 10 minutes or until the edges are firm and slightly golden brown. Transfer cookies to wire racks; let cool.

6. Drizzle each cookie with a small amount of melted white chocolate.

Song Suggestion:

"Rock and Roll Christmas" by George Thorogood and the Destroyers

Sky River Bakery Chocolate Crinkles

These cookies have a double shot of chocolate and espresso, helpful for staying up late on Christmas Eve.

Ingredients *(48 cookies)*

½ cup vegetable oil

4 squares unsweetened chocolate, melted

2 cups sugar

2 teaspoons vanilla

2 cups flour

2 teaspoons baking powder

1 teaspoon salt

2 teaspoons finely ground espresso

4 eggs

1 cup powdered sugar

Directions

1. Preheat oven to 350°F.

2. Mix oil, chocolate, and sugar. In a separate bowl, sift together flour, baking powder, salt, and espresso.

3. When chocolate mix is slightly cooled, beat in eggs one at a time. Mix in vanilla. Slowly add dry ingredients, mixing until dough forms. Chill 1 hour.

4. Roll dough into 1-inch balls and roll in powdered sugar. Place 2 inches apart on greased baking sheets. Bake 10-12 minutes, until edges are firm and the centers remain moist.

Song Suggestion:

"Dobry Vechir Toby," a traditional old-world carol

Romano Family Biscotti di Natale

*These are baked twice in the traditional fashion, and must
be consumed with a perfect cup of coffee.*

Ingredients *(70 biscotti)*

½ cup butter

⅔ cup sugar

3 eggs

½ teaspoon almond extract

½ teaspoon vanilla extract

2 ¼ cups flour

2 ½ teaspoons baking powder

1 tablespoon grated orange peel

½ cup chopped almonds

¾ cup candied fruit of
your choice, finely chopped

12 ounces white or dark
chocolate, melted

Directions

1. Preheat oven to 350°F.

2. In a large bowl, beat butter and sugar until creamy. Add eggs one at
   a time, beating one minute between eggs. Mix in extracts. Then add
   flour, baking powder, and white pepper, mixing until blended. Fold
   in almonds and fruit.

3. On a floured board, form dough into two logs. Place each log on a
   parchment-lined baking sheet and flatten slightly.

4. Bake for 25 to 30 minutes. Cool slightly, cut diagonally into ½-inch
   slices. Return biscotti to the oven for another 7 to 10 minutes, until
   crisp. When cool, dip one end of each biscotto into melted chocolate.
   Lay on wax paper until chocolate is set.

Song Suggestion:

"Adeste Fidelis," performed by Andrea Bocelli

Bo Crutcher's Potato Chip Cookies

Further proof that anything can be improved by the addition of potato chips. But don't tell anyone about the secret ingredient. Just watch them disappear.

Ingredients *(30-40 cookies)*

1 cup shortening

1 cup white sugar

1 cup brown sugar

2 eggs

1 teaspoon vanilla

2 ½ cups flour

1 teaspoon baking soda

2 cups potato chips, coarsely crushed

6 ounces butterscotch flavored chips

Directions

1. Preheat oven to 350°F.

2. In a large bowl, combine the sugars, shortening, eggs and vanilla. Add dry ingredients, mixing well. Stir in crushed potato chips and butterscotch chips.

3. Drop by rounded spoonfuls onto a lightly buttered cookie sheet.

4. Bake 10 to 12 minutes, or until edges are firm and lightly browned. Cool on a wire rack.

Song Suggestion:

"Have Yourself a Merry Little Christmas" by Twisted Sister

Noah Shepherd's "Roll Over" Dog Biscuits

Never forget the critters at Christmas.

Ingredients *(24 biscuits)*

2 cups whole-wheat flour

¾ cup rolled oats

½ cup powdered milk

1 egg, beaten

5 tablespoons vegetable oil

¼ cup water

1 cup applesauce

Directions

1. Preheat oven to 350°F.
2. In a large bowl, combine all ingredients to make a thick dough.
3. Knead on a lightly floured surface until no lumps remain. Sprinkle with flour, and roll out to ½-inch thickness.
4. Use cookie cutters or a small drinking glass to cut out desired shape. Place on an ungreased cookie sheet and bake until edges are lightly browned, about 22 minutes.
5. Let biscuits cool at least 1 hour before serving. Keep remaining treats in an airtight container.

Song Suggestion:

"Christmas is Going to the Dogs" by Eels

Polvorones (Mexican Wedding Cakes)

Un deseo cordial de la navidad para todo el mundo.

Ingredients *(36 cookies)*

2 cups flour

1 ⅓ cup pecans

1 cup butter, room temperature

2 teaspoons vanilla extract

1 cup sugar

½ teaspoon cinnamon

½ cup confectioners sugar

Directions

1. Preheat oven to 325°F.

2. Place flour and pecans in food processor and pulse until nuts are chopped. Add butter and vanilla and process until smooth. Add sugar and cinnamon and process to form a smooth dough, but don't overprocess.

3. Form dough into one-inch balls and place on a greased baking sheet. Bake 15-20 minutes, until firm but not brown. Cool on wire racks.

4. Dust the cooled cookies with confectioner's sugar through a sifter or strainer.

Song Suggestion:

"The Gift" by Stephanie Davis

Christmas Cookie Cut-Outs

No cookie exchange would be complete without cookies cut and decorated by the little ones. Keep plenty of colored icing and sprinkles on hand. These cookies are very tender, so don't roll them out too thin, or they'll break.

Ingredients *(About 36 cookies, depending on the size of your cookie cutters)*

1 ½ cups butter	2 teaspoons vanilla
1 cup powdered sugar	pinch of salt
1 egg	3 cups flour

Directions

1. Preheat oven to 325°F.
2. Cream the butter at high speed. Add the sugar, egg, vanilla and salt.
3. Slowly add the flour to form a thick dough. Chill the dough for about an hour.
4. On a floured surface, roll the dough about 3/8-inch thick and cut out with cookie cutters.
5. Bake on ungreased cookie sheet for 8-12 minutes, until the edges are light brown.
6. When cool, have the kids decorate with frosting and sprinkles.

Song Suggestion:

"Deck the Halls," sung by The Roches

Daisy Bellamy's "May the Best Man Win" Molasses Cookies

So, okay, you were kind of left hanging at the last moment there. If you think it's driving you crazy, how do you suppose I feel? Julian and Logan each have their fans. May the best man win.

Ingredients *(24 cookies)*

¾ cup unsalted butter

1 cup sugar

¼ cup molasses

1 egg

1 ¾ cups flour

½ teaspoon ground cloves

½ teaspoon ground ginger

1 teaspoon ground cinnamon

½ teaspoon cayenne pepper

½ teaspoon baking soda

Directions

1. Preheat oven to 350°F.
2. Line cookie sheets with baking parchment.
3. Melt the butter; mix well with sugar and molasses.
4. Beat in the egg, then slowly add the rest of the ingredients, mixing well to create a wet dough.
5. Line a cookie sheet with foil or parchment.
6. Drop the batter by scant teaspoons onto the parchment. Leave plenty of space, because cookies will spread.
7. Bake 8-10 minutes, just until the cookies darken.
8. Remove parchment from cookie sheet, and let the cookies cool. These cookies are delicious as is, or you can dress them up with a drizzle of lemon icing.

Song Suggestion:

"I'll Be Home For Christmas," performed by Nickel Creek

Acknowledgments

I get by with a little help from my friends—Anjali Banerjee, Carol Cassella, Sheila Roberts, Suzanne Selfors, Elsa Watson, Kate Breslin, Mary Buckham, Lois Faye Dyer, Rose Marie Harris, Patty Jough-Haan, Susan Plunkett and Krysteen Seelen—wonderful writers and eagle-eyed readers.

Thanks to Sherrie Holmes for keeping all my ducks in a row.

Thanks to Margaret O'Neill-Marbury and Adam Wilson of MIRA Books, Meg Ruley and Annelise Robey of the Jane Rotrosen Agency, for invaluable advice and input. Thanks to my publisher and readers for supporting the Lakeshore Chronicles and for inspiring me to return to Avalon again and again.

A very special thank-you and all my love to my daughter Elizabeth, for her help with the recipes and for her marketing expertise. Thanks also to my sister, Lori, for proofreading, and to my mother, Lou, for mothering me no matter how old I get.

My family—the reason for everything—is bigger and more blessed than ever this year. Welcome to the family, Dave.

Susan Wiggs